Lena Diaz was born in
California, Louisiana an
with her husband and tw
romantic suspense author, ... programmer. A Romance Writers of America Golden Heart® Award finalist, she has also won the prestigious Daphne du Maurier Award for Excellence in Mystery/Suspense. To get the latest news about Lena, please visit her website, lenadiaz.com

Julie Anne Lindsey is an obsessive reader who was once torn between the love of her two favourite genres: toe-curling romance and chew-your-nails suspense. Now she gets to write both for Mills & Boon Heroes. When she's not creating new worlds, Julie can be found carpooling her three kids around northeastern Ohio and plotting with her shamelessly enabling friends. Winner of the Daphne du Maurier Award for Excellence in Mystery/Suspense, Julie is a member of International Thriller Writers, Romance Writers of America and Sisters in Crime. Learn more about Julie and her books at julieannelindsey.com

Also by Lena Diaz

A Tennessee Cold Case Story

Murder on Prescott Mountain
Serial Slayer Cold Case
Shrouded in the Smokies
The Secret She Keeps

The Justice Seekers

Cowboy Under Fire
Agent Under Siege
Killer Conspiracy
Deadly Double-Cross

Also by Julie Anne Lindsey

Beaumont Brothers Justice

Closing In On Clues
Always Watching

Heartland Heroes

SVU Surveillance
Protecting His Witness
Kentucky Crime Ring
Stay Hidden
Accidental Witness
To Catch a Killer

SMOKY MOUNTAINS GRAVEYARD

LENA DIAZ

INNOCENT WITNESS

JULIE ANNE LINDSEY

MILLS & BOON

First Published in Great Britain 2024
by Mills & Boon, an imprint of HarperCollins*Publishers* Ltd
1 London Bridge Street, London, SE1 9GF

www.harpercollins.co.uk

HarperCollins*Publishers*
Macken House, 39/40 Mayor Street Upper,
Dublin 1, D01 C9W8, Ireland

ISBN: 978-0-263-32225-5

0424

This book contains FSC™ certified paper and other controlled sources to ensure responsible forest management.

For more information visit: www.harpercollins.co.uk/green

Printed and Bound in the UK using 100% Renewable Electricity at CPI Group (UK) Ltd, Croydon, CR0 4YY

SMOKY MOUNTAINS GRAVEYARD

LENA DIAZ

This book is dedicated to Dr. Tomas A. Moreno and Dr. Lenka Champion. One restored my sight. The other helped restore its clarity. A year and a half after going blind in one eye,

I can see far better than I ever thought would be possible again. I am forever grateful to you both.

Chapter One

Faith Lancaster wasn't in the Smoky Mountains above Gatlinburg, Tennessee, for the gorgeous spring views, the sparkling waters of Crescent Falls or even hunting for the perfect camera shot of a black bear. Faith was here on this Tuesday morning searching for something else entirely.

A murdered woman's unmarked grave.

If she was right, then she and Asher Whitfield, her partner at the cold case company, Unfinished Business, were about to locate the remains of beautiful bartender and single mother of two, Jasmine Parks.

Five years ago, almost to the day, Jasmine had disappeared after a shift at a bar and grill named The Watering Hole, popular for its scenic views and a man-made waterfall behind it. Instead of returning home that night to her family, she'd become another sad statistic. But months of research had led Faith and Asher to this lonely mountainside, just a twenty-minute drive from the home that Jasmine had shared with her two small children, younger sister and her parents.

Faith shaded her eyes from the sun, trying to get a better look at the newest addition to the crowd of police lined up along the yellow tape, watching the techs operating the ground-penetrating radar machine. Once she realized who'd just arrived, she groaned.

"The vultures found out about our prediction and came for the show," she said.

Beside her, Asher peered over the top of his shades then pushed them higher up on his nose. "Twenty bucks says the short blonde with the microphone ducks beneath the crime scene tape before we even confirm there's a body buried here."

"You know darn well that *short blonde* is Miranda Cummings, the prime-time anchor on Gatlinburg's evening news. Toss in another twenty bucks and I'll take that bet. Only I'll give her less than two minutes."

"Less than two?" He arched a brow. "Deal. No one's that audacious with all these cops around."

No sooner had he finished speaking than the anchor ducked under the yellow tape. She tiptoed across the grass wet with morning dew, heading directly toward the group of hard hats standing by the backhoe.

Faith swore. "She's the kind of blonde who gives the rest of us a bad name. What kind of idiot wears red stilettos to traipse up an incline in soggy grass?"

"The kind who wants to look good on camera when she gets an exclusive."

"Well, that isn't happening. She's about to be arrested." She nodded at two of the uniformed officers hurrying after the reporter and her cameraman.

"Double or nothing?" Asher asked.

"That they won't arrest her?"

"Yep." He glanced down at her, an amused expression on his face.

"Now who's the idiot?" Faith shook her head. "You're on."

The police caught up to the anchorwoman and blocked her advance toward the construction crew. She immediately aimed her mic toward one of the officers while her equally bold cameraman swung his camera around.

"Are you kidding me?" Faith shook her head in disgust. "Are men really that blind and stupid? They're fawning all over her like lovesick puppies instead of doing their jobs."

Asher laughed. "They're fawning all over her because she's a hot blonde in red stilettos. You want to go double or nothing again? I can already picture my delicious steak dinner tonight, at your expense."

"I'm quitting while I'm behind. And she's not *that* attractive."

His grin widened. "If you were a man, you wouldn't say that."

She put her hands on her hips, craning her neck back to meet his gaze, not that she could see his eyes very well behind those dark shades. "You seriously find all that heavy makeup and hairspray appealing?"

"It's not her hair, or her face, that anyone's looking at." He used his hands to make an hourglass motion.

She rolled her eyes and studied the others standing behind the yellow tape like Asher and her. "Where's the police chief? Someone needs to put an end to this nonsense."

"Russo left a few minutes ago. Some kind of emergency at the waterfall on the other side of this mountain. Sounds like a tourist may have gotten too close and went for an unplanned swim."

She winced. "I hope they didn't hit any rocks going over. Maybe they got lucky and didn't get hurt, or drown." She shivered.

"You still don't know how to swim, do you?"

"Since I don't live anywhere near a beach, don't own a pool, and I'm not dumb enough to get near any of the waterfalls in these mountains, it doesn't matter." She motioned to the narrow, winding road about thirty yards away. "Our boss just pulled up, assuming he's the only one around here who can afford that black Audi R8 Spyder. Maybe he'll get the police to escort the press out of here. Goodness knows with his history of helping Gatlinburg PD, Russo's men respect him as much as they do their own chief. Maybe more."

Asher nodded his agreement. "I'm surprised Grayson's here. I thought he was visiting his little girl in Missouri. Now that she knows he's her biological father, he visits as much as he can."

"I'm guessing his wife updated him about the search. He probably felt this was too important to miss."

"You called Willow in on this already?" he asked.

"Last night. She's with the Parks family right now, doing her victim's advocate stuff. It's a good thing, too, because it would have been terrible for them to hear about this search on the news without being prepared first."

"Kudos to you, Faith. I didn't even think about calling her. Then again, I didn't expect the word to leak about what we were doing up here this morning. It's a shame everyone can't be more respectful of the family."

She eyed the line of police again, wondering which one or ones had tipped off the media. None of her coworkers would have blabbed, of that she was certain. "At least Willow can tell the family there's hope again."

"That we'll find Jasmine, sure. But all that will prove is that she didn't accidentally drive her car into a pond or a ravine. I doubt it will give them comfort to have their fears confirmed that she was murdered. And we're not even close to knowing who killed her, or how."

"The how will come at the autopsy."

"Maybe. Maybe not."

She grimaced. "You're probably right. Unless there are broken or damaged bones, we might not get a *cause* of death. But if she's buried up here, there's no question about *manner* of death. Homicide." She returned their boss's wave.

Asher turned to watch him approach. "As to knowing

who's responsible, we're not starting from scratch. We've eliminated a lot of potential suspects."

"You're kidding, right? All we've concluded is that it's unlikely that anyone we've interviewed was involved in her disappearance and alleged murder. We still have to figure out which of the three hundred, thirty-five million strangers in this country killed her. Almost eight billion if we consider that someone from another country could have been here as a tourist and did it."

He crossed his arms. "I'm sticking to my theory that it's someone local, someone who knew the area. Out-of-towners tend to stick to the hiking trails or drive through areas like Cades Cove to get pictures of wildlife. There's nothing over here to attract anyone but locals trying to get away from the tourists."

"I still think it could be a stranger who travels here enough to be comfortable. We shouldn't limit our search to Gatlinburg, or even to Sevier County."

"Tennessee's a big state. How many people does that mean we have to eliminate, Ms. Math Whiz?"

"The only reason you consider me a math whiz is because you got stuck on fractions in third grade."

"I'd say ouch. But I don't consider it an insult that I'm not a math nerd."

"Nah, you're just a nerd."

He laughed, not at all offended. She reluctantly smiled, enjoying their easy banter and the comfort of their close friendship. As handsome and charming as he was, it baffled her that he was still single. She really needed to work at setting him up with someone. He deserved a woman who'd love him and appreciate his humor and kind heart. But for the life of her, she couldn't picture anyone she knew as being the right fit for him.

"Play nice, children." Grayson stopped beside them, impeccable as always in a charcoal-gray suit that probably cost more than Faith's entire wardrobe. "What have I missed?"

Asher gestured toward Faith. "Math genius here was going to tell us how many suspects we have to investigate if we expand our search to all the males in Tennessee."

"No, I was going to tell you *if* we considered all of Tennessee, the total population is about seven million. I have no idea how many of those are male."

Grayson slid his hands in the pockets of his dress pants. "Females account for about fifty-one percent of the population. Statewide, if you focus on males, that's about three and a half million. In Sevier County, potential male suspects number around fifty thousand." He arched a dark brow. "Please tell me I'm not spending thousands of dollars every month funding this investigation only to narrow our suspect pool to fifty thousand."

They both started talking at once, trying to give him an update.

He held up his hands. "I was teasing. If I didn't trust you to work this cold case, you wouldn't be on it. Willow told me you may have figured out where our missing woman is buried. That's far more than we had at the start of this. If the case was easy to solve, someone else would have done it in the past five years and Sevier County wouldn't have asked us to take it on. Give me a rundown on what's happening. I'm guessing the German shepherd is part of a scent dog team. And the construction crew standing around is waiting for guidance on where to dig. The guy pushing what looks like a lawnmower—is that a ground penetrating radar machine?"

Faith nodded. "The shepherd is Libby. She is indeed a scent dog, a cadaver dog. Although Lisa, her handler, prefers to call her a forensic recovery canine." She pointed at various small clearings. "Lisa shoved venting rods in those areas to help release potential scent trapped under the ground to make detection easier."

"It's been five years," Grayson said. "I wouldn't expect there to be any scent at all."

"Honestly, Asher and I didn't either. But after our investigation brought us here as the most likely dump site, we contacted Lisa and she said there would absolutely be scent. One study showed cadaver dogs detecting a skeleton that had been buried over thirty years. And Lisa swears they can pick up scent fifteen feet deep."

"Impressive, and unexpected. I'm guessing those yellow flags scattered around mark where the dog indicated possible hits. There are quite a few."

"A lot of flags, yes, but Lisa said it amounts to six major groupings. As good as these types of dogs are, they can have false positives. Other decomposing animals and vegetation can interfere with their abilities. And scent is actually pulled up through the root systems of trees, which makes it more difficult to find the true source. There could be a hit in, say, three different areas. But the decomposition actually originated from only one spot. Thus, the need for the ground penetrating radar. Lisa recommended it, to limit the dig sites. Asher called around and found a company already in the area." She motioned to Asher. "Where'd you say they were?"

"A cemetery near Pigeon Forge. The GPR company is ensuring that an empty part of the graveyard doesn't have any old unmarked graves before a new mausoleum is erected. Originally, I was going to ask a local utility company to bring over their GPR equipment. But what I found online is that it's more effective if the operator has experience locating the specific type of item you're searching for. Kind of like reading an X-ray or an ultrasound. The guys from the cemetery know how to recognize potential remains because they tested their equipment on known graves first. To find the unknown, you start with the known."

"Bottom line it for me," Grayson said.

Asher motioned to the guys wearing hard hats. "As soon as the radar team tells us which of the flagged sites has the most potential, the backhoe will start digging."

"How soon do we think that will happen?"

"Everybody stay back," one of the construction workers called out as another climbed into the cab of the backhoe.

"Guess that's our answer," Faith said.

Lisa and her canine jogged over and ducked under the yellow tape to stand beside Faith. Asher held up the tape for the GPR team as they pushed their equipment out of the way. The anchorwoman and her cameraman were finally escorted behind the tape as well.

Thankfully, they were a good distance away—not for lack of trying. The blonde kept pointing in their direction, apparently arguing that she wanted to stand beside them. No doubt she wanted to interview the radar people or maybe the canine handler. But Lisa had asked the police earlier to keep people away from her dog. By default, Faith and the small group she was with were safe from the reporter's questions.

For now at least.

Their boss formally introduced himself as Grayson Prescott to the others, thanking them for the work they were doing for his company. And also on behalf of the family of the missing woman.

"How confident are you that we'll find human remains in one of the flagged areas?" Grayson asked the lead radar operator.

"Hard to say. We didn't check all of the sites since the sediment layers in those first two areas seem so promising. They show signs of having been disturbed at some point in the past."

"Like someone digging?"

He nodded. "There's something down there that caused distinctive shaded areas on the radar. But false positives happen. It's not an exact science."

"Understood."

The backhoe started up, its loud engine ending any chance of further conversation.

The hoe slowly and surprisingly carefully for such a big piece of equipment began to scrape back the layers of earth in the first of the two areas. Ten minutes later, the men standing near the growing hole waved at the operator, telling him to stop. They spoke for a moment then loud beeps sounded as the equipment backed up and moved to another spot to begin digging.

Faith sighed in disappointment. "Guess hole number one is a bust."

"Not so fast," Asher said. "They're signaling the forensics team."

A few minutes later, one of the techs jogged over to Faith and Asher, nodding with respect at Grayson.

"We've found a human skull. That's why they stopped digging. We'll switch to hand shovels now and sifting screens to preserve any potential trace evidence and make sure we recover as many small bones as possible."

Faith pressed a hand to her chest, grief and excitement warring with each other. She'd been optimistic that their research was right. But it was sad to have it confirmed that Jasmine had indeed been murdered. She'd only been twenty-two years old. It was such a tragedy for her to have lost her life so young, and in what no doubt was a terrifying, likely painful, manner.

"You don't see any hair or clothing to help us confirm that the remains belong to a female?" she asked.

"Not yet, ma'am. An excavation like this will take hours,

maybe days, because we'll have to go slowly and carefully. But as soon as the medical examiner can make a determination of gender, the chief will update you. Since the GPR hit on those two sites, we'll check the second one as well. Natural shifts underground because of rain or hard freezes could have moved some of it. We also have to consider that the body might have been dismembered and buried in more than one area."

She winced. "Okay, thanks. Thanks for everything."

He nodded. "Thank *you*, Ms. Lancaster. Mr. Whitfield. All of you at UB. Whether this is Jasmine Parks or not, it's someone who needs to be recovered and brought home to their loved ones. If you hadn't figured out an area to focus on, whoever this person is might have never been found."

He returned to the growing group of techs standing around the makeshift grave. Hand shovels were being passed around and some of the uniformed police were bringing sifting screens up the incline.

"Looks like our work here is done," one of the radar guys said. "We'll load up our equipment and head back to Pigeon Forge."

"Wait." Asher pointed to the backhoe operator, who was excitedly waving his hands at the techs. "I think you should check out all of the other groups of flags too."

Faith stared in shock at what one of the techs was holding up from the second hole.

Another human skull.

Chapter Two

The sun had set long ago by the time Asher, Faith, Grayson and Police Chief Russo ended up in UB's second-floor, glass-walled conference room to discuss the day's harrowing events. Asher glanced down the table at the power play happening between Russo and Grayson. Across from him, Faith gave him a "what the heck is going on" look. Just as confused as Faith, all he could do was shrug his shoulders.

Russo thumped his pointer finger on the tabletop, his brows forming an angry slash. "Six bodies, Grayson. Your investigators led my team to the graves of six people. I want to know how that happened and who the hell their suspect is, right now. I don't want to wait for them to cross their t's and dot their i's in a formal report. The media's already all over this and I need something to tell them. Make your investigators turn over their files to my team so we can run with this."

Grayson leaned forward, his jaw set. "And this is why I refused your request for Asher and Faith to go to the police station. You'd be grilling them with questions as if they were criminals. Treat them with respect or the next person you'll speak to is Unfinished Business's team of lawyers. And you won't get one more word about what UB has, or hasn't, found in relation to this cold case."

Faith cleared her throat, stopping Russo's next verbal volley. "Can we please bring down the temperature a few degrees? We all want the same thing, to figure out why our belief that Jasmine Parks was buried on that mountainside turned into the discovery of a serial killer's graveyard. Because that's exactly what we've got here, a serial killer. No question. And now that his personal cemetery is all over the news, we have to expect he's already switching gears and making new plans. He could change locales, go to another county or even another state and start killing again—unless we work together to stop him."

"Unfinished Business will do everything we can to bring the killer to justice," Grayson said, still staring down Russo. "But if Gatlinburg PD can't be civil, we'll continue this investigation on our own."

The staring match between Russo and Grayson went on for a full minute. Russo blinked first and sank back against his chair as if exhausted. He mumbled something beneath his breath then scrubbed his face, which was sporting a considerable five-o'clock shadow.

Grayson, on the other hand, seemed as fresh as he had when he'd first stepped out of his Audi this morning. He could use a shave, sure, but there wasn't a speck of lint on his suit and the stubble on his jaw gave him a rugged look that appeared more planned than accidental.

Asher didn't know how his boss always managed to look so put-together no matter what was going on around him. Kind of like Faith. She, too, looked fresh, as beautiful as always, while Asher's suit was rumpled and his short dark hair was no doubt standing up in spikes by now. Russo was just as bad, maybe worse. He seemed ready to drop from the stress of the unexpected discoveries in his jurisdiction.

The chief held up his hands as if in surrender. "Okay, okay. I may have been too harsh earlier."

"*May* have been?" Grayson shook his head. "You practically accused Asher and Faith of being the killers."

Russo winced and aimed an apologetic glance at the two of them. "I didn't mean to imply any such thing."

"Russo," Grayson warned.

"Okay, all right. At the time, the implication was on purpose. It seemed impossible that you two could have stumbled onto something like that without some kind of firsthand knowledge. Still, I know you both better than to have gone there. It was a knee-jerk reaction. My apologies." He frowned at Grayson. "Talk about overreacting, though. You sure are touchy tonight."

"With good reason. I cut short a visit with my little girl to come back here. And then the police chief acts like a jerk instead of being grateful that Asher and Faith's hard work is going to bring closure to six families who have never known what happened to their loved ones."

Russo's expression softened. "I'm glad you're finally getting to establish a relationship with your daughter after thinking she was dead all these years. How old is she now?"

Grayson still seemed aggravated with his friend, but his voice gentled as he spoke about Lizzie. "She's about to become a precocious, beautiful, nine-year-old. And she's delighted to have two sets of parents around for her upcoming birthday. Twice the presents."

The chief laughed. "I imagine it will be far more than twice with you as her dad."

"Actually, no. Willow and I have come to a co-parenting agreement with Lizzie's adoptive parents. They didn't know she'd been abducted when she more or less fell into their laps as a baby. And they raised her all this time, giving her a loving, secure home. I don't want to upstage them or even try to replace them. Willow and I are being careful about not trying to outdo them in the gift department so that we don't unduly influence her toward us because of material things. We want her to stay grounded and continue to love the Danvers and, hopefully, grow to love us as well. But not by trying to buy her affections."

"You're a better man than me. I'd use every advantage at my disposal to win my little girl over, including suing her foster parents for custody. But I sure do admire that you're putting her interests above your own."

Grayson's mouth twitched in a rare smile. "If you're trying to soften my disposition with flattery, game well-played. I can't stay mad at you for long. Too much water under that bridge." He motioned to Asher and Faith at the other end of the table. "It's getting late and every one of us will be besieged tomorrow by reporters and families of missing persons wondering whether their loved ones are among the dead who are still being dug up on that mountain. Asher, Faith, just answer the chief's main question now and we can reassemble bright and early tomorrow to brief his team about the rest of the investigation. Does eight o'clock work for you, Russo?"

He nodded. "I'll limit my entourage to two of my best detectives and one crime scene tech so we can all fit in your conference room with your full team. Appreciate the cooperation."

Grayson nodded as if the two of them hadn't come close to blows a few minutes earlier.

Asher glanced at Faith, silently asking for her help. He couldn't remember the chief's main question at this point.

She took mercy on him and filled in the gap. "The chief wants to know how we knew where to dig."

"Right. Thanks. I got lost there for a minute."

"That's why I work with you. To keep you straight," she said, deadpan.

"And I appreciate it." He winked, earning another eye roll and a quick wave of her hand, signaling him to hurry up.

"The best answer to your question, Chief, is that it was geographical profiling. But it wasn't traditional profiling. We only had one victim to work with, not sets of data from several different victims. We couldn't extrapolate and come up with a good hypothesis of where the killer might live, which is traditionally how we'd use geographical profiling. Instead of focusing on what we did, or didn't, know about the killer, we created a geographic profile of our victim. We found out everything we could about her and built complex timelines for what she did every day in the three months before she disappeared. It was a painstaking process and involved performing dozens of interviews of just about anyone who'd known her."

Russo and Grayson were both sitting forward, looking as if they were about to pepper him with questions that would probably have them there until midnight. Hoping to avoid an inquisition, Asher hurried to explain.

"Our goal, initially, was to determine Jasmine's routine and mark all of the spots that she frequented on a map, from her home, to her work, where she bought groceries, where her doctor and dentist were, friends' homes, movie theaters she favorited—"

"You're talking victimology," Grayson said.

Asher was always impressed with how much his billionaire businessman boss and former army ranger had picked up on police procedures since starting his cold case company a few years ago. Back then, he'd had one purpose—to find out who'd murdered his first wife and what had happened to their infant daughter who'd gone missing that day. And he and Willow—a former Gatlinburg detective—had done exactly that. In truth, his knowledge of police procedures rivaled both Asher's, as a former Memphis detective, and even Faith's, who'd received numerous commendations as a detective in Nashville.

"Victimology, exactly. We'd hoped to zero in on the locations in her routine that would lend themselves the most to allowing an abductor to take her without being seen—which, of course, is what we believe happened. We came up with three most likely locations. From there, we worked as if we were the bad guy, scouting each one out to see how we would have kidnapped someone in that area and where we might have taken them."

Grayson frowned. "Maybe it's my lack of law enforcement background. But this isn't making sense to me. Not yet anyway."

Faith exchanged a nervous glance with Asher before jumping into the conversation. "What Asher's saying, in his adorably convoluted way, is that we came up with one main potential crime scene for the abduction as our working theory."

Asher grinned, wondering if she realized she'd said *adorable*. Slip of the tongue most likely. Nothing personal toward him.

Unfortunately.

"Instead of our theory leading to a suspect," she said, "it led us to ask questions about what would happen with the body after he killed her. There was really only one area near that location that made sense—a place not frequented by tourists, with very little traffic around it, close enough to the abduction site that the risk of being caught while transporting a victim in his car was low. It made sense that he'd take her into a wooded area, do whatever awful things he wanted to do, then dispose of her in the same location. Thus, the mountainside we were at this morning."

Grayson interjected another question before either Faith or Asher could cut him off. "What made you so confident in your theory that you arranged to have a cadaver dog, a ground penetrating radar team and Russo's techs all waiting there for a discovery that might not have happened?"

"It wasn't as bold as you think," Asher said. "We went over and over our theory, doubting our conclusions. We even spoke to one of our FBI profiler contacts about what we'd come up with. His suggestion was to get a cadaver dog out there first, which is what we did. Lisa and her forensic canine came out a few days ago and she was confident there was something there. Based on her track record, we went to Chief Russo. He agreed to send techs and officers out this morning in case the GPR team came up with a potential gravesite. Lisa had the dog rerun the route once everyone else showed up and it alerted on the same areas."

Russo swore. "You didn't explain this flimsy geographical profiling theory when we spoke. You said your months of investigating had you confident that was where Ms. Parks was buried. Sounds to me like you're lucky we found anything at all and I didn't waste all of that manpower for nothing."

"Russo," Grayson warned again.

The chief held up his hands. "Okay, okay. Your theory proved out. But finding a veritable graveyard of victims was never something I anticipated. *None* of us expected it. I get that. But when it happened, I wasn't prepared to deal with the fallout. That dang anchorwoman." He shook his head. "My guys should have escorted her out of there the minute she arrived. This whole thing is blowing up all over the news, along with that tourist's accidental death at Crescent Falls this morning." He shook his head in disgust. "First time we've had a death there in over twenty years, but now everyone's raising Cain saying it's not safe."

He eyed Grayson again, his expression a mixture of aggravation and stress. "A killer's graveyard found a football field's length from where a hiker drowned today is horrible for tourism. The park service is going to conduct a full-blown safety study of Crescent Falls. I'm getting calls from the tourism council, the mayor, and even the governor, asking when all of this will be resolved. Even TBI is threatening to park themselves on my doorstep."

Faith leaned forward in her chair. "Calling in the Tennessee Bureau of Investigation isn't a bad idea. We believe that one of the six bodies is Jasmine Parks. But we don't have a clue who the others might be. If TBI can explore missing person cases and narrow down the timeframes and locales to give a list of potential IDs to the ME, that could jumpstart the victim identification process."

Grayson was nodding his agreement before she finished. "That's a good idea. We could drive that part through Rowan, our TBI liaison. I'll alert him tonight and ask him to attend our meeting tomorrow morning. Sound good, Russo?"

"Works for me. This all started because we don't have the budget to work our cold cases. Now we suddenly have six to look into and everyone demanding action." He eyed Grayson. "Speaking of resources—"

"You'll have our full support. If necessary, I'll bring in contract investigators to temporarily expand our team. That's standard procedure here when the scope of work increases like this. We can ramp up quickly. TBI can do some of the grunt work for both of our organizations. And we'll coordinate the logistics together, you and me, so we can impact your budget as little as possible. Fair enough?"

Russo's brow smoothed out and he actually smiled. "More than fair. Thanks, Grayson. I owe you."

"That's how I prefer to keep it."

Russo laughed and stood. "I'll see you all in a few hours. Hopefully, tomorrow will be a better day than this one was." He opened the door and strode toward the stairs.

Asher and Faith stood, ready to follow Russo.

"Just a minute." Grayson crossed to the glass wall that

looked down on the main floor below with its two-story-high ceiling. What would have been called a squad room at a police department was affectionately called the war room by Unfinished Business's investigators.

He watched as Russo headed through the empty room, everyone else having gone home for the night. And he waited as Russo went into the parking lot, the view through the one-way glass walls allowing those inside to see out but no one outside to see in, even with the lights on. It was only once Russo's car was backing out of his parking space that Grayson turned around, an ominous frown on his face and his eyes the color of a stormy night.

"No one leaves this conference room until you tell me why you both just lied to the chief of police. And to me."

Chapter Three

Asher watched Grayson with growing dread. "What makes you think we're lying?"

"Don't even go there with me. I was in Special Forces and learned interrogation techniques from the best. I've also been playing in the big leagues in the business world for years. I know when someone's not being straight up. You and Faith just told a whopper with that story about using a new type of geographical profiling. What I want to know is why."

Faith's green eyes were big and round as she met Asher's gaze. Both of them slowly sank back into their chairs.

"Wanna draw straws?" Asher asked her.

"Coward. I'll tell him." In spite of her brave words, she seemed nervous as she answered Grayson. "We really did try to do what we said, map out everywhere our missing person had been, her usual routine at least. And we tried to figure out what areas made sense as the best ones where she'd have gone missing. But, well—"

"There were too many," Asher said. "With no witnesses to the abduction and no forensic evidence. We hit a wall. Couldn't make any headway."

"So we, uh, we…" Faith swallowed hard and squeezed her hands together on top of the table.

Grayson's brow furrowed. "I've got all night. But I'd rather spend it at home with my beautiful wife than in a conference room trying to draw the truth out of two of my extremely well-paid employees. I deserve the truth and I want it. Now."

She let out a deep breath then the confession poured out of her in a rush. "We sent letters to ten serial killers in prison and offered a deal. If they'd put us on their visitation list and agree to speak to us, we'd go see them. In exchange for their opinions on which of our potential locations would make the best dump site, we'd put four hundred dollars in their prison accounts."

Grayson stared at her a long moment then cleared his throat. "And how many of these despicable murderers took you up on this bribe?"

She chewed her bottom lip before answering. "All of them."

Another minute passed in silence. Then, his voice deadly calm, Grayson said, "Let's see if I have this straight. You gave four thousand dollars of my money to the scummiest excuses for human beings so they would give you their *guesses* on which of the areas in Gatlinburg they would choose to dump a body. Is that what you're telling me?"

She winced. "Sounds way worse when you phrase it that way. But, um, yes. That's basically what we did."

He blinked, slowly, then looked at Asher. "Let me guess. This was your harebrained idea?"

Asher cleared his throat. "Actually, I believe it was."

Grayson leaned back in his chair. "And how many of the sites they chose did you send the cadaver dog team to?"

"How many?" Asher asked. "Total?"

"That's what the phrase *how many* means. *In total*, how many sites did the cadaver K-9 sniff out before you hired an expensive ground penetrating radar team, construction workers with a backhoe and, on top of that, lie to Chief Russo that your brilliant deductive reasoning determined that mountainside this morning was most likely where our missing person's body would be located?"

Asher stared up at the ceiling as if counting. Then he straightened his tie. "Um, pretty much it was—"

"One," Faith said. "Just the one. The dog hit on it and we felt confident that we were going to find…something. If we told Russo about asking serial killers for opinions, he'd have laughed us out of his office, in spite of the cadaver dog. So we exaggerated the geographical profiling theory in case he asked questions. We needed something to make it seem more—"

"Legit? Reliable? Worth a substantial expenditure of resources in spite of how busy Gatlinburg PD is and how tight Russo is with his budget? Since the whole point of us taking on this cold case was to keep him from having to use his funds and resources, you do realize I'll have to reimburse him for his expenses from this morning?"

Faith clenched her hands together on the table. "We believed strongly that our—"

"Educated guess?"

"We believed we had a high probability of finding Jasmine Parks. And we were somewhat desperate for a break in the case. So, we, um, we lied. And, yes, we cost Unfinished Business—you—a lot of money today. But wasn't it worth it, sir? By all accounts, the clothing and jewelry found on one of the skeletons makes it seem highly likely that we've found Ms. Parks. Plus, we've found other missing people."

"That doesn't sound like an apology for lying to the chief of police and your boss."

She glanced at Asher. "In our defense, sir, we never intended to lie to you. We didn't expect you to even be there today. Our hope was that after we located Ms. Parks's remains, no one would care how we did it."

Grayson stared at her a long moment, his eyebrows arching up toward his hairline. Then a deep rumble started in his chest. His shoulders shook and he started laughing so hard that tears rolled down his cheeks. Still chuckling and wiping away tears, he pushed back his chair and headed for the conference room door.

"Willow's going to love this one." He laughed again as he left the room.

Faith stared at the closed door, her eyes wide.

Asher turned in his chair to watch Grayson cross the war room below, his cell phone to his ear as he no doubt updated his wife about what had happened. "I hope this means we're not fired." He turned around. "Maybe we should have taken advantage of his amusement and went ahead and told him how much that GPR team cost."

"Oh, heck no." Faith stood. "We'll let that one slide in under the radar with the rest of the team's monthly expense reports and hope he never notices."

He stood and held the door open for her. "Now who's the coward?"

She lightly jabbed his stomach with her elbow, smiling at his grunt as she headed out the door.

He hurried to catch up to her as she descended the stairs. "Where are you off to so quickly? Got a hot date?"

"Yep. His name is Henry." She headed across the room to her desk and retrieved her work computer and purse from the bottom drawer.

"Ah. Your laptop. Henry Cavill. If you're going to name a piece of metal and plastic, couldn't you come up with something more exciting than the name of some scrawny actor? Cavill. Seriously. He's so two years ago."

"So is my laptop. Let me guess. You think I should have named it Asher?"

"It does have a nice sound to it."

She rolled her eyes and headed toward the open double

doors just a few steps from the exit. Asher tagged along with her.

"I think you've rolled your eyes at me a hundred times today. It's getting a little old."

"Then maybe you should stop doing things that make me want to roll my eyes."

"Ouch."

A low buzzing sounded from her purse. She stopped at the building's main exit and pulled out her phone.

Asher moved to the door. "Sorry, princess. Are you waiting for me to open this for you? Allow me—"

"Wait." She stared at her phone, her face turning pale.

He stepped toward her, frowning. "What's wrong?"

In answer, she turned her phone around. "I had my News Alert app set to buzz if any local updates went out. This is from a local evening newsbreak."

Asher winced at the picture on the screen. "Poor Jasmine. Poor Jasmine's family. It was bad enough when the news vultures paraded her pictures on TV this afternoon. Here they are doing it again. We don't even have confirmation from the medical examiner that it's her. I mean, you and I both know it is, based on her jewelry and—"

"Asher. Look at that picture again."

He frowned and took the phone from her. Then he saw it, the name beneath the photo. He blinked. "No way."

Faith's eyes seemed haunted as she stared up at him. "The odds against this happening have to be astronomical. What the heck is going on? How is it even possible that a handful of hours after we find Jasmine Parks's body, her younger sister is abducted?"

Chapter Four

Faith yawned as she pulled into the parking lot of Unfinished Business the next morning. It had been a late night for her and Asher. Or, rather, an early morning. They hadn't left UB until after three. They'd pored over their files and explored the databases at UB's disposal to gather every bit of information that they could about Leslie Parks, the younger sister of Jasmine, who'd been only fifteen years old when Jasmine went missing. But nothing they'd found gave them a clue about who might have taken her. And they hadn't discovered anything to tie the two abductions together.

Other than the obvious—that they were sisters—their age difference meant their lives had been more or less separate and different. Leslie had been a sophomore in high school when Jasmine got her job bartending. It wasn't like they'd frequented clubs together or hung out with the same friends. That left two distinct possibilities.

Either whomever had abducted Leslie was a completely different person than the one who'd abducted Jasmine.

Or both abductors were the same person.

The first option seemed ludicrous even though it was technically possible.

The second was terrifying.

Had the person who'd taken Jasmine kept an eye on her

family all these years, waiting for the perfect opportunity to hurt them again? Had the perpetrator decided that he wanted to destroy the family's relief at finding their daughter's body by visiting more horror and pain on them? Faith couldn't even imagine the sick, evil mind of someone who'd want to do that.

She yawned again and pulled to a halt at the end of the third row. She'd never had problems finding a parking space here before. Unfinished Business was located near the top of Prescott Mountain, owned by Grayson Prescott, whose mansion was essentially the mountain's penthouse. No one else lived in this area and UB was the only business up here. People who came to UB were employees, law enforcement clients, or experts assisting them with their cases. So why was the parking lot full?

"Serves me right for sleeping late, I suppose." She sighed and drove her sporty Lexus Coupe out to the main road and parked on the shoulder. Just as she was getting out of her car, Asher's new black pickup truck pulled in behind her.

She leaned against her driver's door, waiting for him.

"Morning, Faith. Did your army-green toy car get a flat or something?" He eyed her tires and started toward the other side of her car.

"Just because you traded your old car for a shiny new truck doesn't mean you should make fun of my Lexus. It's metallic green, not army green. And the only reason it seems small to you is because you're so tall. It's perfect for a normal-size person."

He leaned over the other side. "I'm normal size. You're pint size." He winked then stopped in front of her. "No flat. What's the problem? Need me to wind up the hand crank on the engine?"

"Ha, ha. There's nowhere to park. The lot's full."

He glanced at her in surprise then scanned the lot behind them through a break in the trees. "Can't remember that ever happening before. Guess Russo brought more of his team than he said he would."

"I think it's more than that. Look at the placards around the license plates on some of those SUVs up close to the building. They name one of the big rental car companies. My guess is TBI sent a bunch of investigators, maybe even the FBI if Russo invited them in on the case. Six bodies discovered all at once lit a fire under law enforcement."

"That and a pushy local anchorwoman," he grumbled.

"I thought you liked all that makeup and hairspray?"

"I liked her curves, and those sexy stilettos. Doesn't mean I like *her*."

Faith laughed. "Then you're not as hopeless as I thought."

"Gee. Thanks."

She smiled and they headed through the lot toward the two-story, glass-and-steel office building perched on the edge of the mountain.

"Let's hope that fire gets them cooperating and working hard to find Leslie Parks before she ends up like her sister," Asher said.

"Let's hope. Maybe they'll let us in on the action to find Leslie since we've been investigating her sister's case for several months."

"I'm sure they will. Who else is better qualified? And finding her quickly is urgent."

Three hours later, Faith and Asher were forced to stand out of the way in the war room as the TBI director, Jacob Frost, and an army of TBI agents used the power of a warrant to confiscate Faith's and Asher's work laptops and their physical files and flash drives from their desks.

Fellow investigator, Lance Cabrera, and their team lead, Ryland Beck, stood with them near the floor-to-ceiling wall of windows on one side of the cavernous room. Faith wasn't sure if they were there for moral support or to keep her and Asher from attacking the TBI guys. Other UB investigators—Ivy, Callum, Trent, Brice—tried to work at their desks amid the chaos. But from the way they kept glancing around, they were obviously distracted. How could they not be? The agents were like locusts, buzzing around and swarming the entire room.

"I'm so mad, I could spit." Faith glared at any TBI investigator dumb enough to glance her way as they ransacked her desk.

"Yeah, well," Asher said. "It is what it is."

"How can you be so nonchalant about this? They pick our brains in the conference room for hours, have us review every detail of our investigation. And then they shove a warrant in our faces and steal our files. On top of that, we're ordered not to work the case anymore. These idiots are going to use our hard work to give them a jumpstart. Then once they solve this thing and catch the bad guy and, hopefully, rescue Leslie, it will be all glory for them and nothing for us." She shifted her glare to Ryland. "Stop trying to edge in front of me as if you think I'm going to draw down on these guys. I'm not that stupid. I'm way outgunned."

His eyes widened. "You're outgunned? Is that the *only* reason you aren't pulling your firearm?"

"It's the main one," she practically growled.

He swore beneath his breath.

Lance laughed and clasped Ryland on the shoulder. "I think that's my cue to leave this to our fearless leader."

"Gee, thanks for the help," Ryland grumbled.

Lance only laughed again and headed to his desk.

Asher grinned. "Look on the bright side, Faith. With all of these suits on the case, and the resources they can bring to bear, they've got an excellent chance of solving this thing and rescuing Leslie. I don't like being pushed aside any more than you. But if it means saving a life, I'll bow out gracefully."

She put her hands on her hips. "Have you forgotten that

the TBI worked Jasmine's case when it was fresh? And yet here we are, five years later, finding her body for them. What makes you think these yahoos will do any better with her little sister's disappearance?"

Ryland eyed Asher. "Gun-toting Annie Oakley here does have a point."

Asher's smile faded. "She does. Unfortunately." He glanced up at the glass-enclosed conference room at the top of the stairs on the far end of the room. "Grayson is still arguing with Russo and Frost about this hostile takeover. Maybe he'll make them see reason and keep UB involved."

A few moments later, Grayson yanked open the conference room door and strode to the stairs. His face was a study in anger as he took them two at a time to the ground floor.

Faith crossed her arms. "Looks like Russo and Frost saw reason." Her voice was laced with sarcasm. "Good call on that one, Asher."

"I can't be right all the time. It wouldn't be fair to you mere mortals."

She gave him the side-eye. "Careful. I'm in a really bad mood."

"Darlin', when are you not in a bad mood?"

Her eyes narrowed in warning.

"Follow me," Grayson ordered without slowing down as he passed them.

"O…kay," Asher said. "Come on, Faith. Ryland, where are you going? The boss said to follow him."

"I'm betting he meant the two of you. Good luck." He grinned and headed for his desk.

"Traitor," Faith called after him.

He waved at her from the safety of the other side of the room.

"That's it. I'm going to shoot him." Faith reached for her pants pocket.

Asher grabbed her arm and tugged her toward the door. “Shoot him later. The boss is waiting.”

They rushed to catch up. Grayson was standing in the elevator across the lobby, texting on his phone and leaning against the opening to keep the door from closing. When they reached him, he gave them an impatient look as he put his phone away. “Nice of you to join me.”

“My fault.” Asher practically dragged Faith inside.

She said a few unsavory things to him, yanked her arm free, then immediately regretted it when it felt as if she’d ripped her skin off. “Ouch, dang it.”

“Well, I didn’t expect you to yank your arm or I’d have loosened my hold. I just didn’t want you to jump out of the elevator and shoot anyone.”

Grayson briefly closed his eyes, as if in pain, then punched the button for the basement level, one floor down. It was the only part of the building underground. But it had the absolute best views since the entire back glass wall looked out over the Smoky Mountains range.

In spite of that view, Faith could count on two hands the number of times she’d been down there. The basement was where the forensics lab was located, as well as the computer geeks. She didn’t speak biology or chemistry and, other than knowing how to run her laptop, she didn’t speak tech either. Well, unless she counted Asher. He reminded her of Clark Kent, about as bookish as they came but also tall, broad-shouldered and decent-looking. Okay, more than decent. He put both Clark Kent and his alter-ego to shame in the looks department. But Asher was the only person who spoke technology that was patient enough to word it so that it made sense to her. There just wasn’t any reason for her to go down to the basement level and listen to other techies.

As the elevator opened, she looked out at the many doors

on the far wall with some trepidation. "Grayson. Why are we here?"

She and Asher followed him as he strode down the hallway to the glass wall at the end.

"Where are we going?" she whispered to Asher.

"Since we passed the lab entrance and the storage rooms, I'm guessing the nerd lair."

She let out a bark of laughter then covered her mouth. This wasn't the time for laughing. Not when a young girl's life was at stake, if she was even still alive. And not when her own desk upstairs was being violated, her laptop stolen, more or less—warrant or no warrant. Just thinking about it had her blood heating again.

Grayson stopped at the last door and glanced at them over his shoulder. "Wait here."

When the door closed behind him, Faith whirled around. "What the heck?"

Asher shrugged as if he didn't have a care in the world and leaned against the wall beside the door, his long legs bracing him as he stared out at the mountains. His navy blue suit jacket hung open to reveal his firearm tucked in his shoulder holster. It had Faith longing to pull hers from the pocket of her black dress pants to head upstairs and set a few people straight. She eyed the elevator doors, wondering if she had enough time to do that before Grayson returned.

"Dang. Absolutely gorgeous," Asher said, recapturing her attention.

Since he was looking at her now, she blinked, not sure what to say.

He grinned and motioned at the windows. "We should make the IT department come upstairs to the war room and let us take over their subterranean paradise."

She glanced toward the view that she'd only barely noticed,

then shook her head. "Nah. Too distracting. Grayson knew what he was doing when he put us facing the parking lot."

His grin widened as he continued to look her way. "Definitely distracting. I'll agree with that."

She shifted uncomfortably, her face heating. "Um, Asher, what are you—"

"The view." He motioned to the windows. "I agree it would be hard to focus on work with that to look at all day."

Her face heated with embarrassment. For a moment there, she'd misread him and thought he was actually flirting. Really flirting, not the teasing he normally did. She cleared her throat and leaned back against the opposite wall. "I wonder how the computer guys manage to maintain their focus."

"They don't strike me as the outdoors types. I doubt they even notice."

"I'm told they get used to it." Grayson stepped through the door that neither of them had noticed opening. Once again, he motioned for them to follow him to the elevator.

Faith gave Asher a puzzled look.

He shrugged, seemingly as perplexed as she felt. Before she could recover, he grabbed her hand and towed her after him.

Grayson leaned out the door. "You two coming or not?"

"Coming," they both said as they hurried inside.

"Where to now?" Faith asked.

Grayson's jaw tightened.

"Sorry, sorry. I've obviously aggravated you." She pressed the button for the first floor. Since the only thing on the second floor was the catwalk around the war room that led to Grayson's office and the large conference room, it was rare that anyone ever took the elevator to the second floor.

He sighed heavily. "I'm far more aggravated at the situation than at either of you. Russo shouldn't have called TBI without our liaison talking to them first so we could arrive at an agreement. Instead, he made his own arrangement with TBI, letting them wrestle our case away. I'd bet a year's profits from all of my companies that you two could figure out who this serial killer is way before those bureaucrats." He glanced first at her then at Asher. "That is, if you were allowed to work the case. Which, of course, you're not."

The elevator doors opened and he strode into the lobby. But instead of heading into the war room, he continued toward the exit.

Again, Faith and Asher hesitated, not sure whether they were supposed to follow him or not.

"Uh, boss," Asher said. "Did you want—"

"Hurry up." Grayson flung one of the double doors wide and jogged down the steps. At the bottom, he turned and looked up at them. "Faith, did you bring a purse today?"

She blinked. "Um, I'm female, so, duh." Her face heated. "I mean yes."

"Go get it."

"Go…what?"

Asher gently grasped her shoulders and turned her toward the building. "Get your purse, darlin'."

She sighed and hurried to the war room. The TBI jerks had finished ransacking her desk and had everything they were taking boxed up and on a dolly. Lucky for them, they weren't in punching range. After retrieving her purse, she headed outside.

"Where are you two parked?" Grayson asked when she reached the bottom of the steps.

Asher motioned toward the road. "We didn't leave UB until after three and both got here later than we intended this morning. There wasn't a single parking spot to be had. Both of us are on the shoulder of the road."

Grayson's jaw flexed. "They'd better hurry and get out of here while I'm still in a good mood."

Asher choked then coughed when Grayson frowned at him.

Grayson headed for the road, and this time they didn't hesitate to follow but were forced to jog to catch up. Once they reached Faith's car, she leaned against the driver's door, slightly out of breath. The fact that Asher, who'd jogged with her, wasn't even breathing hard had her regretting that she'd missed so many workouts to focus on the case these past few months.

"Boss, please," she said between breaths. "What's going on? Are we in trouble? Are you…are you firing us?"

For the first time that morning, he smiled. "Why would I fire two of my best investigators?"

Faith gave him a suspicious look. "You tell everyone they're you're best investigators."

"That's because it's true. I only hire the best. And, no, I'm not terminating your employment."

Asher leaned beside her against the side of the car. "Yesterday you were pretty upset when you found out we'd—"

Faith elbowed him in the ribs, not wanting him to remind their boss about a sore subject.

He frowned and rubbed his side.

Grayson chuckled, which had Faith even more confused. "You two are *officially* ordered to stand down, to not investigate the Parks cold case in any way. The case, after all, belongs to Gatlinburg PD, and they've rescinded their request for us to work on it. We'll no longer have access to any of the physical evidence. That's all being transferred out of our lab back to Gatlinburg PD's property room, or TBI's, if they decide to take it into their custody. And all of the files are being stripped from your computers and the physical files confiscated. I'm supposed to ask whether either of you have any additional files, printed or electronic, at your homes."

Faith's face flushed with heat. "This is ridiculous, Grayson. We're not children, even if we tend to bicker back and forth. It's just how we are, like brother and sister."

Grayson's brows rose and he glanced sharply at Asher in question.

Asher cleared his throat. "Exactly. Brother and sister. You were saying, Grayson?"

Grayson hesitated then smiled again. "I was asking whether you have any files, because, *per our contract* with TBI and all the eastern Tennessee counties that we work with, we always defer to law enforcement regarding their cases. They remain the owners and can fire us at any time, which is what they're doing on this particular one. Therefore, *since Russo and Frost told me to ask you*, not to mention the warrant they got, I'm *required to do so*. Think very carefully before you answer because I have to pass your answer along to them. *Do you have any more files pertaining to the Parks case?*"

Faith tried to decipher the odd stresses he'd put on various words and phrases. Since when did he care if Russo told him to do something? Or even if he had talked a judge into giving him permission to take their data? Grayson always did what he felt was best, no matter what. It kind of went with the territory of being a billionaire and not worrying where your next paycheck was coming from.

She pictured her home office with reports and notes on the Parks case arranged in neat stacks on the top of her desk and filed in drawers. There was even a large map on the wall with the geographical profiling information they'd worked on. She probably had more documentation there than she had at UB. Still, there were quite a few files she didn't have copies of. If she wanted to sneak and continue to work the case, she'd have to spend considerable time reconstructing that missing data. But Grayson was ordering them to stop. Wasn't he?

"Faith?" Grayson prodded. "Nothing about the Parks case is at your home. Right?"

"To be completely honest, in my home office there—"

"Isn't anything on this case," Asher interjected. "Neither of us keeps copies of files at home. Ever."

That was a whopper of a lie, since they *all* kept information on active investigations at their homes to save time. Grayson knew that. It wasn't a secret. Having the data at home allowed them to jump on tips and take any documents they needed with them to conduct interviews or further their research without having to go to the office first.

Asher continued his lie. "Absolutely no notes, pictures, affidavits from witnesses, recordings of some of our interviews, maps, theories, plans for future interviews, or copies of any of the files that TBI confiscated here at UB." He gave Faith a hard look. "Isn't that right?"

She frowned. "Well, actually, it's—"

"Excellent," Grayson said. "I can truthfully tell Russo and the TBI that you told me that you don't have anything related to the Parks investigation outside of the office. I hope you're beginning to understand the situation."

Faith blinked, the lightbulb finally going off beneath Asher's hard stare. "As a matter of fact, it's suddenly becoming clear, sir. Confusing, but clear. If that makes sense."

"Glad to hear it. We've been ordered to no longer work this investigation. If we do, we could suffer legal consequences. All of us. And the future of UB could be at risk." He frowned and glanced back at the building. "Or, at least, the way that UB operates today, with quite a bit of control leveraged by those we contract with."

His look had hardened and he mumbled something else beneath his breath that had Faith thinking he was already revamping their future contracts in that business-savvy brain of his.

He smiled again. "We all know what a...*stellar* job the TBI and Gatlinburg PD do with cold cases. I'm *officially* ordering both of you to stand down. Again, do we understand each other?"

Since the whole reason UB existed was that Gatlinburg PD and TBI *hadn't* done a great job and Grayson's first wife's murder had gone unsolved for years, Faith definitely understood him now. "Crystal clear, sir."

Asher nodded his agreement. "Loud and clear. Sometimes Faith is a little slow but she catches up eventually."

Grayson laughed. "You're going to pay for that remark."

"He certainly is." She glared her displeasure.

"I can handle her."

She gasped with outrage.

"Hold that thought." Grayson took out his wallet and handed Faith a platinum-colored credit card. The thing was heavy and actually made of metal. She'd never seen a credit card that fancy before. "As compensation for this disappointment, I'm sending both of you on vacation. Use that card for anything you need. Don't file expense reports or contact anyone else at UB about your...vacation. After all, the police and TBI might be here off and on while working the Parks investigation. I wouldn't want you interfering with that in any way. Still clear?"

They both nodded.

"Take however much time you need. When you feel like you might want to come back, for whatever reason, rather than come to UB, come up to the house. In fact, I'd appreciate it if you check in with me every now and then with a status of your...vacation."

Faith stared at the credit card in her hand. It was probably the kind with no spending limit. The kind people used to purchase multimillion-dollar yachts without blinking an eyelash. Her hand shook as she carefully tucked the card into her purse and zipped it closed.

"One more thing." He reached into a suit jacket pocket and held up a flash drive. "Since you'll be out of the office for a while, I had IT put copies of some upcoming cases on there, just in case you wanted to review them before coming back to work."

Asher swiped the flash drive before Faith could. "Thanks, boss. We'll take it from here. We won't come back to UB until you tell us to."

"Enjoy your vacations. And be discreet."

Asher pressed a hand to his chest as if shocked. "Discretion is my motto."

Faith snorted. "More like your kryptonite. Don't worry, Grayson. I'll keep him in line." She quirked a brow. "I can handle him."

Asher grinned.

"See that you do." With that, Grayson strode toward the building.

Faith eyed the flash drive in Asher's hand. "What do you think's really on that? Obviously something about the Parks case, but what?"

"Backups. Every night IT backs up the network."

"How do you know that?"

"I know a lot of things you'd be surprised about. I'm not just a handsome face."

She laughed.

He rested an arm on top of her car, facing her. "If I'm right, everything that TBI just took away has now been given back to us. I hope you didn't have visions of white sandy beaches and views of sparkling emerald-green water dancing in your head. This is a working vacation. We're going to secretly continue the Parks investigation. And, hopefully, we'll figure out the killer's identity in time to send an anonymous tip to the police so they can rescue Leslie."

Faith snatched the flash drive. "My house is closer than yours."

Chapter Five

Asher stepped inside Faith's foyer with her then moved into the family room while she locked the front door.

"Ash!" Suddenly his arms were filled with soft, warm curves as a young woman threw herself against him. "It's been too long." She squealed as she continued to hug him.

"Uh, hey, Daph. Need to breathe here," he teased as he gently extricated himself from her grasp. Just in time, too, because Faith was now glaring at him from beside her younger sister. "If I'd known you were home from that joke you call a university, I'd have come over much sooner."

"Hey, my Tennessee Vols can smash your Memphis Tigers any day."

"Says the sophomore who still hasn't been to her first football game."

Daphne rolled her blue eyes, reminding him of Faith, who tended to roll her eyes when she was exasperated—which was often. But where Daphne's eyes were blue, Faith's were sparkling emerald-green that lit up whenever she smiled. And even though she and her sister both had blonde hair, Faith's was darker, a shade she called dirty blonde. Asher called it pretty.

"I don't have to go to boring games to show school spirit."

He laughed. “I suppose not. Why aren’t you in Knoxville? I thought you were taking classes over the summer semester.”

“Finals finished up a week ago and I have another week before summer classes start. I figured I’d catch up with some friends and grace my big sis with my amazing presence.”

It was Faith’s turn to roll her eyes.

“I head back a week from tomorrow,” Daphne continued. “I told Faith to tell you I was home.”

“I must have forgotten.” Faith’s tone clearly said she *hadn’t* forgotten. “And his name is Asher, not Ash. Want a soda anyone? Water?” As if deciding the crisis of Asher holding her sister had passed, she moved into the kitchen area and opened the refrigerator.

“I’m good,” Daphne said. “I know Ash would like a high-test soda. But since you only have diet drinks around here, get him a water.”

Asher chuckled. A cold bottle of diet cola was soon thrust into his hands.

“Asher doesn’t drink the hard stuff anymore,” Faith said. “He’s trying to watch his weight.” She stood beside her sister, a water bottle clutched in her right hand.

“That can’t be true, Ash. You hiding some extra pounds beneath that suit jacket?” Daphne started to run a hand down his flat stomach.

Faith knocked her hand away. “We have work to do. I thought you were meeting some of your high school buddies for lunch.”

Daphne’s eyes widened and she pulled her phone out of her jeans’ pocket to check the time on the screen. “Shoot. They’ll be here soon to pick me up. I need to finish getting ready. Don’t worry, Ash. I’ll say bye before I leave.” She waved at him and headed down the hallway toward the back of the house.

As soon as Daphne was out of earshot, Faith said, "Leave my sister alone."

"Whatever do you mean? We were just catching up."

"She's jailbait. Don't. Touch."

"I think you're confused about what that word means. Daphne's twenty, a legal adult."

"I'm not confused at all about the definition of jailbait. It means that if you touch her, I'm going to jail. Because I'll shoot you."

He chuckled. "Careful, darlin'. Your jealousy is showing."

"I'm serious, *Ash*. My sister is off limits. It would make things too…awkward working with you."

He leaned down to her, enjoying the way her eyes widened and her breath hitched in her throat. True to her stubborn personality, she refused to back away, which was what he'd counted on. When his lips were mere inches from hers, and her expression had softened from anger to confusion, he turned his face to the side and whispered in her ear.

"You going to stand there all day, Faith? We have work to do."

He headed for her home office on the front right side of the house, chuckling when he heard her swearing behind him and jogging to catch up.

Seeing the empty spot in the middle of the incredibly neat and organized stacks of paper on her desk, he paused and turned around. "Organized chaos, as usual. But also kind of bare-looking without your work laptop to put there."

"TBI jerks." She paused beside him. "I'll have to dig up Daphne's old laptop, the one she ditched after I bought her a new one for school. Hopefully, I can find a power cord that fits."

"I still can't believe you never use a personal computer when you aren't working. Everyone has a computer in this century."

"It keeps me sane not going anywhere near one when I'm

not working. I'm a TV girl in the evenings. It's called relaxing, recharging. You should try it. You work way too hard."

"Maybe you can teach me this TV concept—after we do everything we can to save Leslie."

She blinked, her eyes suspiciously bright. "Poor Leslie. She's twenty, Daphne's age. Just two years younger than her sister when she disappeared. She has to be so scared. Assuming he hasn't already—"

"He hasn't. I don't think so, anyway. If it's the same guy who took Jasmine, then he's toying with the family. He'll keep her alive long enough to send them pictures or a token of some sort to prove he has her, so he can cause them more pain. If it's not the same guy, it could be a copycat. He heard about the first daughter on the news and decided to go for his fifteen minutes of fame by taking the other daughter. Again, if that's the case, I would think he'd keep her alive until he milks all the attention out of this that he can get. Either way, I choose to believe that we have some time. Not a lot, but we might have enough to find her before it's too late."

"That's not usually the case in abductions, especially if it's an abduction by a stranger."

"True. But with all the media attention on this one, it's automatically different. The statistics don't talk to this particular situation. I say we have a chance."

"I pray you're right. The odds of finding anyone alive more than a few hours after being taken like this are abysmal."

"But not zero."

Her smile was barely noticeable, but a smile nonetheless. "Not zero." She squeezed his hand in thanks before looking down at the stacks of paper on her desk.

He let out a slow breath and focused on not revealing how that touch, that barely-there-smile, affected him. She didn't think about him the way he did about her. There was no changing it. And even if he were to try, now was the worst possible time.

She rifled through one of the stacks of paper, somehow managing to keep it aligned and neat at the same time. "To believe it's the same guy who abducted Jasmine, we have to accept that he's stayed in the area all this time. That supports your theory that her abductor was a local. Of course, that burial ground we discovered pretty much confirms it, unless all of the victims there were part of a spree of killings done years ago and the killer moved on somewhere else. Maybe he was just passing through, if that's what killers like him do. Someone completely unrelated to the original incident abducted Leslie. Coincidence."

"That's a hell of a coincidence." He leaned against a corner of the desk, careful not to disturb her papers, and crossed his arms.

"Yeah. It would be. Let's toss that aside for now, assume he *is* local, is still around."

"Same guy."

She nodded. "Same guy who killed Jasmine. Although, we're making leaps of logic without evidence. We don't have confirmation from the medical examiner that we've found Jasmine among all those bodies." She shivered and ran her hands up and down her arms. "If it wasn't for the media, no one would even realize that we suspect Jasmine is among the dead. The timing of Leslie's abduction is too quick, just a few hours after the first media report that mentioned Jasmine. That makes me think this really is a crazy, devastating coincidence. Lightning doesn't strike twice in the same place." Her eyes were unfocused, her thoughts directed more inward than on anything in front of her.

"World War Two, the Sullivan brothers."

She frowned and looked up. "The Sullivan brothers?"

"Five brothers who all died in 1942 during the Second

World War. Lightning does sometimes strike twice in the same place. Or *more* than twice in the Sullivan case."

"And this is why I'm not a history buff. Stories like that are too depressing."

He smiled. "I'll try to keep my depressing historical references to a minimum in the future."

She smiled, too, the shadows of grief lessening in her eyes. "It's actually impressive how much trivia you store in that amazing brain of yours."

He waggled his eyebrows and flipped his suit jacket open, resting his hands on his belt. "If you think my brain's amazing, you should see my—"

She lightly tapped his arm. "Stop it. You're such a guy. Be back in a few. *If* I can find that dang computer and the cord." She hurried from the room.

He sighed at her inability to see him as more than a friend. His jokes fell flat, his lamebrain attempts to get her to see him as…more, never seemed to gain traction. He was about to sit in one of the two office chairs that Faith kept behind the desk because they worked together so much, but Daphne entered the office.

"'You're such a guy,'" she mimicked her sister. "The woman's blind. You need to jump her bones before you're both in retirement homes."

He coughed to cover a laugh. "And you need to quit stirring the pot. Faith doesn't think about me in that way. I doubt she ever will."

"Then do something to open her eyes. Something outrageous. I'm no longer living at home. She can't use me as an excuse to make *you* go home when you're here working late. There's absolutely nothing to stop you two from going at it like rabbits except that she's an idiot."

He coughed again, nearly choking at her amusing audacity. "Daphne, you really do need to stop—"

The sound of footsteps on the hardwood floor outside the office heralded Faith's return. After setting a power cord and a bright pink laptop on the desk, she hesitated, eyes narrowed suspiciously as she glanced back and forth between them. "Why did you both stop talking when I came into the room? What's going on?"

"Nothing. Unfortunately." Daphne winked at Asher then pulled her sister close for a quick hug and kissed her cheek.

Faith stepped back, a serious look on her face. "No barhopping. It's too dangerous. Come back here if you and your friends want to drink. If the worst should happen, leave bread crumbs—not actual bread, of course, but some kind of clue to help me find you. You're going to the mall, right?"

"The mall? Seriously? I'm not sixteen anymore. And it's not barhopping, it's plain, clean, having fun. Everyone goes to bars—men, women, young people, old people. It's a place to unwind, catch up, stop off on your way home. You really need to loosen up."

"Daphne—"

"Relax, smother-mother. I wouldn't want you to have a heart attack worrying about me. We're just going to a movie." She wiggled her fingers at Asher. "Have fun, you two. Don't do anything I wouldn't do."

Faith shook her head as her sister jogged out the office door. "Don't stay out too late. Text me once you get there and before you leave. And make sure that Find My Exasperating Sister app is turned on this time."

Daphne raised a hand in the air without looking back. A moment later, the sound of the front door closing had Faith letting out a deep sigh.

"She's going to be the death of me."

He shoved his hands in his pants pockets, mainly to keep from doing something dangerous—like pulling Faith in for a hug. "If you get this worried when she's in town with people she knows, how do you survive when she's at school with thousands of strangers?"

She shuddered. "Don't remind me. It's hard, harder than you can imagine. She's like my own kid. I practically raised her."

In spite of his misgivings about her potential reaction, the lost look on her face had him taking her hand in his. "You were about her age now when your parents died, weren't you?"

She nodded, tightening her hand in his rather than pulling away, probably not even realizing it. But he felt that touch all the way to his heart, and only wished she'd accept more.

"She was a preteen, a baby in my eyes. I'm surprised my whole head hasn't gone gray just getting her to this stage. I'll probably never have children of my own. The worrying would likely kill me."

"Oh, I don't know. Maybe if you ever meet the right guy, you'll change your mind."

She shook her head. "Fat chance of that. I'm always working or trying to recover from working by bingeing TV shows. Heck, I spend more time with you than anyone else. When would I ever have a chance to meet a guy?" She chuckled and tugged her hand free. "Come on. We've—"

"Got work to do. I know." His heart was a little heavier as they rounded the desk.

Chapter Six

Faith smiled as Asher walked into the office several hours later carrying a plate of sandwiches, a bottle of water for her and a diet cola for him. "You're going to make some lucky woman an amazing husband someday. She'll enjoy being waited on. You certainly spoil me."

He gave her an odd look then smiled, making her wonder what that look meant. "Make any breakthroughs while I was slaving away in the kitchen?" He set the plate and drinks down to one side, away from the color-coded folders and papers on the desk.

"Not yet. I can't believe it's been…" She glanced at the time display on her phone on the corner of her desk and grimaced. "Over four hours since we started researching Leslie Parks and we still don't have a clue about what happened to her. It would help if TBI and Gatlinburg PD weren't so stingy about sharing their info. If it wasn't for the news reports, we wouldn't even know that she was abducted from her home."

"Speaking of news reports, the TBI press conference is supposed to start soon." He took the remote from one of her desk drawers and turned on the TV beside the massive map on the far wall that they'd used when trying to find Jasmine's grave.

After turning on closed captioning and muting the sound,

he took the largest of the two ham and cheese sandwiches he'd made and enthusiastically began scarfing down his very late lunch, or early dinner since it was past four in the afternoon.

Faith shook her head. "I don't know how you don't get fat."

"Why?" he asked around a mouthful. "It's just a sandwich. No chips or cookies."

She motioned toward hers. "Twice the size of my sandwich and you're a third of the way through in one massive bite."

He took a drink before answering. "I'm hungry. Besides, I'm twice your size. Of course, I eat twice what you do. I'm surprised you don't blow away in a strong wind. I'll be even more surprised if you finish half of your sandwich."

She took a large bite just to prove him wrong and then promptly ruined her point by choking on her food.

He laughed and pounded her back until she waved him away, begging for mercy. Her eyes were watering as she coughed in between laughs.

Finally, she drew her first deep breath and wiped her eyes. "Serves me right for trying to compete with you."

"I'll always win," he promised. "No matter what the contest."

"I'm pretty sure there are more ticks in my win column than yours right now."

He shook his head. "No way. You still owe me over our bet about that anchorwoman."

"Dang. I forgot about that. I guess we're eating steak tonight. Well, maybe not tonight. Not with it this late already. And time's our enemy with Leslie missing."

His expression turned serious. "Rain check. Definitely. Hopefully, by this time tomorrow, we'll—"

"Asher. Turn up the sound. The press conference is starting."

He grabbed the remote. "Look at Frost, front and center.

Always wants to preen for the cameras, even when he has nothing to say."

"The camera loves him just as much as he loves it," she admitted.

He gave her the side-eye. "If you like the stoop-shouldered, gray-haired, senior type, I suppose."

She laughed. "He has a sprinkling of gray, enough to make him look debonair. And he's not a senior or stoop-shouldered."

"If you say so."

About ten minutes later, he held up the remote. "Heard enough of this nonsense?"

"Definitely."

He muted the sound again. "In spite of all their talking, what they actually have is a big fat nothing."

"That's my take, too," she said. "Basically all they did was confirm what we already knew—that she was abducted from her home. The abductor sure is bold."

"Calm, cool, able to snatch a young woman from her house in broad daylight without anyone noticing. That's not the act of a first-timer. He's confident, patient. I guarantee he's done this before."

She sat back beside him, arms crossed. "That supports the theory that he's the same perpetrator who took Jasmine. Five years later, more mature, confident, experienced."

"Agreed. Maybe we've been going at this all wrong. We've been approaching it like we do all our cases, trying to gather as many facts about the victim as we can and build a timeline. That hasn't gotten us anywhere and it's what TBI and Gatlinburg PD are doing—Investigation 101—by the book. Let's throw the book away, make a leap in logic. We already assumed that Jasmine was one of the bodies. Let's assume we also know we're dealing with the same perpetrator and see where that takes us."

"What if we're wrong and we waste time chasing that theory?"

"Then we'll be no worse off than we are now. We have nothing to show for all the hours we've been working. Come on. Grayson wanted us to work on this because we know the case. Let's use that experience, jump in where we were on Jasmine's investigation and see where it leads."

She sat straighter. "You're saying build off our geographical profiling we were already working on."

"Absolutely. If it's the same guy, then he's lost his favorite burial grounds. He needs somewhere new. A place he can take his victim that's secluded, quiet, and offers options for… whatever he wants to do."

She rubbed her hands up and down her arms again. "A place where he can dispose of the body, too, just like we theorized in Jasmine's case."

"A theory that proved true. Same guy, same—"

"Habits," she said, feeling more enthusiastic now.

He pushed back from the desk. "I'll get the map."

"I'll clear some space."

He strode across the room and carefully pulled the three-foot-wide map off the wall where they'd taped it months earlier.

She stacked their papers and folders into neat piles on the floor.

He grinned as he waited. "Even when you're in a hurry, you're organized."

"Cleanliness is next to godliness." She frowned. "Wait. Wrong quote." She shrugged, brushed a few crumbs off the desk and then dumped them in the garbage can while he smoothed out the map on top.

"Colored pens?" he asked.

"Here, on my side." She opened the bottom left drawer and selected two markers. "Red this time? We used blue for Jasmine."

"Works for me." He took one and they both got on their knees on their chairs and leaned over the map. "We know the Parks live at the same address as they did when Jasmine went missing. So we can start with a red circle around that."

She drew a large circle around the house that already had a blue circle from when they began noting areas where the first sister had been known to frequent. "I wish we had time to talk to our convicts again."

"Let's cross our fingers that we can use the same reasoning they told us about to think like Leslie's abductor. Our theory is it's the same guy, so he'd have the same thought process."

"Right. Scary to make all these assumptions without facts, but I'm game to try." She drew another red circle around a horse ranch business for taking people on trail rides in the Smoky Mountains foothills.

He seemed surprised by what she'd circled. "Stan's Smoky Mountains Trail Rides. We talked through all the tourist traps when making our first pass on the map for Jasmine. I can't imagine Leslie's abductor trying to sneak her past people lining up for trail rides."

"We're trying to think outside the box, right? The TBI and police are covering the box. They're following standard protocols, performing *knock and talks*, canvassing Leslie's neighborhood trying to find someone who saw something out of place, noticed some stranger in an unfamiliar car, that kind of thing. We did all that with Jasmine and found nothing. No one in her neighborhood or even the immediate surrounding area had any useful information to help with the investigation."

He was starting to look as enthusiastic as she was feeling. "You're saying skip all that, because we covered it once already, again assuming we have the same perpetrator. We cover the places outside law enforcement's current search zone, places they won't get to anytime soon."

"Now we're on the same wavelength again." She tapped the circle she'd just drawn. "This place seems promising to me. It's not all that far from the burial site and yet has many similarities. Familiar types of surroundings and advantages could place this in the killer's comfort zone. That's what the convicts told us, that they typically had specific types of territories they considered theirs, places where they felt secure. That's where they hunted."

"And where they buried their dead."

She grimaced but nodded her agreement.

He ran his fingertips across the map, exploring the topography symbols that showed many of the waterfalls in the area, major trails, elevations of the various foothills and mountains. It also showed the roads in the vicinity of the stables. "I rarely go out that way, don't even remember this place. It's not on a main thoroughfare between Gatlinburg and Pigeon Forge, or any other towns. There wouldn't be much traffic to worry about. And there should be pull-offs since it's in the foothills, safe places where someone can park their car to take pictures of the mountains."

"Places where a killer could pull off the main road and no one would think anything of it. He could park in one of those and walk Leslie onto the trail-riding land."

He considered the map again then gave her a skeptical look. "Theoretically, sure. But the land around that ranch has rough terrain, steep climbs. I don't see anyone making it up those foothills without a horse, which is kind of the point of running a trail-riding business there. Leslie's picture is all over the news. Her abductor wouldn't want to risk someone seeing him try to lead her into the mountains. The weather is mild today, perfect for sightseeing or riding. That place has to be crawling with tourists right now, even if it is getting late in the day. I say we skip the horse ranch and look down this main road for something more appealing to our killer. Someplace more isolated."

"I'd agree with you, except that today is Wednesday. This particular business is only open on weekends. No tourists to worry about."

He arched a brow. "You sound sure about that. I know you didn't call them to schedule yourself a trail ride. You hate horses."

"I don't hate them. They hate me."

"You got bucked off as a kid and stepped on once as a teenager. Deciding all horses hate you because of those two minor incidents is rather extreme."

"Minor? You should have seen the bruises I had from being thrown. They lasted for weeks. And the beast who stepped on my foot broke two bones. It still hurts sometimes, all these years later."

He grinned. "One of these days I'll get you on a horse again and you'll change your mind."

"No way. Unlike you, I didn't grow up around them. And I don't intend to do anything to change that going forward."

"Back to my original question. Why do you know so much about this place?"

"Daphne's been visiting, remember? She went trail riding with some of her friends last week. I did some of the research for her, called around, made the reservations. She didn't want to wait for a weekend, so we marked this place off her list. She ended up at a place in Pigeon Forge."

"Makes sense. What doesn't make sense is for a trail-riding business to only be open two days a week. Seems like they'd lose a ton of money limiting their options like that in a town that lives and dies by the tourism dollar."

"I asked Stan Darden, the owner, about that when I called. He said he and his son, Stan Darden Junior, used to run the place seven days a week. But the father is retiring and downsizing. It's just the two of them now during the week, taking care of the remaining horses. They have others who help on weekends, earning enough for him to help offset the maintenance costs. That's the only reason he keeps it open anymore, so he can afford to keep his horses."

"I wonder what the son thinks about his dad essentially letting the business die instead of giving it to him. Regardless, I agree we should take a look. With only the two Stans around during the week, our perpetrator could easily park down the road, like we said, walk Leslie onto the property, maybe staying in the tree line on the peripheral edge. Once he's out of sight of the main house and doesn't see any activity at the stables, maybe he takes her into an empty stall or tack room. If he's comfortable with horses, he could even take a couple out and escape into the foothills with her. The roadblocks the state police likely have on the main highways in and out of the area won't stop someone on horseback from escaping through the woods. How far is this place from the Parkses' residence?"

"About twenty minutes, like where he took Jasmine. It's just in a different direction from her home. But get this—it's only five minutes from his makeshift cemetery, in the same geographical area where he feels comfortable. If TBI or the local cops aren't considering this ranch, I believe we should."

"Agreed."

She wrote a note on the map, naming the ranch as their first place of interest. "What other promising locations should we focus on?" She ran her finger on the map down the road past the trail-riding place, studying the names and descriptions they'd put on it earlier. "Maybe this house here. It's isolated. No neighbors anywhere around to speak of. I can search property records, see if it's occupied full-time or a vacation rental. It's one of the places we were going to research next for Jasmine if the scent dog hadn't hit on our original location."

When he didn't respond, she glanced at him. He seemed to be lost in thought as he stared at the map, his brows drawn down in concentration.

"Faith to Asher, come in. What's going on in that brilliant but math-challenged mind of yours?"

"What?" He glanced up, seemingly surprised. "Oh…the stables. There's something bothering me about those." He drummed his fingers on the table. "Stables. Horses. I heard something earlier, somewhere."

"About horses?"

He nodded. "I can't remember where, or why…wait. The news. That's it." He grabbed the remote control.

"What, Asher? Tell me."

"The press conference, after it was over. There was a story on the ticker the news runs along the bottom of the TV about some stables. But I didn't pay attention to what it said." He pressed the rewind button until the feed was at the end of the press conference. Then he fast-forwarded and reversed several times, frowning at the TV. "Yes, there." He pressed Play.

She stared up at the screen, reading the captions. "Blah, blah, blah…okay, same stables I circled. A horse broke out of its pen this morning. They're warning motorists in that area to be careful in case the horse wanders onto the road."

"Not exactly, darlin'. *Two* horses went missing."

She frowned. "Okay, two. But they said the horses broke out of a pen. They didn't say *went missing*."

"No. They didn't. *I'm* saying it. What if they didn't break out? What if someone *took* them and made it look like the horses escaped on their own? Not long after Leslie was abducted?"

She checked their notes on the map, around the red circles, the distances between them. "When did the horse thing happen?"

"Early this morning. The owner, or whoever was checking on the horses, realized they were gone around ten."

She stared at him. "Leslie went missing just after nine. Twenty minutes from the horse place."

He smiled. "Stables."

"Whatever. That's enough time for our perpetrator to drive there—if they did go to this place—leave his car on a pull-off, steal the horses and—"

"Force her at gunpoint or knifepoint to ride up into the foothills. He doesn't have to know the area. The horses do. They're trained to follow the trails. Once he gets high enough, far enough, he could go off-trail, take her somewhere isolated where no one ever goes."

They both stared down at the map, considering the possibilities, talking about other potential hiding places. But they kept coming back to the stables.

"It's a long shot," he said. "We have no evidence either way, just supposition."

"And it assumes the killer is comfortable with horses."

"He's comfortable outdoors, has been in this area for years. It's not a huge leap to assume he could be familiar with horses given that there are so many horse-riding businesses around the Smokies. But, honestly, even a novice could handle a trail horse. That's the whole point. They're docile and trail-trained so tourists who've never sat on a horse before are safe around them. Once you're on their back, they practically guide themselves."

"You'd still need a saddle. A novice wouldn't know how to put one on. I sure wouldn't."

"If he chose this place, he either has the background to prep the horses or—"

"He forced one of the ranch hands to do it. Or, I guess it would be the son, or father, since they're the only ones there during the week."

He shook his head. "That didn't happen or the news would have said that. They always go with the most sensational story angle. Someone being forced to saddle some horses would definitely be a bigger story than a small note about motorists watching out for horses on the loose. I'm a transplant around here. Horses didn't escape all that often where we lived, if ever. You've told me your family visited here a lot on vacations. How common is it for this kind of thing to happen? Ever heard of that on the Gatlinburg news before?"

She stood. "No. Never. We need to check this out. Now. We should call the TBI. Let them handle it. Goodness knows they can wrestle up a lot more manpower than we can to search for her. Maybe they can get a chopper up and—"

"Scare Leslie's horse into plunging down the side of a mountain? A trail horse is docile, but it's still a horse. A chopper could spook it. Regardless, do you honestly think the TBI would put even one person on this if we called? What would we tell them? That we're working a case we're not supposed to be working? That we drew some circles on a map and guessed that some horses that got out of their stalls *might* have been taken by the bad guy? With absolutely no proof whatsoever? What do you think they'd do with that information?"

She frowned. "They'd laugh us off the phone. Then they'd complain to Grayson that we broke the rules of UB's contract with law enforcement, not to mention the warrant. They'd try to get us fired. Or worse, arrest us."

"And while they're comparing jock straps to see whose is bigger, Leslie is all alone with a serial killer. Maybe she's at these stables, maybe not. But so far, that's our best educated guess. If Leslie was Daphne, what would you do?"

She grabbed her purse from near one of the stacks on the floor. "You drive. I'll call Grayson."

Chapter Seven

As Asher's truck bumped along the pot-holed gravel road into Stan's Smoky Mountains Trail Rides, he shook his head in disgust.

Faith straightened in the passenger seat from studying their map. "You see something?"

"Neglect. That barn on the left must house the stables. Doesn't look like it's seen a paintbrush in decades. Paddocks beside it are muddy and full of weeds. Only thing to recommend this place is that pond and the gorgeous waterfall coming down from those foothills at the end of the pasture. It's probably a great location for selfies. Tourists might come here just for that, especially if there are more falls up the mountain where they go trail riding. As for everything else, rundown is a nice way to describe it. Look at the fence around the pasture. Half the rails are broken or missing, with large gaps between a lot of the posts. No wonder some horses got out. It's probably not the first time."

"So much for our theory that the killer stole them."

"I still want to talk to the owner, get his take on it. If he's home."

"I doubt it," she said. "I must have called him five times on the way here. It rolls to voice mail."

"Doesn't surprise me that he doesn't bother checking his

messages all that often. By the looks of this place, I don't think this Stan Darden guy is all that worried about attracting new business."

"He answered when I called last week. Maybe that was lucky timing on my part."

Asher's hands tightened on the steering wheel. "Or maybe something has happened to him."

Her worried gaze met his. She folded the map and put it in the console between their seats. "I'm guessing that building off to the right is the office. Might double as their house too. None of the other outbuildings seem big enough for anything besides storage."

Sure enough, when he pulled his truck up to the small, weathered, single-story building, a rusty sign on the faded blue door proclaimed it as the Office.

He cut the engine and popped open his door. "You want to call about that place down the road you marked on the map? Find out if it's occupied or not while I see if someone will answer the door? We can check the other place when we're done here."

"If we don't find Leslie."

"If we don't find Leslie, yes. You said Grayson was sending Lance to help us search. Can you call him first, get an ETA?"

She pulled her phone from her pants pocket. "Will do."

By the time he reached the office door, his boots were mired in mud and the hems of his dress pants were suffering the same fate. He sorely regretted not changing out of his suit before they'd headed out here. But that would have meant a trip to his house, in the opposite direction. They didn't have time for that.

He tried the doorknob, but it was locked, which made sense since the place only did trail rides on weekends. But if this was also their residence, he'd expect to see some dirt or mud on the front stoop from them going in and out. The stoop was one of the few things around that seemed clean.

Maybe Stan Senior and Stan Junior were both in the stables and hadn't taken a phone with them. Seemed odd, but if they were mucking stalls, the possibility of a phone falling and getting dirty or even trampled by a horse might make them think twice about taking it along. That would explain them not answering Faith's calls on the way here. They could even be in town, maybe enjoying an early dinner. There weren't any vehicles parked on the property, at least from what they'd seen driving up.

Several knocks later bore no results. The place was quiet, seemingly deserted. He stepped to the only window on the front and tried to peer between the slats of the blinds. They'd been turned facing up, no doubt for privacy. All he could make out was the ceiling fan's blades slowly turning. Looking back at the truck, he motioned to Faith that he was going to take a circuit around the building.

As he walked the perimeter, he checked for any signs that would indicate that someone had been there recently. Everything appeared to be in order, no evidence of a break-in, no trampled-down grass.

When he hopped back inside the truck, he said, "It doesn't appear that anyone's been here in the last few days."

"Someone had to have been at the stables this morning to report the horses missing."

"If they were, they didn't go to the office. Keep a careful eye out. Nothing we've found so far rules out that our perpetrator took the horses."

His jaw tightened as the truck bumped across the gravel toward the dilapidated barn. "I sure hope the owner takes better care of his animals than he does his property. Did you find anything out about the place down the road that we want to check?"

"I spoke to the owner and his wife, who live there full time. Neither of them have seen anything unusual. And they have dogs, lots of them, by the sound of the barking in the background. Mr. Pittman, the husband, said the dogs run loose on his property. If anyone had been out there, he'd have known about it."

"We can probably move that place lower on our list of potential spots then. What about Lance?"

"He's on his way. But he won't be here for another forty-five minutes or so."

"Forty-five? He doesn't live that far from this place, fifteen minutes at the most if he takes the highway route."

"He was out of town conducting an interview when Grayson called and told him to come back. The rest of our team is either at UB or working other critical investigations. Do you want me to ask Grayson to send someone else?"

Asher thought about it then shook his head. "No. I'm sure Grayson weighed priorities when he assigned Lance to help. No doubt TBI and Gatlinburg PD are all over him right now and he has to be careful with appearances in regard to Leslie's case. Lance is the right guy for this. He and I go riding every now and then. If we do end up on horseback in the mountains, he'll be an asset."

Her slight intake of breath had him glancing at her as he parked by the barn. "You okay?"

"Um, fine. I just…didn't think about us actually, you know—"

"Riding a horse?"

"Yeah. That."

He smiled. "If we find evidence to support our theory that the bad guy might have taken Leslie up into the foothills above this place, how did you think we were going to go after him?"

"I guess I didn't think that far ahead." She drew another shaky breath.

He gently squeezed her hand. "Don't stress over that possibility. Let's take it a step at a time and see if we find evidence to lead us in that direction. Okay?"

She gave him a weak smile.

He led her along the least muddy, cleanest path he could find to the entrance but she was still cursing up a storm by the time they stopped.

"Why didn't we change into jeans before we left?" she grumbled. "These pants are ruined."

"You can take them off if you want. I don't mind."

She laughed. "You're impossible. And, no, I'm certainly not going to walk around a bunch of smelly animals bare-assed."

His throat tightened. "Does that mean you're not wearing any—"

"It *means* mind your own business. You're not getting me to take off my pants."

He couldn't help grinning at the embarrassed flush on her face.

"Shouldn't we be looking for shoe prints, or something?" Without waiting for his reply, she stomped into the building.

Asher chuckled and followed her inside.

She hesitated a few feet in, her nose wrinkling. "That smell. Ugh. I don't know what Daphne likes about horses. This same smell was all over her when she got home after riding with her friends the other day. Took two cycles in the washing machine to get rid of it."

"It's the smell of freedom. The freedom to go anywhere you want, see the sights, enjoy nature as it was meant to be enjoyed."

"I can enjoy it just fine with my two feet on the ground. And no horsey odor."

He laughed.

A shadow moved off to their right. He and Faith immediately drew their guns, pointing down the darkened aisle between two rows of stalls. There was a tall, brawny man standing in the shadows, a horse not far behind him.

"Show yourself," Asher demanded.

"Whoa, hold it. Don't shoot." He stepped into the light shining through the open door of the main entrance, his jeans faded and dirty, his blue-plaid shirt just as faded but relatively clean. He held both of his hands up in the air. His brown eyes were wide with uncertainty as he glanced back and forth at them. "If you're here to rob me, there's no cash on hand. I swear."

"Who are you?" Asher demanded as he and Faith continued to aim their pistols at him.

"The owner. Well, future owner. My dad, Stan Senior, owns this place. I'm Stan Junior. He's going to turn the place over to me once I get enough sweat equity built up." He shook his head as if embarrassed he'd shared so much. "Would you mind putting those guns away, or at least pointing them in another direction? I'm not armed and I swear I won't fight you. Nothing here is worth my life. Take whatever horses you want. You can get decent money for some of them."

While Asher wondered at Stan Junior's categorization of his dad turning over the business when Stan Senior had told Faith he was downsizing it, Faith called out, "Let's see your ID."

His dark eyes flicked to her with a flash of annoyance. "DUI. Lost my license. I haven't bothered yet to get one of those identification cards."

"You live here? On the property?" Asher asked.

His gaze returned to Asher. "You're kidding, right? In that dilapidated building Pop calls an office? No way. I live with my girlfriend in town. Dad drove me here this morning to feed the horses. That's when we discovered the gate was open and a couple of trail horses missing. He called it in and left me here to handle the search." He mumbled something unflattering about his father under his breath. "Why are you asking about this and pointing guns at me? What the heck is going on?"

Asher studied the blond-haired man, noting the tension around his eyes. Of course, anyone having guns pointed at them would be worried. That alone didn't mean he was hiding anything. "Where's Stan Senior?"

He rolled his eyes much like Faith tended to do. "My old man? Who knows? Probably off spending my inheritance. Maybe he went back to his place in Pigeon Forge. It's a heck of a lot nicer than anything around here." A flash of anger crossed his face. "Way nicer than me and Rhonda's place in town. You going to rob the place or not?"

The man was either a really good actor or he was the thirtysomething-year-old, entitled brat he appeared to be. Asher glanced at Faith. She subtly nodded, and they both holstered their weapons.

"We heard some horses went missing this morning," Asher explained. "We came by to see if they'd been located yet and whether you think they went missing on accident or on purpose."

Relief flooded the man's face as he dropped his hands to his sides. "You're cops? Why didn't you start with that? Dad called you guys hours ago. It's about dang time someone came out to help instead of just talking to us on the phone. Do you have any idea what a twelve-hundred-pound animal can do to a car if it runs out in the road?" He frowned. "Wait a minute. On purpose? You think someone stole them?"

"You don't?"

He shrugged. "Hadn't really considered it before. I suppose it's possible. Shouldn't you be taking this down? Writing up my statement or something?"

"We're not police officers," Asher said. "We used to be, but now we both work in the private sector."

Stan's brows drew down in confusion. "Private sector?"

Asher gestured to Faith. "This is my partner, Faith Lancaster. I'm Asher Whitfield. We work on cold cases for a company called Unfinished Business."

"Cold cases, huh? What's that got to do with our failing trail-riding operation?" Again, he sounded aggravated, as if his complaints about the place were an ongoing argument with his father.

This time it was Faith who explained. "We were investigating a cold case, but got sidelined to work on a recent abduction. The missing horses story on the news got us wondering if the perpetrator might have taken them to head into the mountains with his captive."

His eyes widened. "Cool. I mean, not cool that someone got kidnapped or whatever. But thinking they could be at our place might put us on the map, know what I mean? Could be good for business."

Asher clenched his jaw. He didn't like this guy one bit. "More importantly, a woman's life is at stake and we're trying to find her."

"Oh, yeah. Of course. What can I do to help?"

A whinny sounded behind him in the near darkness.

Stan let out an exasperated breath. "Coco's calling. I just got her saddled and she's getting impatient." He headed down the darkened aisle.

Asher strode after him, not wanting to let him out of his sight.

Faith followed, but stayed well out of reach of the impressive bay mare standing in the middle of the aisle, a white blaze on its face and flashing white stockings on its legs.

"Now that's a nice piece of horseflesh." Asher couldn't resist smoothing his hand down its velvety muzzle, earning a playful toss of the mare's head and a gentle nudge against his shoulder.

Stan tightened the cinch on the mare's girth. "She's one of two bays. The other over there is Ginger. Do I sense another equestrian aficionado in our midst?"

Asher chuckled. "Aficionado might be too strong a word. But I grew up around horses. I know quality when I see it. This mare is gorgeous. Not what I expected in a trail-riding operation."

"They wouldn't be here if it wasn't for me. Dad's stock is the usual docile, follow-the-leader kind most places around here use. I insisted on getting a couple of decent mounts for the two of us when we need to ride the fence line or chaperone tourists up into the foothills. The bays are just as surefooted as a trail horse, but they're bigger, stronger, with more stamina."

He roughly patted Coco's neck, causing her to nervously shy away. He frowned and yanked the reins, making the mare grunt in protest and forcing her back beside him.

Asher stiffened, instantly on alert. For a man who worked with horses daily, Stan didn't seem all that good with them. Asher exchanged a quick glance with Faith and saw his suspicions mirrored in her eyes.

"I don't mean to be rude or whatever," Stan said. "But neither Dad nor I have seen anyone else out here today. And I haven't seen any signs of a break-in. I'm guessing the horses got out on their own. And If I don't get going soon for round two of my search for them, I'll lose what daylight I have left."

"Round two? If you've been searching for them and haven't found them yet, why did you return to the stables?" Asher asked.

Junior gave him an impatient look. "I've been searching all morning. I was hungry and tired. Any other *important* questions?"

"Take us with you," Asher said.

Stan's eyes widened. "What? Why?"

Faith put her hand on Asher's arm. "I'm fine waiting here. Once Lance arrives, I can update him and send him after you two."

"Um, hello," Stan said. "What are you talking about? Who's Lance?"

"Lance Cabrera, a guy we work with. Give us a minute," Asher said. "Saddle that other bay and a trail horse."

"But why—"

"We believe the man who abducted a woman this morning may have stolen your two horses and is in the foothills above your ranch right now. If you go up there by yourself and stumble across him, your life is in danger. You can be our guide and let Faith and me take care of any trouble that comes along."

Junior's eyes widened, but he didn't argue anymore. Instead, he ducked into what Asher supposed was a tack room and hurried out with another saddle. "Give me a few minutes."

After he headed into the other bay's stall, Faith whispered, "Asher, don't ask me to do this. I can't get on one of those things."

Stan stuck his head out of the stall. "If you're worried the bay is too spirited, I've got a four-year-old gelding that's as calm as can be."

"We won't need the gelding," Faith insisted.

"Yes. We will."

Faith frowned.

Stan Junior disappeared back into the stall.

Asher led her a few feet back up the aisle, out of Stan's earshot.

She shook his hand off her arm. "You're not talking me into this. I'm not riding that, that, that…"

"Horse?"

"Gelding." She shuddered. "Sounds even scarier than the word *horse*. What does that even mean?"

"A gelding is a male horse that's been castrated."

Her eyes widened. "Castrated. How cruel."

"It's no more cruel than neutering a dog to avoid unwanted litters of puppies who end up being euthanized. Besides, castrating a horse makes it more docile, easier to control. And it helps keep the peace in the stables. Trust me, you don't want randy stallions trying to kick down their stalls to get to the mares all the time."

"So I take it a gelding would be your ride of choice?"

He grinned. "Hell no. I'll take a randy stallion any day of the week. That fire and attitude makes riding much more of a challenge."

Faith waved a hand as if waving away his words. "We're getting off track. I'm not going to ride one of those things." She crossed her arms. "And you're not making me."

If it had been anyone else, he'd have laughed at her childish-sounding words. But this was Faith. And he could see the fear in her eyes that she was struggling so hard to hide.

Asher gently pulled her arms down and took her hands in his. "It's okay. I'm not going to try to force you to ride a horse—"

"Good. Because I don't want to have to shoot you."

He smiled. "That's kind of the point, though. The shooting part. I need backup, someone who's as good a marksman as I am—"

"Pfft. I'm way better."

"Perhaps."

"I always beat you at target practice."

"I'd say it's more fifty-fifty. Regardless, I need backup." He glanced toward the stall where Stan was working before meeting her gaze again. "You're the only other qualified person here right now to help me if things go bad."

"That's not fair. You're trying to guilt me into going with you."

"No. I'm making sure you're aware of the facts and that your horse prejudice doesn't blind you to them."

She swore.

"If Leslie is up there," he said, "and I find her, I'll need your help to make sure we can rescue her and that the bad guy…" Again he glanced toward the stall. "Doesn't get a chance to hurt her—or worse. I need your skills and expertise, Faith. I know how hard this is for you. And I wouldn't ask if it wasn't important. But if you stay here and I get into trouble, the time it takes for you or someone else to reach me might mean compromising Leslie's safety."

Her face turned pale. "Lance is on the way." She jerked her phone out and checked the screen. She winced. "Thirty minutes, give or take."

"Okay."

Faith blinked. "Okay?"

He feathered his hand along her incredibly soft face. "It's okay. You stay here. When Lance arrives, tell him which way we went. Send him after us."

A single tear slid down her face and she angrily wiped it away. "You know darn well I'm not going to stand around for thirty minutes while you go up there without backup." This time it was her turn to look toward where Stan was saddling the other bay. She lowered her voice. "And we both know you might need backup sooner rather than later. Something's off with Stan."

"I agree," Asher whispered.

She sighed heavily. "Get me that stupid gelding."

He grinned. "That's my girl." He pressed a kiss to her forehead. "Thank you, Faith."

She made a show of wiping his kiss away. "I hate it when you use psychology on me. Thank me with an expensive dinner, assuming I survive this escapade. This cancels out the steak dinner I owe you, by the way."

The sound of metal jangling had both of them turning to see the other bay, Ginger, being led out of her stall to stand beside Coco.

Stan glanced their way. "I'll get the gelding and—"

"Never mind," Asher said. "Ms. Lancaster will ride double with me. The guy coming to back us up can saddle the gelding himself. Like you said, there's not much daylight yet. We need to get going."

"Backup? Cops?"

"The coworker I mentioned before. He's already on the way—"

Stan suddenly vaulted into Coco's saddle and jerked her around in a circle toward the open doors behind them.

Asher swore and sprinted after him, yanking out his pistol. "Stop or I'll shoot!"

Stan kicked Coco and they took off outside.

Faith ran to the doors beside Asher, her pistol drawn like his, both of them aimed toward the fleeing figure of Junior on horseback, racing toward the foothills.

She swore. "We can't shoot a man in the back."

"I'm more worried that if we kill him, and he's got Leslie up in those foothills, we may never find her." Asher shoved his pistol into the shoulder holster beneath his suit jacket and jogged back to Ginger. As soon as he stuck his foot in the stirrup, the saddle slid off the horse and slammed to the floor, sending up a cloud of dust and hay.

Faith ran over to him, waving at the air in front of her face. "What happened?"

Asher grabbed the girth strap, swearing when he saw it cut in two. "He sliced the strap that secures the saddle." He shoved the useless saddle to the side, yanked off what looked like a rug from the horse's back and then pulled Ginger to the nearest stall.

He reached for the top of the stall's wooden slat wall, but his suit jacket pulled tight across his shoulders. After shucking it off and tossing it aside, he was able to climb the wall to mount the horse.

Faith rushed toward him then scrambled back again to give the horse a wide berth. "Asher! What are you doing? You need a saddle—"

He slid onto the horse's back and yanked the reins free from the post, gently patting her neck to settle her down. "No time. Odds are that Stan Junior, or whoever he is, has Leslie. If he hasn't killed her already, he's about to. Unless I can stop him." He clucked to the mare and turned her around to face the exit.

"Wait!" Faith bravely moved to the side of the horse again, standing her ground even when the horse tossed its head. Faith extended her hands toward him. "Swing me up, or whatever. You said we'd ride double."

"Not now. I'm sorry, Faith. It would slow me down." He kicked the mare's side and sent her racing out of the stables at a full gallop.

Chapter Eight

Faith clenched her fists in frustration as she watched Grayson in his business suit, minus the jacket, clinging to the back of the huge red horse, scrabbling over rocks and up the hillside. Soon, they disappeared into the trees. The man was fearless. And competent in ways she'd never imagined. Who rode bareback up a mountain at a full run? Chasing a man who may or may not be a killer?

With no backup.

She cursed herself for the coward that she was and whirled around. Whipping out her cell phone, she strode back inside the building and punched one of the numbers saved in her favorite contacts list. As she held the phone to her ear, she peered into the first stall. A doe-eyed red horse, much smaller than the ones that Stan and Asher were riding, stared silently back at her. Was that a gelding? How was she supposed to recognize a gelding? She bit her lip, then leaned down and peered through the wooden slats. She couldn't even tell if it was a boy or a girl, much less whether it had been castrated.

Jogging to the next stall, she looked in. This time a gray-and-white horse stared back at her, the dark spots on its rump reminding her of one of those spotted dogs. What were they called? Dalmatians maybe? It was pretty and seemed nice.

But it was too big. She couldn't even imagine the terrifying view from its back. On to the next stall.

The phone finally clicked. "Hey, Faith. Sorry it took so long to answer. I was—"

"Lance. How soon will you be here?"

"Nice to talk to you too. I'm guessing another fifteen minutes or so. Traffic in town is crazy with all the tourists—"

"Forget the tourists. Step on the gas. Asher's all alone on the mountain chasing the guy we think is the killer. He needs backup. And I..." She cleared her throat. "I couldn't get on a damn horse and help him."

"I'll be there as fast as I can." The engine roared. Horns honked. The phone clicked.

Faith shoved it in her pocket and hurried down the line of stalls, looking at each horse. There were eight in all. Every single one of them was intimidating. But the first horse was the smallest. She prayed it was the gentle gelding.

Running back to the first stall, she was relieved to realize the horse already had the leather thing on its head. She glanced around for the reins. There, hanging on a hook right outside the stall. It was a long leather strap with a clip on one end. That must be it. She grabbed it and opened the door with trembling hands.

"Here, horsey, horsey." She held out her hand. The horse nickered softly. "Well at least you aren't trying to bite me. Good sign, right? We're going to be friends, okay?" Forcing herself to shuffle forward, she reached out then gently feathered her hand down the horse's neck as she'd seen Asher do earlier. The horse didn't seem to mind. It turned its head and shoved its nose into a metal can hanging from the wall, then snorted.

Drawing a deep breath, Faith inched forward then quickly clipped the rein to the round metal ring at the end of the leather contraption on the horse's head. It didn't even flinch.

She let out a breath and smiled. "This isn't so bad. Come on, horsey, horsey. This way." She gently tugged the rein. The horse snorted again, as if disappointed, but it left the metal bucket and docilely followed her out of the stall.

Faith looped the rein around the same metal hook it had been hanging from earlier and the horse patiently stood waiting.

Even though she was feeling more confident, she knew there was no way she'd be able to stay up on a horse without something more than its mane to hold on to. She glanced at the saddle Stan had sabotaged. She needed something like that, only smaller. Something she could actually lift. Hadn't Stan pulled that saddle out of one of the rooms on the other side of the aisle?

Yes, there. The door on the end. She ran to it and yanked it open. Her heart sank when she saw the jumble of leather reins and saddles stacked all around and hanging from hooks on the wall. She had no idea which one to try. But all of the saddles closest to the door seemed too big and heavy. There had to be something more manageable for her, lighter, or she wouldn't even be able to get it on the horse.

Near the end of one of the stacks was exactly what she'd hoped to find, a small, lightweight saddle. It looked odd, with two knobs sticking up on the end, not at all like the one Stan had used. But she supposed a saddle was a saddle, and she'd be able to hold on to both the knobs if she needed to. She hefted it, relieved that it weighed no more than a large sack of potatoes, and carried it to the waiting horse.

"Now what?" She looked at the horse, who looked at her, perhaps a bit skeptically. Then it closed its eyes and proceeded to ignore her.

"That's fine," she said. "Just stand there like that. Let me do the work. Don't move, okay?"

She sent up a quick prayer then tossed the saddle up on the

horse's back. It whinnied in alarm and bumped against the stall. Faith spoke calming, nonsensical words and managed to keep the saddle from sliding off. As soon as the horse settled down again, she went to work trying to figure out how to keep the saddle from falling off. The amount of buckles and pieces of leather were confusing. But she knew there was one big strap that was supposed to go around its stomach. Asher had called it a girth strap, hadn't he?

Running over to the saddle that Asher had tried to use, she studied the sliced piece of leather. Keeping that picture in her mind, she ran back to the horse and figured out which strap seemed about the same.

A few minutes later, she stood back to admire her handiwork. Everything looked right, as near as she could tell. And when she'd tugged on the saddle, it'd stayed in place.

"Okay. Now, how do I get up?"

The horse aimed a sleepy glance at her then closed its eyes again.

"You're no help," she grumbled. Asher had climbed the boards of the stall to get on his horse. Without any stools or ladders in sight, she supposed she'd have to do the same thing. It took several tries, but finally she gingerly lowered herself down on the saddle. The horse didn't move at all.

She chuckled with satisfaction. "Boy, will Asher be surprised. Let's get this party started, Red. Is that a good name for you? Asher needs us." She patted its neck before tugging the other end of the rein off the hook where she'd hung it. Something wasn't right. It was clipped to the horse's headgear on one side, but the other end had a handle of sorts, not a clip. Didn't Asher's reins hook on both ends?

She wound the rein around her hand to shorten it and then experimented by tugging it. The horse dutifully turned around, facing the exit doors.

Faith shrugged. Maybe she wasn't doing it exactly right, but it was working.

"Yah, horsey."

It didn't move.

She wiggled in the saddle. "Come on. Giddy up, Red. Let's go."

The horse turned its head and gave her the side-eye.

"Great. I picked the broken horse. Come on. Go." She wiggled in the saddle again. "Go, dang it. Come on."

"Faith, stop!"

She turned in the saddle to see Lance running toward her. The horse decided at that moment to move. It trotted out the stable doors with Faith desperately sawing back on the rein. Red jerked to a stop and started turning in a circle.

Lance was suddenly there, grabbing the rein from her hands and pulling the horse to a stop again. "Faith, what the heck are you doing? Trying to kill yourself?"

"I'm trying to help Asher. I told you he needs backup." She frowned. "How did you get here so fast?"

"Ran every light in town. Come on, let's get you off of there."

She gladly let him pluck her from the saddle. But instead of him vaulting up and heading into the mountains, he turned and jogged back to the stables with the horse in tow.

Faith stood for a moment in shock then jogged after him. When she ran inside, she was even more surprised to see her saddle falling to the floor and Lance shoving the horse inside its stall.

"Lance, stop. Don't waste time being picky about which horse you use. Asher needs you."

"That's why I'll grab a horse big enough to support me without buckling under my weight. I'll use a saddle I can sit in, not an English sidesaddle." He shook his head. "Why they even have one of those at a trail-riding place is beyond me.

Instead of a lunge line and a halter with no way to steer the horse, I'll use reins and a bridle. For goodness' sake, have you never ridden a horse before?"

"A couple of times. Didn't end well," she admitted.

"No kidding."

She crossed her arms and moved out of his way as Lance led a larger, dark brown horse out of the next stall.

"Tack room?" he asked.

"If you mean where are the saddles and stuff, in there." She pointed to the door at the end.

He strode inside. A moment later, he emerged carrying one of the big heavy saddles, a small rug and a handful of leather with metal jangling from it.

"Can you call Asher and get GPS coordinates for me?" He spoke soothingly to the horse and tossed the rug on its back.

"I don't want to distract him or give his position away if he's trying to sneak up on the bad guy. But I can use my Find Asher app and tell you exactly where he is."

He chuckled as he settled the saddle on the horse's back. "You have an app on your phone to locate Asher?"

"More or less. It's the same app I use for my sister. It'll locate his phone."

"Works for me." His fingers moved with lightning speed as he buckled and tugged and adjusted the fit of the saddle. A few minutes later, he'd ditched the leather contraption—the halter, she remembered he'd called it—and replaced it with another that looked almost exactly the same except that it had metal hanging off the end that he slipped into the horse's mouth, and rings on both sides to hook leather straps to it.

Now she understood why her rein hadn't looked right. It wasn't a rein. It was whatever that lunge line thing was that he'd mentioned. She clenched her hands, embarrassed that she'd done everything so wrong. But also grateful that Lance had gotten there when he had and knew what he was doing.

He hoisted himself into the saddle and turned the horse using a subtle motion of his legs without even using the reins he'd looped over the front of the saddle. He held his phone and arched a brow. "Coordinates?"

"Oh, yeah. Right. Texting them to you now."

His phone beeped and he typed on the screen, nodded and slid his phone into his shirt pocket. "Text me the coordinates every few minutes. I'll adjust my path accordingly. And call Grayson, give him an update. I didn't get a chance to call him during my Mario Andretti race here."

Before she could answer, he looped the reins in his hand and kicked the horse's sides. It whinnied and flew out of the building.

After watching to make sure Lance was going up the same trail that Asher had, Faith headed inside and pressed the favorites contact for Grayson. He answered on the first ring.

"Faith, it's about dang time I got an update. What's the situation? Found any evidence of our abductor or Leslie being at those stables you were checking out?"

"Maybe, maybe not." She updated him on everything that was happening as she carried the English sidesaddle, as Lance had called it, back into the tack room. As she answered Grayson's questions, she idly fingered the various pieces of equipment hanging from the walls, wondering what they were. One she recognized: a whip. She was glad that neither Asher nor Lance had used one of those on their horses. When she reached the end of the large, messy room, she stumbled on something on the floor and fell against the wall. When she looked down to see what she'd tripped over, she sucked in a sharp breath.

"What's wrong?" Grayson demanded.

She bent to flip back the rest of the little rug. Her hand shook as she lifted another, larger rug beside it. "Oh, no."

"Faith? What is it? Speak to me."

"Based on their physical resemblance, I think I just found the Dardens—Stan Senior and the real Stan Junior. They're dead."

Chapter Nine

Asher knelt to study the hoof prints in the dirt. They appeared to be fresh, and they were about the same size and depth of the prints his bay was leaving. He was on the right track. He just hoped he reached Stan before Stan reached Leslie.

He was about to mount his horse again when a whinny sounded through the trees. Close by, maybe twenty, thirty yards. And since he didn't hear the sound of the horse's hooves, it must be stopped. Easing his gun out of his shoulder holster, he held it down at his side, leaving his bay to munch on the grass beneath the trees as he crept through the woods.

A few moments later, he heard another sound. A whimper. His hand tightened around his pistol and he sped up, as quiet as possible but as quickly as he could. There, up ahead, through a break in the trees, he saw what he'd been looking for. Leslie. She was alive, thank God. Naked, she was standing on a five-or six-foot-long piece of log, cowering back against an oak tree, her head bent down with her hair covering her face. But he didn't need to see her face to know it was her. The height, weight, dark curly hair, the mahogany color of her skin…everything matched the missing girl's description.

Asher peered through some bushes, looking for Stan or his horse. His arms prickled with goose bumps as he continued to wait. Everything about the situation—that whinny, Leslie whimpering against a tree in a small clearing—screamed setup. It was a trap. But where was Stan?

Another whimper had him looking at Leslie again. Even from a good twenty feet away he could tell that she was shivering, the air up in the mountains a good fifteen, maybe twenty, degrees cooler than in the valley. He scanned the surrounding area again. He desperately wanted to run into the clearing and help her. But if he got ambushed and killed, that wouldn't do her any good. She'd still be Stan's prisoner.

Where the heck are you? Where are you hiding, you lowlife?

And then he saw it. A rope, mostly hidden by leaves and small branches, trailing along the ground in the middle of the clearing. One end snaked into the trees on the far left side. The other went directly to the piece of wood Leslie was standing on. It was tied around it.

He jerked his head up, looking above the girl. Sure enough, a second brown rope that almost completely blended in with the bark of the oak tree ran around from the back of the tree down behind Leslie. Asher realized immediately what was happening. Stan had tied that rope to a branch in the back of the tree, the other end around Leslie's neck. Sure enough, the sound of another whinny had the girl lifting her head revealing the hangman's noose around her neck.

Stan had led him there to watch him kill his victim.

A wicked laugh sounded from the shadow of the trees, making Asher's gut lurch with dread.

"Show yourself, Stan. Or are you a coward?"

"I'm no coward, Investigator," he yelled from the shadows. "But I'm not stupid either. You'll let me go to try to save the girl." He laughed. "If you can."

The rope attached to the log grew taut, as if someone was

pulling on it. "Yah! Go, go, you stupid nag," Stan yelled to his horse.

Asher swore and sprinted through the bushes and into the clearing, running full-out toward Leslie. The sound of horse's hooves echoed through the trees. Leslie's eyes widened with pleading and fear as he ran toward her, her skin turning ashen.

The rope snapped against the ground.

The log jerked forward.

Leslie screamed as her feet slipped out from beneath her.

FAITH COULD BARELY breathe with all the testosterone surrounding her. Didn't the TBI hire any women these days? In spite of Frost's agents pushing in on her from all sides, she refused to give up her front-row position at the hood of Frost's rental car. Chief Russo had spread a map on top of it and everyone was crowded around as he and Frost gridded out the search area for the nearby foothills. While no one had heard yet from Asher, Lance had texted Faith an update not long ago that he was on Asher's trail and hoping to team up with him soon in the search for Leslie and her abductor.

The roadblocks that Russo had set near the Parkses' residence were in the process of being moved closer to the stables. Frost discussed the possibility of getting a chopper into the air with infrared capabilities, and whether they could get it in position before dark.

Faith cleared her throat. When that didn't get their attention, she rapped her knuckles on the hood. "Director, Chief, we—Asher and I—discussed a chopper earlier and he was worried it could spook the horses. I understand your men who volunteered to search on horseback are skilled in riding. But a spooked horse is still dangerous, especially if our missing woman is on it. I don't want anyone getting hurt, especially Leslie Parks."

One of the special agents frowned at her. "Look, lady—"

Grayson shoved his way in beside her, frowning at the agent. "That's Ms. Lancaster to you. She's a highly decorated, former police detective, who, as a civilian investigator, has solved half a dozen cold cases that various Tennessee law enforcement agencies, including the TBI, couldn't."

It was hard not to smile as the man's face turned red, but Faith managed it, somehow.

Effectively dismissing the agent, Grayson turned his back on him and addressed Russo and Frost. "If Asher thought it was too dangerous to bring in a helicopter, I trust his instincts. As to the search, your people and mine are anxious to saddle up and follow Detectives Whitfield and Cabrera's trail, but you've blocked access to the tack room. We're losing daylight, and we potentially have an innocent victim up in those mountains, as well as my men, who may need backup. Instead of waiting any longer for the medical examiner to arrive and remove the bodies, why not have your crime scene techs get the equipment that we need out of that room right now?"

Frost's brows drew together. "We can't risk messing up the crime scene. A defense attorney could argue it's contaminated and have any evidence we collect thrown out. We wait for the ME."

Faith rapped her knuckles on the hood again. "You won't even have a perpetrator to bring to court if he gets away while everyone's standing around planning. There's no telling what he could be doing to his captive. We don't even know if Asher and Lance have found her, or the perpetrator. They need our help. We need to get moving."

Grayson gave her a subtle nod of approval and turned his intimidating stare on his friend, Chief Russo.

Russo gave him a pained look. "Okay, okay. We'll nix the chopper idea, for now at least. And we'll stop waiting for the ME. We've already photographed the room. The bodies are at the far end. My techs, and only my techs, will pull out whatever equipment is needed. The fewer people in the crime scene, the better. Contamination is a real concern."

Grayson motioned to Ivy Shaw, one of the UB investigators who'd driven out because of her experience with horses. She nodded and ran toward the building's side entrance, waving for the rest of the half dozen agents and UB investigators who'd volunteered to search via horseback to follow her.

Frost obviously wasn't happy with Russo's decision, but it was the chief's jurisdiction. So he didn't argue. "I'll finish mapping out search grids for those who will follow on foot. Ms. Lancaster has the GPS information. Someone borrow her phone or load up her app, whatever it takes so that both search teams can use the coordinates to find Whitfield and Cabrera."

The sound of a vehicle's tires crunching on the gravel road announced the arrival of the long-awaited medical examiner's van. It pulled up to the main entrance to the stables a good thirty feet away.

Russo plowed through the crowd around the car to reach the ME. Faith stepped back, rounding the hood of the vehicle to follow them into the building.

A hand firmly grasped her arm, stopping her. Grayson. She glanced up in question.

He let go and shook his head. "I know you've been frustrated at the wait, but everything's in motion now. Give the ME and techs the space they need to get the equipment out and protect the evidence at the same time. We'll be saddled up and off on the hunt soon."

"'We'? Are you planning to go along? You ride?"

He gave her one of his rare smiles. "I'll let the younger guys handle this one. But, yes, I ride every now and then.

Willow and I both do. We really need to get you over your fear of horses. You're missing out on a lot of fun."

She stared at him, her face growing hot. "Who told you?"

"You did. By your reactions when giving me the update about what happened earlier. You glossed it over, saying Lance arrived and wanted to head after Asher instead of you. But I know that if you were comfortable riding you'd have been right beside Asher instead of following later."

Her face burned even more, realizing that he knew she'd been a coward.

He put his hand on her shoulder. "Stop feeling guilty for not going with him. It made far better sense for a skilled horseman like Lance to tackle the job. You'd have been a liability."

"Gee. Thanks."

He squeezed her shoulder and let go. "Just keeping it real, Faith."

She reluctantly smiled then critically eyed the rag-tag deputies and TBI agents who'd said they could ride. None of them inspired the confidence that her fellow teammates did, or her former army ranger boss. But at least they knew the difference between a lunge line and reins—not that she'd ever make that mistake again. "They need to hurry up."

"It won't take long to reach him. Your GPS app will guide them, and they won't have to go slowly like I'm sure Asher had to initially while searching for a trail to follow. How far away is he now?"

She checked her phone and frowned. "That doesn't make sense. What's he…he's turned around. He's coming back *toward* us, fast."

Grayson bent over her shoulder to look at the screen. "At that speed, it won't take long for him to get here." He looked up at the foothills. "Contact Lance. See if he knows what's going on. If he doesn't, risk contacting Asher. He's obviously not trying to be quiet or careful anymore. It's not like we'll give away his position by making his phone buzz."

Her fingers practically flew across the screen as she sent Lance a text. Daphne would have been proud of her new-found fast texting abilities. Apparently, stress improved her typing skills.

When Lance didn't text her back, she speed-dialed his number. She tried Asher, as well, with the same results. "Neither of them is texting or picking up. I don't like this. Something's definitely wrong. Asher is pushing his horse too fast, taking risks in the rough terrain."

She checked the GPS again, her stomach sinking. "Asher's riding *recklessly* fast. Do you think Fake Stan could be chasing him?"

Grayson shook his head no. "Asher wouldn't run from a fight. Maybe the trail went cold and he's hurrying back to get a search party together before dark."

She studied the trees at the top of the ridge. She didn't doubt Asher's bravery. He wouldn't run from a fight, *unless it was the only option left*. Maybe he was hurt and had no choice. His gun could have jammed. Or Fake Stan could have ambushed him and—

"He's fine, Faith. They both are. Stop worrying. That's an order."

She clenched her fists in frustration. "You can't make someone quit worrying by ordering them to stop."

The clatter of hooves had both of them turning to see the search party finally emerging from the barn. Seven horses were saddled and being led outside. As they mounted, one of them lifted his phone and called out to her. "Ready for those coordinates, Ms. Lancaster."

She hurried over and gave him the information. "But you might want to wait. Looks like Asher is on his way back. He should be here any minute."

Flashing lights had her turning again to see an ambulance pull up beside the van. She whirled back toward Grayson. "Did you call for an ambulance?" She ran to his side. "You heard from Asher, didn't you, but didn't tell me? He's hurt. I knew it. He—"

"Faith, no. I haven't heard from Asher. Russo asked for the ambulance earlier in case we find Leslie, as a precaution. Are you this worried about Lance too? Or is it just Asher?"

She blinked. "Both of them, of course. They're…they're my teammates. And friends. Why would you even ask?"

"No reason." But his amused tone said otherwise.

Russo shouted from the stable doorway for Grayson.

"Better see what he wants." He jogged toward the chief.

Faith watched him go as she pondered his question. *Are you this worried about Lance too?* In all honesty, no, she wasn't. But that didn't mean anything, not really. She cared about both of them. They were her coworkers, her friends. She didn't want either of them hurt. Was Asher special to her? Yes. Of course. They were close, *best* friends. But that was only natural since they worked together much more often than they did with anyone else. Their team leader, Ryland, tended to assign both of them to the same cases when an investigation required more than one investigator. It was because they complemented each other's skill sets. Together, they got results quicker than apart. It didn't mean there was something more to their…relationship. Not the way Grayson's tone had implied.

She shook her head. He was acting as if she had a crush on Asher, or maybe he had one on her. That idea had her chuckling. Asher often flirted with her. Grayson must have taken it wrong. It was Asher's way of teasing her.

Wasn't it? Had Grayson seen more to the flirting, like maybe that it was…real?

No, no. She wasn't going down that path. She was tired

and concerned for both men. That's all it was. She was way overthinking this because her emotions were raw. Period.

She clenched her hands at her sides as the search party trotted across the weed-filled pasture toward the foothills. They must have decided not to wait for Asher. She just hoped they weren't really needed, that he would be here soon, and that he was okay.

And Lance, of course. She hoped he was okay too.

A big red horse emerged from the trees at the top of the nearest ridge.

"Asher," Faith breathed, relief making her smile for a moment, until she realized how recklessly he was urging his horse down the rock-strewn incline. From her vantage point, it looked like the horse would tumble off a ledge with every hop-skip step it took.

Behind him, Lance followed on the big brown horse, his gun out as he kept turning and looking at the trees behind them. Faith looked up at the trees, unable to see anything in the gloom beneath the thick forest canopy. Were they being pursued as she'd feared?

The two men met up with the search party halfway across the pasture. Asher turned slightly to say something to Lance. That's when Faith caught the gleam of the late afternoon sunlight on Asher's golden, *naked* skin. She'd seen his shirt and thought he was wearing it. Now, she realized he wasn't. It was draped around a petite woman sitting on his lap, her head pressed against his chest.

Faith's breath caught in her throat. Was that Leslie Parks, so still and unmoving against him? Why would she need Asher's shirt? The obvious answer was that Leslie didn't have any clothes of her own, which had Faith wishing she could kill Fake Stan right now, assuming Asher hadn't already.

When his horse shifted slightly, she got a better look at the shirt. Her stomach churned with dread and fear.

Grayson came up beside her and rested his hands on top of the fence. "He found her. Son of a… He really did it. You both did. You found her."

"She hasn't moved, not once. Her eyes are closed too. And the shirt she's wearing, it's—"

"Covered with dark splotches." His voice was tight with worry as he straightened. Neither said the word both of them were thinking, the word that thickened the air with tension.

Blood.

The shirt was covered with blood.

Please let her be alive. Please, God. Let her live.

A moment later, Ivy and the group of men on horseback raced toward the hill, heading in the direction that Asher and Lance had just come from.

Asher clutched Leslie against him and urged his horse forward again, probably using his legs to guide it the way Faith had seen Lance do earlier. Lance rode up to Asher's side and motioned to Leslie. Whatever he was saying made Asher's mouth tighten in a hard line, but he didn't say anything.

His own face a study in anger and concern, Lance urged his horse forward, reaching the open gate ahead of Asher. He glanced at Grayson before stopping by Faith.

"Get the EMTs, Faith. Hurry."

The urgency in his tone had her running to the ambulance, even though she wondered why he didn't ride his horse over there and alert them himself. Once the EMTs had their gurney out with the wheels down, and had placed their boxes of supplies on top to follow her, she turned to see where Leslie and the others were. They were only about fifteen feet away.

"Be careful of her neck," Asher warned.

Lance had dismounted and stood beside Asher's horse, helping him lower Leslie into the waiting arms of the EMTs as they rushed over. As soon as they put her on the gurney, her eyes fluttered open and she moaned.

"She's alive," Faith whispered, smiling in relief.

Lance said something to the EMTs. Asher shook his head, looking angry. The EMTs both nodded at him before rushing toward the ambulance with Leslie.

Faith ran to the horses to congratulate Asher and Lance, and ask about Fake Stan. But her mouth went dry and logical thought was no longer possible as she finally got a good look at Asher up close, astride the big horse. Half-naked, incredibly *buff* Asher. Where had all those rippling muscles come from? Had they been there all along and she'd never noticed? She couldn't help admiring his equally well-defined biceps. Had she ever seen his biceps before? When would she have had the chance? He was always wearing long-sleeved dress shirts and suits.

Her greedy gaze drank in the small spattering of hair on his chest and the long dark line of it going down his flat belly to disappear beneath his pants. Goodness gracious. Asher was *hot*!

She swallowed and forced her gaze up, fully expecting him to have noticed her practically drooling over his body. No doubt he'd tease her mercilessly over that. But he wasn't even looking at her. His eyes were half closed, his face alarmingly pale. And Lance and Grayson were holding on to his upper arms on either side of the horse, as if they were afraid he was about to fall.

Her stomach dropped. She'd been so intent on ogling him that she hadn't realized that something was wrong, terribly wrong. She stepped closer to his horse, stopping just shy of its head and those huge square teeth.

"What's wrong?" she asked. "Asher?"

"Let's pull him down on this side," Lance said to Grayson, ignoring her question. "Careful."

Fear seared Faith's lungs as they pulled him sideways out of the saddle.

He staggered then crumpled to the ground in a slow-controlled fall, with Lance and Grayson helping him. But instead of laying him down, they held him up in a sitting position.

"I've got him," Grayson said. "Tell one of those EMTs to get back here, now, in spite of Asher insisting they look after Leslie first."

Lance jumped up and ran to the ambulance.

Faith dropped to her knees in front of Asher. "What's wrong? Asher, look at me." His eyes were closed now. He seemed to be concentrating on just…breathing. "Grayson?" Her voice broke as she scooted to Asher's side and started to slide her arm around his shoulders.

"Faith," Grayson warned. "Don't touch his back."

She froze then leaned over to see behind him. The haft of a large knife protruded from beneath his left shoulder blade.

She sucked in a startled breath. "Asher. Oh, no." Her hands shook as she gently cupped his face. "Whatever happened, it will be okay." A single tear slid down her face as she kissed his forehead. "It's okay. We'll take care of you." She glanced over her shoulder toward the ambulance. "Hurry, Lance!"

When she looked back, Asher's eyes were open and staring into hers. They were glazed with pain, his breaths shallow and labored. But in spite of his obvious pain, his mouth quirked up in that smile she knew so well.

"We found her, Faith. We found Leslie. Alive." His voice was gritty, barely audible. "He told her he killed Jasmine, that he was going to kill her too." Asher drew a ragged breath, turning even more pale as he struggled to speak.

"Don't try to talk, Asher," she pleaded.

"Had to…" Asher rasped. "Had to grab her, hold her up. The noose would have snapped her neck." He choked and dragged in an obviously painful breath.

Faith stared in horror, the word *noose* sickening her. But her curiosity would have to wait.

"That's when he threw the knife."

"Stop talking, Ash. Just breathe. In, out, in, out." Her hands shook as she stroked his short dark hair back from his forehead.

His smile widened. "You called me Ash."

"Did I? My sister's bad habits are rubbing off on me. It won't happen again."

His answering laugh turned into a cough. Frothy, bright-red blood dotted the corners of his mouth.

Her gaze shot to Grayson. His answering look was dark with concern. He grasped Asher's upper arm tighter with both hands, carefully supporting him. "Faith, call 9-1-1. Get a medevac chopper out here. *Yesterday.*"

Chapter Ten

A slow, rhythmic beeping and the sound of muted voices tugged Asher up through thick layers of lethargy. He struggled to open his eyes, but the feat seemed beyond his abilities. His eyelids were too heavy, like a weight was pulling them down.

Tired, so tired.

Everything ached. His chest and back were on fire. A sharp piercing pain stabbed him with each breath he took. Did that mean he was alive? Where was he? Who was talking?

Most of the voices seemed familiar. He lay there in a fog of pain and confusion, desperately trying to capture snatches of the conversation to figure out what was happening. The last thing he remembered after getting Leslie to safety was Faith calling him Ash. It was the first time she'd ever done that.

Faith.

That was one of the voices he heard. Smart, beautiful, frustrating Faith. She was here. But where, exactly, was here?

Beep. Beep. Beep.

"Pneu…mo…thorax." Faith's voice. "What the heck is that?"

"A collapsed lung. The knife the assailant threw went into his back and…"

The voices trailed off. Waves of confusion threatened to push him under.

No. He needed to wake up. Hospital. He must be in a hospital. The unfamiliar voice had to be the doctor, talking to Faith and… Grayson. And Lance. Those were the other voices he was hearing. He struggled to capture more of the conversation.

"—missed any major organs…"

More murmurs he couldn't catch.

Beep. Beep.

"—But will he be okay?" Faith's voice again. "Will he make a full recovery? Will he be able to walk…"

Be able to walk? Had the knife that Stan had thrown hit his spine? He tried to move his legs, wiggle his toes. He couldn't. Raw fear sliced through him.

Wake. Up.

"I think he's in pain." Faith's soft, warm hand gently clasped his. "Please, give him something to take the pain away."

No, no medication. Need to wake up. What's wrong with my legs?

Another beep. The fire eased. He let out a deep breath, no longer feeling as if his lungs were going to burst out of his chest.

"Can you hear me, Asher?" Faith, her hand still clasping his. He wanted to squeeze it, stroke her fingers with his. But he couldn't. Would it be possible to feel her hand touching his if he had a spinal injury? Maybe he was just too drugged up to move. He had to know. He struggled again to open his eyes.

"It's okay, Asher," she said. "Don't fight the drugs. Rest. If you can hear me, you're in a hospital, in Knoxville. The chopper brought you to the Trauma Center at the University of Tennessee Medical Center—"

Beep.

"When you saved Leslie from being hung by her captor's trap, and he threw his knife at your back, it pierced a lung and—"

And *what*? If he could just open his eyes. *Wake up!*

"Doctor, he's restless. I think he's still in pain. Please. Help him."

No. No, don't. I have to know.

Liquid sleep flooded his veins. If he could yell his frustration, he would have as the darkness swallowed him up again.

BRIGHT LIGHT SLANTED across Asher's eyelids. He turned his head away, raising his arm to block it out.

His arm. He'd raised it. He tried to open his eyes. The lids twitched, as if in protest. But then they opened. He could finally see. As he'd suspected before, he was in a hospital room, lying in a bed, with an IV pole to his left. That must be the beeping he'd heard, or maybe the monitors just past it, showing his vital signs. The bright light was the sun glinting through the shades on the window to his right. There was no one else in the room. Faith was gone.

A pang of disappointment shot through him, followed by a cold wave of fear. *Will he be able to walk again?* Faith's words ran through his mind. Drawing a shallow breath that, thankfully, was far less painful this time, he tried to move his toes. The sheet over his feet moved up and down. He laughed with relief then sucked in a sharp breath at the fiery pain that seared his lungs.

When the pain finally dulled, he took a tentative, shallow breath. It still hurt, but not nearly as much as when he'd laughed. He was still groggy, exhausted. This time, he didn't fight the pull to sleep. He closed his eyes and surrendered.

It was dark when he woke again. The sun had set long ago. But once his eyes adjusted to the darkness, the lights from the IV pump and other equipment in the room was enough for him to make out some details.

To his left was an open door, revealing the dark outline of a sink and a toilet. Another narrow door to the right of that was likely a small closet. The wall stopped a few feet beyond that, no doubt leading to the alcove that concealed the door into his hospital room.

Asher slowly turned his head on the pillow, trying to make out more details he hadn't really paid attention to earlier. There was a digital clock on the far wall, announcing it was nearly midnight. Beside it, a small impossibly old-fashioned-looking TV was suspended from the ceiling. An equally old and uncomfortable-looking plastic chair was tucked against the wall. It was a typical private hospital room, small but efficient. And when he finally looked all the way to his right, he noticed something else. Or rather, some*one*.

Faith.

He smiled, his gaze drinking In the soft curves of her beautiful face as she lay sleeping, curled up in a reclining chair pulled close to his bed. Her shoulder-length hair created a golden halo above her head, glinting in the dim lights from the equipment. And there was something else he could just make out, the thick, pink blanket tucked around her. It looked suspiciously like the one he'd given her last Christmas as a joke, knowing she hated pink. She'd graciously thanked him and he'd laughed, assuming she'd toss it in the garbage as soon as he'd left. And yet there it was.

He wanted to wake her, to see her green eyes shining at him, her soft lips curve in that smile he loved so much. He wanted to thank her, for being there for him. And he wanted to know what was happening with the case.

Was Leslie recovering from her injuries? Had the TBI and police caught Stan? With their combined manpower, the roadblocks, and with Stan only having about a thirty-minute head start, they must have captured him. Asher had desperately wanted for him and Faith to be the ones to bring Stan to justice. But as long as the killer could no longer hurt anyone else, that's what mattered. For now, it was enough. It had to be.

Chapter Eleven

Faith shifted into a more comfortable position on the side of Asher's hospital bed. He sat a few feet away in the reclining chair eating breakfast, frowning at her. He'd barraged her with questions the moment she'd entered the room. And she had a few for him as well. But she'd refused to discuss anything other than reassuring him that Leslie Parks was in good condition and home with her family. Since this was Asher's first solid food since being admitted to the hospital, Faith wanted him to eat as much as possible. He needed to regain his strength. He'd obviously lost weight. And he was still far too pale for her peace of mind.

He washed down some scrambled eggs with a sip of water, glaring at her the whole time.

"Okay, okay," she relented. "You've done really well and haven't tried to murder me while waiting to interrogate me. I'll take that as a win. Two more bites and we'll talk. Big bites."

"You're worse than my instructor at the police academy," he grumbled.

"I'll take that as a compliment."

"It's not."

She laughed. "Eat."

He wolfed down the rest of his eggs then tossed his fork

onto the tray. "Enough. Where's our killer being held? Did TBI take him into custody or is he in the local jail?"

Her amusement faded. "Unfortunately, neither. They never managed to catch him."

He choked on the water he'd just sipped.

Faith started to rise to check on him, but he held up a hand to stop her. "I'm okay," he rasped then cleared his throat and shoved the rolling tray away from his chair. "How the hell did he get away?" He coughed again, his eyes tearing from the water going down the wrong way.

"We can discuss all of that in a minute, when you recover from almost drowning from a straw."

His eyes narrowed in warning.

"It's so good to see you out of bed and finally lucid," she added, her cheerfulness returning. "How are you feeling this morning, by the way?"

"Angry and disgusted. How did the TBI and police screw this up? Stan only had a half hour's head start in rough terrain. They should have closed down that mountain until they found him. What day is it anyway? How long have they been searching for him?"

"I'm fine. Thanks for asking. In spite of several uncomfortable nights sleeping on that recliner waiting to see if my partner would ever wake up." She grabbed the pink blanket that she'd left on the foot of his bed last night and covered her legs. "Is this room cold to you? Maybe I should adjust the thermostat—"

"Faith."

"Normally, if you took that tone with me, I'd be out that door and wouldn't come back without an apology and some serious groveling. But I'm feeling exceedingly generous right now. I guess almost losing your best friend does that. I'm very glad you didn't die, in spite of how irritating you're being this morning."

He rolled his eyes.

She laughed. "Getting my bad habits?"

He inhaled a deep breath then winced.

She was immediately off the bed, tossing the blanket behind her. Leaning in close, she gently pressed her hand against his forehead, the same way she'd checked him for fever dozens of times over the past few days as he'd slept. "How bad is the pain? I can call the nurse and ask her for—"

He grabbed her by the waist and pulled her onto his lap.

She blinked up at him, so astonished that she didn't immediately try to get up.

His arms wrapped around her like a vise, making the decision for her. She was trapped, unless she wanted to wiggle and push her way off him. In his weakened state, it wouldn't be that difficult. But she didn't want to cause him any pain, either, so she let him win this round.

She tapped his left arm where some tubing was taped against the back of his hand. "Careful. Don't mess up your IV."

"I don't even need one. I should pull the thing out and be done with this place. They've kept me so drugged up, I haven't been able to think clearly, let alone stay awake long enough to get any information. If you hadn't showed up a few minutes ago, I was going to start calling everyone at UB until someone gave me an update on the case. I'm not letting you go until you answer every question I have. First, what are they doing to try to catch Stan—"

She covered his mouth with her hand.

This time it was his turn to look surprised.

"The most important question," she corrected him, "is about your prognosis. Do you even know what happened? What injuries you have? Have you spoken to the doctor?"

He pulled her hand down. "I haven't spoken to anyone, except you, and the guy who delivered my breakfast tray. I feel okay. I can wiggle my toes. And I got from the bed to this chair without any help, so I figure I'm going to live."

She blinked. "Wiggle your toes?"

He smiled. It was a small one, but the fact that he was smiling at all was huge.

"I was worried earlier," he said. "I think it was the first day, after surgery. You asked the doctor about me being able to walk again and—"

"You heard me?"

He nodded.

"I'm so sorry." She gently pressed a hand to his chest. "I should have been more careful in case you were able to understand me even with all those drugs in your system. The knife the bad guy threw at you missed your spine, as you've obviously figured out. It punctured your lung, which is why you had such a hard time breathing. It'll take a while to fully recover. And they had to stitch up muscles, so you have to be careful. I definitely shouldn't be on your lap—"

He tightened his hold. "You're not escaping until we're through talking."

"You do realize that I could make you let me go by punching you in the chest."

"But you won't. Because you don't want to hurt me."

"Yes, well. Friends don't generally hurt friends. So there is that. Your prognosis is excellent. It was scary there for a while, touch and go, because you'd lost a lot of blood. You were bleeding internally, in addition to the collapsed lung. But Grayson had them fly you up here so the trauma-one team could take care of you."

"They should have flown Leslie up instead of me."

"Leslie wasn't in nearly as bad a shape as you. She was terrified, shell-shocked. But physically she only suffered some bruises and minor cuts and scrapes. We got to her before he did his worst. She has you to thank for that. You saved her life, very nearly getting killed yourself." Her hand tightened against his chest. "Lance told us what you did. He arrived in that clearing right as it was happening. You saved Leslie from being hanged. And you threw yourself between the perpetrator and his knife. You shouldn't have taken chances like that. You nearly died."

"I did what I had to do. We're both alive. That's what matters. Leslie told you he's our guy, right? That he killed Jasmine too? She whispered to me that he hated Jasmine because she ruined everything, that she was going to tell the police about him. That goes along with our theory, that Jasmine saw something she shouldn't have. Put two and two together, figured out he was bad news. That's all Leslie said, though. I couldn't really talk and she just sort of…stopped. Are you sure she's okay?"

"She's okay. Promise."

He gave her a curt nod, looking relieved. "We need to find Stan and put him away before he hurts another woman."

Faith stared up at him. "You really haven't spoken to anyone about the case, have you?"

"If I did, it was in a half-awake state and I don't remember anything."

"Well, I'll answer your very first question, about how long you've been here. Since Thursday evening. Today is Sunday morning, so that's—"

"I slept for almost three days?"

"The doctor wanted you to be still and rest to let your body heal. You weren't quite in a drug-induced coma, but close. It was scary to watch you sleeping so deeply, so long."

His eyes widened. "You were here the whole time?"

Almost every single minute. "Of course not. I was here off and on. I wanted to make sure you were okay. That's what friends do."

Asher frowned down at her then sighed. "Well, as your *friend*, thank you for looking out for me."

"You're very welcome. Now, may I get up?"

INSTEAD OF LETTING her go, his arms tightened. "Tell me about the hunt for Stan first."

"Stan Darden Junior isn't our serial killer. The guy you went after, the man who took Leslie, we don't know his real name yet."

"I was worried that might be the case. But I'd really hoped he was Stan. At least that way we'd know his identity. More importantly, the real Stan would be okay. He's dead, isn't he?"

She nodded. "We found him and his father in the tack room."

"Good grief. I got a saddle out of there and didn't even notice. Where were they?"

"Hidden under some horse blankets behind some piles of equipment at the very back. There's no reason you would have noticed. Lance pulled some stuff out of there and didn't see them either. The only reason I discovered them was because I was anxious while waiting for you and Lance and went exploring."

He gently squeezed her waist. "I'm sorry you found them. I'm sure it wasn't a pleasant sight."

She stared up at him. "I'm a cop, or I used to be. It goes with the territory. Are you sure you didn't hit your head?"

"I must have. Goodness knows it wouldn't make sense otherwise for me to worry about you, us being just friends and all."

The bitterness in his tone had her studying his face.

"What?" he asked.

"Are you in pain? You don't seem...yourself."

"I've been sleeping for three days and have been shut out of my own investigation. Of course I'm not myself."

"*Our* investigation. And no one shut you out. I was just going to tell you that Lance has been filling in, helping me, while you're recovering."

He frowned. "Has he really?"

She frowned back. "Yes, of course. No reason to get surly about it. He's not trying to steal the case. He wants to help us."

His jaw tightened, but he gave her a crisp nod. "What have you both found out? Anything?"

"A lot and nothing, kind of like where you and I were. It's been one step forward, two steps back. Lance worked with Gatlinburg PD to put together a timeline of events based on cell phone records and neighbors who saw Stan Senior and the real Stan Junior the morning that Leslie was taken. Our theory that the abductor drove Leslie to one of the turnoffs near the ranch and parked his car there is correct. They found the car, but it was stolen."

"Of course. It being his own car would have been way too easy."

"It's not a total dead end. The car was taken in a neighborhood about ten minutes from Leslie's home. Since no other vehicles were found ditched around there, the belief is he walked to that location from his own place, or hired a car to drop him off."

"He wouldn't have hired a car. Too easy to trace."

"I agree. So does the TBI and Russo. They're canvassing that neighborhood with a sketch of the perp based on my and Leslie's eye-witness accounts. Now that you're up and about, I'm sure that Russo will want to send his sketch artist here to see what you remember so they can refine the drawing."

"Not necessary. You're better at details like that than me. I doubt I can add anything."

She smiled. "Was that a compliment?"

"Nope. Just a fact."

"Oh, brother."

He grinned.

She laughed. "It's good to see the old Asher is still in there somewhere." She smiled up at him, relieved. But as he stared down at her, something changed. His eyes darkened, his face tightened. And for the first time ever around him, she felt… confused, unsure, and a little afraid of whatever this…this tension might mean.

Asher was her friend, her best friend. She treasured that closeness and didn't want to lose it, or change it. She was already struggling not to see the image of his drool-worthy chest every time she closed her eyes. What she really needed to do was to get off his lap and put some distance between them before they crossed a line they could never uncross.

Before she could figure out how to extricate herself without hurting him, he tightened his arms around her. And then he was kissing her. It happened so fast, like him pulling her onto his lap, that she didn't react immediately. Her mind was in shock. This was *Asher.* His mouth was actually on hers. His very warm, insistent, and unbelievably *expert*, lips were doing sensual things that had her toes curling in her shoes.

A little voice of warning cried out somewhere in her dazed mind telling her to push him back, get up, and stop this insanity. But that voice became a whimper of pleasure as he deepened the kiss. This kiss eclipsed every other kiss she'd ever had or even dreamed of having.

She didn't want to push him away. She wanted…more. More of his mouth on hers. More heat. More… God help her, she wanted more *Asher.* Her fingers clutched at his hospital gown, pulling him closer as she pushed her soft curves against his hard planes. Their bodies fit together as if made for each other. Even the evidence of his arousal pressing against her bottom wasn't enough to make her stop. She was helpless to do anything but *feel.*

When she pressed the tip of her tongue against his mouth,

he groaned and swept his tongue inside. Heat blistered through her, tightening her belly. Every reservation, every lingering doubt was viciously squashed into oblivion. She refused to pay attention to the warnings, the doubts. She didn't want to think right now. All she wanted to do was to enjoy him, to answer every stroke with one of her own, every ravenous slide of his mouth with an equally wild response.

His warm, strong hands speared through her hair as he half turned, pressing her back against the recliner. When he broke the wild kiss and his warm mouth moved to the side of her neck, she bucked against him, her fingers curving against his shoulders. Her heart was beating so fast she heard the rush of it in her ears. Trailing her hands down his hospital gown, she caressed his mouthwatering chest muscles, and continued the long, slow slide of her fingers toward his impressive hardness pressing against her hip.

A knock sounded on the door, followed by a vaguely familiar voice. "Mr. Whitfield, it's the doctor, making rounds."

Reality was a bucket of ice water, snapping Faith back from the precipice. She practically leaped off Asher and whirled away from him just as the doctor stepped inside, a stethoscope hanging around his neck.

His brows rose. "Should I come back?"

Faith's cheeks flamed. She absolutely refused to look at Asher. "No, no. I was just, uh, leaving."

"Faith, don't go," Asher called out. "Please."

Mortified about what she'd done, what she'd almost done, with *Asher*, she grabbed her purse from the vinyl chair on the other side of the room and escaped out the door.

ASHER SWORE AND leaned back against the chair.

The doctor gave him a look of sympathy. "Bad timing. Sorry, pal. But at least you appear to be doing better. This is one of the few visits where I've caught you fully awake." He sat on the side of the bed where Faith had been only moments earlier. "I'm Doctor Nichols, in case you don't remember."

"I have a vague recollection of hearing that name before. Faith told me I've been here since Thursday, three days. I would have thought it was only one."

"You've been heavily sedated to keep you from moving around too much. The man who stabbed you in the back used a two-inch-wide serrated hunting knife. Thankfully, it only nicked your left lung, otherwise those jagged edges would have shredded it. But it did a number on the muscles in your back, damaged some nerves, collapsed the lung."

"That explains why everything hurts. Thanks for patching me up." He glanced at the door, silently willing Faith to return.

"I can get the nurse in here to give you more pain meds."

"No, no. They just put me to sleep. I need to talk to my coworkers and get updates on the case I've been working. But thanks. Thanks for everything. Sounds like you saved my life."

"I can't take all the credit. There was another surgeon with me, and an excellent trauma team to help pull you through. It's a good thing your boss insisted on medevac. You'd lost a lot of blood and were fading fast. It's doubtful you'd have survived an ambulance ride and subsequent treatment at a hospital without a level-one trauma team."

"I appreciate everything, believe me. But I'm ready to go home. When can I get out of here?"

"Don't mistake the fact that you were able to move from the bed to a chair to mean you're ready to be discharged. You're not."

Asher frowned at him. "I have a job to do, a killer to catch. I really need to get out of here."

"Ignore him, Doc. He's a terrible patient." Lance strode into the room, nodding at the doctor before smiling at Asher.

"Good to see you finally back from the dead. Gave us all quite a scare."

Lance clasped his shoulder then moved back. "Sorry to interrupt. Faith told me you were awake and I wanted to see for myself. Please, finish whatever you're doing, Doctor."

Nichols looked back at Asher. "When you got here, you had a pneumothorax—a collapsed lung. By itself, that usually requires a good week at the hospital so we can monitor for any breathing issues or signs of infection. But, on top of that, you had major surgery to reconnect muscles and repair nerves. If you get out of here before *next* Sunday, I'll be surprised."

Asher swore and proceeded to argue with the doctor.

After a few minutes back and forth, Nichols shook his head. "This isn't a negotiation, Mr. Whitfield. I understand you're involved in an important investigation. I'll release you as soon as possible. But it won't be one minute before I deem it safe for you to go home."

Once the doctor conducted his exam and left, Asher eyed Lance. "You have to help me."

"No way. I'm not breaking you out of here. I won't have that on my conscience if something goes wrong. You're here like the doc said, until it's safe for you to leave."

"We'll see about that," Asher grumbled. "You said you spoke to Faith. How is she?"

"Hard to say. She was in a hurry to leave, said she had an errand. Barely stopped in the waiting room long enough to let me know you were awake. Did something happen between you two? She seemed upset."

He squeezed his eyes shut. Damn. He hadn't meant to upset her. He'd gotten caught up in the moment and had finally done something outrageous, as Daphne had encouraged him to do so many times. Had he opened a door with Faith? Or slammed it shut?

"Asher? You okay?"

Hell no. "I'm fine. Tell me about the search for the killer. Faith said you were working on the timeline. When did he get to the ranch? Why was he in the stables when Faith and I got there? Where was Leslie when he was in the stables? How—"

Lance held up his hands, laughing. "I can see why Faith was in such a hurry to get out of here. You probably drove her nuts with all your questions." He crossed the room and grabbed the extra chair, then sat in front of Asher. "Since you didn't call the bad guy Stan again, I'm guessing you heard the *real* Stans, junior and senior, were murdered and stuffed in the back of the tack room long before you and Faith arrived."

"I heard. I'd hoped to stop this guy before he hurt anyone else."

"Don't beat yourself up. The cops had five years to find him. You and Faith found him in a few months. We've got his description, a BOLO out on him. Every law enforcement officer in eastern Tennessee will be on the lookout, with the picture the sketch artist made after talking to Leslie and Faith. They swabbed the hilt of that knife he threw at you and sent it away for DNA testing. That could break the case wide open."

"Only if he's in the system already."

"Pessimist." Lance chuckled. "We also know, thanks to both you and Faith, that he's good with horses. Maybe he's employed at one of the horse-riding operations around Gatlinburg or Pigeon Forge."

Asher glanced at the door again, worries about Faith making it difficult to focus. Or maybe it was the drugs. It was getting harder and harder to stay awake.

"I wouldn't characterize our killer as being good with horses," Asher said. "He doesn't have the patience or empathy for them. Not surprising for a sociopath. I admit I bought into him being Stan, though. He spun a detailed convincing story about his dad and girlfriend, and him inheriting the business. Either he got that info from the real Stan before killing him, or he's a good actor."

"Probably both. We'll never know how much time he spent, or didn't spend, talking to Junior before killing him. Unless we catch him and he confesses, gives us details. The girlfriend part seems to be made up. None of Stan's friends were aware of him dating anyone, let alone living with them as he'd told you and Faith."

Asher nodded. "What about Leslie Parks? Physically, I'm told she's more or less okay. But we both know she had to have gone through hell."

Lance's smile faded. "No doubt. Thankfully, he didn't have a lot of time with her, relatively speaking. From what he told her, he was planning on holding her for days, maybe weeks, torturing her before killing her. Considering what could have happened, her physical injuries are minor. Psychologically...well, I can't speak to that. I'm sure it's going to take a long time and some intense therapy to move past this, if that's even possible."

Asher refused to glance at the door again, not wanting to clue Lance in to just how worried he was about Faith. He really needed to talk to her. But what would he say? How could he fix this? Did he even want to? He didn't want to go back to the friend zone. He wanted her right where he'd had her, in his arms. Hell, he wanted far more than that.

"You okay, buddy?" Lance asked.

"Just thinking about the case," he lied. "What about the other bodies we found in his Smoky Mountains graveyard? Have they been identified yet?"

"As expected, Jasmine Parks is one of them. They've identified three of the others so far. No known cause of death, unfortunately, since all the ME had to go on were skeletons.

No knife marks on any of the bones to indicate stabbing. No bullet holes or shell casings." Lance pulled out his cell phone. "I'll pull up the latest update."

Chapter Twelve

Once again, Faith was saying goodbye to her little sister. It was bittersweet since they hadn't seen much of each other during Daphne's college break. Work, as it often did, had interfered.

Daphne slung her backpack over one shoulder and leaned into the open passenger door of Faith's Lexus. Her orange-brick dorm at the University of Tennessee towered like a monument behind her. "Thanks for the ride, sis. Give Ash my love when you visit him at UT Med today. You're taking him home soon, right? Hasn't he been there for almost a week?"

"Today would be a week. They flew him up last Thursday. I'll tell Ash*er* you said hello when I see him."

"Give *Ash* a kiss for me too." Daphne winked, laughing when Faith gave her an aggravated look.

Faith watched her sister until she safely entered the dorm. Then she turned the car around and headed back to the main road. She wouldn't see her baby sister again until next week, when she returned to Knoxville to take her out for pizza at one of the campus hangouts. It was a tradition. Faith did her best never to miss pizza night, although the day of the week they chose depended on both of their schedules.

While Daphne sometimes called Faith her smother-mother instead of her big sister, she was mostly teasing. She understood Faith's longing to see her only blood relative, especially because Faith's career, her glimpses of the dark side of humanity, made her worry so much about Daphne's safety. The only reason Faith hadn't switched to a job in Knoxville when Daphne decided to go there for school was that Daphne had made her promise not to. Their compromise, in exchange for Faith paying Daphne's tuition, was that Faith could text her whenever she wanted. What Faith really *wanted* was to text her sister several times a day to make sure she was okay. But she didn't want her sister to resent her. So she kept it to one text a day. Most of the time.

The two of them had always been close, and that had only solidified after they'd lost their parents. They'd had no one else to lean on except each other. It was the main reason Faith had given up her career as a police detective in Nashville when the opportunity at Unfinished Business had come along. The move to Gatlinburg had been a smooth transition, since it was like a second home anyway. Their family had vacationed there dozens of times over the years. But mainly she'd made the move because cold cases would be much less dangerous than active homicide investigations. She and Daphne were already, technically, orphans. She didn't want Daphne having the extra burden of losing her only sibling. Faith wanted to be Daphne's rock, to be the one person she could always rely on and trust. That was why Faith was struggling with guilt as she drove down the highway. She'd broken that trust by lying about Asher. He wasn't in the hospital.

He was already home.

He'd been discharged yesterday, Wednesday morning, several days ahead of the doctor's prediction. Lance had told her that the doctor gave in because he was weary of Asher's constant requests to go home. Lance had been the one who'd driven Asher back to Gatlinburg.

If it wasn't for Lance's updates, she wouldn't have known

what was going on. She hadn't been brave enough to visit Asher herself, not since that earth-shattering kiss. She hadn't taken his calls, either, or replied to his texts. She was a coward, avoiding the inevitable, having a face-to-face discussion about what had happened between them. If it was up to her, she'd never have that discussion.

She wanted, needed, the closeness, the friendship that the two of them had always shared. The thought of crossing that line had never even occurred to her until that devastating kiss. Well, it had really first occurred when she'd seen his naked chest. But it was only a fleeting thought at that time and she'd quickly discarded it. Now, having sipped at the well of Asher, she wanted to dive in and let him consume her.

She tightened her hands on the steering wheel. This obsession with him had to end. Yes, they'd crossed the friendship line. And she'd glimpsed something truly amazing on the other side. But she also knew what had happened to several of her friends who'd dated coworkers. Inevitably, if the relationship didn't work out, things ended awkwardly and they lost the friendships they'd once treasured. One of them would end up transferring to another department to escape the awkwardness of seeing each other every day. There wasn't another department to transfer to at UB. And even if there was, Faith had no interest in that. She didn't want to *never* see Asher again.

She cherished their closeness, the teasing, being able to finish each other's sentences. She craved it, needed him in her life. And she was terrified that if they pursued…more… she could lose him completely. The idea of him not being around was devastating, unthinkable. That's why she desperately wanted to repair the damage that had been done. She had to try to put things back the way they used to be.

Tomorrow morning, the entire UB team was having a mandatory meeting at Grayson's mansion. Their boss had specifically ordered her to be there. He knew she'd hit a brick wall on the case without Asher there to bounce ideas back and forth. And he'd no doubt heard that she'd stopped visiting Asher at the hospital. For the sake of the investigation, he wanted their partnership repaired ASAP.

Their killer was still on the loose. No one had a clue who he was or where he might be. The DNA and fingerprints from the knife had yielded no hits on any law enforcement databases. And even though blasting the composite sketch of the killer across the media had resulted in tons of tips, none of them had panned out so far. It was Grayson's hope that she and Asher could work their magic, build on their research, and figure out once and for all how to stop the killer. That meant she had to clear the air between the two of them *today.*

Somehow.

Over an hour later, Faith pulled her Lexus up the familiar, long, winding driveway to a two-story log house teetering on the edge of one of the Smoky Mountains. In the past, she'd looked forward to the view from the two-story glass windows off the back of the house. Today, she dreaded it. But there was no turning back now. Asher was standing at the front picture window, looking out at her, no doubt alerted by his perimeter security system that a car had turned into his driveway.

After cutting the engine, she grabbed her backpack of files on the Parks case. All too soon, she arrived at the nine-foot-tall massive double doors. Before she could knock, one of them opened.

A disheveled, bleary-eyed Asher stood in the opening. He was barefoot, wearing sweatpants, dark blue ones that matched the blue button-up shirt he had on, no doubt because trying to pull a T-shirt over his head would have been too painful.

He hadn't shaved in days. And it didn't look as if he'd

even brushed his hair this morning. Had *she* done that to him? Or was he in pain? Goodness knew his body still had a lot of healing to do.

"Faith. Hello." His deep voice was short, clipped, bordering on cold. He made a show of glancing over her shoulder. "Your wingman, Lance, isn't with you?"

Her cheeks flushed with heat. "That tattletale. I told him not to let you know that he was feeding me updates. I just wanted to make sure you were okay."

"You could have done that by visiting me yourself. Or at least responding to one of my texts."

She held her hands out in a placating gesture. "I'm here now."

Friendly, welcoming, smiling Asher was nowhere to be found. Instead, a stoic stranger blocked the entryway, his expression blank, unreadable.

Her heart seemed to squeeze in her chest as she realized she'd made a terrible mistake. Avoiding him hadn't salvaged their relationship. It may very well have destroyed it.

Regret had her blinking back threatening tears. "We need to talk." When he didn't move or speak, she added, "Please?"

Still nothing. Was he going to shut the door in her face? She waited, hating how awkward things were between them right now. It was an unfamiliar feeling, the exact kind of feeling she'd been trying to avoid by not letting their relationship change.

Clearing her throat, she hoisted the backpack higher on her shoulder. "Okay, well, I guess I'll see you at Grayson's tomorrow. Sorry I didn't call first. I'll just—"

He sighed heavily and turned away, heading toward the back of the house. At least he'd left the door open. It was a start.

ASHER STOOD WITH his back to the two-story windows in the great room, watching Faith enter. It took every ounce of self-control he had not to run to her, pull her in for a hug, a kiss, anything to reassure himself that he hadn't destroyed his chance with her. Because, surely there was a chance, or had been, based on the way she'd responded to his kiss.

He very much wanted her in his life. But he didn't want to return to the friend zone. Having tasted heaven, he craved it and refused to settle for anything less. He'd already wasted two years pretending, of listening to her chat about her dates with other men as if he was one of her girlfriends. It never seemed to occur to her that there was a reason he never dated, that he didn't pay attention to any woman but her. All this time he'd been hoping that she'd finally open her eyes to what was right in front of her. Well, he was done with that. He couldn't live like this anymore. Something had to give.

She set her backpack on the dining table at the far left end of the open room, and glanced around as if she hadn't been here hundreds of times. The true detective that she was, she noticed the setup of bagels and pastries on the kitchen island that he normally kept empty.

"I know you didn't set up that pretty display. And I'm pretty sure that fancy cake dome didn't come from your kitchen. Did Ivy stop by and bring that?"

He crossed his arms and leaned against the side of the stone fireplace. "She came to visit. Everyone from work has come by. Except you."

Faith winced.

"But," he continued, "Ivy didn't bring that over. My mom did."

Her eyes widened, sparkling emerald green in the sunlight coming in through the back windows. "I thought your parents were in France, visiting some friends."

"They'd still be there, if it was up to me. I didn't want to worry them. But Grayson called them. They flew in Monday."

She glanced around, as if looking for signs of them being there. "They aren't staying with you?"

"They left an hour ago, heading back to Florida."

"Tampa, right? Your dad always entertains me with stories about his fishing excursions there and—"

"Why are you here, Faith?"

She winced again then started toward him, stopping a few feet away. He had to admire her for that. He'd been an unwelcoming ass so far and she was facing him head-on. That's the Faith he was used to, not the one who'd run earlier this week.

"Why are you here?" Asher repeated, not sure what to expect. Was this an official goodbye? Had he scared her so much she was quitting her job, leaving Gatlinburg? Maybe going back to Nashville? The thought of that sent a frisson of fear through him. But he wasn't backing down. In the few minutes that she'd been here, he'd made his decision. Going backward wasn't part of it.

She took his right hand in both of hers. "You look tired. Do you feel okay? Any trouble breathing?"

"I'm sure I look as ragged as I feel. The pain's at a steady four now. But that's much better than the eight or nine a few days ago. I imagine I'll live."

"I'm so sorry you're hurting. Do you want to sit down? Can I get you some pain meds?"

"I'll get them myself once you tell me why you're here."

She sighed and gently ran her thumb over the back of his hand. "You know you're my best friend in the whole world, right?"

That soft slow stroke of her thumb was killing him. He had to force himself not to tighten his grip, pull her to him and seek another taste of heaven.

"I used to think I was your best friend," Asher said. "Now I'm not sure."

"My fault. I treated you horribly. It's unforgivable, really, to leave and not come back. I should have been there for you. That's what friends do. They take care of each other. I didn't do that. And I'm sorry, deeply sorry. Do you think you can forgive me?"

"No."

Faith blinked and tugged her hands free. "No?"

"There's nothing to forgive. You ran because you were scared. I get that. And I respect, and appreciate, that you finally came back to face me."

A look of relief crossed her face. "Thank you. I was worried I'd ruined everything. That you wouldn't want to be around me anymore. Your friendship means everything to me and I don't want to destroy it because of one moment of insanity between us." She laughed awkwardly. "I don't know how it happened. We were both tired, and I know you were in pain and…well, let's just put that behind us and pretend it didn't happen. I brought my case files with me and we can—"

Asher stepped closer, forcing her to crane her neck back to look at him. "I refuse to pretend that amazing, scorching, earth-shattering kiss didn't happen. I've been trying to make you see me as more than a friend for almost two years now. We clicked right away, had fun together. I get that you were glad to have someone welcome you and show you the ropes at a brand-new job. But we started off wrong. I was patient, too patient, and never let you know how I really felt. Well, I'm letting you know now. My interest in you has never been just as a friend. I want you, Faith. And I'm not going to pretend anymore that I don't. I'm done with pretending."

When she simply stared at him, in obvious shock, he decided not to pull any punches. He laid it all out in the open so there would never be any misunderstandings again.

"While we're working, I'll do my best to keep it professional. But when we're off the clock, or having that downtime you mentioned, we're just a man and a woman. And this man very much wants to treat you like a woman, in every way. If you can't deal with that, you can run again, go home. I'll ask Grayson to assign me another partner to help with the Parks case."

Her cheeks flushed. "Assign someone else? It's my case too. I'm not going to stop working on it. You're not replacing me, not on this investigation."

"Then you have a choice to make. Work with me, knowing my feelings for you are anything but…tame. Or we let Grayson decide which one of us continues working on the Parks investigation and which one gets reassigned to something else."

Her hands fisted at her sides. "I don't want to risk him reassigning me. You don't play fair."

He leaned down until their faces were only a few inches apart. "Darlin', if I played fair, I'd never get what I want. To be perfectly clear, what I want is you. In my bed."

Her face flushed an even brighter red as she took several steps back. "Well, I can tell you right now. *That's* never going to happen. And you're not kicking me off this case."

He smiled. "Good to know, about the case. That means we'll continue to work together day in and day out until we solve this thing. You'll have plenty of time to realize you're underestimating yourself."

Her brows drew down in confusion. "Underestimating myself? What do you mean?"

He moved close again, so close that her breasts brushed against him. "You've had a taste, a very small taste, of how good it could be between us. And, like it or not, you're curious. You're wondering just how much better, and hotter, it could get. And one day…maybe not today, maybe not for a while yet, you'll want to scratch that itch."

Her mouth fell open in astonishment.

"When you reach that point," Asher continued, "when you decide you've wondered enough and are ready to discover just how good it will be between us, all you have to do is crook that pretty finger of yours and I'll come running."

Her jaw snapped shut and she smoothed her hands down her jeans. "Well, then. I'll be careful not to…crook my finger. I wouldn't want *you* to get the wrong impression. Now, if you're through feeding that tremendous ego, we both have work to do. On the case."

"Of course. After you." He motioned in the direction of his office.

She grabbed her backpack from the table, then headed down the hallway.

When the door closed behind her with a loud click, he swore beneath his breath and strode into the kitchen to grab some pain pills. Shaking his head as he popped a couple out of the bottle, he swore again. What had gotten into him? He knew the answer to that. Daphne. Faith's sister had pushed him, over and over, telling him to be bold, to do something outrageous to let Faith know how he felt. Well he'd done that and more.

He'd been waiting far too long, moving at glacial speed. Either she'd decide she wanted him or she wouldn't. But he was through spending his life trying to make her notice him. If it was meant to be, great. If not…well, he'd cross that bridge if it came to that. They'd work the case, hopefully solve it. Then it was up to her. If the answer was no, or even to wait longer, he was done.

His bruised ego applauded his decision. But his heart was already mourning the expected end, that Faith would never care about him the way he cared about her.

He glanced down the hallway toward the closed office door. Then he returned to the kitchen and grabbed a bottle of beer from the fridge. He didn't care that it was technically still morning. As the saying went, it was five o'clock somewhere. He popped the top, grimacing at the pain in his back as he tilted the bottle.

Chapter Thirteen

It had been a concerted effort yesterday, but Asher had done his best to *behave*, to act professionally and as platonically as possible so that Faith wouldn't feel uncomfortable. They'd spent the day poring over her research, and that of TBI and Gatlinburg PD, from when he'd been in the hospital. And they'd brainstormed various theories, not that they'd made much progress. She'd gradually relaxed and they'd fallen into their old routine of easy camaraderie. It was a good day, far better than he'd expected when it began.

When she'd fallen asleep at his desk in the early morning hours, he'd wanted to carry her down the hall to the guest room. But his still healing shoulder wouldn't cooperate. Instead, he'd urged a mostly-asleep Faith to shuffle to the couch with his help. He couldn't get her to go the extra distance to the guest room without her sleepily threatening to shoot him. Chuckling, he'd tucked the infamous pink blanket around her, the one she'd left at the hospital when she'd run out. He'd been curious about how she'd react when she woke and saw it. Her laughter the next morning had him smiling when he heard her from his master bath where he was brushing his teeth.

She'd gone home to shower and change, leaving the pink blanket neatly folded over the back of the couch. He hadn't tried driving since getting hurt but he was thinking he'd have to either give it a try or call Lance for a ride to Grayson's mansion for the morning UB meeting. But Faith had surprised him by pulling up and offering her services as his chauffeur.

Approaching Grayson's mansion was just as awe-inspiring this morning as it was every time Asher saw it. Honey-colored stone walls sparkled in the morning sun. A giant portico shaded much of the circular drive out front, with enough space for half a dozen cars beneath it.

Massive windows that Grayson had added in a recent renovation reflected the trees and English gardens out front. They were made of bullet-resistant, one-way privacy glass, just like the windows at Unfinished Business. And they went floor to ceiling in every room.

"How many square feet do you think this place is?" Faith asked as she parked behind Lance's white Jeep. "You could fit four or five homes like mine inside, and my house isn't exactly tiny."

"No clue. I've never asked. Have you ever seen the whole thing?"

"Don't think I have, actually. Maybe we should ask for a guided tour someday."

"In our spare time?"

She smiled. "Maybe we'll have time for a real vacation one day, instead of the fake one we had to work for the Parks investigation." She cut the engine.

"We?"

Her smile faded. "I mean, you know, both of us, our own vacations. I didn't mean to—"

He gently squeezed her hand. "I was teasing, Faith."

"Oh. I knew that."

He grinned.

She rolled her eyes.

"I've missed this," he said. "A day isn't complete without you rolling your eyes at me."

"Well, now that I know how much you love it, I'll be sure to do it more often."

He laughed and they both got out of her Lexus and headed inside.

As he closed one of the double doors behind them, which was even larger than the ones at his place, he leaned down next to her ear. "I'm always surprised when a stuffy English butler doesn't answer the door here. But then, Grayson doesn't stand on ceremony, in spite of all his money. He's pretty down to earth."

"He's not what people expect, that's for sure." She took a turn around the magnificent polished wood and marble entryway. "I think he's got a dozen employees running this place. But half of them are elderly and have lived here longer than he has. It's more of a service he's giving them than the other way around, making sure they can live out their days in style instead of being relegated to some retirement home."

Willow stepped out of the double doors to the left that led to the library. "And if he hears you talking about how wonderful and kind he is, he'll turn ornery and resentful. He's not good at taking compliments."

Faith hugged her. "I'm so glad the two of you ended up together. You're the perfect couple, yin to his yang and all that."

"He's perfect for *me*, that's for sure. Now, let's get this party started. You're the last two investigators to arrive. The rest are already here—Ryland, Lance, Brice, Trent, Ivy. Even Callum put his current case on hold to be here for the meeting. He drove in from Johnson City last night. The only one missing is our resident TBI liaison. Rowan is negotiating the access to evidence in some of our cases but will be here later. No need for us to wait. There's a breakfast buffet set up in the library. After that, we'll get down to business."

The library was exactly that, a two-story-high room that was filled with books. But it was also the equivalent of a family room with groupings of couches and recliners in several different areas. Or, they would have been, except that some of the groupings had been combined into one big U-shaped cluster in the middle of the room for the meeting.

On the opposite wall to the windows, the buffet that Willow had mentioned was set up. It contained an obscene amount of food running the gambit from fruit and bagels to eggs, biscuits and gravy. To a stranger, it might seem wasteful. But everyone at UB knew the truth. Nothing went to waste here. Grayson was generous and shared everything with the staff and any of the temporary workers in the gardens. No doubt the kitchens were bustling right now to ensure that everyone got plenty of fresh, delicious food. And if there ended up being too much for the staff and their families, it would be taken to a local food bank.

True to Faith's caring nature, in spite of the prickly exterior she often showed the world, she fussed over Asher, making sure he ate far more than he really wanted.

"You have to regain your strength," she said, bringing him a second glass of orange juice. "And you need plenty of vitamin C to help your muscles heal."

He eyed the glass without enthusiasm. "I guess that explains why you're trying to get me to drink a gallon of this stuff. I don't really care much for orange juice, to be honest."

"Doesn't matter. It's good for you."

Lance, sitting on a nearby couch, started laughing.

Faith narrowed her eyes. "What's so funny?"

He shrugged, still grinning. "Just beginning to understand why your sister calls you a smother-mother."

She gasped. "Who told you that?"

He pointed at Asher.

"You *didn't*." She crossed her arms.

He started drinking the juice to avoid answering.

She sat back, her expression promising retribution later.

He couldn't help grinning when he finally set the juice down. But before Faith could make him pay, Grayson and Willow stood.

"Thank you all for coming here," Grayson said. "Rather than have this status meeting in the conference room at the office, I wanted to have it at our home because this is a special occasion. Asher, thank God, is with us today when he came close to dying a little over a week ago. Willow and I are both extremely grateful that you're on the road to recovery and back with the team."

Everyone clapped and cheered. A few whistled. Asher shook his head, motioning for everyone to stop.

Faith subtly moved her hand on the couch between them, gently pressing her fingers over the top of his hand.

He glanced at her in question and she simply smiled. He knew she was thanking him, as the others were. But her private gesture moved him more than all the others combined.

Before Asher could say anything, Grayson cleared his throat and the noise died down.

"I'll add one more thing," Grayson said. "Asher risked his life to save the life of another. That's rare. Even more rare is for someone to help another by *actually* giving them the shirt off their back."

Asher groaned at the corny joke.

"Willow and I would like to compensate you for your loss." Grayson pitched something at Asher.

He caught it against his chest, shaking his head when he realized what it was.

A shirt.

Soon, shirts were being tossed at him from everyone there, the last from Faith, who was laughing as it landed on top of the small pile of clothes on his lap.

"Very funny, everyone," he said dryly. "Hilarious." He made a show of checking the tag on one of them and tossed it at Lance. "Someone must have meant that one for you. It's a small."

Lance, who was just as big as Asher, tossed the shirt back. "Then it's definitely for you, little guy."

Faith started folding the pile of shirts.

"Thanks, darlin'," Asher whispered.

She avoided his gaze but subtly nodded.

"All fun aside," Grayson said, "we're all busy and have a lot of work to do. Ryland, you want to give your status first? We can end with Faith."

He nodded and began updating the team on his current case. They each gave updates, as they normally did each morning whether at UB or via remote link, depending on where each of them was working that day. They bounced ideas off each other and made suggestions. When it was Asher's turn, he gave a quick summary of what had happened when Faith zeroed in on Stan's Smoky Mountains Trail Rides as a potential place for Leslie Parks to have been taken.

"You know the rest. We were lucky to find Leslie. But, unfortunately, the killer got away. Faith can tell you what happened after that since I was out of commission for a bit."

"He totally glossed over the details that some of you haven't heard," she said. "The perpetrator strung up Leslie with a noose around her neck. He had her stand on a log and had a rope tied around it, with one end trailing into the woods where he was hiding. As soon as Asher found Leslie, the perp yanked the rope. Asher dove at Leslie, grabbing her legs against the tree just as the log upended her. If he hadn't done that, her neck would have snapped. Then the coward in the woods threw his knife at her to finish the job. But Asher twisted his body in between the knife and Leslie, again saving her life. Leslie told me that knife was headed straight for her heart. Even with the knife embedded in his back, puncturing a lung, Asher managed to get the noose off Leslie and mount a horse with her to bring her back to the stables."

Willow, seated with Grayson across from them, went pale. "I had no idea just how bad it was up there. Good grief. We really are lucky you survived, Asher."

"I appreciate it. But it's over. I'm doing fine." He motioned to Faith. "You worked up a timeline based on yours and Gatlinburg PD's research. Want to tell them about that?"

She took mercy on him by taking over, speaking to all of the research she'd done in the past handful of days.

"The perpetrator walked Leslie into the stables, stole the two horses and forced her to ride up into the foothills. He was rough, slapped her around, gave her some shallow cuts with that same knife. Mostly, he terrified her, telling her the awful things that he was going to do. Thankfully, he never got to the point of carrying out those plans. Asher rescued her before the perp could assault her in the way he'd planned."

Ryland leaned forward in his chair to Faith's left. "Why did he return to the stables and leave her up in the foothills? And why kill the two he left in the tack room?"

"Leslie said that when Stan Darden Junior rode into the foothills searching for the horses, he stumbled right onto them and saw Leslie tied to that tree, being tortured. Stan, again, the real one, tried to intervene. But the perp got the better of him and stabbed him. Stan was able to stagger to his horse and take off, presumably to get help. You can all pretty much guess what happened after that. Our bad guy took off after Stan. He caught him and butchered him at the stables. Then he did the same to Stan's father when the noise alerted him and he came outside looking for his son."

Ivy winced across from Faith. "How awful. That poor family."

"I know." Faith shook her head. "It's so sad. Such a useless waste of life."

Asher took up the tale. "It appears that he was getting a fresh horse, hiding the bodies and grabbing supplies so he could head deeper into the mountains with Leslie at about the time that Faith and I arrived."

Faith nodded. "Leslie hasn't spoken to anyone aside from me that first day. We were both together because the police wanted us to help the sketch artist make a composite of the man who attacked her. Immediately after that, she gave me the basics that I just told you. But after that, she stopped talking, wouldn't even speak to the detectives on the case. I think she's been in shock, unable to face the trauma of what happened. I'm hopeful that she'll agree to speak to Asher and me, given that he saved her life. Willow, as our victim advocate, you've already made inroads with the family. Do you think you could speak to them, see if Asher and I can interview Leslie? Today if possible?"

"Absolutely. Her well-being will be my first priority, of course. But if she's up to it, and her family agrees, I'll let you know right away."

"That's all I can ask for. Thanks."

Willow smiled.

At that moment, Rowan Knight arrived. Nodding at Asher, he went directly to Grayson and handed him a piece of paper. They spoke for a moment before Rowan turned to leave. On his way out, he tossed a shirt at Asher and grinned as he hurriedly left.

Asher chuckled and added the shirt to the pile that Faith had set between them just as Grayson handed the paper to Faith.

"The medical examiner," Grayson said, "with the help of a forensic anthropologist, identified the final two victims. Those are their names, brief descriptions including limited background information on them, as well as their last-known addresses."

Faith summarized the findings for everyone, reading the pertinent details out loud. "Victim number five identified as June Aguirre, female, Hispanic, twenty-six years old. She was single, had a steady boyfriend—Nathan Jefferson. Lived in Pigeon Forge. Occupation, branch manager of a credit union. Disappeared on her way home from work in downtown Gatlinburg and was never seen again. That was five years ago." She blinked. "Wow, she disappeared one *day* before Jasmine Parks."

Asher frowned. "That's a heck of an escalation, from about six months between our earlier victims and only one day between those last two. Definitely something we need to pay attention to. What about cause of death? The ME couldn't come up with one on the other victims. Anything on June Aguirre?"

Faith reread the short summary then shook her head. "Manner of death, homicide. Cause of death, undetermined."

She flipped the paper over. "Victim number six is Brenda Kramer, female, white, twenty-three. Also single, with a steady live-in boyfriend—Kurt Ritter. She was a lifelong resident of Gatlinburg. After high school, she took two years off to travel. When she came back, she began attending business school. She was one year from graduation when she disappeared one night after partying with friends. Her boyfriend said she never made it home. That was seven years ago. And before you ask, cause of death again is undetermined." She grimaced. "This is weird. Some smooth river rocks were found in the victim's pocket. Could that be significant?"

"Were there rocks found with the others?" Grayson asked.

"Not that I recall. Asher?"

"I'll double-check, but I don't think so. I remember one of the victims had really hard dirt caked on what was left of their clothes. The ME speculated it might have been mud at the time the body was buried. That could mean two of the victims had been in or near water shortly before their deaths. Or it could be as simple as someone hiking and picking up rocks. And the other getting caught in the rain and getting muddy before they were kidnapped. I'm not seeing how rocks or mud can help us, but we'll note it, see if it ties into anything else we've found."

Grayson crossed his arms, his brows pulled together in a frown. "Seems thin, agreed. I know it's been years since the murders and the only thing the ME has to go on are skeletons, but can't we get her to at least speculate about possible causes of death? Like strangulation? Isn't that a common COD in serial killer cases?"

Asher nodded. "It's actually one of the most common ways serial killers murder their victims. But usually that breaks some bones in the throat, and that will be found during the autopsy. Since none of our victims had their hyoid bone broken, strangulation doesn't seem likely. Lack of tool marks or splintered bones on any of our victims also makes it seem unlikely they were stabbed. There weren't any bullet holes in any of the bones, no bullet fragments. So shooting is highly unlikely."

"What about poison?" Grayson asked. "There was some hair found with some of the victims. Can't they test the hair for toxins? I seem to remember hearing that hair continues to grow for some time after death. If that postmortem hair contains toxins, could it prove someone ingested some as a cause of death?"

Faith smiled. "Changing professions, boss? Wanting to become one of your investigators?"

"I don't want to work that hard," he teased. "But I'm as frustrated as I'm sure you and Asher are. Just asking questions that come to mind."

"They're good questions. Questions that Asher and I have discussed as well. Or, we did, when discussing the earlier victims. With June and Brenda added to the mix, I'm sure we'll rediscuss all of that. Poison is one of the things we can't rule out. Even with hair growth after death, to have enough concentration of toxins in that hair to detect would only happen if the poison took a long time to kill the victim. The heart would have to be pumping long enough to circulate toxins all over the body and to end up in hair follicles in large enough concentrations to detect. I can't see a serial killer dosing victims over a long enough period of time for the poison to show up in postmortem hair deposits."

Asher nodded his agreement. "It's also rare for men to use poison to kill. That's more of a female killer's method of choice. We know our killer is a white male in his early thirties. That matches our latest FBI profile on him, and the eyewitness accounts—namely Leslie's, Faith's, and mine. The profile also said he's likely single, never married, and has difficulty holding down a steady job. He'll resort to hourly, cash jobs, possibly outdoors, like landscaping or construction. That goes along with his comfort up here in the mountains. This location is his domain, where he feels most at ease. He likely started killing in his mid-twenties, which would go right along with our first victim having been killed seven years ago. As often happens with serial killers, there was likely a trigger at that time that sent him over the edge from hurting and murdering women in his fantasies to actually doing it."

"Don't forget the trauma he believes the killer suffered during his childhood, as a preteen or early teen," Faith added. "That supposedly had a major impact on his world outlook, maybe even began his hatred for women. It might help explain his depravity, but I don't see how that helps us figure out who he is other than looking for some kind of childhood trauma in any background searches we do in the hopes of narrowing any potential suspect lists down."

"Faith and I speculated that hanging could be his go-to for how he kills, since he tried to hang Leslie Parks," Asher said. "But she called the ME about that possibility shortly after we rescued Leslie. That's when the medical examiner explained about the hyoid bone and lack of any other broken bones in our victims. With hanging, it's possible *not* to break the neck. But she believed it unlikely that at least one of the deceased wouldn't have showed some kind of bone injury if they were all hung. Then again, we're assuming our killer is consistent with how he kills. Most are. But some do change it up. They learn from their mistakes, adjust their weapon of choice."

"What about a signature?" Lance asked. "Even if a serial killer changes how he kills, there's usually one thing, a ritual or whatever, that's always the same. It could be as simple as how he binds his victims, or that he kisses their forehead before killing them. Is there anything at all you've been able to piece together as his signature, given that you only have the skeletons, some hair, and fragments of clothes and jewelry?"

Faith shook her head no as she handed the paper to Asher. "With so little to go on as far as physical evidence in each of the graves, we don't even have a theory about his signature. It's something we debate often but neither of us has anything concrete to offer there."

She motioned toward the paper that Asher was studying. "These two latest victim identifications, on top of the information we have on the others, means that the killer's first victim was Brenda Kramer. The rest, in order of when they were killed, are Natalie Houseman, Dana Randolph, Felicia Stewart and June Aguirre. Jasmine Parks is the last victim, five years ago. There aren't any other bodies in that makeshift graveyard. TBI brought in their own scent dog team and reexamined the entire mountainside with ground penetrating radar. Six victims, total. He kills one every five to six months, then his last two only one day apart. After that, nothing. One thing I want answered is why he escalated from his routine of about six months between kills to one day between his last two."

"No clue about the one-day-apart thing," Lance offered. "But I didn't think serial killers stop killing by choice. Either they die, are incarcerated, or incapacitated in some way that makes it impossible for them to continue. Have you explored the incarceration angle?"

"We have," Asher told him. "We actually hired a computer expert for that because we had a massive amount of data on intakes and releases of prisoners from the Tennessee prison system to analyze. He wrote a program that compared all of that data with the dates that our victims were killed and the gap since Jasmine's disappearance and Leslie's abduction. Some of the more recent convicts to be released could theoretically have abducted Leslie. But our computer guy was able to exclude most of them because they were incarcerated during times when some of the other victims were killed. We ended up with only five potentials and were able to rule them out because their photos don't match our killer."

"That thorough analysis pretty much proves he wasn't incarcerated during that time gap," Lance said. "Unless he was incarcerated in another state, which I'd consider a low probability given that he's choosing and murdering people here. He's comfortable, knows the area. Maybe he hasn't stopped killing at all and is burying the more recent bodies in another personal graveyard, perhaps on another remote mountainside."

"Possibly," Asher said. "But it's all speculation without any facts at this point. It's rare, I agree, that a serial killer stops or *increases* the amount of time between kills. Generally, the time decreases as the desire to kill grows stronger and they can't resist it as long. But there are known documented exceptions. One is the BTK killer—Bind, Torture, Kill—out of Park City, Kansas. He killed several victims months apart and then went years without killing anyone before he started up again."

"Regardless of whether our killer did or didn't…pause," Faith said, "we know he's killing again. He would have killed Leslie for sure if you hadn't stopped him. This is one of those areas Asher and I have discussed, and we both lean toward your way of thinking, Lance. We believe there probably is a second graveyard somewhere. We just haven't found it yet."

Grayson shook his head. "Russo and Frost will go ballistic if that's the case. But it's not like I can tell them there may be more bodies without having an idea of where to look."

Asher shrugged then winced when pain shot up his back. He breathed shallow breaths until the pain began to subside then continued. "I'd be comfortable saying the second graveyard, if there is one, would be in the area we already speculated about in our earlier geographical research. If you draw a circle of about twenty-minutes' travel time around the graveyard we already found, I'd bet big money that if he does have another burial site, it'll be in that circle."

"Absolutely," Faith said.

Asher went on. "If most of us agree that there's probably another graveyard, maybe we should get TBI involved, at least. The police don't have the resources to hunt for it. But TBI sure does. We could share our geographical theories and research, and they could go on a wild-goose chase, if that's what it is. Let them decide whether or not to look into this theory. They already pulled all the missing person cases of females in a thirty-mile radius of Gatlinburg for the past ten years to help the ME identity the victims we already have. They can use those as a starting point, see which cases don't have any good suspects already and focus on those as potentially being the work of our serial killer."

Grayson crossed his arms. "Why would they want to do that? Shouldn't they focus on the known victims first, see if that can help lead them to the killer?"

"They're already doing that," Faith said. "So are we. And none of us has gotten anywhere. New cases, new to us anyway, might offer links we haven't seen before, some new evidence that might break the case wide open."

"When you put it that way, it makes sense. I'll pitch that to Russo and Frost."

"Can you also pitch them getting any evidence from the two newly identified victims to our lab?" Asher asked. "I know there wasn't any viable DNA and no hits on the national database for the fingerprints found on the knife the perp used to stab me. Maybe we'll get lucky and get a hit off of evidence found with Kramer's or Aguirre's bodies."

Ryland joined the conversation. "You mentioned hits on the national database, AFIS. What about local law enforcement that might not be linked to AFIS, or that has minor, even nonviolent arrest records they've never bothered to enter into the system. Maybe Ivy or Lance can pursue that angle. You two are wrapping up a major case right now. Can one of you finish that up and the other pursue the fingerprints?"

Ivy glanced at Lance. "I can probably take it. You okay doing the wrap-up?"

"No problem. And I'll help you as soon as I'm done."

Asher smiled. "Thanks. That's a great idea. Fingerprints are as good as DNA if we can get a hit."

Ryland pulled out his cell phone. "I'll text Rowan to contact the TBI about pursuing those other missing person cases. As for the rest of UB helping you two…unfortunately, most of us are heavy into some pretty urgent cases ourselves right now. Contact Ivy if you come up with anything urgent for her to pursue."

Lance motioned with his hand. "Don't hesitate to call me if there's something you need help on. If I can fit it in, I will."

Asher glanced at Faith in question. "Victimology on the two newly identified victims?"

"Absolutely. That would be perfect. Lance, Ivy, add that to your to-do list if and when you can assist. I'm sure that even working this on a limited basis, you can pull together information on Aguirre and Kramer faster and better than TBI and Gatlinburg PD combined."

Lance laughed. "You're laying it on thick there, Faith."

She smiled. "Maybe a little. Anything you can find on them and send to Asher and me would be appreciated. That will allow us to focus on Jasmine and Leslie and any clues we can glean from the other victims that we've already been studying."

"Sounds like we have a plan," Grayson said. "Asher, do you need Faith to provide any further updates on what she's worked on while you were in the hospital? I know it's early and this is the first time you've seen each other since you were released from the hospital—"

"Actually," Faith said, "I brought him up to speed last night."

"At my place," Asher said. "She slept over."

She gasped. "On the couch! Alone!"

He grinned.

Several of the others started laughing.

Grayson coughed and glanced at a wide-eyed Willow.

Faith narrowed her eyes at Asher, in warning.

He chuckled. He was fine airing his attraction to her out in the open, even if Faith wasn't. Heck, everyone at UB had probably known for a long time how he felt about her. She was the only one he'd foolishly hid it from, waiting for her to wake up and give him some kind of signal.

"I'm glad you're both together again," Grayson said.

Faith's eyes widened. "Working, you mean."

He arched a brow. "What else would I mean?"

Her cheeks flushed pink and she crossed her arms as the others laughed again.

Willow lightly punched Grayson's arm and gave him a warning look. "I think what my husband meant to say is that he's glad you're an investigative team again."

"Absolutely," he said. "That's what I meant." He winked at Willow.

Faith's face flushed even redder. If Asher survived the car ride back to his house, he'd count himself a lucky man.

Ryland addressed Lance and Ivy. "Keep me in the loop when you update Asher and Faith. If anyone else on the team frees up, I'll send them your way."

"Thanks, Ryland." Faith's cheeks were still flushed. "And thank you, Lance and Ivy. I appreciate any help I can get on this. Even from Asher, for what little that's worth."

He grinned at her teasing. She sat a little straighter, getting back into the groove of bantering with him and taking his humor in stride. It felt good. And when he winked again, and this time she actually smiled, it felt even better.

He was going to enjoy this. And he was going to give it his all—to the case and to his pursuit of Faith. He'd take nothing less than a win in both arenas.

Chapter Fourteen

Last Sunday, Faith had been visiting Asher in the hospital in Knoxville. This Sunday, she was with him again. But they were in her car driving to Pigeon Forge and distant parts of Gatlinburg that she'd never been to before, doing what she'd called knock-and-talks when she was a police officer. They'd been visiting people from the lives of June and Brenda, looking for anything to link them to the other victims.

So far, talking to Nathan Jefferson about June, and to Kurt Ritter about Brenda, the only link they'd found was that June used the same grocery store as one of the earlier victims.

"What's next?" Faith asked as she headed back toward downtown Gatlinburg.

"Lunch? I'm starving."

"Finally getting your appetite back?"

"Been trying to lay off the pain pills so I don't get addicted to those things. Seems like my appetite's rising with the pain level."

She gave him a sharp look. "If the doctor was worried about addiction, he'd have told you to stop taking them. He didn't, did he?"

"Not in so many words. But I researched the medication. I know the dangers. And I don't want to end up hooked. Stop worrying. If the pain gets much worse, I'll take something over the counter. But I'm through with prescription meds."

She thought about arguing, but the smother-mother teasing still smarted. And even though she was struggling to forget their scorching kiss and to think of Asher as only a friend again, she also didn't want to be thought of as a "mother" in any capacity to him.

Their relationship had become way too complicated. She could barely sleep at night, tossing and turning, thinking about him. Thinking about every *inch* of him. The thoughts she had were waking her up in a sweat the few times she did get to sleep. She was surprised she hadn't caught the sheets on fire with the fantasies that she was having. And every single one of them revolved around him.

Faith cleared her throat and tried, again, to focus. "Where do you want to eat?"

"You okay? You seem a little flushed."

She flipped the air conditioner vent toward her. "It's a little warm today. Where do you want to go?"

He didn't appear to believe her excuse, but he didn't push it. "You in the mood for a burger?"

"I'm always in the mood for a burger. Johnny Rockets? Smokehouse Burger?"

"You read my mind. Can't remember the last time I had one of those amazing creations."

"Probably last Christmas, is my guess. Daphne was at her then-boyfriend's family's house and your parents were off on another trip. To Italy, I think."

"Yep, Christmas was Italy. The summer before that was Spain."

"Oh, yeah. I remember the Spanish candy they brought back. *Huesitos.* I loved the white-chocolate ones. Anyway, since we were both alone, we decided to find a Chinese place and drown our sorrows together."

He grinned. "The Chinese place was closed but Johnny Rockets was open. I'd forgotten about that."

"I'll never forget. You stole my onion rings."

He laughed. "You weren't going to eat them anyway. You couldn't even finish your cheeseburger."

She pulled into a space in front of the diner with its yellow, red and blue sign above the door declaring it the home of The Original Hamburger. "We've had some good times, haven't we, Asher?"

"Yes. We have. And I wish you'd call me Ash."

"No way. Too intimate. If I start calling you that, you'll know something's wrong."

"You called me Ash at the stables."

"I was under tremendous stress. You were hurt. Like I said, something was wrong."

He laughed and they headed inside.

Several hours later, they were back at his house, sitting at the dining room table, this time with both their laptops open. She stared at the pictures of all six victims on her screen then stretched and sat back. "I don't get it. This serial killer is breaking all the rules."

"Rules? Like what? Waiting six months between most of his kills, then possibly killing no one else for the past five years?"

"I'm not even pursuing that angle right now. I've been studying the victims, looking for similarities, and I'm not finding many aside from him choosing only female victims. Serial killers usually kill the same race as them. Our killer is white, but his victims are white, Black, and Latino. We've estimated him as mid-thirties. But his victims' ages range from early twenties to early forties. I could overlook all of that if they had similar physical features of some type, like if they all had straight dark hair. But they don't. I can't get a lock on this guy. My former life as a Nashville detective didn't give me much experience hunting this type of predator. You took some FBI serial killer courses at Quantico. What's your take on these inconsistencies?"

"I learned just enough to be dangerous. But one thing that they taught me is that a large percentage choose victims because of things they have in common that don't have to do with their physical attributes. It could be as simple as occupation or geography, and opportunity. Each one fulfills a specific need in him at the time that he kills them."

"That doesn't help me at all."

He shrugged then winced.

"When was your last pain pill? Over the counter or otherwise?"

"It's been a while. I'd hoped to avoid taking any more meds. But I'm ready to wave the white flag and grab a couple of Tylenol."

She wished he'd take something stronger. It wasn't like him to reveal that he was in pain, so he was probably in far more pain than he was admitting. She tapped her nails on the tabletop while he headed into the kitchen. "I haven't heard from Willow today. Have you?"

"Not a peep. Leslie must be really having a hard time if Willow can't convince her to talk to us." He downed some pills with a glass of water.

"She's the only known survivor of this killer. Something he said, or did, could be the key that ties everything together. And she may not even realize she holds that key."

"Don't pin your hopes on her. She may *never* speak to us. We have to figure out a path without her."

Faith sighed. "I know, I know." She waved at her computer and the pictures of the victims, guilt riding her hard that she hadn't yet figured out how to get justice for them. "It's so much easier said than done."

"We need a break, a distraction to get our mind off this, even if only for a few minutes. Then we can come at it fresh."

"A distraction sounds good. What would that be?"

"I can think of something to distract you." The teasing tone of his voice had her glancing sharply at him. When she saw he was holding up a half gallon of chocolate ice cream, she started laughing.

"Gotcha." He winked. "With or without whipped cream?"

"Duh. Definitely with. I'll help. You don't need to be scooping that with your back still healing." She headed into the kitchen and grabbed the scoop while he got out a couple of bowls.

"I'm guessing your mom bought this for you," she said as she filled their bowls. "She always loads you up with junk food every time she visits."

"I wouldn't have it any other way." He grabbed the whipped cream and put two dollops on top of each of their bowls.

She stared at the chocolate mountains. "What was I thinking? That's more than we could both ever eat."

"Speak for yourself." Asher took a huge spoonful and shoved it into his mouth.

She laughed and did the same, although she went for a much smaller spoonful. They both stood at the island, shoving empty calories into their mouths.

"I'm totally going to regret this tomorrow," she said. "When I get on the scale. Maybe you should finish mine. You still have some pounds to put back on."

"Don't mind if I do." He shoved his empty bowl away and pulled her half-eaten one to him.

She rinsed his bowl, put it in the dishwasher, and then turned around. She froze at the sight of him licking his spoon. His eyes darkened as he stared at her and slowly slid the spoon into his mouth. Her own mouth went dry as he scooped up some more and swirled his tongue around it before consuming it, all the while his heated gaze never leaving her.

"Stop, stop." Her voice was a dry rasp. She closed her eyes, blocking him out, and took a deep breath then another and another.

"Stop what, Faith?"

His tone had her eyes flying open. "Oh, my gosh. How do you do that?"

"Do what?"

"Lower your voice that way. You sound like…like—"

"Like what?"

"Like…sex! Just. Stop." She ran past him down the hall to the guest bedroom and slammed the door behind her.

ASHER DROPPED THE spoon into the bowl, at a loss for what had just happened. He'd made her mad and didn't even know how he'd done it. He'd been enjoying the ice cream and break from the case when he'd noticed the alluring sway of her bottom as she'd rinsed the bowl. When she'd turned around, his gaze had fallen to her lips and all he could seem to think about was the feel of them when he'd kissed her, the heat of her mouth when he'd swept his tongue inside.

The curve of her neck had him sucking on the spoon as he'd thought about sucking that soft, perfect skin as he'd done in the hospital. And her breasts, so soft and firm, pressing against his chest. Her words, asking him to stop, had truly surprised him, brought him crashing back to reality. His voice sounded like sex? He didn't even know he had that superpower. How could he not do something in the future if he didn't even know how he'd done it in the first place?

He scrubbed his hands across his face, cursing the situation. He was frustrated, in pain, and on edge. Nothing in his life seemed to be going right these days, either professionally or personally. And he was just plain tired.

Since it was too early for bed, Asher did the only other thing he could think of to try to ease his aches and pains and take his mind off all the stress, if only for a few minutes. He headed into his bedroom and strode into the bathroom to take advantage of his steam shower.

Washing away the aches and pains was much easier than washing away his worries about the case, and Faith. Even though they didn't have the answers they wanted on the investigation, they'd done so much digging that he felt they had to be close to a resolution. That's how these things typically went. Days, weeks or even months of work with little to show for it and all of a sudden that one puzzle piece would appear that made the entire picture come together. As for his relationship with Faith? That was still very much a puzzle. And he wasn't as optimistic that he'd ever find the missing piece.

After towel-drying himself, he wrapped the towel around his waist and headed into the bedroom for some fresh clothes.

"Oh…oh, my… I'm sorry."

He turned at the sound of Faith's voice. She stood at the foot of his bed, holding her phone, eyes wide as she stared at his towel. He glanced down, just to make sure he was covered, then strode to her, stopping a few feet away.

Her gaze jerked up to meet his, her cheeks that adorable shade of pink they turned whenever she was embarrassed.

"I didn't mean to… I mean I did, but it's still early-*ish* and I thought you had come in here to grab something and I… Oh, gosh, I'm sorry." She whirled around.

He gently grabbed her arm, stopping her. "Faith. No harm done. What's wrong?"

She drew a deep breath and turned. "An email from Ivy. She sent me a file of open missing person cases in Gatlinburg. There are a depressingly large number. Most are old, several years. But one is recent, two days ago. I opened it and…well, look." She held up her phone.

Asher frowned. "I think you're showing the wrong picture. That's June Aguirre."

"No. It isn't. It's a woman named Nancy Henry. They aren't even related, but they look as if they could be twins. Just like Leslie and Jasmine could have been twins if it wasn't for their age difference. Please tell me what I think is happening isn't happening. Did our guy take her?"

He took her phone and studied the screen. "You're right. They could be twins. But we shouldn't jump to conclusions. It could be a huge coincidence. For all we know, she may have run off with her boyfriend or gone on a trip without telling whoever reported her missing."

"I know, I know. But what if she didn't? What if our guy is responsible? What if he's furious that we took his trophies, the bodies he'd buried. And he wants to replace them with look-alikes? Have you ever heard of a serial killer doing that?"

"No. Doesn't mean they wouldn't or haven't. I don't think we should panic and alert anyone without something more than a hunch. We need to look at those other missing person files."

"There are a lot. It will take hours."

"We'll put on some coffee. We're going to need the caffeine."

Her gaze fell to his towel for a moment before she took her phone. "I, um, I'm sorry about…earlier. The ice cream incident. I'm…on edge. Saying really stupid things right now. It wasn't you. It was me. I really am sorry."

He grinned. "The 'ice cream incident'?"

"Don't make fun of me."

He pressed his hand to his chest. "Never."

She smiled. “I really am sorry, for the stupid things I said. And for slamming my door like a child.”

“Does this mean my voice doesn’t sound like sex after all?”

Her eyes widened. “I, um—”

“Kidding. And I shouldn’t tease you when you’re this serious. I’m sorry too. It was a misunderstanding.”

Her gaze dropped to his towel again. “Right. That’s all it was. A…misunderstanding. I’ll get that coffee going.” She ran from the room.

He stared at the empty doorway, more confused than ever—about the case, and especially about Faith. So much for his shower clearing his mind.

Several hours later, with a quick, light supper behind them and numerous phone calls with Lance and Ivy, they finally had their answer about the look-a-like theory. He set his phone down on the dining room table and sat back, rolling his shoulders to ease the ache from hunching over the computer for so long.

“It was a good theory,” he said. “Worth looking into. At least we know that Nancy Henry is safe and sound.” He grinned. “Even if she did run off with a new boyfriend and ghosted her old one. Russo’s canceling the missing person’s report now.”

She shut her laptop. “I wish his people were that diligent about closing out paperwork on their older missing person cases. We chased after two other look-alikes for hours before finding out they were both found within days of the reports being filed and no one canceled the alerts. We’re back to nothing.”

“No, we’re back to reexamining what we have, taking a fresh look. Something will shake out. When nothing makes sense, go back to step one.”

“Victimology,” she said.

"Exactly. It's too late to start on that now. Let's both get a good night's sleep and come at this fresh in the morning. You're welcome to stay over again, in the guest room this time, not the couch. You'll be much more comfortable there."

"I think I'll take you up on that. I'm too tired to drive home. Thanks, Asher."

"Of course. Anytime."

They both stood and headed in opposite directions, him to the main bedroom on the left side of the house, her to the guest room on the right.

"Hey, Asher?"

He turned around. She was still in the opening to the hallway on the other side of the great room. "Yeah?"

"It was a good day. I mean we didn't solve the case. But we worked hard, explored a lot of angles."

He smiled. "It was a good day."

"Asher?"

He chuckled, wondering why she was acting so timid all of a sudden. "Yes, Faith?"

"Thank you. Thank you for…for being my friend."

His stomach dropped at the dreaded *friend* word. Keeping his smile in place was a struggle. "It's my pleasure."

She smiled, looking relieved. Then she headed down the hall, away from him.

He fisted his hands at his sides as he stared at the now-empty hallway. Suddenly the idea of facing his very lonely bedroom was too much. Instead, he headed into the kitchen and grabbed a cold bottle of beer.

Chapter Fifteen

Asher blinked and looked up at the ceiling above his bed. Something had woken him. He turned his head then sat straight up, startled to see Faith standing a few feet away, twisting her hands together.

"Faith, hey. Is everything—"

"Kiss me."

The fog of sleep instantly evaporated, replaced by a fog of confusion. He scrubbed the stubble on his face. "Sorry, what?"

"Kiss me, Asher. I can't sleep. I need to get you out of my system. I have to stop thinking about what happened between us. You have to help me forget."

"You want me to help you forget that we ever kissed? By kissing you again?"

"Yes. No. I mean…yes. Just…kiss me, okay? If you don't mind?"

"Oh, I definitely don't mind. Can I brush my teeth first?"

"No. Yes, yes, probably a good idea. Go ahead. Hurry."

He started to the flip the comforter back then hesitated. "You might want to turn around."

"Why? I don't…oh. You mean you're…"

"Naked as the day I was born."

She whirled around.

He chuckled and grabbed some boxers from his dresser before heading into the bathroom.

When he came back out, he left the bathroom door open to provide better light. Not that he expected her to still be there. He figured she would have lost her nerve and run off again. Once again, she'd surprised him. She was still there, standing by the bed, wringing her hands. He padded across the carpet to stand in front of her.

"Still want to do this?"

"Yes, I… You don't have a shirt on."

"You want me to put one on before I kiss you?"

"Yes. No."

He grinned. "Are you even awake?" He waved his hand in front of her face. "Are you sleepwalking? Because you aren't making much sense and that's not like you at all."

"Believe me, none of this makes sense to me, either, except that I can't sleep because all I do is think of your damn golden gorgeous chest and your mouth and your tongue and… just do it. Kiss me."

He settled his hands around her tiny waist and leaned down.

"Wait." She pressed her hands against his chest, sucked in a breath as if she'd been burned and then snatched her hands away. Her breathing quickened as she stared at his chest, her gaze trailing down to his boxers. She squeezed her eyes shut and took a deep breath. "No tongue. Just a quick soft kiss on the lips."

"Faith."

"Yes?"

"Look at me."

She frowned and blew out a breath before opening her eyes. "What?"

"Explain it to me again, why you want me to kiss you? Not that I don't want to. Believe me, I do. But I don't want you to regret this later. I'm not sure you're thinking straight right now."

"I'm thinking as straight as I possibly can. I've been doing nothing but think for the past few hours. This is the only solution that I can think of."

"To get me out of your system?"

"Yes! I have a theory."

"A theory."

"I believe that I've built up that earlier kiss in my mind, made it seem way more…incredible than it actually was. If I have something to compare it to, I think I'll realize it was just the shock of it happening in the first place that has me in a dither."

He tried hard not to laugh. "You're in a *dither*? Is that what this is?"

"Don't laugh at me. This is serious."

"Of course. Forgive me. You want a quick soft kiss to make you forget the other kiss. Got it. Are you ready?"

She drew a shaky breath. "Ready. Oh, and I brushed my teeth too. It's all good."

He laughed. At her frown, he said, "Sorry."

"Just do it." She tilted her mouth up toward him and closed her eyes.

He slid his arms around her and gently pulled her against his chest.

Her eyes flew open.

He lowered his mouth to hers.

"Wait. No tongue. Remember, just a quick soft kiss."

"No tongue. Got it."

"Stop laughing. I hear laughter in your voice."

He arched a brow. "Would you rather hear sex in my voice?"

"No. Good grief, anything but that. Just hurry up, I need to get this over with."

"Ouch. My ego just limped off somewhere."

"Sorry. We're just friends, remember? I need to get things back the way they are."

"By having me kiss you."

"Exactly, we—"

He swooped down and kissed her, wildly, dragging his mouth across hers, nibbling on her lips.

She gasped against him and pushed at his chest, stepping back. "That wasn't soft!"

"Sorry. Should I try again?"

"Hang on a sec." She closed her eyes, frowned, then opened them again. "It didn't work. You definitely did it wrong."

"Because you're still not thinking of me as just a friend?"

"Exactly."

He grinned.

"It's not funny."

"It kind of is, actually."

"Once more. Soft. Not…wild like that. A quick soft kiss. That should do it."

"One quick soft kiss coming right up."

She pressed against his chest. "No tongue."

"Scout's honor."

"You weren't a Scout."

"I could have been."

"But you weren't. No tongue. Promise."

"Promise."

She gave him a suspicious look then relaxed her shoulders and closed her eyes again. "Let's get this over with. I really need to get some sleep tonight."

He was laughing when his lips touched hers. True to his promise, he gave her a gentle, tender kiss that about killed him not to deepen. When he ended the kiss, he inhaled a shaky breath, shocked at how such a brief, chaste touch had affected him.

Faith kept her eyes closed, her breaths sounding a bit uneven. When she finally looked up at him, the dazed look on her face had him instantly hardening. If she risked a quick glance down, there'd be no doubt about what she was doing to him.

He cleared his throat. "Did that work?"

She considered then slowly shook her head, looking disappointed. "Not even close. There's only one more thing I can think of to try."

"I can think of several things."

She put her hands on her hips "I don't mean that. We're definitely not doing *that*."

"Pity."

She blew out a frustrated sigh. "I need you to kiss me one more time."

His erection was becoming painfully hard now. He grimaced.

"Are you in pain? Do you need me to get you a pill?"

"No I'm… I'm fine. What kind of kiss this time?" Good grief, it sounded as if he was offering her up a menu.

"I think, in order to wipe out the memory of our first kiss, you're going to have to kiss me like that again."

His erection jerked. He cleared his throat again. "Like the first time? In the hospital?"

"Please. If you don't mind. I really think reality won't live up to the fantasy. That's my hope anyway."

His throat tightened. "You fantasize about me?"

"Just kiss me. I need a good night's sleep and—"

He covered her mouth with his and swept his tongue inside. He slid one hand in her thick hair, tilting her head back for better access. The other, he slid down her back to the curves he'd wanted to touch for so very long, pressing her against him. He expected his hardness to shock her into running away. Instead, she moaned and fit her body more snugly against his, cradling him with her softness.

It was like a switch had turned on inside both of them. The kiss at the hospital was incinerated by this one. Both were wild to touch, to taste, wanting more, and more, and more. He whirled her around, pressing her against the bedpost, worshipping her mouth with his, tasting her sweetness, her sassiness, everything that was Faith. Lava flowed through his veins, burning him up. For the first time since he'd been stabbed, the constant pain in his healing back faded into oblivion. All he felt was *Faith.*

He lifted her bottom, fitting her even more perfectly against him, moving his lips to the side of her neck. She shivered and moaned, bucking against him. Holding her with one arm beneath her bottom, he raked back the comforter and began to lower her to the bed.

Her eyes flew open. "Stop!"

He immediately set her on her feet and stepped back, even though it nearly killed him. "Are you sure?"

"Yes! We can't… I mean I want…but we can't…damn it." She stared up at him in shock and pressed a hand to her throat. "That kiss didn't work *at all*."

He motioned to his straining erection. "It worked for me."

Her eyes widened as she looked down. She stood transfixed, then slowly stepped toward him, her hand raised as if to stroke him.

He started to sweat, yearning for her touch, waiting, hoping.

She suddenly snatched her hand back. "What the hell am I doing?" She swore a blue streak and ran out of the room, cursing the entire time until the door down the hall slammed shut yet again.

He groaned and rested his forehead against the cool bedpost, struggling to slow his racing heart. More than anything, he wanted to follow her, to get on his knees and beg if he had to. Faith. She'd always been in his heart. Now she was in his blood. He wanted her so much he ached. And there wasn't a damn thing he could do about it.

He drew a ragged breath and strode into the bathroom for yet another shower. A cold one.

WHEN THE MORNING sun's rays slanted through the plantation shutters in Asher's bedroom, he was already dressed and ready to start the day. He'd chosen jeans and a loose, button-up shirt as he'd been doing since his confrontation with the perpetrator up on the mountain. His back was too stiff to make shrugging into a suit jacket remotely comfortable.

He tapped his fingers on his dresser, dozens of other useless minutiae running through his mind. None of it mattered. None of it was what he cared one bit about. All he was doing was putting off the inevitable. Facing Faith this morning and seeing what kind of a mood she was in today.

Would she blame him for whatever the hell had happened last night? Walk out? Tell him they were done? No longer friends, no longer work partners, nothing? Or would she smile and lighten his heart, be the friendly, fun woman he loved so damn much? Or would she be a mixture of the two? The only thing he knew for sure was that standing in his bedroom avoiding a potential confrontation wasn't going to make things better. And it wasn't going to solve the case either. He had to face Faith head-on and go from there. Somehow.

He strode to the door and pulled it open, almost running into Faith. He grabbed her shoulders to steady her, then let go.

"Faith. Good morning. Are you—"

"It's Willow." She held up her phone. "Leslie Parks is ready to talk to us."

Chapter Sixteen

Faith had never been more grateful for a phone call than this morning when Willow told her that Leslie was ready to talk. She'd been dreading facing Asher after last night. There was no way she could pretend anymore that she thought of him as just a friend. But she was still so shocked at the turn of events that she didn't know what to do.

She was a coward twice over, again not wanting to have an honest, tough conversation. Thankfully, he must have picked up on that and he hadn't even brought up what had happened. But how long would he wait? And how long was it fair to keep him waiting? It wasn't a secret how he felt about her. He deserved to know how she felt about him. But how *did* she feel? He'd been firmly in the best friend category for nearly two years. Thinking of him in any other capacity was…confusing. And it had her on edge.

After going home for a shower and change of clothes, she'd returned, ready to take him to the Parkses' home. Her already high anxiety went off the charts when he said he was going to drive his truck instead of being chauffeured in her car. He'd insisted it had been long enough, that he needed to give it a try to see how it went. The only reason she'd backed down and didn't argue was that he'd readily agreed if it was too difficult, too painful, he'd pull over and let her drive.

When they reached the Parkses' neighborhood and turned onto their street, Asher groaned and pulled to a stop. "Newshounds. They're camped outside Leslie's home."

Faith fisted her hand on the seat. "That pushy brassy-blonde anchorwoman's leading the pack. I can practically smell her hair spray from here. Every time I see her it makes me want to dye my hair brown."

He chuckled. "I'm sure Miranda Cummings is a very nice person. You should give her a chance. Maybe you two could become great friends."

"Not even in my worst nightmares. What's the plan? Sneak in from the backyard? We could call ahead, let the Parkses know."

"That would only give the media more fodder for gossip if someone spotted us. I don't want to give them a video clip for their prime-time broadcast. And I can't imagine Grayson being happy seeing us climbing over a fence on the news, even if we do get the homeowner's permission."

"Good point. The direct approach it is."

"Should I take your gun, to keep Miranda safe?"

"Probably. But I'm not giving it to you."

He smiled and drove farther down the street. But he was forced to pull to the curb a good block away because there was no available space any closer. "Looks like we're hoofing it from here. No shooting, Faith."

"If she thrusts a microphone in my face, I'm not responsible for my actions." She smirked and popped open her door.

Asher jogged to catch up and she immediately slowed, glancing at him in concern. "I'm sorry. I didn't mean to make you hustle like that. How's your back? Breathing okay?"

He surprised her by putting his arm around her shoulders. "Getting better all the time. See? I couldn't do this a few days ago."

She ducked down and gently pushed his arm off her shoulders. "And you can't do it today either."

"Spoilsport."

She laughed. He smiled. And her world was right again. At least until they reached the walkway to the Parkses' home and the anchorwoman recognized them.

"Don't look now," she whispered. "The bulldog and her cameraman are running over as fast as her stilettos will allow."

"Then we'll just have to run faster." He winked and grabbed her hand, tugging her with him, double-time, up the path.

Faith didn't even have a chance to worry about his injuries or try to stop him. She had to jog to keep up with his long-legged strides. But they made it to the front door before Cummings and her cameraman could maneuver around the other media to cut them off.

The door swung open and Mr. Parks waved Faith and Asher inside, firmly closing the door behind them.

He shook his graying head. "Danged rude reporters. They haven't left since the day you found our Jasmine. Neighbors have to bring us groceries so we don't get mobbed going outside. The police had people out here the first couple of days. But then they left, won't do a thing about it."

Faith took his hands in hers. "Mr. Parks, we're so sorry for your loss. We truly are, and everything you and your family are going through."

He patted her hand, smiling through unshed tears. But before he could respond, Mrs. Parks ambled into the foyer. "Lawd, Ms. Lancaster. You don't have anything to apologize for, you or Mr. Whitfield. If it weren't for both of you, we'd never have gotten our Jasmine back. We were finally able to give her a proper burial. And thanks to you, Mr. Whitfield, our baby, Leslie, is home safe and sound. If we'd lost both of them, I just don't think we could have made it. You saved our little family."

Faith held back her own tears as Mrs. Parks hugged Asher. She was probably the only one who noticed him slightly stiffening when Mr. Parks squeezed his shoulder and patted him on the back. But just as Faith took a step forward to warn them to be careful, he gave her a subtle shake of his head. She understood. These people had suffered one of the most painful losses possible, the loss of a child. If hugging him or pounding his back gave them some comfort, his physical pain was a small price to pay.

The four of them sat in the modest family room for a good half hour, with Asher and Faith being showed the family albums and listening to the couple reminisce about their precious Jasmine.

Mrs. Parks grabbed a stack of pictures from an end table and fanned them out on top of the last album. "These are from her funeral. I don't think we could have gotten even one more person in the church if we tried. And look at all those flowers."

Faith looked at every picture then carefully stacked them again and handed them back to her. "Jasmine was obviously well loved. She must have been a very special young woman."

"Oh, she was. She definitely was. Her two babies are half grown now and just as smart and precocious as she was." Her smile dimmed as she exchanged a suffering look with her husband. "'Course, we don't get to see them near as often as we'd like to. Their daddy moved an hour away from here."

Her husband patted her shoulder. "We see them once or twice a month. They're healthy and happy and love their nana and papa. That's what matters."

"I suppose." She didn't sound convinced.

Faith reached across the coffee table and squeezed her

hand. "I'm sure no grandparents feel they get to see their grandchildren enough."

"Honey, you got that right. Can I get either of you some coffee, some pie? I made apple pie last night when Leslie said she was thinking about calling Mrs. Prescott this morning, just in case. You have to try my pie."

Faith glanced at Asher for help.

He leaned forward, gently closing the last photo album. "Maybe we can have a piece of pie to go. Right now we'd really like to speak to Leslie, if she's still okay talking to us. It could really help with the investigation. We want to get justice for Jasmine, and for what Leslie went through. It's also urgent that we catch this man before he hurts someone else."

"Oh, goodness. And here I've been rattling on and on." She dabbed at her eyes. "Charles, check on Leslie. See if she's ready."

"I'm ready, Mama," a soft voice said from the hallway off to Asher's right. She nodded at Faith and gave Asher a tentative smile. "You're the man who saved me."

He stood and smiled down at her, offering his hand.

When she took it, instead of shaking it, he held it with both of his. "And you're one of the bravest young women I've ever met. You're a survivor, Leslie. Don't let what this man did define you. You're going to go on and do amazing things with your life."

Her eyes widened and she seemed to stand a little straighter. "You think so? You think I'm brave?"

"I know so."

She cleared her throat and nodded at Faith, who'd moved to stand beside him. "I don't think I know anything that will help you catch him. But I'll answer any questions that you have, if I can."

"Thank you," Faith said. She looked around the small

house. "Is there somewhere we can go to talk privately? No offense, Mr. and Mrs. Parks. It's just that sometimes survivors feel more comfortable talking without their loved ones in the same room."

They exchanged surprised looks, but Mr. Parks overrode whatever his wife was about to say. "Of course. Leslie, take them to Jasmine's room. They might want to see her pictures anyway. You can answer any questions they have about her too."

Leslie didn't seem enthusiastic about his suggestion. But she waved Faith and Asher to follow her down the hall. The last room on the left was a surprising combination of adult and child. The full-size bed on one wall had a contemporary, grown-up feel with its country-chic bedding and subdued tones. But the other side of the room boasted a bunk bed with bright blue football-themed blankets and pillows on top, and a fluffy pink comforter with white unicorns dancing all over it on the bottom.

"I never come in here since…" Leslie's voice was small, quiet. "Mama cleans it every week as if she expects Jazz to come through the door and pick up where she left off."

"I can tell she loves both of you very much." Faith motioned to the big bed. "Do you think it would be okay if we sit on her bed so we can talk?"

Leslie shrugged then sat. "Don't guess it matters now. She's in Heaven. I wonder if mama will keep cleaning the room."

Per the plan that Faith and Asher had worked out on the way over, Faith did most of the talking. They figured it would be easier for a woman who'd been victimized by a man to talk to another woman. Asher pulled out a chair from the small desk along a wall with a collage of pictures and spoke up just a few times to ask questions that Faith didn't think to ask.

To Faith's disappointment, the only thing Leslie told them

that was new information was that the killer had zapped her with a Taser to abduct her when she was out walking in her neighborhood. She'd have to remember to tell Chief Russo so he could send someone back to where Leslie had been abducted to search for the tiny Anti-Felon Identification confetti tags that shoot out of Tasers when fired. If the killer had legally purchased the cartridges used to deploy the darts, the tags would trace back to him. But she wasn't hanging her hopes on a legal purchase.

Leslie also said the man who'd abducted her had zip-tied her wrists together and then threatened her with a large, wicked-looking knife—likely the same one that he'd used to stab Asher—to get her to do what he'd wanted.

When Leslie couldn't think of anything else to tell them in response to their questions, Faith pulled the stack of photos out of her purse that she'd printed off before leaving Asher's home.

"Leslie, would you mind looking at these? I know it's been five years since your sister went missing, but if any of these people seem familiar, let me know. We're wondering whether your sister knew any of them. Their names are on the back of each picture."

Leslie dutifully looked through the photos and read each name. When she handed them back, she shook her head. "I don't recognize any of them. But I didn't hang with her and her friends. She was older than me. She'd graduated high school before I even started. I'm sorry. I guess I haven't been too helpful."

"You've been a huge help. We don't know which details will be important until the case all falls together."

Leslie nodded, but didn't seem convinced.

Asher leaned forward, his elbows resting on his knees. "Leslie, you were with your abductor for several hours. The sketch you and Ms. Lancaster helped the police artist draw is very good. But it's impressions, thing like how he spoke, certain word choices he might have used that stood out, things that don't show up in a sketch that might help us too. Faith and I spoke to him. But we weren't with him all that long. Neither of us picked up on anything unique or different that might make him stand out. Is there anything at all that you can think of that we may have missed?"

She started to shake her head no then stopped. "Well, it's probably not important."

"What?" Faith asked. "Tell us."

"I'm sure you noticed too. Maybe not him." She motioned to Asher. "But you probably did. His eyebrows."

Faith blinked. "Uh, his eyebrows? What about them?"

Leslie rolled her eyes and Faith suddenly realized how irritating that could be. Maybe she should work on trying to break that annoying habit herself.

"They were dark," Leslie said. "You know, really dark. Guys don't pencil their brows, at least none that I know. His blond hair didn't match his brows." She shrugged. "Like I said, probably doesn't help. But I think his natural hair color is a very dark brown, like his eyebrows. He either bleached his hair lighter or he was wearing a wig as a disguise."

A knock sounded on the open door and Mr. Parks stood in the entry. "Everything going okay?"

Asher stood. "Yes, sir. I think we're finished. We appreciate you allowing us to come into your home. And thank you, Leslie. You've been very patient with our questions."

She smiled, and Faith noticed the hero worship in her eyes. Asher had earned a life-long fan when he'd rescued Leslie. There might even be a little infatuation going on there. Faith couldn't blame the young woman. She was in the throes of a major crush on Asher herself. And still so shocked she didn't know what she was going to do about it.

Asher motioned to the large photo collage on the wall

above the desk. "Mr. Parks, would you mind if I snap some pictures of those? Just the ones of your daughter, Jasmine, and her friends?"

He shrugged. "Help yourself. She sure had a lot of friends, a lot of people who loved her." He smiled and tapped one of the pictures that showed Jasmine and four other young women in a bright yellow raft going over a four-foot waterfall that began a series of small rapids, probably class twos, maybe a few threes, too, just enough to make the trip exciting without being too dangerous for beginners and intermediate rafters. All of the women were smiling and appeared to be having the time of their lives.

"That there is the first time she ever went white-water rafting," Mr. Parks continued. "See her sitting right up front, holding that rope instead of a paddle? That's some kind of trick the guides show them, riding the bull or something like that. She wasn't afraid at all and jumped up front to give it a try. 'Course her best friend told me the secret, that she fell into the water right after the guide took that picture." He chuckled. "She'd have hated it if I knew that." His smile disappeared and his expression turned sad. "Come on, Leslie. Let's give these nice people a few minutes to take their pictures."

Faith exchanged a sad smile with Asher then helped him by moving some of the photos out from behind others so he could get good shots of all of them.

It took another half hour to extricate themselves from the home. Mrs. Parks was obviously going through grief all over again with the discovery of her oldest daughter's body. And she desperately needed to talk about her. Asher was far more patient with her than Faith, who'd been trying to edge them toward the door much sooner than he did.

When they did finally leave, they had an entire apple pie in a large brown paper bag. They'd tried to turn it down, but when it became clear that Mrs. Parks would be offended if they didn't take it, Asher had graciously accepted her gift and kissed her on the cheek.

Faith grinned at him once they got through the media gauntlet and were back in his truck heading down the road.

"What?" he asked. "Did I miss a joke somewhere?"

"I just think it's cute."

"Cute? You think *I'm* cute?"

"No. I mean yes. No secret there. You're an extremely handsome man. But I'm talking about the Parks women. It's cute that both of them have crushes on you."

"I sure hope not. Can we go back to that part about you thinking I'm extremely handsome?"

"Nope. Your ego's healthy enough as it is." She held up her phone. "And I'm busy trying to reach my baby sister."

"Your daily text?"

"Not every day."

"Mmm-hmm."

"Seriously. I try not to hover."

He laughed. "I can't imagine what you think hovering looks like."

"Whatever. I just worry about her. One text a day isn't hovering. It's caring."

"So you admit it's daily."

"I'm through with this conversation." She scowled as she stared at her phone. "She hasn't answered yet."

"Give her a few seconds."

"It's been far more than that. I texted her on the way to the Parkses' house. That was almost two hours ago."

"If you're really worried, why not call her?"

She checked the time. "No. I think she's in her chem class right now. I'll wait." She set the phone beside her. "Did you catch anything I missed in what Leslie told us? I didn't feel as if we learned anything new. Well, except that maybe our killer dyes his hair. Or wears a wig. I suppose that's something."

"It's a good reminder not to get thrown off by hair color if we see someone who fits his description in any other way. But, I agree. Nothing really new. I do want to review those pictures I took in her bedroom. Most of them appeared to be from the bar where she worked. I'd like to review them closely to see whether our killer could be in any of the background shots. Maybe he's been at that bar before and that's how he zeroed in on her as his target."

"Can I see your phone?"

He pulled it out of his jeans' pocket and gave it to her.

She flipped through the snapshots he'd taken of Jasmine's photos. Nothing stood out. The pictures taken at The Watering Hole, the bar where she'd worked, didn't reveal anything surprising. It was just a bar. Not one of the sleazy ones, more like a bar and grill. The grill part took up one side and the bar the other. Jasmine looked so young and happy, posing with other young people who could have been friends or patrons, or both. It was so heart-wrenching knowing her life would be cut short not long after many of these had been taken.

Faith was about to hand the phone back to Asher when something in the background of one of the shots caught her attention. She tapped the screen then enlarged the shot.

"No way."

"You found something?"

"Maybe." She grabbed her own phone, flipped through her photos, then stopped and compared it with one on Asher's phone. "It's her. June Aguirre is in one of the background shots. And if I'm not mistaken…give me a sec." She flipped through more photos on both phones until she could compare two more shots. "Asher, another one of our victims is in this picture, at The Watering Hole, where Jasmine worked. It's victim number three, Dana Randolph. That makes three of our victims so far—Jasmine, June and Dana. I think we've found our link."

Chapter Seventeen

"Dana Randolph," Asher said. "The married mother of two? She's at the bar?"

"Sort of. I mean yes. She's definitely there. But I don't think she's barhopping. It appears that she's sitting with her family at that high-top table. The kids certainly favor her. You know how when a restaurant is really busy, they offer to seat you in the bar area to eat? I think that's why she's there."

"Nothing about the bar came up in any of our interviews with victims' families."

"We've been trying to build timelines, come up with places everyone frequented. If they didn't go to this place very often, it might not have even occurred to them. This could be the tie-in we've been looking for. Maybe our killer is a regular and picks his victims there. When we interviewed the staff at the bar who were there when Jasmine worked there, we were focused on friends and enemies, anyone she knew and interacted with a lot. Every single person we checked out from that bar failed to raise red flags."

She set both phones down and shifted to face him as he turned the truck onto the long winding road up the mountain to his house. "I can almost see the gears turning in that mind of yours. You have a theory?"

"A possibility more than a theory. Something to check

out. What if none of the people we looked into at the bar came up as persons of interest because the killer was never after Jasmine?"

"Okay. You lost me there. Explain that one."

"You've seen two of the victims in the crowd, assuming that second one really is Dana Randolph. That's a heck of a coincidence that three of our six victims had been to that location. If we can prove the other three had at least been there, that's our link."

"I'll bet I can prove all six have been to the same fast-food chains too."

He smiled. "You've got me there. However, the bar where Jasmine worked isn't a chain. It's the one location. And it's not in downtown Gatlinburg with all the tourist spots. It's more out of the way, a place for locals. I think it's unlikely it's just a coincidence that they've all been there before. I think that's where the killer saw them and decided to go after them."

"All right," she said. "I'll go with that, for now. How does that explain your earlier statement that Jasmine was never a target? Wait. I think I know where you're going with this. The others were a target, but Jasmine saw something she wasn't supposed to see? Like maybe she started realizing some of the missing person stories she was seeing on the news were of people she'd seen in the bar, and she'd seen them all with our killer. He killed her to keep her from talking."

He nodded. "Possibly. Like I said, the theory could be far-fetched. But it does fit the evidence. It would explain why no one mentioned anyone fitting our killer's description as being one of her friends, or a regular who caused problems. If he didn't interact with her, if he kept to the background to try not to be noticed, then he wouldn't be on anyone's radar who knew her."

"That really does fit," she said. "The last victim before Jasmine, June Aguirre, went missing one day before her. Maybe Jasmine saw the killer with June, didn't think anything about it at the time. But the killer knew she'd seen him and decided to make sure she couldn't tell anyone once June's disappearance hit the news. It makes sense with what we know, or think we know anyway. What about Leslie, though? How does she fit in this? Why take another victim from the same family?"

"The media hasn't made a secret that we found his victims' graves because we were trying to find Jasmine. If the theory holds that he killed Jasmine because she saw him take June, or even because he believed she was beginning to suspect him for some other reason, that could make him even angrier that because of Jasmine again, he's lost his private graveyard."

She nodded. "He was angry at Jasmine all over again, so he wanted to hurt her. But with her gone, the next available outlet for his anger at her was to hurt someone she loved. Leslie."

Asher parked beside her car in the garage, grabbed the bag with the apple pie, and followed her into the house. "We need to review those pictures more in-depth and set up interviews with the bar staff again, those still working and the ones who no longer work there who knew Jasmine."

Faith chewed her bottom lip as she looked down at her phone again.

"Daphne still hasn't responded to your text?"

"Nope. I'm getting really ticked off about it too. She knows how much I worry."

"Go see her." He set the pie in the refrigerator. "I mean it. It's almost time for your weekly pizza night anyway. Re-interviewing everyone from the bar is going to take days. You heading to Knoxville to see your sister isn't going to jeopardize the investigation. I'll get Lance to help me. And Ivy's still tracking down those fingerprints. Maybe she'll get a hit soon."

"Are you sure? I mean I'd feel like a heel taking off right now. But I keep thinking about how guys that get out of prison sometimes go after prosecutors, judges, even their own defense attorneys, wanting revenge for them having gone to prison in the first place. This guy knows you and I are on his trail because of the stables. And it's been no secret in the media that we're the ones who discovered his graveyard and took away his trophies, the bodies of his victims. What if he goes after us, after our families, out of revenge?"

"I think that's a stretch. But you should still check on Daphne in person. It's the only way you're going to reassure yourself that she's okay. Do you want me to go with you? Or one of the others from UB?"

She shook her head. "I appreciate the offer. But, no. Someone needs to direct the others, explain what we've found, our theory. I'll head to her dorm, yell at her for letting her phone battery die, or whatever, and worrying me. Then I'll join you at the bar. Two and a half hours max. I'll still be able to help you with those interviews." She dug her keys out of her purse and headed toward the garage.

Asher stopped her with a hand on her arm. "Did you check that Find My Sister app on your phone?"

"It's turned off."

"Have you ever known Daphne to turn it off?"

"Only once, back when she was in high school. I lit into her for it and she's never done it again. Ever."

"I'm going with you. You can call Grayson about your concerns on the way to Knoxville."

She blinked back threatening tears of gratitude. "Thanks, Asher." Without even thinking about it, she wrapped her arms around his waist and hugged him. When she realized what she was doing, and that her arms were pressing against his healing injuries, she stiffened in shock. "I'm so sorry. I'm probably hurting you."

She started to pull back but he tightened his arms around her. "I'm fine. You need to stop worrying about me so much."

She hesitated. "I'm not hurting you?"

"Just the opposite. I'd like to stand here forever holding you. But I know you're worried about your sister." He kissed the top of her head again then sighed and stepped back. "Let's go."

They'd just gotten into his truck when her phone buzzed in her purse. She gasped and held up a hand to stop him from backing out of the garage. "It's Daphne. She finally texted me."

He leaned over and started laughing when he read the screen.

She gave him an aggravated look. "It's an endearment."

"Smother-mother's an endearment?"

"It is!"

"Sure. Okay." He grinned.

"Whatever. Just give me a minute to see if she really is okay." She reread the text.

Hey, smother-mother. Sorry—my battery died. Is something wrong?

Faith typed a reply.

Everything is fine. Just worried when no answer to my texts or call.

"Go see her, Faith. It'll make you feel better."

She almost denied it, but he was right. Seeing her sister, safe and sound in person, would calm her nerves. And maybe, just maybe, they could talk out her confusing feelings about Asher. Daphne might tease her. Okay, she'd definitely tease her. But in the end, she would hopefully help her see things more clearly, figure out what she should do.

"If you're sure, I think I'll take you up on that," she told him.

"Of course. I'll head to the bar and start setting up interviews. I can show the picture on my phone to the owner, see if it jogs his memory about regulars back then, even if they didn't pay attention to Jasmine. If Lance can't help, I'll get Ryland to send some others out there, even if he has to pull in some temporary consultants. We'll get it done. Don't worry about the case. Do what you need to do."

She took his hand in hers. "You really are a wonderful friend and partner, Asher. Thank you."

He gave her a pained look then nodded. "Call if you need me."

Her heart twisted at that look. But she didn't have time to try to sort things out with him right now. She really needed to see Daphne, to rid herself of this nagging feeling that things *weren't* okay, in spite of the text.

Asher backed out of the driveway while she idled in his garage, texting Daphne again before she got on the road.

Daphne, where are you?

My dorm. Why?

Stay there. Don't let anyone in. If anything seems off in any way, call security.

You're scaring me.

Don't be scared. It's just a case I'm working. Has me uneasy. I'm coming to see you.

Oh brother.

I'll make it up to you. Pizza on me.

Sounds good.

And turn your Find My Annoyingly Independent Little Sister app back on.

Have to plug it in first. Battery almost dead.

She was halfway to Knoxville when the last text that Daphne had sent flashed in her mind again. Something about it was bothering her. She pulled to the side of the highway to reread it.

Battery almost dead.

That didn't seem right. She scrolled to one of the earlier texts.

Sorry—my battery died.

Bad word choice or something else? If her battery had died, the assumption was that she had it plugged in so she could text Faith after that. So why, after Faith asked her to turn on her app, would she then say her battery was *almost* dead?

"You're overreacting, Faith. You're overreacting."

But even as she said the words out loud, her fingers were flying across the keyboard, sending another text.

Daphne. Call me.

Nothing.

Faith tried calling her sister.

No answer.

She texted again, called again. Still nothing.

She turned on her app. A few seconds later, it stated Daphne's phone could not be found. What was going on?

Suddenly a text came across, with a picture.

She screamed and immediately swung her vehicle around, almost crashing into a car that had to swerve to avoid her. Ignoring the honking horn, she slammed the gas, fishtailing until her wheels caught and shot her car back down the road toward Gatlinburg.

Her hand shook so hard she struggled to press the favorites button on her phone for Asher. When it finally buzzed him, he answered on the first ring.

"Everything okay?"

"No. God, no. I'm heading back to Gatlinburg. Asher, he's got her. He's got Daphne."

"Hold it. Slow down. I can't understand you. Try again."

She clenched a hand on the steering wheel, her knuckles going white. "It's *Daphne.* That bastard has her. He texted me a picture of her, bruised, bleeding. Oh, God, Asher. I recognized the background in the photo. The killer's got Daphne *in my house.*"

Chapter Eighteen

Faith swore in frustration as she yanked her car to the side of the road a good two blocks from her home. There were dozens of police cars parked along both sides, their red and blue lights flashing off the bushes and trees that covered the mountain. Several unmarked, dark-colored SUVs, likely the TBI, were scattered around, some parked in her front yard. Her driveway was taken up by a big black SWAT truck. Farther down the road, on the far side of her property, an ambulance waited.

Her stomach churned at the image branded in her mind of Daphne's bruised and blood-streaked face. She'd hoped the police would have rescued her by now. But part of the SWAT team was just now creeping up toward the front door. Others headed around the side of the house, no doubt to cover any exits—not that there were any. There was no backyard. Her home, like so many in the Smokies, looked like a typical one-story ranch in front with an expansive yard. But the back was on stilts, drilled into solid bedrock deep in the mountain. The basement didn't have any doors out back, just a few, small, high windows that let in light. The only real access to that basement was through the stairs inside the house.

She checked the loading of her pistol, then shoved it back in her pants pocket and took off running toward her house.

She'd only made it halfway before at least a dozen officers surrounded her, guns drawn, ordering her to stop.

Holding her hands in the air, she froze. "I'm Faith Lancaster. That's my house. My sister's inside."

"Show some ID," the nearest policeman ordered.

She swore, wishing some of them were cops she knew. There wasn't time for this. "My purse is in my car, back there."

"Check her for weapons," he told another policeman.

"Oh, for the love of…my pistol's in the front right pocket of my jeans. Yes, it's loaded. I'm a former police officer, a detective with Nashville PD. I work for Unfinished Business now."

She wanted to shout at them to let her go. But she knew how out of control and dangerous things could get really fast. Everyone was hyped up on adrenaline and. She endured a humiliating pat-down after one of them took her pistol away.

"There, I'm unarmed now. Please, let me go. I need to talk to the SWAT commander. I need to know what's happening. I can give him intel on the layout of my house and—"

"They already have intel on the layout of your house. I gave it to them."

She turned at the sound of Asher's voice. Grayson and Russo were with him, ordering the police to lower their weapons.

"Asher, thank God." She ran to him and grabbed his hands in hers. "What's going on? Why haven't they gone inside yet? Have they got eyes on Daphne—"

He squeezed her hands and pulled her to the side, leaving the bosses to deal with the group of anxious police.

"They had to secure the scene first, get a negotiator to try to make contact."

"What? Are you kidding? He's a freaking sociopath. Forget negotiations. Get my sister out of there!" She reached for her gun then stopped. "One of the cops took my pistol. I need to get it back and—"

"And nothing. We'll worry about that later. Faith, listen to me. SWAT's about to go in. You need to wait out here and—"

"I'll go with you. I can help. Just need my gun." She frowned and looked around for the cop who'd taken her pistol. The police were all huddling behind the cars parked in her yard now, using the engine blocks for cover as they aimed their pistols at the house. "What are they doing? Daphne's in there. Tell them to put their weapons down."

He lightly shook her and she looked up in question.

"Faith, we're going in, right now. You need to fall back, get somewhere safe to wait this out."

She frowned as he motioned at someone behind her. "We? You're going in too?" Her eyes widened. "Wait, you're wearing a SWAT vest. Hell, no. Asher, what are you thinking? You can't go in there with the SWAT team. Your back—"

"Is fine. And you know damn well I was SWAT before I switched to detective work. I need to do this, for you, for Daphne. God willing, I'll protect her and bring her out in just a few minutes. But you have to calm down, get to cover and—"

"No. *No.* If anyone's going in there, it's me. Give me your gun and I'll—"

He glanced past her again. Suddenly strong arms wrapped around her middle, anchoring her arms against her sides.

She bucked, squirming, trying to break the hold. "What the…let me go."

Asher jogged across the front lawn, away from her, weapon drawn, joining the SWAT members on the porch.

"Get your hands off me now!" She tried to slam the back of her head against whoever was holding her.

Swearing sounded in her ear. "Stop fighting me, Faith. It's Lance."

She immediately stopped. Then he picked her up and jogged with her arms still clasped against her sides. She kicked with her legs, twisting and desperately trying to get loose.

"Lance, damn it. Where are you taking me? That's my sister in there."

"Which is why—ouch, stop kicking me! You're too emotionally involved to help. You'll only endanger her. Seriously, Faith, will you knock it off?"

He stopped with her beside the last police car in the long line of them parked against the shoulder and finally set her on her feet. As soon as he let go, she took off running.

He swore and grabbed her again. He yanked her up in the air and stuffed her into the back seat of the patrol car, then slammed the door.

She screamed bloody murder at him and pounded on the glass. "Let me out of here!"

He leaned in close. "It's for your own good. I'll let you out as soon as the place is secure."

She could barely hear him through the thick, bulletproof glass. She pounded on the window again in frustration then showed her appreciation with a rude gesture.

He mouthed the word *sorry*, then jogged back to her house to join the others watching the SWAT team.

Faith had never been so frustrated in her life. A little voice in her head told her that Asher and Lance were right in keeping her from trying to go in and rescue her sister. But her heart told her she couldn't wait and do nothing when Daphne was in danger.

As she watched from almost too far away to see the action, her front door was busted in and the SWAT team, along with Asher, ran into the house.

Her shoulders slumped in defeat. Daphne's life, her safety, was now completely out of her hands. She dragged in a deep, bracing breath and pulled her phone out. She wasn't about to sit in this police car while they—hopefully—brought Daphne out. She needed to be right there for her and ride with her in the ambulance.

Please let her be okay. Please.

She thumbed through her favorites in her contact list, searching for Lance so she could tell him to let her out of the car.

The back door swung open.

She jerked her head up. Before she could even react, a policeman reached in and grabbed her phone out of her hands and tossed it into the woods.

"Hey, what are you—" She stared in horror at the face staring back at her. Stan. No, not Stan. Fake Stan, the killer. As her stunned mind finally realized what was happening, she drew back her fist to slam it into his jaw.

The door swung shut and her fist struck the window. She swore, shaking her aching hand, blood trickling down her knuckles.

The driver's door jerked open. He hopped into the driver's seat, closing the door on her screams for help.

He glanced at her in the rearview mirror through the thick plexiglass that separated them. And smiled.

THE HOUSE WAS eerily quiet. And clean, neat, as it always was. Nothing seemed out of place, as you'd expect if a madman had busted inside and kidnapped someone. Everything seemed...off.

Asher knew his job, to wait for the team to clear the main level before accessing the basement. But he also knew that a young woman he and Faith both loved very much was right now at the mercy of a killer. He'd seen the picture that Faith had sent him and knew right where she was when the picture had been taken. He wasn't waiting one more second to help her.

He sprinted into the kitchen and rounded the end of the row of cabinets to the staircase behind the wall that led to the lower level.

Ignoring one of the SWAT members frantically motioning from across the room for him to wait, Asher headed downstairs. Although he desperately wanted to take the steps two at a time and sprint into the basement to rescue Daphne, he also knew that getting himself killed wouldn't help her. So, instead, he stealthily moved down the stairs, gun out in front of him, avoiding the spots he knew from experience would creak. At the bottom step, he ducked down behind the wall that concealed the stairs so his head wasn't where the killer would expect if he shot at him. Then Asher quietly peeked around the wall.

Daphne was tied to one of the support posts about twenty feet away. Her mouth was duct-taped and her hands were zip-tied above her head to the post. Her ankles were zip-tied together, but not to the post. She was wearing shorts and a T-shirt, both dotted with blood in a few places, probably from the small cuts on her face that had dripped onto her clothes. Her chest was rising and falling with each breath she took. She was alive.

His mind cataloged all of those details in a fraction of a second as he swept his pistol back and forth, looking for the killer.

The sound of something knocking against a pole had him swinging back toward Daphne. She was twisting her tied feet back and forth, hitting the pole. Her eyes were wide and frantic above the gag as she watched him.

Seconds later, several SWAT team members emerged from behind the wall that concealed the stairs. He motioned to them to secure the basement and ran to Daphne. She seemed desperate to tell him something and every instinct in him was screaming to pull off her gag. The feeling that all was not as it seemed, that had hit him the moment he'd entered the house, was now an all-consuming feeling of dread.

He loosened the edge of the duct tape on her cheek. "This is going to hurt, Daph."

She nodded.

He ripped the tape off in one long swipe.

She gasped at the pain, sucking in a sharp breath.

"Where's the man who did this to you?"

She blinked, tears running down her face. Then her eyes widened again. "Asher, where's Faith? Where's my sister?"

"She's outside. She'll greet you when we get you out of here. Are you hurt anywhere else besides your face?"

She ducked away from his hand when he tried to brush the hair out of her eyes. "Are you absolutely sure Faith's safe?"

He frowned. "Safe? What are you—"

"It's a trap," she said. "All of this. I'm bait, to get Faith here. It's her he wants."

"Ah, hell." Asher took off running, taking the stairs two at a time and sprinting through the house. At the ruined front door, he paused, only to make sure none of the police outside mistook him for the killer and opened fire.

"Clear," he yelled, motioning inside.

Russo ordered his men to lower their weapons and they started running toward the house.

Asher sprinted down the porch steps, searching the groups of TBI agents and other police until he spotted Lance with Grayson, standing behind one of the police cars a short distance away. He ran up to Lance, dread and worry making his blood run cold when he didn't see Faith and didn't hear her swearing at him for not allowing her to go into the house.

"Where is she?" he demanded, turning in a circle before whirling back around. "Lance, where's Faith?"

"I put her in the back of a patrol car to keep her from interfering."

"Where? Show me."

Lance frowned. "Is Daphne not okay? Is that why you're—"

"Daphne's fine. She was bait. He wants Faith. Where the hell is she?"

Lance's eyes widened. "The last police car, way down there." He pointed and Asher took off running again.

His heart slammed in his chest, his healing lung and back protesting with twinges of pain as he raced down the row of cars. Each one was empty, lights flashing but no one inside. When he reached the last car and looked through the back window, he fisted his hands and whirled around.

Lance and Grayson both stopped in front of him, gasping for breath.

"She's not here. Is this the right car?" Asher demanded.

Lance's brows drew down. "Well of course it—wait, no. No, it's not. This is one of the Sevier County Sheriff's cars. The last one was a Gatlinburg PD patrol unit. It's…it's gone."

Grayson whipped out his phone and stepped away from them.

Lance motioned at some of the police, drawing their attention. As they jogged up to them, Asher pulled out his own phone.

"I never use this thing," he mumbled as he opened an app. "Hopefully I can figure out…there. Right there, that dot. That's her."

Lance stepped beside him, looking down at the screen. "Is that Faith's infamous find-Asher app?"

"She calls it a number of different things, depending on who she's tracking. She made me put it on my phone to track *her* in case we ever got split up. Her phone is that dot. It's not moving, it's…" He jerked his head up. "Right over there. In the woods."

He and Lance both drew their weapons and rushed to the trees. They swept their pistols in an arc, each covering the other as they followed the blinking dot on his phone. Less than a minute later, Lance swore and crouched over the bloody body of a man dressed only in his underwear. He pressed his fingers against the side of his neck and shook his head. “He’s gone. Throat’s slit. He’s not our perpetrator.”

“He’s a policeman. I met him earlier.” Asher bent down and picked up a small brightly colored piece of paper with a number written on it.

Lance stood. “What is that?”

“AFID. Anti-Felon ID confetti tags. Some Taser canisters shoot them along with the darts to help identify who pulled the trigger on a Taser. It’s only useful if the ID numbers trace to a legal buyer though.”

“This guy was Tased then his throat slit. Why?”

Asher checked his phone again then stepped around the body and walked a few more yards into the woods. His stomach sank with dread. “I found Faith’s phone.” It lay discarded on a bed of leaves and pine needles.

Lance stood and crossed to him. “Oh, man.”

The sound of shoes crunching on leaves and twigs had Lance and him whirling around, guns drawn.

Russo held his hands up. “Hey, hey. Only friendlies here. Everyone holster your guns.” The uniformed police officers with him slowly put away their weapons. Lance and Asher did the same.

Grayson stepped around Russo and stopped in front of Lance and Asher. “What have you…oh, no.”

Russo knelt by the body. “Sweet, Lord. It’s Sergeant Wickshire.”

Asher glanced down at Faith’s phone then at Grayson. “It was a setup from the beginning. Daphne said the man who abducted her didn’t want her. He told her she was bait, to draw in Faith. We played right into his hands. He must have killed Sergeant Wickshire, took his uniform, then drove off in the car with Faith in the back seat. She was supposed to be safe there. Instead, we delivered her directly into the hands of her enemy. And because of me, she doesn't even have her gun to defend herself." His voice broke and he took a steadying breath. "We have to find her. We have to find her before it's too late." He ran back toward the road with Lance and Grayson running after him.

Chapter Nineteen

This time when he ordered her to stop, just past a group of pine trees, Faith did. Running right now wasn't an option, not when he'd already proved he wouldn't hesitate to Taser her. When he'd opened the rear door of the police car, she'd jumped out and taken off. But he'd been prepared. The twin dart wounds on her back attested to that. And if that wasn't enough incentive, the lethal knife sheathed at his side was more than adequate to keep her following orders.

At least until she could figure out how to escape without getting killed.

"Head uphill, up the path."

She hesitated, thinking about all the scary movies she'd seen where the too-dumb-to-live heroine went up instead of down, sealing her fate.

The razor-sharp tip of his knife pressed against her back, cutting into her flesh. She gasped and arched away from it, then started up the incline.

One step, two, three. The sound of his footfalls joined hers, following behind. He certainly wasn't dumb, staying close enough so she couldn't escape but far enough back so that she couldn't simply whirl around and shove him down the mountain.

Being helpless and forced to pin her hopes on someone else

coming to her rescue was a foreign and uncomfortable feeling. But the way things looked, if no one figured out where she was and helped her, she wasn't going to make it off this mountain alive.

In spite of her longing for one of her UB teammates or the police to find her, she silently prayed that Asher didn't. Oh, she knew he'd try. If the roles were reversed, she'd do everything in her power to find him too. But even though to most people he might seem healed and back to normal, she'd seen his winces of pain often enough to know the truth. He wasn't at a hundred percent, which made him vulnerable. She didn't want him risking his life to save hers. She'd rather die than have that happen.

That realization had her blinking back tears of shock. Good grief. When had he become so important to her? She'd always treasured his friendship. But now he was so much… more. In spite of her determination to not risk the loss of their friendship to a romantic relationship, she'd utterly and completely failed.

She loved him.

Completely.

Hopelessly.

Loved him.

Please, God. Don't let Asher be the one to come for me. Let it be someone else, or no one at all. Protect him. Keep him safe.

"Quit daydreaming. Move." The knife pricked her back again.

She swore and started up the mountain.

RUSSO AND GRAYSON stood with Asher, discussing the circles he and Faith had drawn on the map currently spread out on the hood of his truck. Asher was explaining the colors of the circles and which ones he recommended that the police focus on as phase two of their search for the missing police car, and Faith. Everyone available was searching for her, and had been for the past forty-five minutes or so. But they'd found nothing. They needed a more focused approach, to think like the killer, and find her before it was too late. That was why Asher had stopped his seemingly fruitless searching and raced back to his house to grab the map.

He couldn't even consider that they wouldn't find her and save her. Even now, just the thought of her not being around left a big, gaping hole in his future. Who was he kidding? Without her, there *was* no future as far as he was concerned. Hell, if she wanted to be only friends and couldn't see him as anything else, he'd take it, pathetic as that was. He'd rather be her friend than to lose her completely. What mattered most was that she was happy. And safe. God, he wanted her safe.

He motioned above them, speaking loudly to be heard. "Chopper's been over this area for several minutes now. Heard anything from them yet? That police car has to be close by, even if the killer ditched it for another car. Otherwise, your men would have found some witnesses who saw it go down the mountain."

Russo grimaced.

Grayson exchanged a surprised look with Asher. "Russo, don't start holding back information now. Faith is our teammate, our family. We deserve the truth. We *need* the truth if we're going to find her."

The chief let out a deep breath. "I know, I know. I just don't want to get anyone's hopes up. The chopper pilot thinks he saw sunlight glinting off something in the woods just around the curve at the bottom of the mountain, before the stop sign. My guys are checking it out right now."

"Get us an update," Grayson told him. "Now. Every minute counts."

"On it." Russo pulled out his phone to make the call.

Asher's own phone buzzed. He checked the screen. "It's Lance. I have to take this." He stepped away from the hood, holding his hand over his left ear so he could hear Lance over the sound of the helicopter circling above.

"Lance, tell me you have something."

He listened for a moment then swore. "Don't give up. Someone at The Watering Hole has to know this guy. You're using the police sketch, right? Telling people to picture him with dark hair, too, not just blond? Someone there has to know him, or remember him, maybe what he drives in case he hid that car and used it after ditching the patrol car. Get me a name."

"We're pulling out all the stops, doing everything we can." Lance updated him on what the other UB investigators were doing to help. "We'll find her, Asher. We will."

He swallowed against his tightening throat. "I know. I just pray to God we're not too late."

A solemn group of police officers stepped out of the woods, escorting the medical examiner's team as they finally brought Sergeant Wickshire's body to the ME's van.

Asher's stomach sank as he watched the body bag being loaded. The idea of Faith in one of those shredded his heart. He turned away, still on the phone.

"Lance, check with Ivy. See if she's made any headway with those fingerprints. If we can just get this guy's name, we can figure out where he lives, what he drives, talk to people who know him and can give us insight on places he frequents."

"I'll call her right now. Hang in there, Asher."

Grayson rounded the hood and leaned back against the side of Asher's truck. "They found the police car. It's empty."

Asher nodded. "I figured. Any evidence inside? Anything to tell us what happened? Where they went?"

"There were tire tracks that don't match the police car. One of their forensic guys said they appeared to have been made from a car, not a big truck or SUV. Looks like he hid it there, planning all along to escape in a police car then switch vehicles. What I don't get is how he could have foreseen Faith being put in that last car, well away from where all the police were gathered."

"Easy enough to predict," Asher said. "Every officer in the area would have rushed up here to try to catch the serial killer and rescue his latest victim. Anyone who's ever seen police activity like that knows there will be tons of cars and the cops themselves will all congregate around the action. Police rarely lock their cars in a situation like that. They leave the keys in them in case someone needs to move some of the vehicles out of the way."

"I follow what you're saying," Grayson said. "Since Faith was personally involved, she'd have been kept way back from the action. Which is exactly what happened."

"And we made it even easier for him by putting her in the back of a police car." He shook his head, hating himself right now.

"There's one other thing that Russo told me, about the cop car they just found." Grayson gave him a sympathetic look. "There were some of those confetti ID tags on the ground."

Asher squeezed his eyes shut a moment, a physical ache starting deep in his chest. "He used a Taser on her, probably the same one he used on Sergeant Wickshire. When I catch this guy, I'm going to tear him limb from limb."

"I'll pretend I didn't hear that." Russo joined them. "We've got TBI agents searching those areas you circled on that map. I took pictures of it and sent it to them. Law enforcement volunteers are driving in from neighboring counties to help so we can cover more territory more quickly."

Grayson clasped Asher's shoulder. "What else do you want us to do? Anything. Name it."

Asher raked his hand through his hair. "I don't… I don't know. Damn it. I hate this. I have to do something."

"You already are. You searched up and down the mountain like the rest of us, then rallied the troops and got everyone more organized. You've given her the best chance possible."

"I have to figure this out, figure out where he has her." Asher strode to the front of his truck and grabbed the map off the hood.

Grayson and Russo stepped back as he hopped inside and started the engine. When Grayson tapped on the window, Asher swore and rolled it down. "What?"

"I don't think you should be driving right now. You're upset and—"

"Damn straight, I'm upset. Faith is out there, somewhere, with a sociopath who's killed nine people so far, that we know of. I'm heading up to this sicko's cemetery. Finding it was the trigger for him to go after Leslie. It's probably why he went after Faith too. He blames her, and me, for taking away his personal dumpsite. That location means something to him. There has to be a clue up there, something we've missed, something we haven't thought of."

Russo called out to him as he and Grayson hurriedly backed up to let him turn around in the yard. "My men already searched that area. There's nothing there."

"There has to be. There *has* to be." Asher slammed the accelerator, kicking up dirt and sending his truck racing down the road.

Chapter Twenty

Russo's men had definitely been to the makeshift graveyard. Their fresh shoeprints showed they'd scoured the place, conducting a thorough search. But Asher did his own search anyway. He was more focused on specifics, like finding more of those neon-colored confetti tags shot from the Taser when fired. And he'd also been looking for bread crumbs. Not real bread crumbs, but some kind of sign that Faith had been there. She was smart and careful. If there was any way at all to leave any kind of trail to prove she'd been there, and to give someone else something to follow, she'd do it. But he hadn't found anything to indicate she'd been there.

So much for his theory that the killer would have brought her to this particular mountain.

He dropped to his knees and spread the map out on the ground. It had been the foundation of Faith's and his investigation. It had yielded them the missing Jasmine and her sister. It was proof that they'd done their homework, knew the killer's habits to some degree. The clues had to be right there in front of him. He just had to figure out how to identify them.

Everything to do with this case was concentrated in a twenty-minute travel radius from this mountainside. He'd explained that to Russo when he'd sent his men out searching. With this exact spot as the epicenter, all of the abductions could be placed within the large circle he'd made on the map. Every single one of them. This circle was the killer's comfort zone, where he hunted and where he buried his victims. He lived here, worked here, played his sick games here. So, where in this circle, was he now?

Think like the killer. Put yourself in his head. Where would you go to avoid the cops, knowing that killing a police officer means that every law enforcement agent within driving distance is going to join the manhunt?

I'd go somewhere I'm comfortable with, stay in my twenty-minute circle.

But the police were already looking in the places that they knew he'd been to before. That seemed like a waste of time to Asher. The killer already had his victim. The question was, where would he take her now that he had her? What place had special significance for him? What was the common thread between all of his victims that caused him to choose that special place?

Asher ran his fingers over the topographical symbols, studying the map as if he'd never seen it before. The names of the victims ran through his mind as he studied it. What did they all have in common?

The link that Faith had found between victims was the bar, The Watering Hole. Did something set it apart from other restaurants and bars, make it attractive as a hunting spot to the killer? What about it made it comfortable to him? All Asher could think of that was unique to that bar was the manmade waterfall behind it. Customers loved to take selfies and post them on social media in front of that waterfall. But there were hundreds of real waterfalls throughout the Smoky Mountains. That by itself didn't seem unique at all. What else did he know about the victims themselves? Something that stood out?

Mud. Two of the victims' bodies had dried mud, or what

the experts believed was originally mud, in their hair or on their clothes.

Another victim had river rocks in her pocket.

Jasmine liked to go white-water rafting. What about the others?

He accessed the cybercloud from his phone to read the latest reports his team had been uploading with any information they'd gathered for the investigation. Mini bios had been created for all of the victims. Asher quickly skimmed the ones for the remaining victims he didn't know as much about.

Natalie Houseman owned a boat.

Dana Randolph used to work at the Ripley's Aquarium in downtown Gatlinburg.

Felicia Stewart was an avid fisher. Her favorite spot to fish was off the dock in her backyard.

Some of them had visited or frequented The Watering Hole. The link between all of that seemed obvious—water. Each of the victims he'd just thought about had some kind of water in common. Was that a useless coincidence or a useful fact? Was it possible that the killer had some kind of fascination with water? He certainly seemed comfortable in the outdoors, as evidenced by his taking Leslie up into the mountains. Leslie…wait. There was a waterfall at the trail-riding place where they'd found her. And a pond. Water yet again. Was that another coincidence?

He ran his fingers across the map more quickly now, his instincts telling him he might be onto something. Too many things kept coming back to water of some form or another. There had to be a reason. Or was he off on a ridiculous, unrelated tangent?

Think, Whitfield. Think. What do you know about this guy?

All of his victims were women. Everything else about them varied. Young, older, Black, white, Asian. He didn't have a specific type of person he abducted, except, maybe, that they all had some kind of affinity for water either to work or play. Did the killer resent them for that? Or was it something he liked about them?

The idea that a serial killer would choose his victims because they boated, rafted, liked waterfalls or anything else to do with water seemed ludicrous. Then again, serial killer Ted Bundy chose his victims because they all had long straight hair parted in the middle. What could be more ridiculous than that?

He was onto something. He felt it in his bones.

It all went back to The Watering Hole. Asher knew the killer didn't have Faith at the bar. The place was crawling with cops and UB investigators. But the killer had picked out his previous victims there. Because he frequented the place. It was his hunting ground. He'd likely listened to conversations and discovered interests in his favorite attraction—water—as a part of some recreational activity. He'd chosen them at the bar, stalked them, figured out the best place to abduct them, killed them, then buried them on this mountainside.

Close. So close. The missing puzzle piece was here. He knew it.

He glanced around at the mounds of dirt where the graves had been filled in. Killing them, then bringing them here to bury them didn't feel right. It was a lot more work to carry a dead body than to force a live one where you wanted them to go. It made more sense that he'd kill them right here. But if that was the case, wouldn't he stick to his routine and…try to kill Faith here? There was another puzzle piece. Maybe he did kill them somewhere else and brought them here. But it was harder to move a dead body. Maybe he did it anyway, used a litter or something like that to pull them up the mountain. Seemed crazy to think he'd do that. But, hey, serial killers were crazy as far as Asher was concerned. Trying to understand them was next to impossible. But that didn't mean he couldn't predict what they'd do, not if he sifted through the evidence the right way. Setting aside the logistics question about moving bodies, he explored the next obvious question.

How did he kill the women?

The ME couldn't find an obvious cause of death. But Asher knew the most common way that serial killers murdered their victims was strangulation. Hanging was an obvious choice to strangle someone since he'd tried to hang Leslie. But without any bones broken in any of the bodies they'd found, it didn't seem to make sense that he would have hung them. That threat was exactly that: a threat he'd set up with Leslie to force Asher to choose between going after the killer or saving his victim. Hanging wasn't his method of choice for killing all of his victims.

No obvious stabbing or bullet wounds found with any of the victims. No broken bones. No blunt force trauma. Poison didn't seem likely, either, given their earlier discussion at Grayson's house.

He was left with suffocation of some kind. So how did you suffocate someone without breaking bones in their necks?

He blinked as he stared down at the map again. Water, water, everywhere. How do you take away someone's ability to breathe and explore your twisted fascination with water at the same time?

You drown them.

His phone buzzed in his pocket. He grabbed it without looking at the screen. "Asher."

"It's Lance. We struck gold. Just as you thought, the common link is the bar. Asher, we know who he is. There was a freaking picture of him on the wall, one of dozens of framed pictures showing crowd shots. I grabbed it and showed it to nearly everyone there. I got a name. And right after, I swear, to the very second, Ivy called. She's been visiting every Podunk police force in all the neighboring counties and got a fingerprint match from that knife. It was a small police station that didn't enter the fingerprints into AFIS because it was for a minor arrest, a traffic violation. He—"

"Lance, for God's sake, who is he? Tell me something to help me find Faith."

"Malachi Strom. Get this. He saw his father drown on a family trip when he was only twelve. Then his mother died seven years ago of leukemia. That's when the killings began. Maybe that was his trigger to start killing."

"Water. His father drowned? That's the link."

"Okay, you've lost me now."

Asher quickly explained his theory about water and that he'd drowned his victims.

"How is that supposed to help us find Faith?"

"I don't know yet. Obviously, we can't search every river, stream or waterfall in the county. My gut tells me that's where he's taking Faith, to some body of water. She can't swim, Lance."

Lance swore.

"You said his father drowned. Where did he die? Is it in our twenty-minute circle?"

"Oh, man. Hang on, let me see what Ivy sent."

Asher fisted his hand at his side, torn between frustration and hope as he waited. "Hurry, Lance. Hurry."

"This is it. Yes, yes! It's in that circle you gave us. Holy… it's on the other side of the mountain from the graveyard. Crescent Falls. His father must be the person Russo said drowned there twenty years ago."

Asher's shoulders slumped as hope drained out of him. "He wouldn't have taken Faith there. On a day like today, that place is crawling with tourists."

"No, no, it isn't. Remember a tourist drowned there a while back, the day you found the graveyard? The park system shut it down until they can do a study on the safety measures. It's still closed."

"That's it. Has to be. Get everyone over to the falls. Get that chopper up there. And tell me everything you know about what happened to his father." Asher took off running.

The falls couldn't have been more than a football field away. But by the time Asher reached the parking lot, his healing lung was burning and he was having trouble taking a deep breath. His back ached, but it always ached these days, so he didn't pay much attention to that.

"You okay, buddy?" Lance asked over the phone. "Your breathing doesn't sound so good."

Probably because it wasn't.

Asher tried to take a deeper breath, but every time he did, it felt as if a knife was being stabbed into his lung all over again. Didn't matter. He couldn't let it slow him down, not with Faith's life at stake.

He stopped at the taped-off entrance to the path that visitors used to go to the top of Crescent Falls. Something neon orange on the ground caught his attention. One piece of Taser ID confetti. The Taser hadn't been fired here or there'd have been dozens of them. Instead, someone had specifically dropped one piece.

Faith. It had to be her. He was on the right track. She must have secretly pocketed some confetti after getting Tased beside the police car. She'd left him a bread crumb.

"Asher?" Lance called out. "Give me an update. Are you okay? Have you found anything?"

He studied the path that followed a steep angle up the mountain, winding around rocks and trees. The falls weren't visible from this vantage point. But he could hear them. He was close.

"This is the place. She's here. Tell everyone to hurry." He ended the call, silenced his phone, then ducked under the yellow tape and began jogging up the steep path toward the falls, as quickly as his burning lung and aching back muscles would allow.

Chapter Twenty-One

Faith stood in the knee-deep swirling waters at the top of the waterfall, just feet from the edge, her wrists zip-tied in front of her. Four feet away, the cold dead eyes of a sociopath stared back at her, one hand holding the Taser, the other a wicked-looking knife with a six-inch blade that was already stained with her blood. It was as if he was trying to come to a decision—Taser her yet again or gut her. Or maybe he was going to toss her over the falls and let the rocks and water do their worst.

She couldn't resist taking a quick glance at the edge. It was a twenty-foot drop, maybe more. If she did go over, and managed not to crush her skull or drown, she'd probably be swept to the second tier of the falls and go over again. The pool of water at the very bottom was much deeper than up here. It was where the tourist had drowned a few weeks ago. And that tourist's hands hadn't been tied. If she ended up down there, it was lights out.

Asher was right. She should have learned to swim a long time ago. Although how she could do that with her hands tied was beyond her, even if she knew how.

Asher. Daphne. The two most important people in her life. Just thinking about them had her tearing up. They would take her death hard, assuming Daphne was even okay. This lowlife had refused to answer her questions about her sister. She'd begged him to tell her if he'd left her alive in the basement. His only response was a cruel smile that chilled her more than the water swirling around her legs.

It took all her strength to remain standing as the current pushed her ever closer to the edge. Her teeth chattered, the water brutally cold this high in the mountains. But Fake Stan, the killer she and Asher had been trying to find for months, seemed immune to it as he continued to watch her.

"What do you want from me?" she demanded, not for the first time.

And just as before, he said nothing. He simply kept staring at her with those dead eyes, making her want to vomit.

At least she had one thing to be thankful for. The gashes in her legs from the Taser barbs he'd yanked out no longer hurt. The freezing water had mercifully dulled that pain. Too bad it wasn't high enough to take away the throbbing aches in her back and stomach. The slices he'd made weren't deep enough to kill. But they hurt like hell.

She risked another quick look past the falls to the thick trees lining the steep path below that she'd been forced to climb. Beyond that, around several curves in that path, was a parking lot. But no one had been there when he'd driven into it. No sirens sounded in the distance. No police or friends from Unfinished Business were rushing up the mountain to rescue her. She was going to die, unless she could think of something else to try.

Like somehow freeing her hands so she could put up some kind of defense. The only way she could think of to free them was to cut the zip-ties. To do that, she needed a knife. He was the only one with a knife. Kicking it out of his hands was one option to try. But she'd likely be swept over the falls trying to get the knife. Either way, the end result was death.

As if finally making up his mind about how he was going

to kill her, he holstered the Taser. Then he slowly started toward her, fighting the current, his knife firmly in his right hand.

"Wait," she called out, forced to scoot her feet closer to the slippery edge to keep some space between them. "My sister, please. Tell me if she's okay. You used her as bait, didn't seriously hurt her. Right? Please tell me. I have to know."

He cocked his head like a bird looking at a worm right before it bit its head off.

"The knife usually scares them," he said. "They scream by now, try to run, get swept over the falls. Why aren't you screaming?"

Oh, God. This was how he'd killed all his victims? Forcing them over the falls? Revulsion and dread made her stomach churn.

"Will screaming make a difference in what you do to me?"

A cold smile curved his lips, sending a shiver through her soul. "It never has before." He raised the knife again.

She held up her hands. "Wait."

He lunged forward, the knife high over his head.

She fell backward into the water, desperately scrabbling away, searching for something to hold on to so she wouldn't get swept over the waterfall.

He yelled with rage, leaping at her just as the crack of a gunshot filled the air. Faith screamed and scrambled out of his way as he landed with a splash. He immediately pushed up on his knees, knife raised again.

"Faith! Move out of the way!"

She whirled around, astonished to see Asher running out of the woods toward them, gun raised.

"Faith, behind you!"

She twisted to the side, the killer's arms narrowly missing her as he fell into the water. She scrabbled away, desperately fighting the relentless current as it pushed her toward the edge. But the rocks beneath the surface were slippery and her bound hands so numb she couldn't grip them.

"Faith!"

Another gunshot sounded as she screamed and hurtled over the falls.

ASHER WATCHED IN horror as Faith fell over the waterfall. He splashed through the water to the edge. A guttural roar had him whirling around, gun raised. But the killer was on him before he could fire. They both fell back under the water, jarring the gun loose. The glint of the knife below the surface came slashing at him. Asher grabbed the other man's wrist, yanking hard.

Bubbles blew out of his attacker's mouth as he yelled underwater, the knife coming loose. He kicked at Asher, breaking his hold. They both surfaced, gasping for breath and climbing to their feet. But when the killer ran toward him, Asher ran for the edge of the falls. Faith was down there somewhere, in the water. And she couldn't swim.

He leaped out over the rushing water and fell to the pool below. He landed hard on the bottom then pushed to standing. It was only waist-deep. And there was no sign of Faith here. She must have gone over the second waterfall to the much deeper pond at the bottom.

Running as fast as he could toward the edge, he leaped again just as a splash sounded behind him. He fell to the deep pool below then quickly kicked to the surface.

"Faith!" he yelled. "Faith!"

He twisted and turned, desperately searching for her, hoping to find her on the edge of the pool. Nothing. No sign of her anywhere. He tried to take a deep breath, but his hurt lung had him gasping in pain. Swearing, he drew a more shallow breath and dove straight down. He pulled himself through the water as quickly as he could, both dreading and hoping to find her. His lungs screamed for air, forcing him to surface. He dragged in several shallow, quick breaths, then dove again.

There, on the far side. A shadow on the bottom. He kicked his feet, using the last of his air, refusing to surface no matter how much his lungs burned as he raced underwater. As he reached the dark shadow he'd seen, long tendrils of golden-brown hair floated out toward him. Faith.

He scooped her up and kicked for the surface.

Something slammed into his back. Fiery lava exploded through his veins. But he didn't stop. He kept hold of his precious burden and climbed to the surface. He breached into the air and whirled onto his back, pulling Faith into the crook of his arm, face up. As he kicked with his legs for the shore, he breathed air into her lungs over and over. Kick, breathe, kick, breathe.

He was almost there when a hand grabbed his leg and yanked him under the surface. He kicked out violently, smashing his foot against the other man's face. It broke his hold and Asher again surfaced, half dragging and half throwing Faith out of the water. She landed on her side, still unresponsive.

The water rippled around him, his only warning. He dove back under, grabbing the killer from behind, his arm around his throat. Asher yanked his forearm back in a swift lethal movement, crushing the man's windpipe. He went slack and Asher shoved him away and kicked for the surface again.

He crawled out of the water, feeling oddly light-headed and short of breath. Sirens sounded in the distance. Help was finally on its way. But was it too late? He reached Faith's side and rolled her onto her back; her beautiful face so pale and white, his stomach sank. He gave her three quick breaths, watching her chest rise and fall. Then he began chest compressions.

"One, two, three..." He kept counting, thirty chest compressions for every two breaths, as he'd been trained so long ago. Over and over, he pumped her heart, swearing at her, swearing at him, swearing at the man who'd done this to her, all the while pumping, pumping, breathing, pumping.

"Come on, Faith. Don't leave me. Breathe."

"Asher, Asher, move. Let them help her."

He blinked and realized he wasn't alone anymore. Lance and Grayson were both pulling at him as two EMTs jumped in to take over.

"She drowned," he told them. "She's got water in her lungs. I can't get her heart going. Please, you have to help her."

Grayson and Lance dragged him back as more first responders came to Faith's aid.

Asher desperately jerked sideways, looking back, but he couldn't see her anymore. There were half a dozen people surrounding her on the ground. "Let me go. I need to see her." He twisted and fought against their hold.

"Stop fighting us," Grayson ordered. "Let the medics help her. Where's Strom?"

Asher frowned, still twisting and trying to see Faith. "Who the hell is Strom?"

"Malachi Strom," Lance told him. "Fake Stan. Where is he?"

"Fish food." Asher motioned to the pond. "I crushed his windpipe. Do they have her heart going? Is she breathing?"

"They're working on her," Grayson said. "Stop moving for one damn minute. Is this Faith's blood? Strom's?"

Asher jerked his head back toward Grayson. "Faith's bleeding? I didn't notice any cuts. But I was focused on trying to stop the killer."

"I have no idea." Grayson glanced at Lance. "I think this is Asher's blood."

"The rocks," Asher said. "Probably cut myself on the

rocks. Is she breathing? Let me see her." He coughed, struggling to catch his breath. "My lung's giving me fits." He coughed again, everything around him turning a dull gray.

"Medic!" Grayson yelled. "We need help over here. This man's been stabbed."

Lance swore. "You have the worst luck with knife-wielding homicidal maniacs. We need an EMT over here! Hurry!"

"No, no, no. They need to help Faith." Asher heard himself slurring the words. But he couldn't see anything anymore. "Faith. Have to save...save her." Everything went dark.

Chapter Twenty-Two

Faith sat up in her bed, coughing yet again as she tried to pull the pillows up to support her better.

Asher hurried into her bedroom, a look of concern on his face. “What are you doing? You’re not supposed to overexert yourself. Those were the conditions of the hospital releasing you to go home so early.”

“Neither are you,” she complained as she endured another round of his pillow-fluffing. Finally, she pushed at his hands to get him to stop. “Enough. I’m never going to get out of this bed if you and Daphne don’t let me do things on my own. I need to build up my strength.”

“Which is only going to happen if you rest. You died. You realize that, right? You died and they brought you back. If the water hadn’t been so cold, you’d have had brain damage and you wouldn’t even be here. You got a nasty bacterial infection from that water, on top of everything else, so you need to take it easy, give your lungs a chance to heal.”

“You can turn that same speech on yourself. You were stabbed, again. Had a collapsed lung, again. You were worse off than me when they got you down from the mountain. The only reason you aren’t still in bed is that you didn’t catch the nasty bug I did, and you’re too stubborn to lie down and rest.”

He arched a brow. "Okay. If you insist." He lifted the comforter and slid in beside her.

"What are you doing?"

"Resting. That's what you said you wanted, isn't it?" He gave her an innocent look that had her laughing even though it hurt.

"How do you do it, Asher? You make me laugh even when I'm mad at you."

His expression turned serious. "You've been mad at me ever since you woke up in the hospital three weeks ago. I think it's time you told me why."

She pulled back and looked at him. "You don't get it at all, do you? You don't have a clue."

He held his hands out in a helpless gesture. "I really don't. What's wrong?"

"Other than that we were both almost killed by that… that…"

"Homicidal maniac? That's what Lance called him."

She nodded. "That fits. Malachi Strom. Even his name sounds evil." She shivered.

Asher responded by scooting up against her and putting his arm around her shoulders. "You shivered. You must be cold. Let me warm you."

She rolled her eyes, but the expression was lost on him since he couldn't see her face. "I still can't believe that Strom blamed his mother for his father drowning and went on a rampage after she died, trying to avenge his father. How can one traumatic event as a child make someone into a sociopath who sees all women as his enemy?"

"I don't think it did. I'm not a psychologist or an expert on this in any way, but I personally believe someone as evil as he was is born that way. Sure, environment and experiences play a role. But most people going through that same trauma wouldn't become a serial killer. His brain wasn't wired right. Period."

She shuddered again. "I'm just glad it's over. He's dead and buried now and I can stop thinking about him."

"And you can stop being mad at me? For whatever it is that I did wrong?"

She took his arm from around her shoulders and turned to face him. "What's wrong is that you were still recovering from being stabbed and you jumped off a freaking waterfall. Two waterfalls! How stupid is that?"

He stared at her a full minute before finally clearing his throat. "You're mad that I risked my life to try to save you?"

"Yes!"

His mouth curved up into the most beautiful smile she'd ever seen. "I love you too."

She blinked. "I didn't say that!"

"Sure you did. You care so much about me that you would have rather died than have me die. I feel exactly the same way. I love you too."

She sputtered into silence then shook her head. "I can't love you. I don't want to love you."

His smile turned into a look of commiseration. "I understand. You want to keep me in the friend zone. But it's too late. We passed that threshold when you stuck your tongue down my throat at the hospital in Knoxville."

She gasped. "You stuck yours down my throat first!"

"I remember it differently. But that's okay. We're past that now. Just look." He motioned at the comforter over both of them. "We're in bed. And it's not the first time we've spent the night together." He winked.

She sputtered again.

His look turned serious and he slowly pushed her back against the pillows, his body covering hers.

"Faith. We've been best friends for a long time. I know

you're scared to lose that closeness. I understand it. And I know you didn't think you wanted to cross that line, to let things change. It was obvious. But the truth is I've been in love with you almost from the day I first met you. I zipped past that whole friendship thing and straight into wanting forever with you a long, long time ago."

She stared at him in astonishment. "Did you say…forever? With me?"

He nodded, his gaze searching hers. "My heart belongs to you, Faith. It always has, always will. I'm here to tell you I'll always be your friend, no matter what. But I can be so much more. I want you, Faith. I want you any way I can have you. But mostly, I want you happy. If making you happy means I have to pretend we're just friends, give you that illusion, I'll do it. But I really hope you can see the truth and embrace it."

She stared up at him. "The truth?"

He pressed a gentle kiss against her lips. "The truth that's in your heart. What do you really want, Faith? Tell me right now you don't want me in your heart, in your bed. Don't try to convince me. Convince yourself."

She started to tell him that, of course, she was fine keeping him as a friend, that she didn't want more.

But that was a lie.

She did want him, in every way—her heart, her soul and, most definitely, her bed. But there was one little problem remaining. "I'm scared, Ash."

His hand shook as he gently stroked her hair back from her face. "Whatever you're scared of, we can face it together." He smiled. "Because you called me Ash. I know you're in trouble now. You can't resist me, or your feelings for me. Remember that warning you gave me? If you ever call me Ash, you're in trouble?"

"At the time, I was thinking I could use Ash as a code word if I was kidnapped or something."

He grimaced. "Let's not mention kidnapping again."

"Agreed. But that doesn't take away my real fear."

"Which is?"

This time it was her turn to frame his face with her hands. "That something could happen to you, that I'll lose you. If I let myself love you, give myself to you completely, in every way, how will I ever survive if the worst happens?"

"Ah. So that's it. You love me so much, you don't ever want me to leave. I can live with that."

She laughed. "How do you always change something serious into something funny?"

He grinned. "It's a gift." His smile faded. "I can't promise you that I won't die before you. What I can promise is that as long as there's breath in my body, I will love and cherish you. Take a leap, with me. A leap of—"

"Don't you dare say a leap of Faith. That is beyond corny."

"Then how about a leap of love? Marry me, Faith Elizabeth Lancaster. Marry me and I'll never leave you, so long as we both shall live."

Tears suddenly threatened as she stared up at him in wonder. "Ash, you wonderful, gorgeous, stubborn man. What in the world am I going to do with you?"

"Love me, Faith. Just love me."

And so she did.

* * * * *

INNOCENT WITNESS

JULIE ANNE LINDSEY

Chapter One

Hayley Campbell settled onto the bench at her usual picnic table and unpacked her lunch. The small park, nestled between the public library and social-services department, was her private oasis from 11:00 a.m. to noon, every Monday through Friday. The cooler of sandwiches and drinks at her side was a personal offering to anyone in need.

For Hayley, becoming a social worker had felt more like a calling than a choice, and she couldn't imagine doing anything else. Though at twenty-four, she still looked more like the average high schooler than a legitimate representative of the county. Occasionally, judges, lawyers and local law-enforcement officials tried to overlook her or not take her opinions as seriously as those of her older coworkers. It was an inclination she understood, but never indulged. She did her best to be a voice for the youth of Marshal's Bluff, North Carolina, and anyone else who needed to be heard.

Within a few minutes, a number of familiar faces began to arrive. She opened the large cooler at her side and continued her meal. Folks young and old made their way to her table, selected a drink and sandwich, then waved their goodbyes. She ate and read and watched closely for the one face she always hoped to see. Then, finally, he appeared.

"Hey, you," she said, brightening. She closed her book and set it aside as fourteen-year-old Gage Myers approached.

Composed of gangly limbs and one big heart, he took the seat across from her with a small grin. "Hey."

Gage had lost both his parents in a car accident the year before, and Hayley was assigned his case. Her heart had split wide open for him when she placed him into foster care. His parents had both been only children, and their parents were already deceased. Gage was one of many cases she'd never forget—she was sure of it. But he was something more too.

His olive skin was unusually ruddy as he watched her. His wide brown eyes, heavy-lidded. He looked as if he hadn't slept, but also as if he wanted to run.

Hayley shifted, suddenly nervous and hoping not to seem that way. A gust of wind tossed strands of stick-straight blond hair into her eyes. She tucked the locks behind her ear with care, using the small distraction to further evaluate her friend.

Gage's fingers and T-shirt were spattered with spray paint, a sign something had been on his mind. He used street art to work through the emotions too big to process with words. He'd been in trouble for defacing property more than once, but she'd never found it in her to be angry. His paintings were powerful, and it was a necessary outlet for the teen.

"You okay?" she asked finally, reaching to press the back of her hand against his forehead. "Are you getting sick?"

He rolled those big appreciative eyes up at her, the way he always did when she offered him comfort. "I think I saw something I shouldn't have," he said. "I don't really want to talk about it."

"Okay." She handed him a sandwich, a napkin and a drink. "You want to talk about something else?"

He shrugged and ate quickly, as if he hadn't in a while.

A growth spurt? She wondered. *Or hadn't he eaten breakfast? And if not, why?*

"How're the Michaelsons?" she asked, feigning casual as she fished for information. Gage's foster parents had never struck her as a good fit for the system. But they'd been housing children in need for more than a decade, caring for dozens of youths in that time, and they were one of the rare couples willing to host teenagers. Still, something always felt off when Hayley visited. Maybe Gage had witnessed something questionable there.

He shook his head, as if reading her mind. "It's not them this time." He sighed and glanced away.

She hated his clarification of "this time," but held her tongue, sensing there was more he wanted to say. But she intended to circle back. If there had been other times the Michaelsons were a problem, she needed to know.

Gage's lips parted, but he didn't speak. Something was stopping him.

"You know you can trust me, right?" she asked. "I will always have your best interests at heart, and I'd never take any action without keeping you in the loop. I'm here to be your advocate. Whatever you need."

She wished for the dozenth time that she could foster him, instead of the Michaelsons. Instead of anyone else. She'd try to adopt him if she thought the courts would consider it, but the system liked to see kids placed with couples, preferably married and stable ones. Ones who'd been out of college and in the workforce more than eighteen months, unlike Hayley.

His gaze lifted to something over her shoulder, and his expression changed. He gathered the empty sandwich baggie and napkin from his vanquished lunch and stood. "I'd better go. Thank you for this." He wiggled the trash in his hands. "I needed it, and it was great."

"Wait." Hayley rose and removed another sandwich from the cooler. "Take this. And come back at five when I get off work," she said. "We can talk. If something's wrong at your foster home, you can stay with me while we straighten it out. Let me help you."

He nodded, eyes flicking to the distance again. "Yeah, all right."

She retook her seat. "All right," she echoed, swallowing the lump in her throat. She glanced over her shoulder, in the direction Gage had looked, but saw nothing of interest, then turned back to watch him go. Every fiber in her body urged her to chase after him, but she had no grounds to make him stay. "See you at five," she called, needing the confirmation.

He waved and nodded, then picked up the pace as he strode away.

THE AFTERNOON DRAGGED for Hayley as she attended a court hearing and made several home visits, checking on the other children in her caseload. At the office, she rushed through the paperwork, one eye on the clock and eager to take Gage somewhere safe so they could talk.

She was out the door at five-o'clock sharp, blinking against the bright southern summer sun. The air was thick and balmy, eighty-nine degrees with extreme humidity. The soft scents of sunblock and charcoal grills drifted by. Life in coastal North Carolina was beautiful at any time, but August was Hayley's favorite. She loved the extreme heat and the way everything was in bloom, lush and alive. Laughter carried on the wind, from parks and beaches, ice-cream parlors and outdoor cafés. She couldn't imagine living anywhere else, but she'd be a lot happier in the moment, once she knew Gage was okay.

At five thirty, she gave up the wait and began a slow walk to her car.

The social-services staff parked their cars in a series of spaces along the perimeter of a nearby church's lot. It was a protective measure against potentially unhappy clients, or family members of clients, who lashed out when court appointments didn't go the way they'd wanted. And it was an added level of privacy for workers.

In Hayley's experience, the people willing to destroy private property over a particular outcome probably weren't the ones who should have children in their care. But she also knew the system sometimes failed, and anyone could reach a breaking point when someone they loved was taken from them. She hoped to become part of the solution and a support for those in times of trouble.

She waited outside her car until six, then she called Mrs. Michaelson.

Gage's foster mom claimed she hadn't seen him since the night before, and she accused him of being on drugs before Hayley could get any useful information.

She rubbed her forehead as they disconnected. Gage was not on drugs. His eyes had been clear, if worry-filled, this morning. He'd been alert and on edge, not hung over.

Something else was wrong.

She climbed into her car and started the engine. She had a few ideas of where Gage could be. She'd had to search for him before, in the early days following his parents' deaths, when grief and despair had made him reckless and hostile. She hated to think of him feeling those ways again. Hated to think of him upset and alone.

The drive from Social Services, on the periphery of downtown Marshal's Bluff, to the fringe areas along the warehouse and shipping district was shockingly quick. The landscape changed in a matter of blocks, trading community parks and tree-lined streets for abandoned housing and condemned buildings.

To Gage's eyes, a neighborhood full of blank canvases for his art.

She slowed as small groups of people came into view, scanning each of their faces for Gage. Hayley noticed evidence of his artwork here and there, all older pieces she'd seen last fall.

After a trip around the block, she decided to go on foot, talk to folks, ask for help. She parked her sedan at the curb and climbed out, hyperaware that her pencil skirt and blouse stood out in ways that were unlikely to help her blend. She could thank her appearance in court for that. Typically, she wore jeans and a nice top. Outfits that made her more approachable to the people she helped. Less authoritarian.

Old Downtown was filled with buildings that blocked the bay views. Most were crumbling from age and in need of repair. Windows and doors were barred and boarded. No Trespassing signs were posted everywhere, so property owners wouldn't be sued if someone became injured while inside.

Hayley approached a group of young men on the stoop attached to a former barbershop and offered a small, hip-high wave. "I'm looking for a friend named Gage," she said. "Do you know him?"

The nearest kid, wearing baggy jeans and a long-sleeved flannel shirt, despite the heat, shot her a disbelieving look. "Who are you? His mom?"

Hayley shook her head, saddened by the thought. She'd give just about anything to bring Gage's mom back to him, or to have the honor of caring for him herself, but those things weren't options right now. And all that mattered was finding him and bringing him home safely. "I'm just a friend," she said. "He's about your age. He's an artist. He painted these." She lifted a finger to indicate a small black silhouette on one of the boarded windows.

Gage regularly used the image to depict children like himself, the ones he felt went unseen. Untethered numbers in case files. Kids nobody really knew.

"You know him?" the boy asked.

She bit her tongue against the obvious response. She'd made that clear, hadn't she? "Have you seen him?"

"Nah."

"Thanks." Hayley sighed and moved along.

"Hey," one of the other kids called to her, making her turn around. "Lady, I ain't trying to get in your business, but you shouldn't be down here. Nothing good is gonna find someone like you on this street."

"Noted," she said. "But I'm worried about my friend, and I need to know he's okay. If you see him, I hope you'll tell him I was here."

Dusk was settling, but she walked the neighborhood for nearly an hour as the sun lowered in the sky, eventually blunted by the buildings. She talked to knots and clusters of people along the way. Most were less friendly than the first group she'd encountered. Eventually, she was forced to call it a night, so she started back to her car.

The street was quieter on her return trip—the people she'd spoken to earlier were already gone. Her nerves coiled tightly at the realization she was alone. Wind off the water stirred loose sheets of newspaper and scooted empty plastic bags over broken asphalt, causing her to start and jump. Each sound and movement increased her already hurried pace.

When the breeze settled and silence returned, the echoing clicks of her high heels were offset by a softer, more distant sound of footfalls.

She beeped the locks open on her sedan and wrenched the door wide, tossing her purse onto the passenger seat. She slid behind the wheel with a sigh of relief.

In her rearview mirror, a shadow grew from the space between two buildings, stretching and morphing into the silhouette of a man. He moved pointedly across the street in her direction, barely ten yards away.

She waited, wondering if someone she'd spoken to earlier had something they wanted to tell her now.

Then he raised a gun.

Hayley started the car's engine and jerked the shifter into Drive as the first bullet ripped through the evening air, eliciting a scream from her core.

She peeled away as the second and third shots exploded behind her.

Chapter Two

Marshal's Bluff Detective Finn Beaumont collapsed onto his office chair and kicked his legs out in front of him. His head fell back, and he hooked one bent arm across his eyes. He was tired to his core, exhausted in ways he hadn't been in ages. And it was hot as blazes outside, where he'd spent most of his day, in a dress shirt and slacks, questioning socialites in swimming pools and executives on golf courses.

It'd been one of those days when he'd wondered if he really knew his town at all.

Katherine Everett, a local philanthropist known widely throughout the community simply as Kate, was officially missing. Kate's grandfather had established the largest shipping company in the area and grown it into a national conglomerate. Today, Everett Industries transported goods along both coasts and the gulf, as well as to countless inlet towns. Kate managed the family's estate and funneled her heart and soul into Marshal's Bluff rehabilitation efforts.

Everyone loved her, but she was gone. And after ten hours of interviewing her neighbors, family and friends, Finn was no closer to guessing her whereabouts than the moment he'd received the call this morning announcing her disappearance.

His appreciation for her work and love of his job were just two of the many reasons he needed to find her fast. At twenty-five, he was both the newest and youngest detective on the force, and he had a lot to prove. When people with money went missing, and a ransom note didn't follow, foul play was a scary possibility. According to everyone he'd interviewed, Kate wasn't the sort to take off without letting someone know, and the calendars at her home and office showed a number of appointments happening all week. None had been canceled.

More bad signs.

The phone on Finn's desk rang, and he forced his head up, then stretched to lift the receiver. "Beaumont."

"Detective Beaumont," the desk clerk responded. "I have a social worker here who'd like to see you immediately. Possible missing child and gunshots fired in Old Downtown."

Finn rubbed his forehead. "Anyone hurt?"

"No, sir. Units are en route for follow-up."

He exhaled a long breath. He'd been on the clock nearly twelve hours, but sure. He'd see the social worker. "I guess there's always time for one more crisis, right?"

"That's the job," the clerk said, then disconnected the call.

A moment later, Finn heard the steady click-clack of high heels in the hallway.

He'd gotten nowhere while looking for Kate today, but maybe he could end the shift on a positive note by helping the social worker. He sat taller and straightened the files he'd slung onto his desk earlier, in a hurry to make his next set of interviews on time.

"Finn?"

His limbs froze, and his gaze snapped to his open office door. He'd know that voice anywhere, though he hadn't heard it in more than a year. "Hayley?"

Hayley Campbell had crashed into his life like a freight train during her first few weeks as a social worker. She'd faced off with some pretty rough-looking folks outside the courthouse when they didn't like the verdict about losing their children. He'd intervened before things escalated too far. And he'd asked her out the minute she'd stopped insisting she'd had the situation covered. Shockingly, she'd agreed.

The story of the whirlwind romance that followed was one he thought they'd tell their grandkids. But when he'd proposed a few months later, she said no. And she'd proceeded to ghost him until he stopped trying to reach her or make sense of her reaction.

He'd eventually let it go, but he wasn't over it. He doubted he ever would be. Life was like that sometimes, he supposed. People had to take the good with the bad. And the months he'd spent with Hayley were some of the best of his life.

Now, she stood before him in a pencil skirt and blouse that emphasized every dang curve on her petite little frame. Straight blond hair tucked behind her ears, she had a look on her face he knew all too well. Determination.

"Come in," he said, hoping to sound calmer than he felt. "Have a seat." The desk clerk's words rushed back to him with a slap. "You saw a shooter?"

He pulled a bottle of water from the nearby mini fridge and reassessed her expression when she didn't answer. Now, he could see she was doing all she could to hold herself together. "Talk to me, Hayley."

The sound of his voice seemed to pull her back to him, and she wet her lips. Unshed tears filled her blue eyes as she accepted the water and drank greedily.

Was she in shock?

He scanned her body more carefully, searching for signs of injury or physical trauma.

"I know it's not fair of me to come here like this," she said, voice shaky, "but I need help, and I don't want him to become another case ignored because he's been in trouble before. He hasn't run away. Either something happened to him, or he's hiding because he thinks something will happen."

Finn crossed his arms and sat on the edge of his desk before her. "Okay. I'm missing a lot of pieces, so let's start at the beginning. Who are you worried about? And when did you first know something was wrong? Take your time and be as specific as possible. Especially about this shooter."

She inhaled slowly, then released the breath and began talking about her lunch hour.

Finn took mental notes as she spoke, and a few literal ones on a pad of paper he scooped up, sticking with her as she carefully laid out the details of her day.

"When the first shot went off, I thought, maybe it was because I look like a person with money," she said, glancing at her modest skirt and sensible heels. "In that area, any amount of money is enough, you know?"

He nodded, tongue-tied as he imagined getting his hands on the person who'd taken a shot at his— Finn's brain halted and misfired. His what? Hayley wasn't his anything anymore. She hadn't been in a very long time. He cleared his throat and pushed ahead. "How many shots were fired?"

"Three. But by the second one, I was driving away. I don't think a robber would have persisted like that. I think this has something to do with Gage's disappearance. I called 911 on my way here, but I wasn't going to wait around for them. I needed to talk to you."

Finn's chest tightened at her final words. She'd avoided him for a year, but when she needed help, she still looked to him. That had to count for something.

"All right." He pushed onto his feet and rounded the desk to his chair. "I need to get your official written statement and make a report. You can tell me all you know about… Gage, is it?"

She nodded. "Yes."

"I'll share his description and relevant information with Dispatch and let officers know he's missing, possibly in danger."

"Thank you." She released a long, steady breath. "What happens then?"

"Then I'll follow you home," he said. "It's unlikely the shooter will show up at your place, but an escort might make you feel better. It'll certainly help me."

HAYLEY SMILED, relieved and exhausted. Finn hadn't changed at all in the time they'd been apart. He was still kind and accepting. Still listened and didn't interrupt. And he still had her best interest at heart, even after she'd walked out on his proposal without an explanation. Then she'd hid from him, like a coward, for more than a year. "I'd appreciate it."

An hour later, she pulled into the driveway outside her cottage, several blocks from the bay, with Finn behind her.

Her neighborhood was a series of older homes packed closely together. The tiny yards spilled into one another all the way to the end of each block. It was a blue-collar, working-class section of town, established at the turn of the last century, when most of the male citizens worked on the docks or on ships in some capacity, hence its proximity to the sea. These days, however, her block had more retirees than worker bees. That fact had been a selling point on this property over all the others in her price range. The way Hayley saw it, a block full of retirees likely meant someone was home all the time, which would keep crime low. Witnesses tended to ruin a criminal's day.

She grabbed her things from the passenger seat and climbed out, then met Finn on the porch. Hopefully, she hadn't left anything she'd regret Finn seeing in plain sight inside. She was tidy, but it'd been a while since she'd had company. An errant bra on the couch or coffee table wasn't unheard of at her place, mostly because removing the torture device was her go-to move after a long day at the office.

Hayley turned on the porch light as they entered. "I didn't

expect to get back so late," she said, mostly out of nerves and habit. Finn used to worry about her returning to a dark home.

Her heart rate rose as they stood in the entryway between her living room and staircase to the second floor. The cottage suddenly felt smaller and warmer than she remembered.

She'd furnished the space in hand-me-downs and thrift-store finds, full of colors and textures that made her happy. Mismatched throw rugs and tables she'd saved from the curb on trash day, sanded and given new life with fresh paint.

"Can I get you a glass of sweet tea or a cup of coffee?" she asked.

He looked tired and a little anxious, but the second part couldn't be true. He was Finn Beaumont, a full six feet of handsomeness, with lean muscles, broad shoulders and two perfect, extra large hands.

She resisted the urge to pluck the fabric of her shirt away from her chest.

Her female coworkers always took an extra minute to check their hair and refresh their lipstick before going to the police station or courthouse, just in case they'd see him.

"Sweet tea sounds nice," he said. "Thank you."

Hayley hustled into the kitchen, glad for the moment alone to collect her marbles. She poured a glass of tea from the pitcher she kept in her fridge, then straightened her skirt, took a deep breath and hurried back to the living room.

Finn stood at the fireplace, examining framed photographs on her mantel. She'd replaced the images of her and Finn with snapshots of children from her caseload, their artwork, or pics of her at community events and charity drives. The first photo he'd taken of her on the Beaumont ranch stood at the center of her collection.

The old wooden floorboards creaked as she moved in his direction.

"How's your mom?" he asked, casting a glance over his shoulder.

"She's fine," she said, passing him the glass.

Hayley didn't keep pictures of her mom, or talk about her, for a number of reasons. Her mother didn't bring her joy, peace or any of the other things Hayley needed her home to provide. And most of her memories involving the older woman upset her.

Finn scanned her briefly, then took a small sip of his tea. "You look nice. Were you in court today?"

"Yeah." She moved to the couch and Finn followed. "You look as if you've had a big day too."

He raised his eyebrows then laughed. "I have. But no one shot at me, so there's that."

She smiled.

"And even the worst days have bright spots," he added.

She sat and pulled a throw pillow onto her lap, hugging it to her chest. "How's your family doing? I recommend their ranch for rehabilitation every chance I get. I think some folks take me up on it."

Finn sipped the tea again before setting his glass on the coffee table. "I know my folks appreciate that." He rested his hands on his lap and grinned. "It's been a big year for the Beaumonts. Have you heard?"

She swiveled in his direction, curiosity piqued. "No. Do tell."

"Dean got back with his ex, Nicole. They're engaged now."

Hayley's heart swelled. She loved Dean, and knew he wasn't over his ex, but she'd expected him to move on, not find his way back to her. Did things like that really happen? "That's wonderful," she said, meaning it to her core. "Nicole has the younger sister who stayed at the ranch, right?"

"That's the one." Finn hooked one ankle over the opposite knee. "Nicole came to him for help when her sister went missing. They worked out their troubles, saved the sister and fell in love all over again. They're getting married in the spring."

Hayley pressed her lips together and felt her cheeks heat. The parallels between her situation with Finn and his brother's situation with his ex were hard to ignore. But she wasn't naive enough to think there'd be a way back to him for her. Not after what she'd done. Finn was kind and forgiving, but she'd gone too far.

"And then there's Austin," he began, a dimple sinking into his cheek at the appearance of his mischievous grin.

"What did Austin do?" She'd always liked Austin. He was the oldest of the biological Beaumont boys, third in line of the five, which actually made him a bit of a middle child and a goofball. Dean and Jake had been adopted as young boys, around the same time Austin and Lincoln were born only sixteen months apart. As a result, the brothers were close in every way and inseparable friends.

"He's currently engaged to a local real-estate agent," he said.

She shook her head in awe. "You're kidding?"

"Nope. He took her case when she thought someone was following her. She was right, and we handled that. Now Austin and Scarlet are planning a big Christmas wedding."

Hayley laughed. "I can't believe the Beaumont boys are getting married. Your mama must be elated. She's obsessed with seeing your family grow."

Finn's smile fell a bit, and reality knocked the awe from Hayley's tone.

"Oh—" She winced. "I didn't mean to—"

Finn had proposed long before Dean or Austin, but Hayley had said no.

He lifted a palm. "You had your reasons."

She had, but she also owed him an explanation. The words piled on her tongue, but wouldn't quite fall from her lips.

Silence stretched as he searched her eyes. "I suppose I should get going and let you rest," he said, the words low and thick. "I'll get a neighborhood patrol on your block tonight for good measure, and I'll keep you posted with any updates we have on Gage. You'll do the same?"

"Of course." She rose and walked Finn to the door.

"You still have my number?" he asked, pausing on her front porch.

She nodded.

His gaze flicked over her face once more. "For what it's worth, I'm glad you came to me," he said. "You can always ask me for help. Tomorrow or ten years from now. Won't matter."

She leaned against the doorjamb as her knees went a little weak.

"I mean it, Hayley. If you ever need anything, you can call me. Whether you're having a hard time and just want someone to listen, or you need a background check on your date. Maybe help opening a jar or reaching a high shelf."

She laughed. "Let me guess. You're my man?"

"I will always be your man," he said. Then he turned with a wink and jogged away.

Chapter Three

Hayley arrived at Social Services early the next morning. She hadn't slept well and decided to use the extra time to get ahead on paperwork. But the moment she'd taken a seat behind her desk, her mind was back on Gage.

A call to Mrs. Michaelson had confirmed his continued absence, which meant he was still missing and in trouble. He was a kid alone and on foot. And whatever he'd gotten into possibly involved a gunman.

She shivered at the memory of the silhouette as it had grown from the shadows. She wasn't sure she'd have survived if not for her car.

Gage didn't even have a cell phone.

By the time her coworkers began showing up, Hayley had already moved her laptop outside and set up a hot spot on her phone. If she worked at the picnic table where she ate lunch, it would reduce her chances of missing Gage if he stopped by to see her. Thankfully, her day's schedule was light. No court appearances, and only two home visits. She could keep a lookout from the park most of the day.

Sweat gathered on her brow and across the back of her neck as hours passed and the sun rose in the sky. She'd worn a blue silk sleeveless blouse with tan capri pants and flats. All in all, better suited for running than the prior day's pencil skirt and heels.

She'd struggled to choose between tops this morning and was mildly distressed by the outcome. She'd initially leaned toward a more figure-flattering cream blouse, but ultimately selected the blue because it matched her eyes. And Finn always used to comment when she wore blue.

The resulting internal cringe was nearly painful. She shouldn't be thinking about Finn Beaumont right now, or which color he'd liked on her a year ago. She should be focused on Gage and the gunman.

But since her mind had opened the Finn rabbit hole, she let herself tumble back down for another moment or two.

Two of his brothers were planning weddings. That was unexpected news. Dean never dated after Nicole broke his heart and Austin just never dated. Or, Hayley had never seen him with the same girl more than twice while she was with Finn anyway. Now, Dean had reunited with the woman he loved, and Austin had committed to a local real-estate agent. Whoever she was, she must be special. The Beaumonts certainly were.

Hayley loved the whole family and wanted them to be happy. She wished she could meet the women who'd stolen Austin and Dean's hearts. She wished she could attend the wedding ceremonies and celebrate with them. They were the brothers she'd never had. And now, she never would.

If only she'd been less broken and more understanding of her own damage at the time of Finn's proposal, she'd be part of his family now too. Instead, she'd done what she always did. She'd panicked and she'd run. She hadn't even seen the pattern until it was pointed out to her in therapy. She was working hard on correcting that kind of behavior these days. But until the proposal, she hadn't understood all the ways her emotional damage had shaped her entire life.

A cool breeze picked up, pulling her back to the moment. She glanced around, wondering how long she'd been lost in thought. Then she opened her cooler and unpacked her lunch. The day was slipping away without any good news.

An hour later, she collected her things, ready for her two afternoon appointments.

A large black SUV pulled away from the curb across the street and moved slowly past the social-services building. The fine hairs along Hayley's arms and the back of her neck stood at attention as she watched it disappear around the corner. The vehicle was high-end and new, a familiar make and model, but she'd missed the license plate.

Thankfully, she didn't see the vehicle again all afternoon.

She returned to the picnic table at five o'clock and waited until six before leaving. She traded texts with Finn about the fact neither of them had news on Gage's whereabouts. And she fought the urge to go back to Old Downtown and overturn every brick until she found him.

At six, she began the slow trek to her car.

Intuition prickled across her skin as she scanned the world around her, feeling someone's gaze on her as she moved. She hoped it belonged to Gage.

Kids played in the park and coworkers chatted in the lot, but none paid any attention to her as she passed.

The dark SUV from lunch appeared at the curb across the street, and Hayley's steps faltered. This time, a man in a black T-shirt, jeans and a ball cap leaned against the hood, mirrored sunglasses covering his eyes.

She picked up the pace, wondering, belatedly, if she should've turned back to talk with her coworkers until the man left. But it was too late. Now, he'd know what she drove.

He crossed his arms and widened his stance, appearing to watch her as she unlocked her car door.

She pulled a flyer wedged beneath one windshield wiper into the car with her and locked the door. She raised her phone in the man's direction to snap a photo, but he turned away, then climbed behind the wheel of his SUV and merged smoothly into evening traffic.

A gush of relief rushed over her lips a moment before the three words scrawled across the paper came into view.

Leave This Alone

FINN PACED THE sidewalk outside the pub near the precinct. Hayley's message had been brief but pointed. She was leaving work and on her way to meet him. He'd suggested they chat over dinner, and she'd named the pub they used to frequent.

He'd walked straight out of his office and jogged the block and a half to wait for her.

Her navy blue sedan swung into the narrow parking area beside the pub a moment later, and she climbed out looking on edge.

He tried not to notice the way her pants clung to her narrow hips and trim thighs. Or how the blue of her blouse perfectly matched her eyes. But he couldn't stop the smile that formed at the sight of her sleek blond hair, pulled into the world's tiniest ponytail.

"You okay?" he asked as she reached his side.

"No."

Alarm shot through Finn's limbs as he opened the pub's door and waited while she stepped inside. A million reasons for her answer raced through his mind. None of them were good.

The hostess smiled. "Two?"

"Yeah. A booth if you have one," Finn said.

The young woman's gaze slid over Hayley. "Sure. Right this way."

She led them to a table in the corner and left them with a pair of menus.

Hayley sat near the window, leaving Finn the seat with a

clear view of the door and room at large, which he appreciated. She frowned as she watched the hostess walk away. "I forgot what it was like to go anywhere with you."

"What do you mean?" He glanced around the busy pub, then back at her. Nothing seemed amiss. They'd passed several available tables on their way to this one, but his request had been strategic. "I thought a booth would give us more privacy."

She sighed and pulled a folded piece of paper from her purse, then passed it to him. "This was on my windshield when I left work, and I park at the church a block away from Social Services. That means whoever left it knew which car was mine. I'm afraid it might've been the same person who saw me drive away last night after they shot at me."

Finn raised his eyebrows. "You think the shooter wrote this?"

"I don't know," she said. "But a man was standing outside an SUV, watching me, when I found it. And I think I saw the same vehicle near the park at lunchtime. The guy left when I tried to take a picture of him."

"Did he look like the shooter?" Finn asked, blood pressure rising.

This wasn't the way he'd expected their exchange to go. Hayley hadn't mentioned any of this in her text. She'd just wanted to meet, and he'd assumed, at worst, she was still worried about Gage's absence. At best, he'd thought she might just want to see him again.

Hayley raised her narrow shoulders in an exaggerated shrug. "I didn't get a good look at the person who followed me last night. All I know is Gage never went back to his foster home, and he didn't reach out to me today. I'm doing everything I can to find him, which for the record feels like nothing, and everything about my day was absurdly unremarkable until that appeared."

Finn read the note again. "You think this is a reference to Gage's situation?"

"What else could it be?" she asked. "Searching for him is the only thing I'm doing differently, and Gage said he thought he saw something he shouldn't. I'm guessing whoever is responsible for whatever he saw left this note."

Finn rested against the seat back, telling himself to remain calm and collected. He couldn't let his attachment to Hayley interfere with his ability to do his best work for her. "I'm going to need another formal statement," he said. "I'll put the note into evidence after we eat."

A waitress arrived with a notepad and a smile. "Are y'all ready to order?"

Finn watched Hayley for the answer, allowing her to decide. She hadn't even looked at the menu.

She slid her attention from the woman to Finn and pursed her lips. "Just a soda for me."

"And what can I get you?" the waitress asked, shifting one hip against the table and angling toward him as she spoke.

"You're not hungry?" Finn asked Hayley, confused. "Have you already eaten?"

"No. I'm just shaken."

"You have to eat." He looked at the waitress, who was smiling.

He frowned. "Can we get a basket of chicken tenders to split? Honey for dip. And I'll have black coffee."

"Sure thing, sugar. Anything else?"

"No."

The waitress left, and Hayley rolled her eyes.

"Did you want something different?" he asked.

She used to love chicken strips with honey. Had that changed this year?

She shook her head. "The order was good. Thank you. I'm just— What am I going to do?"

He waited, unsure how to answer without more specifics.

"I know this is bad," she said, pointing to the note he'd refolded and set aside. "I need to know how bad and what to do next."

"Well," Finn began, rubbing a hand along his jaw, "we'll need more information to answer the first part. Should we wait until you've had something to eat before we tackle the second? You look like you're ready to drop."

"No," she said. "And I am." She let her eyes close briefly and tipped her head over one shoulder.

Finn willed his gaze away from the exposed length of her neck.

Her lids opened and she straightened, fixing her attention on him. "I'm being followed by a man in an SUV who knows where I work and what I drive. Gage is still missing, and the man with the SUV doesn't want me looking for him, but I can't stop doing that. Gage's life could be in danger. Meanwhile there's a possibility this guy is the same person who shot at me. I feel sick."

Finn rested his forearms on the table between them and clasped his hands. Apparently they were going to talk about the tough stuff before eating. "You're right to be concerned about all that. I'm doing everything I can on my end to figure out what happened in Old Downtown last night. Officers walked the area you described but didn't find any evidence of the shooting. They're looking for the shell casings from the shots fired. If we find them, we can use ballistics to try to match the gun to other crimes and possibly get a lead on the shooter. I was running on the theory the shooting was a separate issue from the kid's disappearance, but the note makes this personal, and given the big picture, it's smart to proceed as if these things are related."

"Okay," she said softly, sounding frightened but in agreement. "Now what?"

"Now, I think it would be wise if someone looked after you for the next few days while we figure out what's going on here."

Her nose wrinkled. "Like a bodyguard?"

"More like a personal protection detail," he said. "I'll put a cruiser in your neighborhood and assign one to you at work. I'll fill in whenever I can so you're as comfortable as possible while being followed around."

Hayley blinked. "You're going to follow me around?"

"Just until we're sure you're safe."

The waitress returned with a tray and bent low to set it on the table, temporarily blocking his view of Hayley. "Chicken fingers with honey, black coffee and a soda," she said. "Is there anything else I can do for you?" She stood and cocked her hip again.

Finn followed Hayley's droll, heavy-lidded gaze to the smiling young woman. "No. This is everything. Thank you."

She left.

Hayley raised a chicken finger and pointed it at him. "That waitress is hitting on you. Just like the hostess. It's blatant and rude. We could be here together."

He furrowed his brow. "What?"

"You're an actual detective, Finn. You're literally paid to notice details, yet you are oblivious. How is that possible?"

Finn leaned forward, shamelessly enjoying her undivided attention and hint of possessiveness in her tone. "Probably because all I see right now is you."

A blush stole across her beautiful face, and she lowered the chicken. "Fine. You can follow me around, but you have to help me look for Gage too."

"Deal." He was already doing the latter, and he wanted the extra time with her.

She slid her hand over the table, fingers outstretched for a shake.

Finn curled his palm around hers and held tight, letting the intoxicating buzz of her touch course through him. "I will protect you," he promised. "And we'll find Gage. Together."

Chapter Four

Hayley rose with the sun the next morning. Unable to find sleep in more than small bits and patches during the night, she was glad to give up and get moving. She checked her phone with hope for missed news, preferably a message that Gage had been found, or a text directly from the teen saying he was safe. The only waiting notifications were social-media updates from coworkers and a few junk emails she marked as spam.

Disappointment washed over her, but not surprise. Nothing had ever come easily. At least, she supposed, this was familiar territory. Time to set a plan and get to work.

She hurried through her morning routine, dressing for the day and sending good thoughts into the universe, hoping the energy would find its way to Gage. Something to keep his chin up until she found him. And she would find him. Whatever it took. She wasn't sure she'd recover if something happened to the teen. He'd already experienced too much tragedy. He deserved a home filled with love and a safe place to exist while he grieved the loss of his parents. A place he could become the man he wanted to be without all the noise. Somewhere he could focus on his art and express himself freely.

Not on the run. Not alone and afraid.

She willed away the budding tears and pressed the brew

button on her single-cup coffee maker. Then she packed a cooler of sandwiches, baggies of pretzels and cold water bottles while she finished her first cup. She returned the empty mug to the machine and brewed a refill.

Someone knew where Gage was. If she couldn't find him, she could at least find someone to point her in the right direction. All she needed was a lead.

Her thoughts circled back to the SUV outside her office and the note left on her windshield, then to the man with the gun. None of those things were clues to Gage's whereabouts, but they were all clues. She just had to figure out what they meant.

"What did you see, Gage?" she whispered, remembering his worried words to her at lunch, and hating that she hadn't been able to stop this, whatever it was, from happening.

Memories of the gunman sent a shiver down her spine, and she crept toward her front window for a careful peek outside. He knew her car and license-plate number, and her place of employment, so why not her address?

A familiar black pickup truck sat at the curb across the street. Finn was behind the wheel, a laptop balanced on something inside his cab as he typed away, stealing occasional glances into his mirrors and at her front door.

"Of course, you're already outside," she murmured, smiling as she rolled her eyes. "The Beaumont brothers and their big, dumb, hero hearts." She slipped onto her porch when he turned his attention back to his computer, then marched down her walkway in his direction.

As she drew nearer, it became clear he wasn't just starting work a little early. He'd been outside her place all night. He was wearing the same shirt from last night, and his usually clean-shaven face was dark with stubble. His hair pointed in all directions from one too many finger combs, and there was a level of fatigue in his eyes that only came from pulling an all-nighter.

He turned to face her before she reached the center of the street.

"Still got those heightened senses, I see."

He grinned, hooking one elbow through the open window. "Keeps me alive."

"Handy." She stopped at his door and lifted her chin to indicate the mess of empty snack wrappers at his side. "You want to come in for coffee, or are you full of jerky and candy?"

He climbed out and closed his door with a grin. "Coffee sounds amazing."

Hayley inhaled, steadying herself against his intoxicating nearness. Even after a night in his truck, his trademark mix of cologne and sea air seemed to cling to his clothes and skin. The inviting scent of his spearmint gum beckoned her closer. Heat from his body seemed to grip and pull her, as did his sleepy eyes and disheveled hair. Up close, Finn Beaumont was mesmerizing.

Memories of sleepless nights they'd once shared slid into mind, unbidden, raising her body temperature and heating her cheeks. She forced away the images and willed her heart and head to get a grip. Nothing about her bone-deep attraction and attachment to him would help her find Gage, and that sweet missing boy was all that mattered.

"Penny for your thoughts?" Finn asked, voice low and careful.

She shrugged, feigning confidence. "You could've stayed inside, you know. There wasn't any reason to sleep in your truck. I have a spare room."

He rubbed a hand against his stubbled cheek, looking suddenly boyish and shy. "I'll keep that in mind. For now, I think all I need is a little coffee, and I'll be good to go."

She nodded and turned back to her home, leading the way

across the street. "I'm asking a coworker to take some tasks off my plate today and tomorrow. I want to double down on my efforts to locate Gage before much more time passes. I'd hoped to get news during the night, but I haven't."

He nodded as she held open her front door for him. "If we don't make solid progress fast, I'll reach out to Dean and Austin, see if they can help."

Hayley's heart swelled. The duo owned a private-investigations office together, and they were very good. "Thank you."

"Of course. How much of your work were you able to off-load?"

"Most of it. I figure the less time I spend at the office, the less likely I'll be to draw a criminal stalker there. It's a building full of folks trying to make the world a little better for local kids and families. I can't be the reason something bad potentially comes into their lives."

"Always troubleshooting for others," he said with a small smile.

"That's the job."

"That's your heart," he corrected.

Hayley scanned his dark brown eyes. "Kind of like the way you insist on seeing the best in people."

She felt like a failure for not getting the whole story from Gage while he'd been right there at the picnic table with her. She'd failed when she let him walk away. Yet Finn managed to see her in the best light. As if she wasn't at least partially at fault.

"I can reach out to your supervisor," Finn suggested. "Let them know you're part of an ongoing investigation and that you'll be working with Marshal's Bluff PD outside the office for a few days."

"Not yet," she said. "I'm holding out hope that Gage will turn up soon and fill us in on what's happening. Then, I can take care of him while you arrest whoever is behind the gunshots."

She selected a mug from the cupboard and brewed him a cup of coffee, then passed it his way.

"Thanks." Finn accepted and blew over the steamy surface before taking a greedy gulp.

"You're welcome. Thank you for keeping an eye on me last night. Are you headed home to rest now, or are you on the clock for a bit longer?"

He lowered the cup slightly, eyebrows raised. "I've been off the clock since last night. Today's supposed to be my day off, but I'm in the middle of another case, so that was never happening. Why? What do you need?"

"I thought you might come with me to ask around about Gage, but I don't want to add more work for you on your day off." The people who roamed Old Downtown were unlikely to talk to a lawman, but at least some of the folks in Gage's world were likely to be motivated by a badge. His foster parents and siblings, for example. And Hayley could use all the help she could get.

Finn finished his coffee and set the mug on the counter. "Helping you will never be work, Hayley."

She blinked. Something in his tone suggested he might not be as angry with her for running away from his proposal as she'd imagined. That maybe he was over it. And not necessarily over her.

"Where do you want to start?" he asked, moving the mug to her sink for a rinse and allowing her to take the lead, despite a shiny detective badge on the leather bifold perpetually clipped to his pocket.

I'd like to start with a deeply apologetic kiss, she thought, but she pushed the silly notion aside.

"I was thinking I should go back to Old Downtown."

Where she'd been shot at. Where her gut said Gage had been likely last seen.

"I'll drive."

FINN PARKED HIS pickup along the crumbling curb of Front Street in Old Downtown. The area was dreary, even by morning light. There would be more people around as the day commenced, but the danger increased with the population in this neighborhood, and Finn intended to keep Hayley as far away from trouble as possible. Meanwhile, they'd have to settle for questioning the early risers, typically an older, less hostile group.

Hayley swung open her door and climbed down, pulling a large black tote behind her. "Ready?" She closed the door without waiting for his response.

He met her at his back bumper and gave her a curious look. "What's with the luggage?"

He'd assumed it was her work or laptop bag when she'd carried it to his truck. Maybe she thought it would be stolen if she left it behind? "I've got a lockbox behind my seat, if you'd feel better leaving your things in there."

She smiled. "No thanks. I plan to give this away."

Finn frowned. "What?"

"I usually bring sandwiches and water to the office and distribute them at lunch. Folks know they can help themselves. Since I won't be there today, I thought I'd do what I can down here."

Finn opened his mouth to speak, but words failed. He'd grown up in a family that made sure as many folks as possible had something to eat every day. His parents, particularly his mama, were still dedicated to the task. Since becoming a detective, he'd taken a much smaller role in the family's daily efforts, but seeing Hayley's considerate and giving nature in action melted him a little. He'd held out hope of getting over her one day, but clearly that wouldn't be today. Spending time with her on this case would set him back months in his quest to move on, but some sadistic part of him would enjoy the pain.

A woman wearing too many layers of clothing for the increasing heat and humidity appeared on the corner. She eyed him skeptically before taking note of Hayley at his side.

Hayley unzipped her bag and liberated a small bottle of water. She extended it in the woman's direction. "Going to be another hot one today."

The woman froze, but Hayley continued moving toward her.

"You can have this if you want it."

Finn slowed, hanging back to allow the women to interact.

"I have food too. If you're hungry," Hayley offered.

"What do you want for it?"

"Nothing." Hayley passed the water and a small pack of pretzels to the other woman.

"What are you doing down here?"

"I'm looking for the boy who makes those." She tipped her head to indicate a dark patch of graffiti, the silhouette of a child at the end of a long shadow. "He's my friend, and I haven't seen him in a couple days. I'm worried." She dug a sandwich from her sack and passed that to the woman as well. "If you need a place to stay tonight, somewhere cool and safe," she added, "the mission on Second Avenue has openings for women and children."

The woman's expression softened. "You're her, aren't you?"

"Who?" Hayley asked.

"The angel."

Hayley's eyes widened for a moment, but she rearranged her features quickly. Anyone who wasn't staring at her, like Finn was, probably wouldn't have noticed. "Pardon?"

The woman finished the water without answering. She tucked the sandwich into the pocket of her baggy cardigan. "I've got a place around the corner. I don't like the mission. It's too crowded, and there's a curfew."

"If you run into anyone who might need somewhere, will you let them know?" Hayley asked.

"Sure." The woman's gaze flickered back to the graffiti. "He's a nice kid," she said. "Seems right that he'd have someone like you." She lifted her eyes briefly to Finn, then moved away.

Hayley's expression fell with the woman's parting words, and Finn moved quickly to her side. "You all right?"

"Fine." She forced a tight smile. "Worried about Gage. That's all."

He wasn't convinced that was the whole story, but Finn knew better than to push her past her comfort zone. The last time he did that, she'd avoided him for a year.

They moved onward, searching for pedestrians to ask about Gage. Block by block, until her bag was empty. Everyone seemed to know the boy who painted the shadows of children. They were kind and concerned, but no one knew where he'd gone.

Finn's presence could easily have deterred folks from talking to her, but Hayley was just so genuine. Everyone could see it. The tough things she'd been through had somehow strengthened her instead of breaking her. She'd become stronger without becoming hardened. In truth, she was probably softer and more gentle-hearted as a result. People seemed to sense and respect that.

He set a hand on her back when they turned around at the waterfront.

Her narrow shoulders curved in defeat.

Regardless of how many people were willing to talk, Gage

was still missing. Just like the heiress, Kate. And that was incredibly frustrating.

"Hey." The deep bass of a male voice turned them on their heels. A large man approached slowly from a nearby dock. He was tall and broad-shouldered with thickly muscled arms and deep-set brown eyes. He lifted his chin to Finn, then refocused on Hayley.

"Timothy!" Hayley moved quickly in the man's direction, meeting him halfway and smiling widely. "How are you? How's Sonia?"

Timothy's lips twitched as he seemed to be fighting a smile and he nodded. "All good, thanks to you. I heard you're looking for the little tagger."

"I am," she said, jerking her attention to Finn, then back to her friend. "He's missing, and I think he's in trouble. Have you seen him around here in the last day or two?"

"I try not to spend too much time out this way these days, but I heard you were here yesterday, and a friend told me why. I asked around for you." He balled one hand into a fist at his side, then stretched his fingers before letting them hang loose once more. "I encouraged folks to talk. I was just headed your way, to be honest. You shouldn't be down here. This place just ain't for you."

"You heard something?" she asked, ignoring his sage advice.

Finn glanced at Timothy's hand again and imagined it wouldn't take much effort on the mammoth's part to encourage anyone to do anything.

The man's steely gaze flicked to Finn. "What kind of law are you?"

"I'm with the Marshal's Bluff PD," Finn answered.

Hayley declared, "He's a friend."

Timothy rolled his shoulders and refocused on Hayley.

"Some folks saw your boy at the rave a couple of nights ago. They noticed, because he was new, and he was running."

Hayley took a half step back, and Finn leaned forward to steady her.

"Running from who?" Finn asked.

"Don't know," the man said. "But more than one person saw him, so he was there."

"Where?"

"Winthrop's—you know it?"

"Yeah." The old warehouse had nearly burned down several years back. The owners couldn't afford the repairs, and their insurance had lapsed, so the city had condemned it. "That place isn't structurally sound. No one should be in there, especially not a crowd. The whole thing could've collapsed."

The guy made a painfully bland expression. "Not my business."

"Do you know when the next rave will be?" Finn asked.

If ravers recognized Gage because he wasn't a regular, then maybe Finn and another detective could drop in and talk to attendees. Get firsthand information.

"Nah, man. It's a pop-up. Place changes. Day changes. Time changes. You know that, Detective." The last few words were said in a pointed tone, and Finn bristled. He hadn't told Timothy he was a detective, but he was right on both counts. Finn knew all about the raves. They were a thorn in the side of Marshal's Bluff PD. The department tried to bust up the parties anytime they could, but getting wind of one ahead of time had proven impossible, and hearing about a rave while it was in motion was rare. Lots of drugs and money exchanged hands on those nights, along with plenty of other illegal activities, he was sure. "Why'd you ask if I was a detective if you already knew?"

"That wasn't what I asked." Timothy turned dark eyes

back to Hayley. "I asked what kind of law you are. She knew the answer."

Finn considered the words. Timothy had wanted to know if he could be trusted.

With that, the man turned and walked away.

Chapter Five

Hayley chewed her lip as she walked at Finn's side. She'd spoken to a lot of people in a short amount of time. No one had known where Gage was, but several women with children now planned to sleep at the mission, and more than a dozen souls weren't hungry at the moment, thanks to her trip to Old Downtown. Despite feelings of defeat, she couldn't be wholly disappointed in the morning's outcome.

She was especially thankful for Timothy's efforts to acquire information on the missing teen, though she hoped no one had been harmed in the process. Timothy's rage was legendary and the reason he'd lost his little girl to the system last year. The only thing bigger than his temper was his love for Sonia. So he'd taken the required anger-management courses, started working out and joined a local basketball league to burn off the excess stress of his job and being a single parent. He'd gotten Sonia back in only a few months. He did the work and set a good example for his daughter. Hayley had endless respect for that. And sincere appreciation for the lead he'd provided on Gage, thin as it was.

"I know the rave has been over for days," she said, stealing a look at Finn. "But Winthrop's is only two blocks from here."

He slid his eyes to her without missing a step. "You want to go there?"

She nodded. "I know Gage isn't there, and likely no one else will be either, but it's all we've got to go on right now. If we leave without stopping by, I'll wonder if we missed a huge clue, and it will eat at me."

Finn inhaled deeply and released the breath on a slow exhale. "I'd rather send a couple of uniforms to follow up on that, but I don't suppose that'll satisfy you?"

Hayley stopped walking. "It's the only place I know he's been in the last couple of days, aside from visiting me at lunch. I need to see it."

She was certain every protective fiber in Finn's body wanted to get her away from Old Downtown as quickly as possible, but he knew her well enough to understand she wasn't asking his permission. Letting her go alone was more dangerous than going with her, so he'd agree eventually. "Come with me?"

A long, quiet moment elapsed between them. A muscle in his jaw flexed and tightened. Then, he cracked. First his expression, then his stance. "Fine, but I go in first, and you stay with me. Not just where I can see you, but within arm's reach. That place was condemned for a reason. It's unsafe. And it's known to attract trouble."

"Agreed." Hayley turned and headed in the direction of the old warehouse that overlooked the harbor. She concentrated to keep her steps even, though she wanted to break into a run. As if Gage might be there if she hurried. Instead, she slowed her breathing, reminding herself to be vigilant and focused. She had no idea what she might find if she really looked.

Finn increased his pace casually when they got closer to the building, his long strides forcing her to speed up. He placed himself a half step ahead on the sidewalk outside the door, then raised one arm in front of her like a gate.

Hayley stilled, surveying the crumbling, neglected exterior. Winthrop's was a stout, vacant space that had once held boats and shipping containers for the fishing company. The property, formerly home to a thriving enterprise, was now a heinous eyesore. Its charred bricks and cracked windows rotted darkly beneath a scorched metal roof. All evidence of the fire that had bankrupted the owners.

Finn opened the door with little effort, and she followed him inside—they were as silent as two ghosts.

The air was hot and dry, laced with salt from the nearby ocean and ash from the singed interior beams. Litter covered the floor—empty liquor bottles and beer cans, fast-food wrappers and cigarette butts. Ironic, she thought, to smoke in a building that'd nearly burned to the ground.

Finn moved methodically through the space, examining the open areas, then clearing the sections blocked from view by partial walls and pallets of materials from an abandoned reconstruction effort.

Distant sounds of the ocean, bleating tugboats and screaming gulls, traveled in through a large portion of missing wall at the back. Hayley moved to the floor's edge and peered over the steep plummet to the water. Intense sunlight reflected off the crystal surface, while small white wave breaks rolled steadily toward the shore. The drop from the warehouse was survivable, if the unfortunate person landed far enough away to hit the water, or close enough to begin an early roll down the hillside, instead of a midpoint smack against the narrow, rocky shoreline below.

Thankfully there wasn't any sign of Gage, hurt, suffering, or worse, in view.

She imagined him running through the warehouse packed with people and music raging into the rafters, then leaping to his escape.

"You okay?" Finn asked, moving to her side.

"Yeah." She pulled her gaze away from the water, blinking to refocus on him in the shadow of the building. "Notice anything useful?"

He shook his head. "You want to walk the perimeter?"

She led the way back through the front door and around the side of the building. Her skin heated with the late morning sun as they moved over broken asphalt. Humidity tugged at her hair and added beads of sweat to her temples.

When they'd finished the circuit, Finn turned to her, hands on hips. His frown suggested he was as frustrated as she was. "I'm sorry this didn't go better."

"It's not your fault," she said, feeling the pressure of defeat on her chest once more. "At least everyone around here knows I'm looking for him. Someone will deliver the message."

Finn nodded, his keen gaze and trained eyes dragging over everything in sight, probably seeing a lot more than she did in the dirty streets and dilapidated landscape. "I'm in the middle of a missing-persons case too," he said, surprising her with the unexpected disclosure. "I was looking for her all day yesterday and hoping for a win today. I'm not used to striking out twice in a row."

Hayley had no doubt that was true, but she kept the thought to herself. Beaumont men rarely failed at anything they were determined to achieve. "Who were you looking for?" she asked. "I'm sure they'll turn up with you on the case."

She offered a small smile he didn't return.

"Katherine Everett."

"The philanthropist?" she asked, officially stunned.

"Yep."

Hayley raised her eyebrows. "Any chance she'll turn up at a spa retreat in the mountains?"

"So far, she doesn't seem to be anywhere."

"Did you know she's building a shelter and community center down here?" Hayley asked. "She wants to make better use of all these blocks of crime and waste."

"I've heard," he said. "My family's ranch donated to the effort. It's long overdue. People experiencing homelessness should have somewhere safe to stay while getting on their feet."

Hayley's heart swelled at his words. It was easy to forget how steeped in this community Finn and his family were, and that his parents dedicated themselves to the betterment of life for Marshal's Bluff youths. "It's hard enough for people to find themselves in need of shelter. Harder still when the only placement available is in the basement of an old church—not that staying at the mission isn't better than being on the street," she clarified.

"There's a lot to be said for dignity," Finn agreed. "The entire project will add hope to an area that's been without it too long. This town has too many people in need. Kate's project will be an incredible boon."

"It will," she agreed. "The number of kids in our local foster system is beginning to outweigh the number of available families. I don't suppose you've thought of adopting?" Hayley asked.

When she'd dated Finn, he'd talked about wanting children of his own, but he'd make a great role model for any child. He was tough but fair, strong-willed but willing to compromise and loving but never a pushover. All things that struggling youths needed in their lives. For their emotional security and as an example of what a leader and high-quality human should be. "Or maybe becoming a foster parent?"

Finn pursed his lips. "I work too many hours. Kids need routine and reliability, not an adult running off at all hours, or one who's never home for dinner." He dragged emotion-filled eyes back to her. "If I had someone to care for, I'd want them to know they could count on me to be there."

Hayley tucked a swath of windblown hair behind her ear, his searing gaze burning a hole in her heart.

"How about you?" he asked. "Have you considered fostering or adoption?"

"I wanted to foster Gage," she confessed. "I knew the moment I met him. I could be there for him, helping in any way he needed. I could make him feel seen and loved. Support him through his grief. But I also know the system prefers couples and people twice my age for foster families, so I didn't bother throwing my hat in the ring."

Finn frowned. "What happened with him? How'd he end up on your caseload?"

"He lost his parents last year. A drunk driver. Before that, the three of them were a run-of-the-mill, happy family."

Breath left Finn in an audible whoosh. "Oh, man. To go from that to the system—"

"Yeah."

"No relatives?"

"None." Though Hayley certainly felt as if Gage was her family, and she wished she would've asked to foster him when she had the chance. She should've pleaded her case. But at the time, she'd felt the way Finn had described, unsure she had time to be all the things Gage needed. She was gone ten hours a day and often brought her work home. Plus, she'd never been a parent. She had no experience raising a teen, and she'd been a teen not so long ago in the court's eyes. She wasn't sure she'd ever actually been a kid, though. She'd been taking care of herself and her alcoholic mother since she could reach the doorknob to let herself in and out for school and trips to buy bread and eggs. "I didn't try to get him placed into my care, because I knew there'd be a fight in court. I'd have to prove myself, and I didn't want him drawn into all that when he'd just been orphaned. It wasn't fair."

"Most things aren't," Finn replied. "But you're the one out here looking for him now. What about the family he was placed with, what are they doing?"

Hayley bit back a barrage of unkind thoughts about the

Michaelsons. "They have several kids at their place. I'm sure they're doing their best."

Finn narrowed his eyes. "Yeah?"

She looked away. The Michaelsons weren't her favorite foster family, but they seemed to do what they could, and that was more than she could say for some.

"I'm just learning Gage's story, and so far I know you're the one feeding him lunch every day. You're the one he came to see when something was wrong. You know about his art, and there's pride in your eyes when you look at it. Even though you know defacing public property is a crime. I'd say the two of you have chosen one another, regardless of the court's decision. You should see what you can do about that after we find him."

Hayley blinked back tears at the perfection of his words and the sincerity in the delivery. "He's a good kid. He shouldn't be painting the buildings, but he's not hurting anything down here, and he's working through his stuff." She scanned their surroundings in search of Gage's work and spotted an example several buildings away. Finn was right. She was proud of the kid's talent, and his outlet of choice. Plenty of other young adults in his situation would lash out with violence or fall into drug use. Gage chose to send messages to others who felt unseen, and to the system that made them feel that way.

She moved toward the painting in slow motion, drawn by something she couldn't put a finger on.

"What do you see?" Finn asked, falling into step at her side.

"It's unfinished." She lifted a finger to the silhouette when she noticed the missing section. "Why would he leave it like that?"

Finn examined the place where the image ended abruptly. "Out of paint?" he mused.

Hayley spotted a can on the ground across the street and

went to pick it up. She gave the cylinder a shake then pointed the nozzle at the ground and pressed. A thick stream of black emerged.

Finn grunted. "We're not far from the rave location. He said he saw something he shouldn't?"

She turned slowly, following his train of thought. "He could've been standing across the street, painting, when something went wrong. Then he ran."

"Raves are nice and loud," Finn said. "Plenty of people and chaos. Easy place to disappear."

And Winthrop's warehouse had a giant escape hatch in back.

A spike of adrenaline shot through her. She was likely standing where Gage had been when he'd seen the thing that scared him. If she was right, then she knew what he'd been doing and where he'd run to hide. "What did he see?"

She scanned the area with new eyes, searching all the places and things visible from her standpoint. An apparition of heat rolled like fog above the street. The rising sun baked her fair skin.

Finn rubbed the back of his neck. "With a rave going on nearby, there would've been a lot of witnesses if something happened on the street. I'd guess he saw something done discreetly, through a window or in an alley."

"It's not uncommon for people to keep their mouths shut about crime," Hayley said. "No one wants to get involved or become a snitch."

"But Gage ran," Finn countered. "He'd had a safe and normal life last year. So the question becomes, did he run explicitly out of fear, or because he was being chased?"

"Chased," Hayley said, suddenly confident in her answer. "Why run through the rave if not? And why was the can over here, when he was painting across the street, and the rave was down there?"

Finn looked from Hayley to the incomplete artwork, then down the block to Winthrop's warehouse. "The can could've been kicked or blown over—" Finn's words stopped short, and his gaze fixed on something.

"What is it?" Hayley asked, moving closer to watch and listen.

"My gut," he said. "See the big orange *Xs* painted on those doors?"

She followed his line of sight to the set of buildings in question. All were in rough shape, but none appeared any worse than the other structures around them. "It means they're marked for demolition."

"They're being razed for Kate's project," Finn added. "She purchased a large section of adjoining properties. Construction won't begin until next year, but removal of everything in the work zone starts in a few weeks. I read up on all the details after she went missing." He turned to Hayley, eyes wary. "Kate disappeared two nights ago."

"The same night Gage saw something." Hayley considered the unlikely possibility that her friend's disappearance could have anything to do with a wealthy philanthropist. "Kate wouldn't have any reason to visit this place at night, would she?" Or at all? Didn't investors only show up when their projects were complete? To cut a ribbon with giant scissors and make a public speech?

Finn took a step toward the nearest building with a big, orange *X*. He bumped her as he passed. "We might as well take a look around while we're here."

"You don't think the two are connected?"

He tipped his head noncommittally, left then right. "Probably not, but I like to cover my bases."

Hayley stepped aside when they reached the door, allowing Finn to try the knob.

Her heart rate climbed as the barrier creaked open. A wall of heat and sour air sent them back a step.

Finn covered his mouth and nose with the collar of his shirt, while she fought the urge to gag. “Stay here.”

Hayley easily complied, angling her face away, desperate for the fresher air.

A low guttural moan and series of cuss words rose from the detective inside. He crouched over a still form covered in newspapers and raised a cell phone to his ear. “We’ve got a crime scene,” he said.

“Is that…?” Hayley asked.

He glanced remorsefully in her direction. “Yeah.” He stretched upright and returned to the doorway. “This is Detective Finn Beaumont,” he told the person on the other end of his call. “I need the coroner and a CSI team with complete discretion. No lights or sirens. Unmarked vehicles. I’ve just found the body of Katherine Everett.”

Chapter Six

Hayley leaned against a telephone pole on the sidewalk near Gage's unfinished painting while men and women swarmed the street, working the crime scene. The first responders on-site wore plain clothes, as Finn had requested. Those who came later had on ball caps and T-shirts with the Marshal's Bluff PD logo, or the simple black polos of the coroner's office. A handful, presently taking photographs, setting up small, numbered teepees, or swabbing the building for trace evidence, wore lanyards and carried toolboxes with *CSI* emblazoned on them.

Hayley used the massive wooden pole at her back for support and concentrated on her breathing. She didn't need a criminal-justice degree to know what Gage had seen that night. And how much trouble he was in now. There'd be a large bounty on the head of the person who killed Katherine Everett, beloved community member and philanthropist. She and her family's money single-handedly funded two seasonal soup kitchens, kept the lights on at the mission's shelter for women and children and made sure no Marshal's Bluff student left school on weekends, holidays or summer breaks without food. Her family had the means to hunt down anyone with information about her murder. Making Gage a major liability to the killer.

Understanding why anyone would want to harm her was another story.

The coroner had declared the cause of death as blunt-force trauma. The weapon, a broken two-by-four, had done irreparable damage to her skull and brain. The bullet in her chest was unnecessary excess.

A commotion at the opposite curb drew Hayley's attention to a news van, the first of what would undoubtedly be many within the hour. Thankfully, Kate's body was long gone, removed from the crime scene by the coroner as quickly as possible following his arrival. There'd been a brief exam, preliminary findings were recorded, then she was loaded into the van and taken away. The media wouldn't get the salacious photos they hoped for today.

Officers met the crew as they climbed out, directing them to relocate behind the barricades a block away.

Yep, Hayley thought. *Chaos is coming.*

An unmistakable thrumming drew her eyes to the sky, where a helicopter appeared, bearing the local television station's call number in bright red.

Word was definitely out now.

A sharp whistle turned her around and raised an unexpected smile on her lips.

Austin and Dean Beaumont appeared. They strode in her direction, long legs eating up the distance to her side.

Austin lifted her off the ground in a hug, and Dean embraced her the moment his little brother set her free. They smiled broadly, offering warm greetings and reminding her of another reason she'd loved being in Finn's life. His brothers were the very best.

"We just heard about this," Dean said, blue eyes flashing with interest. "We were hired to take the missing-persons case this morning."

"Barely started our research before the call came," Austin added. "This is messed up."

"Agreed," Hayley said.

Dean scanned the bustling scene, then shot the chopper a death stare. "She was a huge proponent of good things here. I can't understand who'd do this."

"That makes two of us," Hayley said.

"Three," Austin countered. "How much do you know?"

Hayley exchanged information with the brothers, falling easily into the familiar rapport. Austin was a Beaumont by blood. Dean and his younger brother, Jake, an ATF agent, had been adopted as kids, not that it mattered, or anyone ever talked about it. Still, in her line of work, and with her heart set on gaining custody of Gage, it warmed her to know families could blend and heal into one perfect unit when enough love and dedication was involved. She had both in spades.

Austin folded his arms, taking in the scene. "You think your missing kid saw what happened?"

She nodded and pointed to the unfinished painting. "I think he was painting when he saw her murder, or the killer leaving the scene, and ran."

Dean scrubbed a hand through thick, dark hair and swore. "That'd put a target on his back. Whoever killed Kate will know her family has the money and connections necessary to find them."

Austin's gaze traveled thoughtfully over the silhouette painted on the nearby building. "Your kid painted this?"

Hayley nodded, pride filling her chest.

"He's good."

"He is," she agreed.

Gage's potential to heal from his unthinkable losses and become a man who made a difference in the world was outstanding. Even if he felt lost sometimes, Hayley could see the warm, bright future out there waiting for him. And she'd stick by him until he saw it too.

"I've noticed these shadow people popping up around here for a few months," Austin said. "I wondered who was responsible." He turned an appreciative look her way. "I'm impressed the artist is just a kid."

Hayley swallowed the lump in her throat. "He's a good kid who's had a bad year, and he doesn't deserve any of this."

Dean gave Hayley a pat on her back, then headed across the street toward Finn.

Austin watched him go, then squinted appraisingly at Hayley.

Goose bumps rose on her skin. It was already unfair that Beaumont men were so disarmingly attractive, but the fact they also seemed to share some kind of mind-reading ability was just too much. She rolled her eyes. "What?"

"Long time no see. Where ya been hiding, Campbell?"

She looked away, in no kind of headspace for the conversation he wanted.

"Okay," he relented, breaking into a ridiculously breathtaking smile. "I get it. We can talk about what happened between you and my brother another time."

"I'm literally never talking to you about that," she said sweetly. "Ever."

"Wrong."

Hayley laughed despite herself. "Goof."

Finn's pain had no doubt affected everyone who loved him. She was sorry about that, but there was only one person she'd discuss her failed relationship with, and it was Finn, not Austin.

"I know some people out this way," he said, changing the subject. "I'll put out some feelers and see what I can learn about your boy. One thing that's always true in this business is that nothing goes completely unseen. If my informants can't dig him up, or won't tell me where he is, I can at least ask them to keep him safe until we find whoever's responsible for this." He tipped his head toward the building where Kate's body had been found.

Unexpected emotion stung her eyes and blurred her vision. The idea strangers might look out for Gage until she could do the job herself pulled her heartstrings. Renegade tears rolled over her cheeks, and she swiped them away.

"Hey now." Austin stepped forward, pulling her against his chest and wrapping her in a hug. He rubbed her back in small, awkward strokes. "We'll find him and bring him back to you safely. That's a promise."

Hayley returned his embrace, holding on tight to her would-have-been brother-in-law and to a thousand silent prayers that he was right.

FINN'S GAZE DRIFTED past Dean's shoulder, drawn to Hayley yet again. He couldn't quite believe she'd dropped back into his life after a year of silence, or that she was really standing across the street right now. Had they actually spent the day together? And how was she so wholly unaffected by their split, when it had broken him completely?

They'd been in love. He'd proposed, and she'd vanished.

The memory still gutted him, but he was glad to see she was doing well. Even at his worst, he'd hated the possibility she was sad or alone. He'd had a horde of family members to comfort and annoy him during the tough times. Hayley didn't have that.

Across the street, Austin's smile faded and he embraced her. Hayley held him tight.

"What do you suppose that's about?" Dean asked.

"It's been a day," Finn answered honestly. And it was barely afternoon. "I'm sure she needed it."

"We all miss her, ya know?" Dean asked.

"I know."

Hayley fit with his family in ways he never dreamed someone could. She belonged with them, if not with him. And he hoped that maybe, after this case was closed, she'd come around more often. She didn't have to be lonely when there was an army of Beaumonts who loved her. If she wanted them, he'd even keep himself in check so she wouldn't feel as if their presence in her life required his.

"You ever find out what happened with her?" Dean asked.

"Why she loved me one minute and disappeared on me the next?" Finn squinted against the southern summer sun. "Nope. And I don't plan on it. If she wants me to know, she'll tell me."

"Funny she didn't call the police about the gunman or her missing kid," Dean said, his tone painfully casual.

Finn frowned. "She came directly to the station."

Dean nodded, keen gaze darting back across the street to Hayley and Finn. "Most people get shot at, they call 911."

"And?"

"She drove straight to you."

Finn widened his stance and crossed his arms over his chest. "Because she's smart."

Dean grinned.

"I plan to find her missing kid as soon as possible," Finn said. "Likely before we figure out who's after him. I'd like to set him up at the ranch until I'm sure he'll be safe elsewhere. I can't promise he won't run again if we take him back to the foster home, and Hayley will want to keep him with her if he doesn't stay there."

"That'd put her in danger," Dean said.

"Exactly. Any idea how many beds are open at the ranch right now?"

"No, but there's always room for one more," Dean said,

quoting their mama. "I'll let her know he's coming when I drop in for dinner."

Finn nodded his gratitude. "He paints those."

Dean followed his raised finger to the painting behind Hayley and Finn. "She mentioned that. Kid's got talent."

"And a heart for people. Probably one of the reasons Hayley bonded with him so quickly."

"He'll be a good fit at the ranch," Dean said. "Lincoln can show him the ropes. Redirect his energies. Give him another outlet while this is sorted."

"Good idea. Lincoln could use a project involving people." Their brother, a recent veteran and current stable hand, spent too much time alone, brooding, with the animals. "He'd be feral by now, if not for Josi."

Dean puffed air through his nose. "I don't know how she puts up with him, but they make it work."

Finn couldn't help wondering how long they'd continue to make it work after Lincoln realized he was in love with the young stable manager, but that answer would come in time.

"Heads up," Dean said, pulling Finn's attention to Hayley and Austin.

The pair headed across the street.

Hayley appeared unsure, as if she might be asked to vacate the crime scene, even with the three of them at her side. Austin looked as he always did, entitled to be anywhere he pleased.

"Hey there, brother," Austin said, offering Finn the quick two-step handshake they'd adopted in high school. "Your girl caught me up on things. Now, what's our move?"

Finn ignored the pinch in his chest at Austin's word choice, then turned to the beauty at his side. "I think it's time to let your office know you'll be out for a few more days. Until we identify Katherine Everett's killer, we'll need a revised plan for your safety."

Hayley nodded. “Okay.”

And Finn would start by accepting that spare bedroom she’d mentioned this morning.

Chapter Seven

Hayley curled on her couch that night with a bottle of water and take-out tacos. She and Finn had left the crime scene shortly after his brothers' arrival, and she'd tagged along when Finn was called to the station. A few hours later, they'd picked up dinner. Nothing about her day seemed real. In fact, she'd spent the past twenty-four hours feeling as if she was trapped in a terrible dream. Gage's fear. His disappearance. The gunman. Now a dead socialite. None of it made any sense.

Still, the truth sat two cushions away, unwrapping his third El Guaco Taco. The urge to poke Finn with a finger, just to make sure she wasn't dreaming, circled in her thoughts. Her one true love, and almost-fiancé, was at her home after a year of silence between them, and planning to sleep over. For her protection. Was any of this even real?

"Ow." Finn turned amused eyes on her. "What was that for?"

She bent the finger she'd poked him with and returned the hand to her lap. "Making sure I'm awake," she admitted. "This day has me questioning everything."

"Well, I appreciate the offer to stay in the spare room," he said, running a paper napkin over his lips. "The truck isn't as comfortable as it looks."

Hayley laughed, surprising herself and earning a grin from Finn.

He gathered their discarded wrappers when they finished, then headed for her kitchen.

"You don't have to clean up," she called, twisting to watch him over the back of the couch as he walked away.

"And you didn't have to let me stay here, but you did." He retook his seat a moment later, a little closer to her this time.

"Do you really think someone might show up here?" she asked, images of the man outside the black SUV flashing through her mind.

Finn offered a small, encouraging smile. "I don't want you to worry, so consider this a favor to me. I always assume the worst where criminals are concerned, and in a worst-case scenario, I can do a much better job protecting you from in here than from outside. Plus, this gives me peace of mind, which means I might get some sleep. I need the rest if I'm going to find Gage and capture Kate's killer as soon as possible."

Hayley relaxed by a fraction. "Have I thanked you for helping me? Because it's all I can think about. I needed someone, and you were the only name in my head. After everything that happened between us, you never hesitated."

"Did you think I might?" he asked, a note of concern in his tone.

"No," she said instantly, and honestly. "But it still feels unbelievable. I owe you—"

"Ten bucks for tacos?" he asked, shifting forward and taking his gaze with him. "Don't worry about it."

Finn might not want to hear it, but she had things she needed to say.

"An apology."

"We don't need to talk about that right now."

"Finn." Hayley swiveled on her seat to face him fully. "We should've talked about this a year ago, but I was a coward."

He shook his head, still not meeting her eye. "It's fine. It's in the past. What matters most now is that you knew you could come to me. I will find Gage, and Dean's talked to our folks. Gage can stay at the ranch until we know he's safe. They're already making room. You and I can visit as often as you want while we find the person who's been following you and hunting him."

Hayley's heart swelled at Finn's casual use of the word *we*. He wasn't pulling the detective card or shoving her away. He certainly had every right, especially when he hadn't let her apologize or explain why she'd vanished on him last year. He deserved so much better.

Finn's phone rang and his lips twitched with the hint of a smile as he looked at the display. He lifted a finger to Hayley, indicating he needed a moment before he answered.

An immediate and nonsensical stroke of displeasure coursed through her. Was he seeing someone? Did she care? She certainly had no right.

"Hey, Mama," he said. "Everything okay?"

Hayley grabbed her water bottle for a long drink, then worked to get her head on straight. She wasn't the jealous type, and she had no claim to Finn. Clearly, all the turmoil from a wild day had scrambled her brain.

"Which channel?" he asked, pulling Hayley's attention to him once more.

She grabbed the television remote and passed it his way.

"Thanks, Mama. Love you." He disconnected the call and navigated to the local news. "They're covering Kate's case on Channel Three."

"I saw the chopper this morning."

"Yeah," he said. "I guess they sent a crew later."

Finn leaned forward, resting his elbows on his thighs as he waited.

Two overly charismatic anchors announced the next segment, and Finn pumped up the volume.

Soon the streets of Old Downtown appeared. Words scrolled across the bottom of the screen announcing "Death of a Philanthropist: Body of Katherine Everett located among trash in abandoned building."

"She was covered in newspapers," Finn complained. "It was meant to disguise the body as a sleeping squatter. They make it sound as if she was tossed beside a pile of garbage bags, or worse. The media always has to sensationalize everything." He kneaded together his hands, visibly annoyed. "They do this junk intentionally for views, and it gets the public all wound up. Then the phone lines at the station are bombarded for a week with citizens worried about a million nonemergency, nonthreatening things."

Hayley tucked her feet beneath her and focused on the television. She knew exactly what he meant. Anytime something bad happened in town, the local news blew it up as big as they could and anxiety rose across the board. Social workers, counselors and medical professionals all saw corresponding rises in their workload for as long as the secondary situation continued being covered.

On the TV screen, a reporter stood outside the building where Kate's body had been found. The sun was low in the sky, the CSI team gone, as she gave the most generic of comments about the day's events.

"This is good," Finn said. "Sounds as if we've kept a lid on the details." The relief in his features touched Hayley's heart.

Finn gave his all in everything he did.

He'd done a lot of very nice things with her once.

She shook away the sudden rush of heat and memories as the camera angle changed, widening to reveal a familiar face at the reporter's side. "A local private detective, Austin Beaumont, has been at the scene all day."

Finn groaned. "This explains why Mama was watching the news. He must've told her he'd be on."

"Why didn't he tell you?" Hayley asked.

The look on Finn's face suggested he could think of a number of reasons his brother hadn't mentioned the on-screen interview, and none of them were great.

"Can you tell us what brought you to Old Downtown today?" the reporter asked. "Were you hired to assist in the investigation of Katherine Everett's murder? Was it Marshal's Bluff PD who reached out to you, or was it a private party?"

Austin sucked his teeth and stared at the camera. "At Beaumont Investigations, we take privacy seriously, and we don't answer questions." He tipped two fingers to the brim of his hat and walked away.

Hayley burst into laughter.

Finn smiled as he watched her. "I thought that was going to go much more poorly. He hates reporters."

"Well, he's smart," she said. "He parlayed that annoyance into excellent business exposure."

Finn lifted the remote, whether to turn the television off or the volume down, she wasn't sure, but her breath caught as a familiar figure and dark SUV appeared on-screen. "What's wrong?" he asked.

Hayley blinked, afraid the man might disappear if she looked away. "I think that's the guy I saw outside the parking lot when I found the note."

Finn paused the television before the scene could change. Then he lifted his phone once more.

A mass of chills ran down Hayley's spine, and a slight tremor began in her hands.

"Ball cap. Sunglasses. Black T-shirt," Finn said to someone on the phone. He pointed the remote toward her television again and the SUV rolled off-screen.

"Dammit," Finn said. "They didn't catch the plate." He wrapped up his call and turned to her. "How do you feel about staying at my place?"

"Not great," she said honestly. "I'm hoping Gage will realize he needs help and come here to find me."

Finn leveled her with his trademark no-nonsense stare. "I understand that, but I can protect you better there."

She dithered, frozen by an impossible choice. How could she risk missing Gage? But how could she know he'd come? If he didn't seek her, and she or Finn were injured as a result of waiting for him, it would be her fault. If she left and Gage was injured after arriving and not finding the help he needed, it would be her fault.

"I can assign someone to keep an eye on the house," Finn said gently. "If Gage comes here, they'll intercept him."

Her heart dropped at the possibility Gage would come to her home for help, and she wouldn't be there.

"I have a guest room too," he reminded her. "It's not the same as sleeping in your own bed, but at least you'll know you aren't in danger."

"I'm not sure I'll be able to rest anywhere tonight," she admitted.

Not with Finn under the same roof.

"What if I remind you that the minute my mama knows you're there she'll be on her way with casseroles and hugs? All shameless ploys to keep you."

Hayley thought of Mrs. Beaumont's warm hugs and casseroles, then pushed onto her feet. Everyone would be safer if she agreed to Finn's terms, and that was all that mattered. "Who can say no to your mama's casseroles?"

"No one yet."

"I guess I'd better get dressed and pack a bag," she said, heading swiftly toward the stairs.

"Mama wins again."

FINN DROVE SLOWLY to his place, watching carefully for signs of a tail. He'd been concerned twice in town, but as the traffic and bustle of Marshal's Bluff gave way to rural back roads lined with farms and livestock, his truck quickly became the only vehicle in sight.

Dean and Austin were already in place. They'd swept the property and posted up as additional eyes to verify Finn and Hayley arrived safely.

The home had been purchased under the name of a limited-liability corporation to increase anonymity. And he'd spent several long weekends outfitting the place with abundant security measures.

Still, an influx of misplaced dread tightened his gut as they drew nearer. The last time Hayley had visited Finn's home, he'd proposed. He'd spent hours preparing that day, lining the driveway and drenching the sprawling trees in twinkle lights. Even longer practicing what he would say. The weight of the engagement ring in his pocket had felt life-affirming. He'd known without a doubt that the woman at his side was meant for him, and he would've done everything in his power to make her happy. Forever.

An hour later, she'd been gone. And his phone hadn't stopped ringing for days as the news swept through his family.

"I forgot how beautiful this place is," Hayley said, pulling him back to the moment.

Security lighting illuminated his home and perimeter landscaping now. Hidden cameras tracked and reported everything to a system inside. Silhouettes of his brothers' parked vehicles came into view at the back of the home as the driveway snaked around an incline.

Two familiar figures moved into view, hands raised in greeting as Finn drove the final few yards.

"Looks like we're all clear," he said, glancing her way.

Hayley's smile was radiant. "I'm always amazed by how intimidating this couple of goofballs can appear."

Finn shifted the truck into Park and considered his approaching brothers once more, trying to see them from someone else's perspective.

They were tall and broad, moving in near sync with long, determined strides. Their expressions were hidden beneath the shadows of plain black ball caps. He supposed, at first glance, or if he squinted a little, he could imagine them as dangerous. But anytime he saw Austin and Dean working together like this, he could only think of the time they'd attempted to build a tree house, only to wind up in a fight over the design that rolled them both off the platform.

Finn climbed out to thank their personal protection detail. They exchanged greetings and farewells, then Finn grabbed Hayley's bags and led her into his home.

He watched from the window as his brothers' taillights shrank in the distance—but he knew they wouldn't go far. Dean and Austin would likely split up and take shifts. One keeping watch on Finn's home, the other running leads on Gage's whereabouts. Like Finn, the PIs wouldn't get much sleep until this was over.

"I'll take your things to the guest room," Finn said, turning back to Hayley. "Make yourself at home. Consider this place yours until it's safe for you to go home."

"Thank you."

Finn moved through the open-concept living space and kitchen to a hallway with three bedrooms and a shared bath. His throat tightened as he fought a wave of unexpected and unpleasant emotions. Now wasn't the time to get nostalgic or wish things had gone differently. They hadn't. And that was life.

"Wow," Hayley said, her voice carrying to his ears. "You've completely remodeled."

He opened the guest-room door and set her bags on the

bed, allowing himself one long breath before squaring his shoulders and heading back. "Yeah."

He'd taken his excess energy out on his home following their breakup, starting with refaced cabinets, new countertops and a farmhouse sink in the kitchen. Refinished floors, new paint and light fixtures everywhere else. He'd barely had a day off in the last year that hadn't involved at least one trip to the local hardware store.

"It's great," she said. "I love it."

"Thanks." Finn emerged from the hallway to find her admiring the kitchen. "Can I get you something to drink?"

She shook her head and her cheeks darkened.

He told himself she wasn't thinking of the things they'd done on his old countertop, and he pushed the thoughts from his mind as well.

"I should probably try to sleep," she said.

"Of course. I've got some work to do so…" He let his eyes fall shut when she passed him, making the trip to her room, not his.

THE SOUND OF the doorbell shot Finn onto his feet the next morning. He stumbled back, knocking his calves against the couch and blinking away the remnants of sleep he hadn't meant to get. A bevy of curses ran through his thoughts as he moved forward, wiping his eyes and hoping to stop the bell from chiming again.

A rush of breath left his chest as he passed the front window. A familiar truck was parked beyond the porch. He checked his watch, then opened the door.

His parents waited outside, smiling brightly as the barrier swung wide.

"Morning, Mama," he said, planting a kiss on her head as she hustled past.

"Morning, baby boy," she cooed, already halfway to the kitchen. She'd tied her salt-and-pepper hair away from her face in a low ponytail and wore jeans with boots and a T-shirt. Oven mitts covered her hands, a foil-covered casserole in her grip.

Finn was still wearing the sweatpants and T-shirt he'd changed into before beginning his online research the night before.

"Dad." He drew the older man into a quick hug, then followed him to the new granite-topped island.

"Morning."

Finn dragged a hand through sleep-mussed hair and rubbed fatigue from his eyes. "Can't say I'm surprised to see y'all, but you could've waited until at least eight."

"We've been up since five thirty," his dad said, adjusting the cowboy hat on his head. His black T-shirt was new and emblazoned with the ranch insignia. His jeans and boots were probably from the year he'd gotten married. "Your mama's been trying to get me out the door since six."

Mrs. Beaumont tucked the casserole into Finn's oven and set the timer. "He came up with every chore under the sun to do before we could leave."

"That's the life of a farmer," his dad said, setting additional dishes and bags onto the counter. "Can't be helped."

"We have farm hands," she countered. "You were stalling."

"You were rushing."

Mama shrugged and turned her eyes to Finn. "Where is Hayley? Can we see her?"

"She's not a puppy," his father said. "And she's probably still in bed. It's barely seven a.m."

"Nonsense. Who's sleeping at this hour?"

Finn raised a hand. "I was sleeping until you rang the bell."

"Silly." His mama fixed him with a no-nonsense stare. "It's time to start your day. We've heard all about what's going on. It was smart of you to bring Hayley here. She's much safer in our hands than alone at her place."

Finn traded a look with their father. His mother's use of the word *our* implied that she planned to stay involved. Probably not the best idea, but there was little to be done about it. No one talked her out of anything. Ever.

"We fixed up the storage cabin for the missing boy. Gage, is it?" she asked. "He'll like it. Tell me about him."

Soft footfalls turned all their heads to the hallway, where Hayley appeared. Her pink cotton sleep shorts and white tank top were slightly askew. As if she'd hurried out of bed without thought of straightening them. Emotion crumpled her features. "Morning, Mama," she said, voice cracking.

"Sweet girl," his mama said, a moment before engulfing her in a hug.

A lump formed in Finn's throat as his father welcomed her back too.

Working this case without getting his heart broken again in the process was quickly disappearing as an option.

Chapter Eight

Hayley sank into the Beaumonts' welcoming arms. Though she prided herself on her fierce independence, there was something about a group hug from good parents, even if they weren't hers, that made everything better. Mr. and Mrs. Beaumont treated the entire world like family. They'd cared for her emotionally since the day they'd met, celebrating her victories, asking about her troubles and supporting her silently when she just needed to be in the presence of someone who truly saw her. She'd missed them horribly for the past year, but the weight of their absence hadn't fully hit until now.

She wiped her eyes discreetly as the couple pulled away. Then she smiled through tears of joy. "It's so nice to see you again."

"We brought food," Mrs. Beaumont said, batting away a few renegade tears. "There's a casserole warming in the oven, and I prepared some sandwiches, potato salad, fruit salad and a cheese-and-cracker assortment for later. There's a lasagna in the freezer, and a pie in the fridge."

A bubble of laughter broke on Hayley's lips. She looked to Finn, and found him smiling as well. The expression sent a jolt of warmth through her core.

Mr. Beaumont carried a pile of plates to the island, arranging one before each stool. Finn poured coffee into four mugs, and their fearless matriarch bustled cheerfully, preparing for the meal.

This could have been Hayley's life.

Every day.

But she'd let fear and unhealed trauma take that from her, and it was too late to get it back.

Hayley shoved aside past regrets and focused on the present. "Did I hear you say you've made room for Gage at the ranch?"

Mr. and Mrs. Beaumont turned to her, pride in their nearly matching expressions.

"We did," Mr. Beaumont said. "We turned one of the small storage cabins into a private space for him. He'll have plenty of room for independence and privacy while still being a stone's throw from us." He turned a thumb back and forth between his wife and himself. "Lincoln will work with him until he finds his rhythm."

Mrs. Beaumont's expression melted into concern. "Is that okay? We haven't overstepped?"

Hayley refreshed her smile, realizing it had begun to droop. "No. Of course not. The cabin sounds perfect. Thank you."

Finn moved in her direction and set a hand between her shoulder blades. "Gage is very important to Hayley," he said, giving voice to her thoughts when her tongue became wholly tied.

She dropped her gaze to the floor. "I should've fought for the ability to foster him the moment we met. I should be the one caring for him."

"You are." Finn spread his fingers and pressed gently against her back, offering the reassurance she craved.

When she raised her eyes to his, electricity crackled in the air.

Mr. Beaumont cleared his throat, breaking the strange spell. He exchanged a look with his wife. "We know quite a few people in positions to help you when the time comes. You can count on that."

Hayley's bottom lip quivered, and she nodded, unable to speak once more.

The Beaumonts had strong ties to everyone in the courthouse and offices related to child and family services. Their ranch was a major player in the rehabilitation and healing of youths. If anyone had the ability to influence related outcomes, it was them.

"Here, sweet girl," Mrs. Beaumont said, approaching and separating Hayley from Finn. "Let me feed you. Then you can tell us all about the boy who stole your heart."

Hayley's traitorous gaze moved to Finn and back to his mother, who'd caught the slip.

Mrs. Beaumont added scoops of casserole and warm, sliced bread to their plates. His father served fruit salad, and Finn delivered the caffeine.

Together, they took their seats and dug in.

Hayley told the Beaumonts all she knew and loved about Gage. Then she shared the little she'd learned about his disappearance. The older couple listened carefully. When the plates were mostly empty, Hayley's heart and stomach full, Mrs. Beaumont turned serious eyes on her son.

"Tell me what you know about Kate's death," she directed Finn.

He caught her up quickly, then refilled everyone's mugs.

"It's a real shame," his mother said. "Kate was a special woman. Her heart for this town and its citizens was huge. She was smart in business and driven by her compassion. I can't imagine who'd want to stop her."

"Was it a robbery?" his dad asked.

Finn shook his head. "Unlikely. She didn't have a purse or identification on her, which could point to a mugging, except that she was still wearing a watch and necklace with a combined value higher than my annual salary. And someone covered her in newspapers. Could've been a sign of regret as much as an attempt to disguise the body. The missing purse was possibly a failed attempt to misdirect the police or hide her identity."

"Any suspects?" Mrs. Beaumont asked.

"None that stand out for now," Finn said, taking a long pull on his coffee. "Finding our young witness will be a major help."

Hayley chewed her lip, reminded again that Gage was in hiding, alone and scared.

"I've got plans to interview the husband and some workers from the charity," Finn said. "We'll visit Gage's foster family while we're out, see if we can make some progress on that end as well."

"I doubt they know anything," Hayley said. "If he'd gone back there, someone would've called me."

"Speaking to the other foster kids could be useful," Finn said. "When I was young, I told my brothers everything."

"Still do," his mother said, looking slightly affronted. "Luckily, I've got a sixth sense for when something is going on with my kids, and I can usually press the weak link for information."

"For the record, I was never the weak link," Finn declared, one palm against his chest.

Hayley smiled, falling easily into rhythm with the family she'd always wanted. The family she could've had.

If she hadn't panicked and blown it.

FINN PILOTED HIS truck into the Michaelsons' driveway an hour later. His parents had hurried away after breakfast to handle business on the ranch, and Hayley had gotten ready quickly for a new day of investigation.

Despite the heat, she'd chosen jeans that stopped midcalf,

sneakers and a blue silk tank top that accentuated her eyes and her curves.

"Here we go," she said, climbing down from the cab.

Finn met her at the front of his truck and reached for her hand. She accepted easily, and he squeezed her fingers before releasing her to lead the way to the door.

The old clapboard home was gray from age and weather. The red front door was battered with dents and dings. An array of toys and children's bikes cluttered the overgrown front lawn and walkway. All in all, it wasn't an idyllic scene, but Finn tried not to judge.

"How many kids are living here?" he asked, scrutinizing the postage-stamp yard and modest home.

"Five," Hayley said. "There are three bedrooms. Three middle-schoolers in one. Gage and a younger boy in another. Mr. and Mrs. Michaelson in the last."

Finn stared into the overflowing trash receptacle as Hayley rang the bell. Beer bottles were visible inside the bags. He had no problem with enjoying a drink or two, but there were more than a few visible bottles.

The door swept open before Finn could point out his concerns.

A woman in her late forties blinked against the sun. Her wide brown eyes were tired, her frame thin and shoulders curved. "Miss Campbell?" the woman asked, clearly stunned to see Hayley, though the disappearance of a child in her care should've made this meeting obvious and inevitable.

"Hello, Stacy," Hayley said. "May we come in?"

The woman stepped onto the porch, pulling her door shut behind her. "Sorry. Everyone is still sleeping. Can we talk here?"

Hayley's eyes darted to the closed door and back. She forced a tight smile. "Of course. This is my friend, Detective Beaumont. We're here to talk to you about Gage."

The woman looked at Finn, skin paling. "I'm not sure what you mean."

Finn flashed his badge, blank cop expression in place. "Can you tell us anything more about his disappearance? Have you heard from him? Any idea where he might've gone?"

She wrapped her arms around her middle, thin dark hair floating above her shoulders in the wind. A T-shirt and jeans hung from her gaunt frame, and heavy makeup circled her eyes. "Gage hasn't been home in a while now. I've asked everyone and searched everywhere but no one has seen him. Teenagers are like that. Always running off and disappearing. Probably one of the reasons it's so hard to find families who will take kids his age."

Hayley's jaw dropped, and Finn pressed a palm discreetly against her back.

"Ma'am, I'm quite familiar with teens and young people who struggle," he said. "I grew up at the Beaumont ranch, have you heard of it?"

She worked her jaw. "Sure."

"I've spent a lifetime in this arena, and in my experience, kids come home when they can. Assuming this is a safe place offering food, shelter and welcoming arms."

"Of course, it is." She tutted and slid her eyes to Hayley. "We offer all those things here."

Finn straightened to his full height, drawing the other woman's attention once more. "In that case, we have to ask what's stopped him from being here these past couple of nights. And every answer I can think of is reason for your concern, not contempt."

"Couple of nights?" Mrs. Michaelson raised an eyebrow. "That kid has barely bothered to spend more than a few hours at a time here in weeks."

"Weeks!" Hayley yipped. "What do you mean? How is that even possible?"

Mrs. Michaelson shrugged. "I told you—teens like their space. I can hardly help it if Gage won't stick around."

Finn opened his mouth to speak, but Hayley beat him to it.

"Why haven't you reported him missing?" Hayley demanded. "Or as a runaway?"

"He's a teen," Mrs. Michaelson said dryly. "They come and go. Besides, he always comes back eventually."

A little gasping sound leaped from Hayley's mouth. Her pointer finger flew up, and Finn grabbed it, covering her entire tiny fist with his.

He gave a small shake of his head when she struggled. "Ms. Campbell has lunch regularly with Gage and had no prior knowledge that there was a problem here."

"Guess he had you fooled too," the woman sneered.

Finn released Hayley and widened his stance, catching Mrs. Michaelson with his most pointed gaze. "You've continued to receive and deposit payments from the state for his full-time care, though you've only seen him a few hours at a time?"

The smug expression slowly bled from her face.

Hayley stiffened. "If you can't be bothered to report one of the children in your care as missing, it's clearly time for a thorough review of your status as a foster family. I'm guessing no children should be staying here."

"Well, good luck finding anyone to take in these teens. Besides, it sounds as if you're the one who dropped the ball on Gage. Not us." She ducked back inside and pulled the door shut hard behind her.

Hayley made a deep sound low in her throat. She turned and stormed up the walkway toward Finn's truck, towing him along by the hand.

Finn spun Hayley to face him when they reached the passenger-side door. The tears in her eyes tore through his heart like talons. "Hey," he whispered, stealing a look at the home before pulling Hayley against his chest with ease. "This isn't your fault. She's in the wrong and trying to project that back on you. Her anger and accusations were redirects. Nothing more." He ran the backs of his fingers gently along her cheek, then tucked a swath of hair behind her ear. "We'll figure this out. Together. Okay?"

She nodded and wiped away a stream of falling teardrops. "Okay."

A red playground ball rolled into view from behind a patch of hedges, and a dirty-faced kid crept out to grab it. He startled when he saw Finn and Hayley watching. "My ball," he said in explanation, moving slowly to retrieve the toy. "I'm not supposed to play out front."

Finn's gaze jerked to the home and back to the boy. "You live with the Michaelsons?"

He nodded.

So much for everyone being asleep, as Mrs. Michaelson had said.

"I'm Finn. What's your name?"

"Parker."

Hayley crouched before him, immediately bringing herself to the child's height. "Hi, Parker. I'm Hayley. Do you remember me?"

Another nod.

"Have you seen Gage lately?" she asked.

"No." The boy wet his lips and dared a look over one shoulder to the home at his back. "But he always comes back for me."

Finn's muscles tightened as he imagined all the reasons a teenage boy would come back for a kid who was no older than eight. "He took care of you when he was here?"

"Yes, sir."

Hayley glanced at Finn in alarm. "How did Gage take care of you?"

The kid hugged his ball but didn't speak.

"You can tell me anything," Hayley promised. "I won't tell the Michaelsons, and if you're unhappy here, I can help you with that."

Something Finn suspected was hope flashed in the boy's eyes.

"Gage shared his food when we got some, and he gave me water when we had to play outside all day. It gets hot. Sometimes we aren't allowed to go in, and I get a headache."

Hayley raised a hand to her mouth, but dropped it quickly away. "Gage is a great kid. So are you. I'm not surprised you're such good friends. Did he help you with anything else?"

"He told us all stories when the grown-ups fought."

"Do they fight a lot?" she asked.

Parker looked at his ball.

Finn considered that a big yes.

"Do you have any idea where Gage is now?" Hayley asked. "We're trying to find him and make sure he's okay."

"I think he went home," Parker whispered.

"Where's—" Finn's words were cut short when Parker suddenly stiffened, turned and ran away.

He darted into the trees along the lawn's edge as the front door opened, and Mrs. Michaelson stepped outside.

"What are you still doing here?" she yelled. "You can't just hang around on my property!"

Finn felt the anger vibrating from Hayley's small frame and opened the passenger door to usher her inside. "We'll sort this out with the courts," he said quietly. "Meanwhile, let's go before we stir up a bees' nest and possibly make things tougher for the kids."

He closed her door and rounded the hood, keeping one eye

on the angry woman in the distance. When he climbed into the cab, Hayley was on her cell phone.

"We need a wellness check at 1318 Sandpiper Lane," she told whoever was on the other end of the line. "I'd also like to request a full and comprehensive review of the Michaelsons."

Finn shifted into gear and pulled onto the street with a grin. It sounded as if smug Mrs. Michaelson was the one to open that can of worms, and Hayley Campbell was going to make her eat them.

The cell phone in his pocket began to ring as Hayley finished her call. Austin's number appeared on the dashboard console.

Finn tapped the screen to answer. "Hey, I've got you on speaker. I'm in the truck with Hayley."

"I'm glad you're together," Austin said. "I swung by Hayley's place, and it looks as if someone's inside. Since it's not you, I'm assuming it's a break-in. Things look secure from the front. They must've used a back door or a side window to enter."

Hayley dropped her cell phone to her lap. "Someone's inside my house?"

"Yep," Austin said. "I saw a light go on behind the curtain."

Finn took the next right, setting a course to Hayley's home. "Have you called it in?"

"Kind of what I'm doing now, Detective," Austin drawled.

Finn cast a look at Hayley's worried face, then returned his attention to the road. "Keep watch. We're on our way."

Chapter Nine

Hayley's muscles tensed as she processed the situation. She shifted and slid on the bench seat as Finn took a final wild turn into her neighborhood. "How long has Austin been watching my house?"

"Since last night. He and Dean have been taking shifts since they left my place."

Panic warred with appreciation in her chest as the truck roared onto her street, then entered her driveway.

Austin's truck stood empty at the end of the block.

Finn unlatched his seat belt and set a hand on the butt of his gun.

"What are you doing?" she whispered, curling nervous fingers around Finn's wrist before he attempted to leave her behind. "Shouldn't you text Austin to see where he is? Or call for backup?"

Finn gave her a pointed stare, and she released him. "I need you to wait here. Lock the doors. Keep your phone at the ready. I'll check the house and report back."

Hayley reached for her door's handle, then she climbed out of the cab.

Finn hurried after her. "What are you doing?" he hissed, speeding around the hood to meet her.

"I'm not waiting alone out here like a sitting duck," she

said. "I'll take my chances with whatever is going on in there. Right beside a trained lawman with a gun."

Finn pursed his lips but didn't argue. He tipped his head toward the front door, and she nodded.

Hayley moved along behind him, attempting to mimic his strides and posture, hoping not to alert the intruder to their presence. She crept up her front steps, then followed his example as he pressed his back to the wall near her door. On the opposite side of her porch, the front window curtain shifted.

Finn raised a closed fist, indicating she should wait.

This time she didn't protest.

The distinct clattering of dishes in the kitchen set her heart to a sprint as Finn reached for the front doorknob.

The door swung open before his fingers made contact.

Hayley's breaths stopped as she sent up a flurry of silent prayers.

Finn cussed and holstered his weapon. "What are you doing?"

"Eating, man." Austin poked his head and shoulders over the threshold, looking both ways before grinning at her. "Hey, Hayley. Come on in."

She nearly collapsed in relief as Finn ushered her through the door. She made a mental note to pinch Austin for scaring her.

His sandy hair was messy, void of his typically present ball cap, and he looked utterly at ease in a T-shirt, jeans and sneakers. He scooped a spoonful of ice cream from a bowl. "Welcome to your lovely home."

"Thanks," she answered, stepping aside so Finn could close the door.

"Ow!" Austin pressed a palm to his biceps. "You pinched me."

"You scared the daylights out of me."

Finn snorted behind her.

"And that's my ice cream," she continued, infinitely thankful to see Austin instead of a dangerous criminal. "Why didn't you call or text to let us know you were okay?" The rich, salty scent of warm grilled cheese reached her nose and she stiffened. "Are you cooking?"

Austin's wide smile returned. "Yeah. You should join us."

She followed his gaze to a narrow figure in the archway beyond. "Gage!"

The teen leaned against the jamb, long, narrow arms wrapped around his middle. His clothes and hair were dirty, and his cheeks were red with exposure from the sun. "I'm sorry—"

Hayley launched herself through the room, cutting off his unnecessary apology. "You're okay! I was so scared. I worried that you were hurt or abducted." *Or worse*, she thought, biting back the tears. She pulled him against her and rose onto tiptoes to tuck his head against her shoulder.

He hugged her back, instantly accepting the embrace. Then his thin body began to shake with stifled sobs.

"You're going to be okay now," she whispered. "I won't let anything bad happen to you. Neither will these guys. Or their family. Or the local police. And you're absolutely not going back to the Michaelsons."

He sucked in a ragged breath, regaining his composure and straightening with effort. He forced a tight smile through the tears. "I didn't mean to scare you."

"I was terrified," she said. "We think we know what you saw, and whoever is responsible for Kate's death might be following me too. Probably looking for you."

His eyes widened. "That's the reason I didn't come here sooner. I was trying to make sure I didn't accidentally bring him here. I've been hiding and waiting until it was safe."

"I'm just glad you're here," she said, sliding her arm around his back and pulling him to her side. "How'd you get in?"

He frowned. "I came through your doggy door."

Austin moseyed in their direction, pulling an empty spoon from his mouth. "You really need to close that up or get a dog. Are you hungry?" He slid past them and headed for her stove.

The doggy door was tiny compared to the boy before her, but she supposed, if he managed to work his way inside, so could someone else. "Noted," she said. "And, yes. Something smells delicious."

Sounds of sizzling butter turned her to the stove, where Austin was loading another grilled cheese. "Good. We can talk over food."

Hayley searched the refrigerator for side dishes. "You are your mother."

Austin winked.

A few sliced apples and washed grapes later, the foursome settled around her small kitchen table. She nibbled on apples, too emotionally jarred to work up an appetite, but deeply satisfied with the turn of events.

Gage had come to her, just as she'd hoped. He trusted her to help him, which meant the world. More, Austin had been there to welcome and feed him. And the Beaumonts had prepared a place for him to stay safely on their ranch. Emotion stung her eyes and clogged her throat as she scanned the trio of men before her.

"Do you mind if I shower?" Gage asked. "I don't have anything else to wear, but I'd really like to wash up. Shampoo my hair. Maybe brush my teeth?"

Hayley nodded and stood, glad to be useful, when it seemed everyone else was doing things for her these days. "Of course. Come on. I have everything you need." She kept an assortment of travel-size toiletries for youths taken into emergency care without time to gather their things. Or others who simply didn't have anything of their own.

"I keep a change of clothes in my gym bag," Finn said.

"You're welcome to wear that while I toss your outfit into the wash. It'll be a little big, but it's clean, and I'm guessing it'll fit better than anything in Hayley's closet."

Gage smiled, and the expression spread to the others.

The Beaumonts were broader, their bodies honed and matured, but Gage wasn't much shorter, and he'd likely be their height in the next year or two. He looked down the six-inch gap in height between himself and Hayley. "You're probably right about that."

Finn made a trip outside and returned with the bag.

Hayley walked Gage to the bathroom, then waited for him to toss his dirty clothes into the hallway.

"HE FIT THROUGH the doggy door?" Finn asked, eyeballing the small rubber flap across the room.

"Yep." Austin grinned. "You remember life at that age. He's a rack of growing bones. And I've got to be honest, I don't think he's eaten in a while."

Finn's jaw locked as he thought of Hayley feeding Gage and so many others lunch each workday. After meeting Mrs. Michaelson, he wasn't sure the kids in her care were getting much else, and he hoped the system moved quickly to review the family and extract the youths in their care.

"How was he otherwise?" Finn asked, knowing Austin would be a good judge. His brother had been around as many troubled teens as he had and would have insight. There was a lot to infer from a kid's general disposition and unspoken vibe. Even Gage's mannerisms were likely to say more than the teen himself. Frequently, a combination of those things would reveal whether or not the individual might be willing to make healthy changes. Or if he was already determined to resist.

"I like him," Austin said, resting his backside against the sink and crossing his arms over his chest. "He was terrified when he saw me let myself inside, but once I mentioned Hayley's name and yours, he relaxed."

"Mine?" Finn worked the concept around his mind, unable to make sense of it. "How did he know my name?"

"Apparently the love of your life still talks about you too."

Finn frowned to stop his lips from smiling. He didn't have to ask how his brother had gotten inside. Austin was quite proud of his lock-picking skills. "Okay. What else?"

Austin held Finn's eye contact for a long beat before moving on. "He's polite, apologetic for his disappearance and the break-in. He stands tall, looks folks in the eyes and he washed his hands before eating. I'd say he was being raised right before whatever happened to his family."

"Car accident," Finn said. "Drunk driver on their weekly date night."

His brother's face paled, and he scrubbed a heavy hand over his hair. "That's horrible. He was where? Home with a sitter? Got a call from the hospital?"

Finn shook his head, feeling heat course through his chest. He'd looked into the case last night when he couldn't sleep, and what he'd found still haunted him. "The sitter fell through, and the kid begged them to go anyway. He was thirteen and convinced he could manage a couple of hours on his own while they had dinner. Mom reluctantly agreed. They ate at a restaurant two miles from home and died just outside their neighborhood. He heard the commotion but didn't think much of it until a sheriff came to the door. Apparently Mom's last words were about her son being home alone."

Austin's eyes shone with emotion, and he cussed.

"Yeah."

"What'd I miss?" Hayley asked, reappearing in the room like a ninja.

Austin spun away, and Finn cleared his throat. "We're just talking through our next steps."

“Good,” she said. “We need a plan.”

“I’ll take his statement after he finishes in the shower,” Finn said. “We’ll have time while his clothes finish washing and drying. We can sit in the living room together. Someplace comfortable.” He watched Hayley carefully, trying to determine her mood and mindset. “You should stick with him—he’s clearly attached to you. He trusts you. We don’t want him to hold back on anything or get scared.”

She nodded, and her lips curled into a small prideful smile. “Agreed.”

Austin pulled the dish towel from his shoulder and hung it over the sink’s edge. “I’ll tell him about the ranch and ask if he’d be willing to check it out. Then we can explain why it’s the safest place for him right now and let him decide if he’s willing to give it a chance. We don’t want him running again.”

“What if he says no?” Hayley asked, uncertainty in her eyes.

Finn lifted an arm toward the living room. Gage would likely finish showering soon, and finding all the adults holed up in the kitchen could give the wrong impression. They were definitely talking about him, but they weren’t attempting to hide it from him. Better to get comfortable in the next room. In Finn’s experience, transparency bred trust, and this kid needed to know they could all be trusted, not just Hayley. “Can we?”

She nodded, and they moved to the next room.

“If he doesn’t like the ranch, he can stay at my place,” Austin said, dropping onto the overstuffed armchair beside the couch. “It’s cozy and well-protected. Food’s not as good, but there are fewer kids and livestock to hassle him.”

Finn rolled his eyes.

“And if you want him to stay someplace completely unconnected to the family,” Austin added, “Scarlet can probably get us access to an empty home for a few nights. We can talk to the owners about paying rent for a few days."

Finn didn't hate that idea. Having a real-estate agent in the family had been surprisingly beneficial to the Beaumonts. "I like that."

The stairs creaked, and their heads turned collectively to see Gage.

His hair was mussed and damp. Finn's clothes hung from his narrow hips and shoulders, as expected, but something strange twisted in Finn's chest at the sight of him. He'd only met this kid an hour ago, but it was easy to understand why Hayley had become so attached. He was kind and vulnerable, but smart enough to make it on his own when he'd thought he was protecting Hayley. The intention alone was priceless.

"Come on down," Hayley said. "We were just talking about our next steps, and we need your input."

Gage's concerned expression morphed into surprise. He followed her request and settled on the couch between her and Finn. "What's up?"

Hayley told Gage about the ranch, and he listened, glancing to Austin and Finn a few times while she spoke.

"Is that where you want me to go?" he asked when she finished.

"I wish I could keep you with me, but I think the ranch is the best option for now," she said. "Until the killer is found, and you're safe again."

His skin paled at the word *killer.*

Finn accessed the recording feature on his phone. "I need to get an official statement from you about what you saw in Old Downtown the other night and anything before or after that you feel is relevant."

Gage took a deep breath and exhaled with a shudder. He rubbed his palms up and down his thighs, then wet his lips and nodded.

"Whenever you're ready," Finn said, pressing the button to begin the recording, then setting the device between them.

Gage set the stage, then spoke about his art, the thrumming bass of the nearby rave and the draw of people to the sound, like moths to the light. "I didn't see anyone go inside the other building, but I heard yelling in the pause between songs down the street. It sounded like a fight. Then the music came back, and I didn't hear the voices anymore, so I went across the street to see if I'd imagined them. I hadn't. There were two silhouettes inside the building marked for demolition. One was Kate. I'd talked to her earlier when a few of us were playing ball in the intersection. She'd explained how she was planning to fix up that part of Old Downtown, and she asked us what we thought was most important in a new shelter or community center. We all had things to say, and she listened. It seemed like she really wanted to get things right. She even said there would be part-time jobs for older teens to work with younger kids, packing lunches and getting them onto their buses for school when it starts again. At first it made sense to me that she'd be there, checking out the area, but it was kind of weird to see she was still there at night. And it was also hard to understand why anyone would argue with her. She was so kind. Still, I saw something move toward her, like a bat, maybe." His skin paled as he spoke. "Then she fell. A few seconds later, I heard a gunshot."

"Were you able to get a look at the person she was with?" Finn asked.

"No. They were behind the wall. I only had a glimpse at her through the broken window."

"Could you tell by the voice if it was a man or woman?" Finn asked.

Gage kneaded his hands together, brow furrowed in concentration. "Not for sure. I heard a woman's voice in that moment between the MC's voice and the next song, but I've been thinking about it, and I'm not sure if it was Kate's voice or not. It could've been a second woman, or it might've been her, and the other person could've been a man."

"Was she alone when she spoke to you earlier, when you were playing ball?" Finn asked.

"As far as I could see, yeah."

Hayley set a hand on his shoulder. "A man took a shot at me in that area, and a man stood outside the parking lot where I park for work."

Austin leaned forward. "Gage, when you ran, did you see who chased you?"

Finn considered the question. It was a good one. Typically, male criminals were more likely to give chase, and women tended to regroup and strategize, but there were exceptions to even the strongest rules. And he couldn't rely wholly on past scenarios to predict the future. Any murderer would have motivation to stop a witness before they reported what they'd seen.

Gage took another long beat to consider before he spoke. "I think it was a man. They seemed big, with heavy foot-falls on the street. And they were close when I reached the rave. I thought I was caught, but the crowd was thick, and that building has a hole in the back wall. I ran to the opening, then ducked and doubled back instead of going out. I hid in the crowd until I thought it was safe to leave. I think whoever it was assumed I left."

Hayley swelled with pride. "That was smart. If they nearly caught you in a footrace to the rave, they might've gotten ahold of you if you'd tried your luck outside again."

He twisted on the cushion to look at her. "I was going to tell you everything the next day, but I kept thinking that maybe no one knew it was me. And maybe if I didn't say anything it would go away. Her body would be found, and the police would handle it. I didn't want to bring you into it or put myself in the spotlight."

She rubbed his back, and Finn's heart gave another heavy thud. Hayley was a natural at comforting hurting people. She had a heart for their pain, an internal drive to comfort. She'd make a perfect foster mom, and he was sure the court would give her a fair shot when this was over. From what he knows about the system between his connections and his family's, he was sure a judge would consider giving Hayley a chance at fostering Gage. The kid clearly accepted her as a mentor and confidante, and she would never let him down.

"Sorry I worried you," he whispered.

"Thank you for coming to me," Hayley responded.

Finn stopped the recording app and stood. They'd been at her home long enough for anyone watching to take notice. It was time to get moving, if they wanted to stay safe. "Who wants to see some livestock?"

Chapter Ten

Hayley leaned forward on her seat as Finn turned onto the long, familiar gravel lane. Returning to the Beaumont ranch for the first time in more than a year was nearly as breathtaking an experience as seeing it for the first time. She wished Gage had ridden with her so she could see his face as they arrived. Instead, he'd gone with Austin, who'd taken the lead in their little two-truck caravan.

She felt Finn's gaze on her cheek as her eyes widened in pleasure. Thick green grass rolled all the way to the horizon, split down the center by a dark ribbon of driveway and interspersed with fencing and livestock in their respective fields. The occasional human in a straw cowboy hat or colorful baseball cap waved an arm overhead as they rolled past.

Outbuildings, a large, impressive stable and several cabins dotted the land, each lovely, but none compared to the sprawling farmhouse before them. The Beaumont home spoke of generations of farmers and the decades of love bestowed upon it by this family.

Mr. and Mrs. Beaumont appeared on the porch as Finn parked his truck beside Austin's.

Hayley had to stop herself from running to greet them again. She hoped Gage would soon feel the same way. She wanted the family who meant so much to her to be important to him as well.

"Ready?" Finn asked, unfastening his seat belt.

"Always." She climbed down from the cab, taking a long beat to enjoy the view. Thick, dark mulch overflowed with bright blooms all around the farmhouse, and the arching cloudless blue sky stretched like a dome overhead.

Gage moved in her direction, nervous energy pouring off him in waves. The tension in his youthful face and posture set her slightly on edge.

"Give it a chance, okay?" She slid her arm beneath his and pulled him close, tipping her head back slightly to look up at his face. "I love this place and these people," she whispered, the words meant only for him. "They're not like anyone else I've ever known, and they're the very best of us. I'm sure of it."

His expression was grim, but he nodded. He was probably thinking of the last time Hayley had taken him to stay with a family. Look at how that had turned out. She needed to ask him more about the Michaelsons, and let him know what she thought of him not going back there for weeks, according to his foster mother, but this wasn't the right time. In this moment, she needed to give him the sense of peace and security he greatly deserved.

"Trust me," she urged, tugging his arm when he didn't look at her. She waited for those concerned brown eyes to fall on hers. Then she smiled. "If you aren't completely comfortable here before I leave, I will take you with me. That's a promise."

Gage pressed his lips together. "Austin said staying with you could put you in danger."

Hayley shook her head. "Staying at my house could put us in danger, but I'm not staying there right now, and I won't ask you to stay anywhere you aren't comfortable ever again."

He scrutinized her for a long moment before turning to the silent crowd on the Beaumonts' porch.

Finn and Austin had joined their parents, along with another brother, Lincoln, and the stable manager, Josi. All watched intently as she spoke to Gage.

"Look at them," she whispered again. "What's not to love?"

They all smiled brightly, eagerly, except Lincoln, who seemed to be sizing up Gage. He was probably already thinking of chores to keep the teen mentally engaged and physically exhausted. Josi looked at the brooding man beside her then elbowed his ribs.

Lincoln grunted and a partial smile bloomed on his face before he shut it down.

Hayley glanced at Finn, wondering if he'd caught the exchange, but his eyes were focused tightly on her. Fresh heat spread over her cheeks in response.

Gage straightened as if prepared for battle. "All right. I can do this. I don't want to put you in danger or cause you any more trouble."

"Hey." She stopped him as he tried to move forward. "You are not a burden to me. Understand? I'm only asking you to give them and this place a try. There's no wrong answer."

He nodded, not speaking.

"You are not a burden to me," she repeated, more slowly this time. "You are my friend, and I'm going to take care of you. These guys are going to help me. By the time I leave today, they'll all be your friends too. If they aren't, I meant what I said. Got it?"

"Yeah."

"Well?" Mrs. Beaumont asked from the bottom of the porch steps, nearly vibrating with excitement. "Will you stay?" she asked. "At least for the tour?"

"Sure," Gage agreed, and the older woman rushed to greet him.

"Can I hug you? I'm a hugger," she explained. "Isn't that right?"

The crowd murmured in confirmation, and Gage lifted his arms.

She wrapped him in a tight embrace, and within seconds, he hugged her back.

Hayley's eyes burned with appreciation. This was the safe place Gage needed, and she would be eternally grateful.

"It's lovely to meet you, Gage," Mrs. Beaumont said as she released him. "This is my family. You'll meet Dean soon, if you haven't already. I believe he's watching Hayley's place now. You know Finn and Austin. This is my husband, Garrett. I'm Mary. And this is Josi and Lincoln."

The family members took turns greeting him while Mrs. Beaumont fussed and Finn made his way to Hayley's side.

"I'm sure this isn't overwhelming at all," Finn teased, nudging her with his elbow.

She laughed, recalling the first time she'd been introduced to the family. The Beaumonts were wonderful, but they could be a lot. Especially upon introduction.

"Are you hungry?" Mrs. Beaumont asked, steering Gage up the porch steps toward the farmhouse door. "I always keep food and snacks on hand. Help yourself anytime. We have meals at…" The sound of her voice trailed off as the group followed inside.

"Do you remember the first time I brought you here?" Finn asked.

"How could I forget?" Hayley turned a bright smile on him. "I thought you were all too good to be true. Gathering around that giant table for dinner, talking and laughing like friends. I was sure it was a show. I couldn't understand how you willingly spent so much time together and still liked one another."

Finn's eyebrows tented, then his expression slid into one of concern. "I sometimes forget my life isn't everyone else's normal. I wish it was."

"Me too."

He set a palm against her back and rubbed gently before pulling away.

Hayley felt the absence of his touch in her core, and maybe in her heart as well. She shook off the unwanted feeling and concentrated on the moment at hand. She needed to be sure Gage was at home on the ranch, then she needed to get back out there with Finn to see what they could learn about Kate's death. The sooner the killer was arrested, the sooner Gage wouldn't be in danger, and she could apply to be his guardian.

The farmhouse front door opened and Gage appeared, chatting with the young blond stable manager. Lincoln followed with his usual frown. All three members of the little group carried a bottle of water in one hand. The guys also held half of a sandwich.

"Not sure how Josi got away without being fed," Finn said. "Then again, she puts up with Lincoln all day every day, so we've suspected she was a magician for a while now."

Hayley laughed and raised her fingers in a wave as the trio passed.

Lincoln slowed. "We're giving the kid a tour."

Josi reached up to smack the brim of his hat. "His name is Gage."

Lincoln glared until she turned away, then grinned as he straightened his hat.

Finn shook his head, having clearly seen the exchange this time. "I don't get them."

Hayley fell into step behind the trio, giving them distance. Finn kept pace at her side.

"Do you have a dog?" Gage asked Lincoln.

"No."

"Really? Why not?" Gage frowned. "Don't they help with herding or something? You've got lots of room and the rescues are always full."

Lincoln looked past the teen to Josi, who grinned.

"He has a point," she said. "We've got miniature cows and donkeys, horses, goats and sheep. Chickens galore. No dog?"

Lincoln stopped suddenly and turned to pin Hayley with a curious stare. "Weren't you getting a dog last year?"

She'd wanted to badly but couldn't bring herself to take the plunge. "I decided I was gone too much to be the parent I wanted to be."

Josi looked to Gage. "Have you ever had a dog?"

The teen's cheeks paled and he nodded. "Larry."

"Where is he now?" Hayley asked, suddenly concerned he'd been forgotten in the chaos of losing Gage's parents. Had he been taken to the pound? Cast off somehow? Left to the streets?

"I got him when I was in preschool," Gage explained. "He died a few months before my parents. He was ten."

Josi's eyes shone with emotion and darted to Lincoln.

"Ten's a good long life for a dog," Lincoln said. "We've had a few over the years that only made it to eight or nine, but they were loved. They were happy."

Gage nodded. "Yeah."

Hayley's stomach tightened with the new knowledge. She'd had no idea he'd lost a lifelong friend and his parents in the same year. "I'm going to get a dog soon," she blurted, drawing the eyes of all three companions.

"Really?" Gage asked, his expression both stunned and hopeful.

"Mmm-hmm," she said, processing the possibility at warp speed. "I plan to work less overtime soon, so I'll be home for dinner every night, and the office is near enough for me to walk him at lunchtime." She could set up her cooler at the usual picnic table before she left. Maybe even bring the dog on some work-related visits.

"Let's go," Lincoln said, clapping Gage on the shoulder. "We'll check out the stable and your cabin while they talk." He lifted his chin to indicate something behind Hayley.

She turned to find Austin making his way across the field.

"Are you running from me?" he called as Lincoln led Gage and Josi through the open barn doors.

"Always," Lincoln hollered, then vanished inside.

Finn set his hands on his hips and turned to his approaching brother. "Any news?"

"Nope. One of my informants says he was at the rave that night. Saw a kid fitting Gage's description tear through the place. That was all he remembered. Most folks were high, so everyone he asked today had no idea what he was talking about."

Hayley groaned. "So there aren't any new leads on who was chasing him."

Or who'd killed Kate.

"So what's next?" she asked.

Finn rolled his shoulders and squinted against the sun. "I'll check in with the officers who stayed in Old Downtown to do interviews. Maybe something someone said will be a clue, even if it isn't a definitive ID of the killer."

Austin rubbed his palms. "I'll head back to the office and dig into Kate's social-media accounts. I'll look at everyone on her friends lists, check out her posts, read their posts, see who she interacted with on the days leading up to her death. The usual."

Familiar laughter turned Hayley back to the barn, where Gage was leading the pack in her direction.

"I like it here," he called. "You were right. I want to stay."

A long breath of relief rushed from her chest. "If that's what you want."

"I do." He smiled widely as he reached her, then wrapped her in a hug. "Thank you."

Lincoln's lips twitched, and Hayley felt her eyebrows raise. The fleeting expression looked a lot like a smile. Three in an hour had to be a new record for him. "In that case," he said, pulling a cell phone from his pocket, "this is for you. We set it up when we heard you were coming. It's got all our numbers in there and Hayley's."

"Seriously?" Gage asked, obviously flabbergasted.

"Yep."

Gage accepted the phone with an expression of pure joy. "This is sick!"

Hayley tamped down the rush of emotion, laughing outwardly at the roller coaster of feelings she'd been on today. "You can call me if you need anything. Even if you're just bored or lonely."

"Or if Lincoln gets on your nerves," Josi offered.

The group laughed, but Lincoln pinned her with his grumpiest of looks.

"I'll be his favorite in a day or two," Lincoln said. "Now let's check out your mini apartment." He turned and headed for the small cabins behind the stable.

Gage shot Hayley a stunned look. "Apartment?"

"Everyone staying on-site has their own space," she explained as they all followed Lincoln. "Those larger cabins belong to Lincoln and Josi. The smaller ones are used for teens staying here on a short-term basis."

"This one," Lincoln said, stopping at the door to a unit near his own, "is for you."

Finn crossed his arms and leaned toward Hayley as his brother unlocked the door. "This one is usually used for storage, so it's a work in progress."

"Ranch was full," Austin added, inserting himself into the exchange. "But there wasn't any stopping Mama when she heard about your situation."

Hayley watched as the group filed inside.

"Are you serious?" Gage's voice carried through the open door to her heart. "Hayley! You've got to see this!"

She darted forward, slipping into the former storage unit before coming to an immediate halt. The Beaumonts had arranged a twin bed and small desk on one wall. A chest of drawers on another. The bed was covered in a navy blue blanket and topped with a puffy white pillow. An oval throw rug covered the floor. The desk doubled as a nightstand with a lamp positioned closest to the headboard. An open notebook contained a two-word message in bright blue letters.

Welcome, Gage!

Hayley looked first at Josi, then at each Beaumont with silent adoration. "Thank you."

Gage dragged his eyes from the notebook to Hayley. "This is where I get to stay while I'm here? In this cabin?"

"Yep," Austin answered, then reached beneath the desk to open the door to a pint-size refrigerator. "We stocked this with drinks and snacks. Kids your age keep ridiculous hours, and we thought you'd rather have some things at your place than go hungry or make the trek to our folks' house at two a.m."

"My place," Gage repeated, awestruck.

Finn shifted, reminding Hayley he was still right there at her side. "Only until we find the person who killed Kate and chased you. I don't plan to let that take long."

Gage's smile filled the room. "How old do you have to be to stay here?"

"At the ranch?" Josi asked.

He nodded. "Hayley said the other kids will be removed from the Michaelsons' home. I looked after them when I could, especially Parker. He's eight."

"You're probably the youngest," Josi said. "We typically host kids closer to high-school graduation. Some are even my age on occasion."

"We look at each applicant on a case-by-case basis," Lincoln said. "Eight is too young to be here, I think. Not everyone we host is in a good place emotionally. You're in danger, and you've been through a lot, but you seem like you've got a clear head. Not all our kids do."

Gage's expression fell, and his brow creased in concern. "Where will Parker go?"

"Someplace nice and safe," Hayley promised. "I'll personally interview each family to be sure they're up to par this time."

"When will he move?" he asked.

"Soon. I've requested a review of the home and one-on-one interviews for the kids. Without the Michaelsons listening or influencing them in any way. The children will have the freedom to speak candidly."

Something in Gage's expression said he didn't think that was good enough, but Hayley didn't press the issue. She told herself to take his willingness to stay with the Beaumonts as a win and she'd let the social workers handling the Michaelsons do their jobs. She had a good team at the office and in front of her.

Finn's phone buzzed and he removed it from his pocket to look at the screen. "If you're set here, we should take off," he said, looking to Gage, then Hayley.

The sudden tension in his jawline set her feet in motion. She gave each of the individuals before her a hug, adding an extra squeeze to Gage before stepping back. "Call me if you need anything, and I'll be here in under thirty minutes."

"I'm good," he assured.

"If anything changes," she said, backing through the door and into the grass.

"Take care of him," she called, turning to follow Finn, who was already moving toward his truck.

He stopped to catch her hand and urge her into a jog.

"What happened?" she asked, on high alert as they launched into his cab and peeled out of the driveway.

Finn placed his portable emergency light on the roof and hit the gas "There was a break-in at your office."

Chapter Eleven

Finn piloted his truck into the lot outside the social-services office. A pair of Marshal's Bluff cruisers were already in place. A uniformed officer stood guard at the door. The building had closed for the day only a short while earlier, so whoever had broken in hadn't waited long to act.

Typically, break-ins were executed under cover of night and at a location with items of high resale potential. Whatever the criminal had been seeking was likely only valuable to one person, and Finn suspected that person was searching for Gage Myers. The timing, when factored in with Kate's murder and the witness who'd gotten away, was too coincidental. And Finn didn't believe in coincidences.

"I can't believe this is happening," Hayley whispered, releasing her safety belt as he pulled his key from the ignition.

He climbed out and met her on the sidewalk. "How do you feel about working the scene together?"

She raised her eyebrows. "You want my help in there?"

As a general rule, he did his best to keep civilians away from crime scenes, but Hayley was familiar with the case and location in ways no one else on-site was, making her invaluable. Not to mention, he preferred to keep her close. For her safety and his sanity. "I'll do the talking and interacting with staff and officers," he said. "You evaluate the office. This is your territory. You'll know better than anyone if something is missing or has been left behind. Take your time and concentrate. If there's a mess, it could be a distraction. If something new has appeared, I need to know that too. The item could be a camera or recording device. Make note of anything that feels off."

Her expression morphed from shock to resolve, and she nodded. "Got it."

Finn held her gaze one moment longer, then took the lead as they approached the officer at the door.

"Detective Beaumont," the older gentleman said, accepting Finn's outstretched hand for a quick shake.

Finn stepped aside, allowing Hayley to pass. "This is—"

"Hi, Don," she said sweetly, pausing inside the small vestibule. "How's Cora?"

"Better every day," the older officer said. "I'll let her know you asked about her."

"Thank you."

Finn matched Hayley's pace as they moved through the quiet hallway. "How do you know Don?"

"Through his wife. She had a pretty serious surgery last month. I brought dinner once or twice. They're good people. Do you know them well?"

"Barely at all." Even in a department as small as his, everyone had a job to do, and it was easy to stay busy. He rarely spent any real time with anyone outside his immediate team.

A pair of men in suits appeared at the open door to Social Services. They bent their heads together as they moved away, each carrying a stack of files and loose papers.

"They work in human resources," Hayley whispered, then waved. "Caleb, Frank."

The men stopped, looking curiously at their coworker.

Finn extended a hand to each man in turn. "Hello, I'm Detective Beaumont."

They both murmured quick hellos.

"What can you tell us about the break-in?" Finn asked.

Their collective attention swung back to Hayley, as they were probably wondering why she was there and was being accompanied by a detective.

The taller of the pair was first to respond. He cleared his throat and forced a tight smile in Finn's direction. "I'm Caleb Morrison, the management leader here. I organize and facilitate the teams. I also act as a liaison between all staff and administration." His gaze slid briefly to Hayley before returning to Finn. "The break-in appears to have been directed at Ms. Campbell or someone on her caseload. Beyond that, I'm not sure."

The heavier man at Caleb's side wiggled his blue-gloved fingers. "I'm Frank Riggs. These files were tossed out of the cabinets in our portion of the offices. We're supposed to see if anything's missing. We barely print anything these days, so unless someone was searching for something from years ago, all this mess was likely for show. Or the result of a hissy fit."

Hayley snorted lightly, then covered her nose with one hand. "Sorry."

Finn fought a smile.

"Someone is hot for one of your cases," Frank said, looking much more serious. "I'd stick with this guy as much as you can until this is sorted." He tipped his head at Finn and scanned him appreciatively. "Shouldn't be a hardship."

Hayley took Finn's elbow in her hand and tugged him away, waving goodbye to Frank and Caleb with her free hand.

"I like Frank," Finn said.

Hayley laughed, and the sound warmed his heart.

A second officer stood guard inside the social-services door and raised his chin in greeting.

Before Finn could ask the man for information, Hayley gasped. He followed her wide-eyed stare to a crime-scene photographer, snapping shots of an absolute disaster. Presumably Hayley's desk.

The rolling chair had been overturned on its mat. All the metal drawers were open. Trinkets, framed photos, toys and keepsakes littered the floor and desktop. Office supplies were fanned across the carpet.

It seemed Frank had been on the right track. This certainly looked like the site of a recent hissy fit. Not at all what Finn had anticipated.

The photographer stepped away, and Finn donned a pair of gloves, then passed a second set to Hayley. "I guess it's time to get to work. Tell me about the space."

The room was large and divided into sections by groups of desks, presumably the teams Caleb had mentioned.

Hayley tugged the gloves over her trembling hands. "This is my desk. These belong to my team members." She swung a pointed finger from desk to desk. "Those are the other teams, and that door leads to Human Resources and Administration." Her voice cracked, and she released a thin, shaky breath.

"You okay?"

"I can do this," she assured him quietly, then crouched to examine the mess.

Finn scanned the bigger picture first, then slowly pulled his attention inward to the single destroyed workstation.

Everything else appeared untouched and utterly ignored.

The office was in need of sprucing up. The carpet was threadbare, while the wall paint was chipping and faded.

"Recognize these desks?" she asked, rising to her feet once more. "They were handed down to us from the police station after your renovations last year."

Finn grimaced. He hadn't recognized them, but he'd certainly noticed they were old.

"They're a step up from what we had," she said, probably reading his expression. "We were glad to get them, and it's nice they didn't go straight to a landfill somewhere. Our desks went to other places in need. A church office and some homeschooling moms, I believe."

Finn made a mental note to circle back to the topic of funding for Social Services when he had more time. His family would surely have ideas on how to help the department who helped everyone else.

"What do you think?" she asked.

"I think someone knew what they were after and where to find it."

"The guy who's been following me," she mused.

Finn nodded, then raised his hand to a passing crime-scene technician. "Are you finished here?"

The young man gave the room a glance. "We're wrapping up now. We've got all we need."

"Anything you can share that might help me?"

"Afraid not," the man said. "No prints. No signs of a break-in. The alarm was triggered at the interior point of entry." He pointed to a keypad on the wall inside the social-services area.

Finn considered that a moment. "Someone accessed the building before closing and waited until the coast was clear to make his way in here."

"That's my guess," the tech said. "I'll get the photos over to you along with lab analysis on a couple small things. Hair. Mud. Probably left by workers or clients, but both were in the line of fire, so I'm taking a closer look." He tipped his head to the overturned chair.

"Appreciate it," Finn said.

"Can I clean up, Ryan?" Hayley asked.

"Okay by me," the tech said. "But Beaumont's the boss."

"Well, don't tell him that too often," she teased. "We'll all pay the price."

Hayley collected an armload of her things from the floor as the tech took his leave. "Ryan and I met a few months ago. His wife teaches second grade, and I had one of her students on my caseload. She introduced us."

Finn shook his head. Everyone who met Hayley was instantly charmed. Not because she was perfect, but because she was honest and real.

She narrowed her eyes, but before she could voice her thoughts, Caleb appeared with a frown.

"Detective?" he asked.

Finn snapped easily back to work mode. "Find something?"

"No. We've been through all the folders. Everything appears to be in order."

"Thank you." Finn set his hands on his hips and looked at the open door to Human Resources. What had made the burglar dig through the paper files? "You took your laptop home with you?" he asked Hayley.

"Yes. Why?"

It was possible that whoever had come for her computer might've tried the filing cabinets as the next most logical place to find information on a case.

"Just theorizing," he said. "The interior alarm was already triggered when they came in, so they had to hurry, then leave empty-handed. Explains the hissy fit."

She grinned.

Finn went to wrap things up with the officers on duty while Hayley rearranged and tidied her desk.

An image of her in his arms at a fundraiser caught his eye upon return. A dozen bright, youthful faces filled the space at their sides. They'd made huge differences for the betterment of their community when they were together. He'd thought they'd grow old doing those same things.

What had gone so wrong? And how had he not seen it coming?

HAYLEY PACKED A few more of her things during a quick trip home, then rejoined Finn in his truck. "Thanks," she said, buckling up for the ride back to his place.

It hadn't occurred to her, until the break-in at her office, that there were a number of little things she'd like to protect in case there was a burglary. She would've been safe at Finn's place, but her precious photos, mementos and keepsakes were irreplaceable too. So she'd been thrilled when he hadn't objected to her picking up a little more of her stuff.

"Any chance you have a spare key on you?" he asked, dropping his cell phone into the truck's cupholder. "And would you mind if Dean or Austin replace your locks with a keypad version as soon as possible? Something we'll be able to monitor? Maybe one of those doorbells with a camera too."

"They can have mine," she said, lifting a key between them. "Whatever makes my home safer is perfect." Especially since she hoped to share the place with Gage when this was over.

Finn took the key and shifted into Drive.

It broke her heart to think of how close she'd come to spending her life with him, and how she'd ruined it by waiting far too long to face her demons.

Soon the familiar home appeared, situated atop a hill with mature trees and plenty of lush green grass. Enough room for chubby toddler legs to run and growing childhood bodies to play. The wide gravel swath outside an attached garage had ample space for guests, family and friends to park. Even enough for future teenage drivers she'd once believed would belong to her and Finn.

Never underestimate how much can change in a year, she thought.

Or the limits on how badly one person can mess up.

A few moments later, Finn unlocked the front door and waited for her in the kitchen while she delivered her things to the guest room. She returned to him with squared shoulders. Things between them couldn't go back to the way they were, but they could certainly be improved. And that started with an explanation for her behavior last year. Finn would never bring up something so painfully personal in the midst of a serious investigation. She, on the other hand, needed to say her piece. She owed him at least that much.

Finn clapped his hands as she emerged from the hallway. "Austin's on his way over to grab that house key, and I've made some sandwiches. Nothing fancy, but I'm hungry and thought you might be too. Also, I'm hoping we can brainstorm."

Hayley froze. The sudden change of mental direction nearly gave her whiplash.

He passed her a plate with a handful of kettle chips and a pickle spear beside a sandwich cut into two triangles.

"BLT," he said. "I microwaved the leftover bacon from breakfast."

She took a seat at the island, unsure she could eat until she got a few secrets off her chest. Her attention caught on a large whiteboard with wheels in the living area.

"For the brainstorming," he said around a mouthful of sandwich.

She blinked. "Right."

Finn wiped his mouth, looking ten years younger at home than he did on the job. He'd turned a baseball hat around on his head and visibly relaxed down to his toes. It was easy to remember he was twenty-five when he was on duty. At home, like this, it was hard to believe he wasn't late for class somewhere. "Now that Gage is safe, we can redirect our attention. Uniformed officers have done preliminary interviews with Kate's family and staff. I'll go over the official transcripts before we start knocking on doors."

He rose and crossed the room to grab his satchel and a laptop. He set the latter beside her plate, then freed a second laptop from his bag. "Are you still a magician when it comes to social-media stalking?"

Hayley reluctantly set aside her need for confession and willed herself to refocus. Finn wanted her help now. The rest could wait.

"Hayley?" he coaxed. "You okay?"

She refreshed her smile. "I believe stalking is illegal, Detective, but I'm still quite good at research."

"Excellent." Finn opened the lid on his laptop. "I was hoping you'd say that. I'm looking for details on all the latest posts and interactions from Kate. Austin usually helps with this, but he's spread thin. If you find something you want him to dig into, he can. Otherwise, let's see how much progress we can make tonight. I'll read all the interviews and anything else that's been added to the case file while you search, and we'll see what stands out."

"Deal." She raised her half sandwich to him in a toast.

Several hours later, her eyes stung, and her body ached from being hunched over the laptop. She stood and stretched.

"Anything?" he asked.

"Nothing's screaming *motive* to me," she admitted, "but I generally see the good in people so—"

He set aside his laptop and turned to face her. "What are your overall thoughts and insights?"

She considered his question and what she'd learned that could be relevant. "I hadn't realized Kate's husband had such a Cinderella story. His family was practically homeless when he met her. The fact his path ever crossed hers is a miracle. For them to fall in love, get married and make it eight years together is probably like winning the lottery. Literally and figuratively." Hayley wasn't sure how she felt about it. Happy for the couple, but also a little suspicious, because money was the number-one reason for divorce—she felt somewhat guilty for thinking the last part.

Finn rolled his shoulders and arched his back, apparently

as stiff and uncomfortable as she'd been. "Paul was poor before they married?"

"Very much. He was working at a YMCA when she came to see how she could help. Then poof. Love."

Finn grunted. "I'll see if there's a prenup. If so, I'll need to know what he stood to lose if the marriage fell apart."

Hayley frowned. "Am I a sappy dope if I really don't want that to pan out? Not another man who vowed to love, honor and cherish his wife only to murder her for her money."

"No." The smile on Finn's face was brittle, and she flinched when her phone buzzed.

"It's my coworker," she said, lifting the device to read the message. "The kids are being removed from the Michaelsons' home tomorrow morning."

Finn's expression brightened a moment before he went into work mode. "That's good."

"Yeah," she said, feeling the first flutters of nerves return. "Finn?"

"Yeah?"

Hayley inhaled deeply, then spoke the words that had been on her heart for a year. "I'm sorry I ran away when you proposed."

He tensed and the air thickened…and all evidence of the carefree young man disappeared.

"It wasn't because I didn't love you, or because I didn't want to marry you, because I did. More than anything." She paused to let him process, then searched for the strength to go on.

His jaw tensed and flexed, but his body was otherwise motionless.

"I've told you my mom drinks," Hayley went on. "That she's unreliable, difficult and mean. I didn't tell you how bad it was growing up with her. It was awful." Hayley nearly choked on the words. Nothing she could say would make it better or believable. If she hadn't lived her life, seen it with her eyes, experienced it herself, she'd never have believed a mother could be like hers. The way she probably still was. "She was supposed to love and protect me. She did not. And she stood by while the men in her life hurt me too." Tears sprung to her eyes, and her chin jutted forward in defiance to everyone who'd tried to make her a terrible, hateful human. "I hadn't dealt with that pain or processed the trauma, and in a very twisted way, your profession of love and desire to protect me felt like betrayal. It triggered all these suppressed, ignored, bottled-up feelings and I just…ran."

The same way she'd run away from her mother's trailer. The way she'd run from almost everything good in her life before it could hurt her too. Only her job had ever given her joy without fear, and that was probably because she worked hard and faced her share of troubles, according to her therapist. She trusted that joy, because she'd felt she'd earned it. "I know now that I don't have to earn love and that I am deserving of it as well. But I didn't know that then."

Finn's Adam's apple bobbed. "You don't owe me an explanation."

"You're right. I owe you a whole lot more. You didn't deserve the pain I caused you. I want you to know I'm getting the help I need, and I'm doing better all the time. I shouldn't have waited so long to get myself together." She locked her eyes on Finn, desperate for him to understand what she couldn't say. She'd do anything to take back the moment she'd ran. Because she knew now, from a healed perspective, he'd have stayed with her through it all. "I didn't believe something as wonderful as you could be meant for someone as damaged as me."

Regret swelled her tongue and halted her words. Then the tears began to fall.

Finn stepped carefully forward and opened his arms as an offering.

Part of her longed to turn and leave.

Instead, she stepped into his embrace and let him cradle her protectively against his chest until the tears ran dry.

Chapter Twelve

The muffled sound of a ringing phone drew Hayley from a restless sleep. She groaned with the crash of memories. She'd confessed her soul to Finn, then she'd cried herself to sleep. He'd barely said a word.

The past few days' worth of tension and fear had poured out of her, along with a lifetime of heartache and pain. She'd only intended to tell Finn as much as necessary to clear the air, but instead a dam had burst. She wasn't able to stop her words or tears until she'd become completely deflated.

Like the man he was, Finn had held her, comforted her, then walked her to bed so she could rest and recover. Despite the fact she'd hurt him. Despite the fact she'd unleashed a torrent of emotion without warning. Despite the fact she'd basically ambushed him. He'd even brought her a cold, wet cloth for her eyes. A glass of water and a couple of Tylenol to prevent a headache.

Hayley rolled onto her side and pulled the pillow over her head in residual horror. Finn hadn't been angry that she'd kept so much of herself from him while they were together. He didn't tell her that none of it mattered now, because they were over. He'd just been there. Strong and silent. Giving her the emotional space to fall apart while he held her together.

Then he'd left her alone with her demons.

At least she wouldn't have to face him for a few more hours. The first rays of sunlight were barely visible on the horizon beyond her window. With a little luck, she'd be ready to face him by the time the day began.

Her ears pricked when the muffled voice in the next room said Gage's name. Instinct made her sit upright and tightened her nerves. She stared at her closed bedroom door, hyperfocused on each low warble as the words came faster, desperate to dissect the meanings.

"I'm waking her now," Finn said suddenly, right outside her room.

Panic pushed her onto her feet. "Come in."

The door opened, and Finn's eyes met hers with alarm.

"What happened?" she asked, fear swirling in her anxious heart and muddled mind.

"Gage is missing."

THIRTY MINUTES LATER, Hayley burst from Finn's pickup and onto the grass outside his family's farmhouse.

Mrs. Beaumont waited on the wide wraparound porch. "Come in. I made breakfast and put on the coffee." She opened her arms to embrace them, then ushered them inside.

Hayley's lip trembled at the warm reception. She was thankful for the love of a mother when she needed it most, even if the mother wasn't hers. "Thank you."

The oversize eat-in kitchen smelled of biscuits and gravy. Beaumont men sat at the nearby table and hovered around an island the size of a boat. Josi filled mugs with coffee at the counter.

The family quieted as they took note of Hayley's arrival.

She stroked flyaway hairs away from her puffy eyes and swollen cheeks. The haphazard ponytail she'd wrangled into place on the drive between homes was already falling over one shoulder. She could only imagine what she looked like.

She hadn't been brave enough to meet her own eyes in the bathroom mirror while brushing her teeth and hair.

Josi passed her a steaming mug. "I'm so sorry."

Lincoln stepped forward, into the space behind the young blonde, before Hayley could form words. "We don't know what happened," he said, jaw tense and eyes hard. "Gage was happy when we left him to settle in for bed. This morning, he was gone. He took his phone, but he won't answer."

"Why would he do that?" Hayley whispered, posing the question to herself as much as to the others.

"That's what I keep saying," Lincoln grumbled. "Doesn't make any sense."

Josi passed Finn a mug when he joined them at the counter.

The warmth of his nearness added a small measure of comfort to Hayley's weary soul.

"Have you thoroughly checked his room?" Finn asked. "Notice signs of trouble? Maybe a note?"

The responding death glare from Lincoln raised the fine hairs on Hayley's neck. "Of course, I have," he said.

Josi shifted discreetly, angling her body by an inch until her shoulder brushed Lincoln's chest.

His gaze flickered to her before jerking back to his brother. "I'm well aware of what to look for when a kid goes missing," he added, only slightly less hostile. "This isn't my first rodeo, and you know it."

Finn raised a palm. "I'm just trying to ask what you found."

"Nothing. That's the problem," Lincoln stormed. "The place is spotless. Nothing's missing except him and his phone."

Hayley thought about Finn's advice to her at the office crime scene. "Did Gage happen to leave anything behind? Something you didn't provide?" Something to suggest he planned to come back?

"Yeah. These," Josi said, pulling a folded row of photo-booth pictures from her back pocket. "I brought them along to help the search party."

Hayley took the strip gingerly. "There's a search party?"

Josi nodded. "They went out about twenty minutes ago. Lincoln went over to wake him around five thirty on his way to the stables. He looked around for a few minutes, thinking he'd just gone out to walk or clear his head. As soon as we realized he was nowhere near, I reached out to some of the farm hands just starting their days, then headed over here to let the Beaumonts know. Lincoln called Finn, and the others fanned across the property. No word so far."

Finn leaned closer, peering at the strip of black-and-white images in her hand. "That's Parker."

Hayley nodded. The pair were closer than she'd realized.

"Who?" Lincoln asked.

"Another boy staying with the same foster family," Finn explained. "He said Gage took care of him whenever he was there."

Fresh alarm shot through Hayley as she dragged her gaze from the photos to Finn. "All the kids are being removed from the Michaelsons' care today. Including Parker."

Josi sucked in a small, audible breath. "He's the boy Gage asked about. He wanted to know how old kids had to be to stay here."

Hayley felt herself begin to nod, recalling Gage's question. In all the chaos, she'd completely forgotten.

Josi had told him Parker was too young.

FINN MARCHED ONTO the Michaelsons' porch at just after eight. He knocked more forcefully than necessary, then waited impatiently with Hayley at his side.

She'd spoken by phone with the social worker who'd reviewed the Michaelsons at her request. The other woman had found the couple lacking and confirmed the children would only be there another few hours. She was on her way to begin the process now.

Finn knocked again.

The front door sucked open with force, and Mrs. Michaelson glared out. A cacophony of voices and noise filled the home behind her. "Ugh," she groaned. "You again. Haven't you done enough? Sending people out here to ask a bunch of questions, disrupt the kids' days and poke through my life. Go away."

"Mrs. Michaelson," Finn began calmly, raising a palm to indicate she would be wise to wait. "We're here to speak with Parker." With a little luck, the kid had spoken to Gage last night. If Gage had used his new phone to call the Michaelsons' residence, Parker might even know where to find the older boy.

The sound of approaching vehicles drew his attention over one shoulder. A cruiser and unmarked sedan pulled into the space behind his truck at the curb.

The sedan was expected, but a uniformed officer was not.

"Why are the police here?" Hayley asked, gaze jumping to Finn.

"Haven't you heard?" Mrs. Michaelson asked. "Parker's gone."

"What do you mean he's gone?" Hayley cried.

A woman in tan pants and a navy blouse jogged up the steps to join them. She frowned at Hayley. "I just got the call. I changed directions and came right over as soon as I heard. I haven't even been to the office."

"I don't understand," Hayley said, eyes pleading. "Are you saying Parker ran away too?"

The uniformed officers were next to reach the porch. Officer Young tipped his head in greeting. "Mrs. Michaelson called to report a missing child this morning. We're here to take the report and interview the family."

Finn pointed to the nearby trash bin, filled to the brim

with beer cans and empty alcohol containers. "You'll want to make note of that. The contents have doubled since the last time I was here."

"Hey now," Mrs. Michaelson protested, opening the door to allow the officers to pass. "Why don't you mind your business," she suggested. "Maybe concentrate on finding Gage, because he's still not here."

Finn held the door when the woman stepped out of the officers' way. He waved for Hayley and her coworker to enter ahead of him, then paused to level Mrs. Michaelson with an icy look. "If you're exposing vulnerable children to parties serving that much alcohol, or worse, you and your husband are putting it away on your own, that is absolutely our business."

Three middle schoolers at the kitchen counter went silent.

"Where's Mr. Michaelson now?" Officer Young asked. "We're hoping to catch him before he leaves for work."

"Already gone," Mrs. Michaelson reported, shoving the door shut behind the crowd. "He's a fisherman. Boat leaves before dawn, and he's always on it."

Hayley and her coworker went into business mode, instructing the children to gather their things.

The officers walked Mrs. Michaelson to the kitchen table to take her statement.

Finn took a spin around the first floor, looking for additional signs of trouble. The rooms were relatively tidy, considering the number of kids under the roof. According to the coat hooks and cubbies on the kitchen wall, there were five children in total at the modest suburban home. Pieces of masking tape with neat black letters spelled the names Gage, Parker, Orion, Wesley and Trent. Hopefully, one of the latter would be cooperative and helpful in finding Gage and Parker.

He paused in the kitchen to listen while Mrs. Michaelson relayed her timeline of events, beginning last night and ending this morning. "Ms. Campbell and I spoke with Parker when we were here before," he said, interrupting. "He said Gage goes home when he takes off. Any idea what that means?"

The officers raised their eyebrows in interest.

Mrs. Michaelson crossed her arms. "No. This is his home. Or it was."

Officer Young pursed his lips, presumably in thought. "Whatever happened to his family's place?"

"I assume it sold," Finn said. "It's been a while."

Hayley reappeared with one of the boys, a pillow and his bag. "I can check the county auditor's site."

"I've got this," Finn said. Dean's fiancé was a Realtor. If they needed any additional information on the home or property, he'd give his brother a call. Hayley had her hands full with more important things.

"Okay." She led the boys and her coworker outside to help settle them in the sedan.

"Where are they going?" Mrs. Michaelson complained.

Finn left the officers to handle the angry woman, then joined Hayley in his truck.

She looked exhausted and disheveled as she climbed aboard once more. "Any chance we can trace the cell phone Lincoln gave Gage?" she asked. "Get a list of numbers he called or everyone who called the Michaelsons' landline since last night? Confirm whether or not Gage contacted Parker?"

"You're certain they're together?" Finn asked, feeling the truth of the words as he spoke. The boys' united disappearance was another coincidence too big to ignore.

She nodded. "I'm sure of it."

"Josi told Gage that Parker was too young for the ranch," Finn said, shifting into Drive and thinking aloud. "Gage thought Parker wasn't safe with the Michaelsons, and this is Gage's way of protecting him?"

"I think so," Hayley said. "Which is hard to get my head

around considering the danger Gage is in. How can he possibly protect a little kid and himself while on the run? Parker would've been safe and happy if Gage would've given us time to place him in another home."

"But Gage is new to the system," Finn said, suddenly more tired than he'd been in a very long time. "You and I know the Michaelsons are the exception to the rule, and that wherever Parker is placed next will likely be filled with love and compassion. But this was Gage's only experience in foster care. He has no idea how good things can be, only how bad they've been."

Hayley raised her cell phone. "I'm going to try Gage's number again." She turned away and left a pleading voice mail, begging him to return to the ranch. She assured him it was okay to take Parker with him, and she vowed to protect them both.

Finn focused on the road, willing the rest of their day to get significantly better than the start.

Chapter Thirteen

Hayley concentrated on her breaths as Finn drove along the bay toward Old Downtown. It seemed like the most reasonable place to start their search for Gage and Parker. Gage was known to spend time in the area, and there were plenty of places for two boys to hole up and hide out. She hated the thought of them being there, especially knowing how many things could go wrong, but she also hoped they were somewhere in those neglected blocks, so she and Finn could find them and bring them home.

Sunlight twinkled off cresting waves and brilliant blue water, creating a postcard-worthy view beyond her window. Warm southern sun heated her skin, the familiar humidity cocooning her through the open window as they slowed for a turn.

Hayley kneaded her hands.

"We'll start on the outskirts," Finn said. "Talk to everyone we see, just like we did that first day. Then we'll move inward, toward the heart of the area, and finally toward the waterfront properties where the rave was held and Kate's body was located."

Hayley crossed and uncrossed her legs, knee bobbing as they rolled toward their destination. "I'm glad it's still early. I'm willing to turn over every piece of trash and rubble down here if needed." And thanks to the long summer days, she'd have nearly twelve more hours of light to do it.

"I don't think it'll come to that," Finn said. "Gage is trying to protect Parker, so he'll be strategic about where he takes him."

She stared into the distance, where traffic vanished along with all signs of grass and trees, replaced with sprawling concrete and desolation, dark storefronts with painted windows and barred doors. "That's what bothers me about him coming here. Gage knows what safe means. He had it with his family. If he's here now, I don't think he plans to stay longer than necessary. Which makes finding them fast even more important."

Finn glanced Hayley's way, his eyes skimming her face, then his gaze dropped to her twisting hands and bouncing knee. "I got the feeling most people in Old Downtown knew Gage, or at least recognized him from his art. He's spent a lot of time down here. His shadow children are everywhere. Chances are he talked to someone long enough to make friends. Maybe he went to them for help with Parker. Maybe he shared something that will lead us to the place he's calling home."

Hayley inhaled deeply and shook her hands out at the wrists. "You're right. I need to stay positive and focused." No more letting her unbearably negative imagination run away.

The truck slowed along the curb near a highway overpass, and Finn's attention moved to his rearview mirror.

"What is it?" Hayley turned, noticing a black SUV behind them.

The other vehicle sat on the previous block, angled against the curb as if it had pulled over as suddenly as they had. The SUV stood out as badly as Finn's truck in this area. It was shiny and new, while the rides parked between them were old and rusted.

"That SUV's been following us," Finn said. "It's not the same make or model as the one from the news, but it's been back there since we turned off Bay View. If we're being tailed because they're also looking for the boys, I need to know. And if we're being tailed for some other reason, I should probably know that too."

Her stomach churned as he opened his door. "Where are you going?" she hissed, reaching for him as he climbed out.

"Stay here, please." Finn turned toward the SUV in question. "Lock the doors."

"Wait!" Hayley gasped as his door closed. She hit the automatic locks, then dialed 911 on her cell phone. She hovered her thumb over the screen, ready to send the call, and twisted in her seat to watch Finn move confidently away. Every horrific possibility charged through her mind as she braced for the pending encounter. Most involved bullets and blood.

The SUV launched forward with a bark of the tires.

Finn lurched sideways, thrown between parked cars.

"No!" The word tore from her throat in a scream as the SUV rocketed past her.

Hayley was on the sidewalk in an instant, racing toward Finn as the SUV rounded a corner behind her. Her sharp, pounding strides ate up the space between the truck and the location where Finn had disappeared. "Finn!"

A low moan slowed her steps.

He rose slowly off the concrete, from the space between parked cars. Palms bloody and arms rubbed raw from wrist to elbow. "Guess they didn't want to talk."

Her grip on the phone relaxed, and she burst forward, wrapping herself around him. "Oh, my goodness!" The force of her attack hug knocked him back against a busted Toyota. "You could've been killed!"

"Just a few scratches," he said, straightening to his full

height, taking her with him. "I'm fine, but I'm getting blood on you."

She released him to better survey his physical damage. "I almost called 911."

"No need." He rolled his shoulders and tipped his head from side to side, stretching the muscles of his neck. "I don't suppose you got a look at the license plate?"

"I wasn't looking for a license plate." Her only thoughts had been of him. "I think you need to see a doctor. Maybe we should visit an urgent care before we keep going."

"I definitely don't need a doctor," he said, testing his fingers, wrists and elbows. Wincing with each move. "I couldn't see the driver. Too much sunlight reflecting on the windshield."

Hayley crossed her arms over her middle, hating that she'd thrown herself at him the way she had. Hating that whoever had tried to hit him would get away with it.

"Hey," he called, following her. "What's wrong?"

"You were nearly killed."

"I told you. I'm—"

She spun to glare at him. "Do not tell me you're fine."

Finn grinned. "Suit yourself."

She turned back to the truck, taking slow, deep breaths to regain her calm. She couldn't think about what would happen if she lost him. Even if she couldn't keep Finn in her life when this was over, the world was a better place with him in it.

Finn opened the driver's-side door and pulled a bottle of water from behind his seat. He unscrewed the lid and poured the contents over his hands and forearms, then used a towel from his gym bag to wipe away most of the blood. A few thin streams sprouted anew. "See? The rest of this will scab up by lunch. I don't even need stitches."

"Keep downplaying what just happened and you might

need a few," Hayley warned. She rounded the truck's grill, reached the passenger's door and climbed aboard.

Finn slid behind the wheel and started the engine. He pumped up the air-conditioning and pointed the vents in her direction. "I'm going to call this in before we move on," he said. He tapped the vehicle's dashboard screen while she buckled up.

Hayley swallowed a sudden wave of panic as he calmly relayed the details of his near death to someone at Marshal's Bluff PD.

The voice on the other end of the line sounded distorted as heat climbed her neck and her ears began to ring. She leaned forward on her seat, fighting nausea and searching for oxygen.

Gage was missing. A killer wanted him dead. Parker was likely in tow.

And she thought she'd seen Finn mowed down by a Range Rover. Had imagined him never getting up again.

Her vision tunneled and she closed her eyes against the dark spots encroaching on her vision.

"Hayley." Finn's steady voice echoed in her ears. "Hey. Are you okay? Can you hear me?"

Her seat belt gave way with a snap, and Finn's big hands curled around her biceps, dragging her toward him.

In the next moment she was across his lap, curled against his chest, face pressed to his neck. "Shh," he said softly. "I've got you, and we're both just fine. I promise."

Hayley held on to his words like a lifeline as he stroked her back and gripped her tight. She pressed her palms to his chest and counted the beats of his heart until she was calm once more.

"Better?" he asked, not missing the release of tension in her body.

She raised her face to his, embarrassed at her unexpected

reaction to the stress, infinitely thankful for his reaction to her. "I thought I lost you again."

His eyes darkened, and his lips parted. His gaze lowered to her mouth. "I'm right here."

Suddenly, every moment with him seemed so much more important than it had an hour before. This was it for her and Finn. They'd find Gage. Finn would arrest the killer. And the man she loved would be out of her life all over again. She hated the future, but she still had this moment.

Before she could talk herself out of it, she burrowed her fingers into the soft hair at the back of his head and urged his mouth to hers. She kissed him tenderly, hoping to convey how truly precious he was to her. She was desperate to show him all the things she hadn't found the courage to say.

And for one terrifying moment, Finn grew stone-still.

She dropped her hand away, pulling back in humiliation. "I am so sorry," she said in a rush, horrified by her unsolicited actions. "I didn't mean to—"

"Hayley." The deep rumble of pleasure in his chest had barely registered before his mouth returned to hers. The gentle sweep of his tongue sent fire through her veins, and the heady mix of joy and desire overtook her. She adjusted her body to better align with his, their hearts pounding together in a staccato rhythm.

"Ms. Campbell?" a deep male voice called, somewhat muffled by the closed windows.

A round of whoops and catcalls followed, returning her rudely to reality.

Hayley scrambled back to her side of the truck as a group of laughing teens came into view outside the windshield. She smoothed her hair as they closed in on the truck.

Finn stared at her, breathing heavy, his lips slightly swollen from her kisses. "Friends of yours?" Finn asked quietly, shifting his attention to the group.

"I only know the spokesman."

He powered down the window and set his bloody elbow across the frame.

"Ms. C?" A young man she recognized as Keith Shane, a former child from her caseload, frowned back. "What are you doing down here?" His attention flicked to Finn and his bloody arm, then back to her. "You okay?"

"Fine," she said, hoping to appear as if it was true and hating her word choice. She'd just yelled at Finn for saying the same thing. And like Finn, she was absolutely not fine. She'd just made out in the front seat of a truck in broad daylight. And been caught. She was supposed to be looking for two missing children. And behaving like a professional grown-up.

Keith crouched to stare boldly through the open window. "So what's going on in here?"

"This is Detective Beaumont," Hayley said, thankful her voice sounded natural and unbothered. "Detective, this is Keith."

The young man's brow rose briefly, then furrowed. His gaze hardened on the detective. "Did he bring you down here for a reason I need to know about?"

Her heart warmed at the kid's protective tone, and she smiled. "Actually, yes. We're looking for two boys. Parker and Gage, ages eight and fourteen. Gage is the artist who paints the shadow children on the buildings. Do you know him?"

The group behind Keith made a few comments in approval of the artwork. Keith took another long look at Finn before turning to confer with his friends.

"If you've seen either boy today," Finn said, voice thick with authority, "we need to know. We have reasons to believe both kids are in significant danger."

The group dragged their eyes from Finn to Hayley, apparently deciding what to do next.

"They aren't in any trouble," Hayley assured them. "I want to protect them, but first I need to find them."

A short, wiry guy in a plain white tank top and navy basketball shorts stepped forward. "I saw that kid at a rave." He glanced at Finn.

"We know about the rave," Finn said. "We know Gage was there. Someone was chasing him. Any chance you got a look at that person?"

The kid nodded. "Yeah, it was an old rich dude."

"How old?"

He shrugged. "I don't know. Thirty."

Hayley felt her breath catch. This was a new lead. "How did you know he was rich?"

"His clothes." The kid plucked the material of his tank top away from his chest. "He was bougie as hell. V-neck T-shirt. Three-hundred-dollar boat shoes. A watch I could hock to buy my ma a house."

"Ever seen him before that night?" she asked.

The kid shrugged. "Maybe. There's been a lot of folks like that around lately. Preparing for the community center, I guess. I figured your boy got caught taking something from him, or maybe he painted on the wrong building."

Finn straightened, giving up any final pretense of casual. "Anything else we should know?"

The teens commiserated. "Nah," Keith said, retaking his role as spokesman. "But I wouldn't worry. That guy never had a chance at catching him. Kids disappear down here for a lot of reasons. And if they don't want to be found, they won't be." The sad smile he offered Hayley implied that she could expect the same result.

She could only hope he was wrong. "Any idea where he calls home?" she asked.

The group traded looks then shook their heads.

Finn distributed his business cards. "If you see Gage or

think of anything that can help us find and protect him, give me a call."

Hayley offered a composed smile. "I'm safe with the detective," she said, noting the lingering concern in Keith's eyes. "He's one of the good ones."

Keith nodded in acceptance, then led his friends away.

Finn powered up the window and set his hands on the wheel. "Well, that was—"

"Embarrassing? Humiliating? Awful?" Hayley offered, feeling latent heat rise over her cheeks.

"I was going to say lucky," Finn said. "Based on his description, we can assume I was right in theorizing that Kate's killer wasn't robbing her. People in expensive shoes don't come down here at night if they can avoid it. They certainly don't chase kids into raves without serious motivation."

"Like getting away with murder," she mused.

"Yep." He shifted the truck into gear and headed deeper into Old Downtown.

Chapter Fourteen

Hayley tried not to obsess over the kiss. She'd acted impulsively but didn't regret it. And he'd kissed her back. Good and right. Her toes curled inside her shoes at the memory. The timing, location and audience were severely unfortunate, but damn…

Had it been more than just heightened emotions that had caused Finn to return the affection? He'd yet to comment on her tearful confession the night before. Not that they'd had time to talk about anything other than Gage and Parker today.

Finn turned onto the street where the rave had taken place and Kate's body had been discovered. The hour was early, and they'd yet to see anyone other than Keith and his friends.

She wet her still tingling lips and pushed aside thoughts of personal problems. Something more important suddenly had her attention. "Do you see all these signs?" she asked. "I didn't notice them when we were here before."

Rectangles of sturdy white cardboard had been affixed to multiple buildings in the area, each marked with the logo of an unfamiliar company.

"Is that an investment group?" he asked.

"Maybe. I've never heard of Lighthouse, Inc. Is it one of Kate's companies?"

"I'm not sure," he said, parking the truck once more.

"What do you think about taking another look at the warehouse where the old rich guy was seen?" He smiled. "I want to be sure we didn't miss anything there."

Hayley agreed and followed him out of the truck, then into the site of the rave. Empty plastic bags and sheets of newspapers blew over the silent, empty street as they entered. Their footfalls echoed in the stillness.

"Stay close," he said, posture tense, clearly on high alert.

She easily complied.

Dust motes sparkled like silver confetti in shafts of sunlight through broken windows. Sounds of the distant sea rose through the missing rear wall to her ears. A Lighthouse, Inc. sign on the broken boards drew her eyes. "Look."

They moved to the back, approaching the sign for inspection.

"Condemned," Finn read. "Marked for demolition. Unsafe for inhabitants and industry." He snapped a photo of the large cardboard warning then tapped his phone screen. "Let's see what Dean can learn about the company."

"They seem to own everything nearby," Hayley said. That had to mean something. "Maybe Lighthouse, Inc. is involved in the community-center project somehow."

Finn stilled. He worked his jaw and slid his gaze over the space around them, posture stiffening incrementally.

Hayley followed his eyes, searching for what had gotten his attention, but seeing nothing unusual. "What is it?"

"I'm not sure." His phone rang, and she started. "Hey," he answered, raising the device to his ear. "We're at the warehouse now—"

The sounds of squealing tires and rapid gunfire erupted from the world outside.

Splinters of wood burst into the air around them, and a scream ripped from Hayley's throat. Finn's body collided with hers in the next heartbeat, jolting them forward.

"Run!" he hollered, thrusting her toward the missing back wall, where nothing stood between them and the sea far below.

"But—" Something bounced and rolled in her peripheral vision as the car roared away, and she recognized the urgency. "Is that dynamite?" she screeched.

Finn jerked her by the wrist, forcing her into a sprint. "Jump!" he yelled a moment before they launched into the air.

Her feet left the warehouse floorboards, bicycling high above the sea.

Their joint freefall began as the warehouse exploded.

Another scream ripped from Hayley. Her ears rang and her vision blurred with the intensity of the boom.

Debris blew into the sky around them. Bits of busted stone and chunks of roofing. Clods of earth and fractured beams. A thousand pieces of instant shrapnel. Some sliced her clothes and others bit her skin.

Then, it was all swallowed by harbor water.

The impact pushed the air from her lungs. Shock separated her mind and limbs, leaving her body to twist and roll helplessly in the dark silence of the sea. She searched for the surface, fighting the pitch and heave of undercurrents, burning with need for oxygen.

Would she survive an explosion only to drown in the waters below?

Demanding hands gripped her waist in the next moment, propelling her upward. She recognized Finn's touch before she saw him. Before she took her next breath.

Her mouth opened and her body gasped as they broke the surface—she pulled sweet salt air deep into her lungs.

"I've got you," he promised, between the raspy breaths and the rhythmic kicking of his legs. "Are you okay?" he asked, treading water as he caressed her cheek and scanned her face with worried eyes.

She opened her mouth to speak, but a fit of coughing erupted instead. Followed by a stomach full of salt water. How much had she swallowed?

Finn pulled her against his chest and began an awkward backstroke toward the shore.

Emergency sirens wailed in the distance, growing louder and more fervent with each inch of progress Finn made.

He towed her through a floating field of charred and busted planks, dodging the larger, most ragged pieces. "Only a little farther," he promised, his breaths coming rougher and shorter.

Slowly, Hayley's mind and body reunited, coordinating her limbs. She helped him paddle until his feet struck the ground below.

"Help is on the way," he panted, setting her gingerly on the rocky shore. "They'll be here soon."

She took a mental inventory of her faculties and scanned her body for injuries. All her parts were accounted for, and the cuts and bruises were shockingly few. Though she'd still have been dead, if not for Finn. "You saved my life."

He dipped his chin in acknowledgement, eyes scanning the top of the hill, where a cluster of onlookers had appeared. Blood lined his mouth, seeping from a split in his lip, and a large purple knot had formed beside his right eye.

"You're hurt." She reached for his hands, pulling him down, certain her shaking legs wouldn't hold her if she tried to stand. "Sit. It could be bad. Adrenaline can cover serious injuries."

He wobbled slightly, then fell to his knees, his body stiff as he winced. His shirt was torn and his arms were bleeding. Suddenly, the scrapes from the earlier road incident seemed like paper cuts in comparison.

Hayley's gaze shot to the warehouse on the hill, or what remained of it. The explosion had demolished the back half, reducing that portion of the structure to rubble. *Exactly what dynamite tended to do*, she thought. And they'd been inside moments before it blew. She sucked a ragged breath as something horrendous came to mind. "What if—" The words were lodged in her throat, unable to break free.

What if Gage and Parker had been there too?

"We were alone," Finn said, offering comfort and apparently reading her mind. He eased into the space beside her then reached for her trembling hands.

"Someone blew up a building to kill us," she said. The words were nonsensical. How could anything so outrageous be true?

Finn gave her fingers a squeeze. "I'm guessing they used C-4 from a nearby construction site, and the one who threw the explosive was probably the same person driving the SUV that nearly hit me." His normally tanned skin was unusually white, and his gaze slightly unfocused.

"I think you should lay back," Hayley said. "You're going to need stitches. I don't know how much blood you've lost. Or if you have other injuries. Did anything hit your head as we fell?" There had been a lot of large debris, and he'd used his body to protect her.

"I'm all right," he said. "Just wondering what's taking the ambulance so long."

"There they are!" someone called from the top of the hill, drawing Hayley's eyes back to the growing crowd. She waved a limp arm overhead.

"Help is coming!" a stranger called. "They're almost here!"

"I can't believe they're alive!" someone else yelled. "That place blew into splinters!"

Finn slumped against Hayley's side, and she wound an arm around him. Hopefully, the crowd was enough deterrent to keep their near-assassin from taking another shot. Neither she nor Finn were in any condition to run again. She wasn't convinced they were even ready to stand.

A collection of rocks and dirt slid over the hill in their direction, accompanied by a pair of EMTs. The men wore matching uniforms and expressions of disbelief while carrying backboards and medical kits.

Hayley knew exactly how they felt.

A long hour later, she and Finn were sequestered in side-by-side ambulances. Hayley's EMT had examined her swiftly, cleaned her wounds, then hooked her up to an IV to replenish lost fluids.

Outside the open bay doors, uniformed officers interviewed the crowd. From what she could piece together, several people had heard the squealing tires that preceded the dynamite delivery, but no one had seen the car causing all the noise or its driver.

Finn strode into view, scowling, with an EMT trailing behind.

"Detective," the medic pleaded. "I haven't finished." He swiped an alcohol pad over the back of Finn's arm as they moved.

"Yes," Finn corrected. "You have. I appreciated the IV and bandages. The rest of this will heal on its own."

Hayley smiled despite herself. "You should go to the hospital and let them check you more thoroughly," she said, watching as he climbed aboard with her.

"I'm fine. I wasn't hit by anything big, and I've cliff-dived from greater heights. I got a little dinged up, but it's been handled. What about you?"

"Oh, I'm super," she said, struggling to maintain her smile. Images of Finn cliff-diving helped. She wished she could've been there to see him make a leap like that for fun.

He looked to the EMT for confirmation. "She's okay?"

"She's going to heal completely, with rest and fluids,"

the man said. "For the record, I don't think either of you are okay. That was quite an experience. You both need to take a few days and rest. Visible wounds or not."

"Noted," Finn said, though he didn't look convinced. He looked like a losing prizefighter. His split lip had swollen, and the knot on his head had grown. "If we're cleared to go, I think we're ready."

Hayley nodded in agreement when he turned her way.

The EMT sighed and removed Hayley's IV. "Fluids and rest," he repeated. "Something over-the-counter for pain."

"Thank you." Hayley waved. She let Finn help her down from the ambulance then along the sidewalk to his truck on the next block.

The day was insufferably hot, the air thick with stifling humidity. A secondary crowd had gathered outside the warehouse remains.

She recognized Dean on the outskirts surveying the scene.

Finn unlocked the pickup as they approached, and Hayley climbed inside.

Her previously soaked clothes were wrinkled and dirty, and had been dried by the relentless heat. She peeled strands of tangled hair from her cheeks and neck. "Are you sure you're okay?" she asked.

"Physically, sure," he said. "But I've been wondering how long we were followed." He eased behind the wheel with a small wince. "Some of what we said after leaving the truck might've been overheard. Maybe even our chat with Keith and his friends."

Hayley tensed, thinking about all the things she'd spoken with Finn about in the time before the explosion. "Someone could know we're looking for the spot Gage called home. They'll be looking for it too."

Finn shifted into gear and piloted the vehicle back toward town, scanning pedestrians and passing traffic with care. "Gage's file mentioned active involvement at his middle school last year. Band. Soccer. Art camps. His parents led a few extracurriculars as well. Let's start there, and see if there's any place he could make a temporary home. Somewhere to relive the better days."

"He attended Virginia Dare middle school," Hayley said. She reached for her phone before remembering it was at the bottom of the bay. "He was part of the swim team too, and I think there's a pool on the property."

Finn stretched across the cab and opened the glove box. He withdrew a handgun and cell phone. "Do you remember the address of his home?"

She searched her memory for the information but came up empty. "No. I'm sorry."

"Would you mind giving your office a call? Asking someone to look in the file?"

She took the device with trembling fingers, and Finn made the next turn toward the middle school. By the time they arrived, she'd gained the information they needed, and Finn had passed it on to his team.

"I'll ask Dispatch to send a cruiser to the house and talk to the new owners," he said. "We'll let them know there's a possibility a couple of kids might show up, try to sleep in the backyard playhouse or elsewhere on the grounds. If that happens, the owners can give the station a call."

Hayley wiped tears from her cheeks, unsure what had prompted them this time.

"You doing okay?" Finn asked.

She shook her head, unable to lie. "I thought I was tough, but this whole situation has been awful. How do you do this every day?"

Finn smiled kindly. "This isn't a typical workweek," he said. "I'm not usually in continual danger, and the good I do is always worth the trouble. I'm sorry you're in the line of fire this week. If I could change that, I would."

"Don't feel too badly," she said. "I brought the fire."

Finn chose a spot in the middle-school parking lot, then turned stormy eyes on her.

A cascade of goose bumps scattered over her skin in the quiet cab, and her lips parted of their own accord. "I kissed you," she whispered. Somehow, that had been the least dangerous yet most traumatic event to occur since breakfast.

Maybe the timing was wrong, but she'd bared her heart to him in words last night and in actions this morning. She needed to know where he stood on the matter. She needed to settle at least this one thing in a time when everything else was beyond her reach. She had no means of getting answers to Gage's whereabouts. Or Parker's. Had no way of knowing who'd killed Kate and wanted to kill her too. But she could ask Finn to be direct with her, and she could get this one issue solved.

"We should talk about that when this is over," he said, turning his attention to something beyond the truck's window. "Looks like the groundskeeper is headed our way."

She followed Finn's gaze to a man in jeans and a navy blue T-shirt with the school's logo.

Grass clippings stuck to the bottoms of his pant legs and a curious look crossed his heavily creased face. He grinned as he drew near. "Finn Beaumont. What brings you around here? How's your family doing?"

Finn climbed out and met the man on the passenger's side. He shook his hand.

Hayley powered down her window, hoping to hide her aching limbs and frazzled nerves by remaining inside the truck.

"Nice to see you again, Eric," Finn said. "The family's good. This is Hayley Campbell. She's a social worker, and we're looking for a former student. He's in foster care now, attending the high school this year. He's gone missing. Runaway, we believe. We're hoping you might be able to help."

The older man accepted the handshake then crossed his arms and listened intently as Finn covered the important details of Gage's story. Eric removed his hat when Finn finished. "I remember Gage. Remember the accident. Hell, I remember his folks. Nice, good people. What happened to them was unthinkable. Our whole community grieved. I hate to hear he's taken off, but his world must be in a shambles."

Hayley nearly choked at the painful understatement. Eric didn't know the half of it. She passed a business card through the open window and into his hand. "If you see him, will you reach out to the police or call me directly?"

"Will do." Eric raised two fingers to his forehead, saluting them as Finn retook his seat behind the wheel and shifted into Reverse.

Hayley sent out another round of prayers to the universe as they motored away.

Let us find those boys before the killer can.

Chapter Fifteen

Hayley tried and failed to rest all afternoon. Her body was sore and fatigued, but her mind was in overdrive. She'd nearly died today while under the protection of a lawman. What chance did Gage have at survival on his own while caring for a kid?

Finn's brothers and other detectives had visited the pool where Gage used to swim, along with a few other spots from the teen's past, but none had revealed any indication the boys had been there.

Meanwhile, Finn and Hayley had returned to his house. Mrs. Beaumont had delivered a delicious lunch, and Hayley had taken a lengthy, indulgent shower, but her tension only increased. She couldn't shake the sensation a giant clock was counting down, and the boys were running out of time.

She dragged Finn's laptop onto the couch with her while he took his turn in the shower. If she couldn't be on the streets searching for Gage and Parker, she could at least keep looking for clues online. She started with the name of the company that had plastered signs all over Old Downtown.

Her initial findings revealed Lighthouse, Inc. to be a small company located in Marshal's Bluff. Real-estate projects seemed to be the business's focus, but it was unclear if Lighthouse, Inc. was an investment group or something else. The website was static, and the accompanying social-media accounts were sorely lacking.

Sounds of the shower filtered to her ears, and Hayley did her best to ignore them. In the big scheme of her current problems, matters of the heart should've been less than irrelevant. But knowing Finn was naked and separated from her by one closed door made it unreasonably hard to concentrate.

She clicked the next link on her web search, and an image of Kate pulled her focus back to where it belonged. The article featured the philanthropist as the keynote speaker at a recent fundraising gala. The caption below the photo identified her and the men at her side. Her husband, Topper, and Conrad Forester, the CEO of Lighthouse, Inc.

Hayley swung her feet onto the floor and opened another browser window, starting a second search. She added Kate and her husband's names to the words *Lighthouse, Inc.* Several links appeared. Each time, the results also mentioned Conrad Forester. Apparently, the trio had golfed together, boated together and attended a number of other community events.

Did they simply run in the same circles, or were they friends outside their work? The three of them? Or only two? If the latter, then who was the third wheel? More importantly, was their connection relevant to the case?

The water shut off in the bathroom, and Hayley rose to her feet. She paced the carpeted space between the couch and hallway, waiting for Finn to appear. She wasn't a detective, but something inside her told her this new knowledge mattered. Finn would know for sure.

When the door opened and he emerged in a clingy T-shirt and cloud of Finn-scented steam, she allowed herself a moment to appreciate the view.

Her eyes met his a heartbeat later, and his mischievous grin suggested he'd noticed exactly how long it'd taken her to pull herself together. "What's up?" he asked, rubbing a towel over damp, tousled hair.

"I think I found something." She pointed over her shoulder, refusing to steal another glance at his nicely curved biceps as he draped the towel around his neck.

"What is it?"

She returned to the couch and passed him the laptop, recapping her concern.

"That is interesting," he agreed. "It makes sense a company involved in real estate would know her. Their work probably brought them together from time to time. The frequent interactions could've made them friends."

"Do you think they were collaborating on the community-center project?"

Finn grinned. "I can think of one way to find out. How are you feeling?"

"Like I could sleep until retirement, but I'm too wound up to rest."

Finn checked his watch. "If we hurry, we might catch Mr. Forester at work before office hours end."

"Then we'd better get moving."

LIGHTHOUSE, INC. WAS housed in a single-story cottage in the shopping district. The former residential property was covered in gray-blue vinyl siding and trimmed in white. A small porch with two steps and a coordinating black handrail matched the roof and front door. According to the sign in the window, the office was open.

Finn held the door for Hayley. "After you."

Seashell wind chimes jangled overhead as she crossed the threshold.

"May I help you?" a young woman in a periwinkle-blue sundress asked. Her long brown hair hung in waves across her shoulders. The welcome desk where she sat was white and tidy, topped with a keyboard and monitor.

Finn raised his detective shield. "We're here to speak with Conrad Forester."

Her eyes widened in response. She looked from Finn to Hayley, then to a set of closed doors on the far wall before managing to recover. "Do you have an appointment?"

Finn wiggled the badge. "Yep."

She nodded shakily. "Right." She turned her focus to the monitor and typed something with her keyboard.

Hayley gave the office a more thorough look while they waited. A small sitting area beside the welcome desk held a couch, a set of armchairs and a coffee table covered in boating magazines. A placard on one of the closed doors across the room identified it as a restroom. The others, Hayley presumed, were offices.

"He'll be right out," the woman said.

Finn turned to stare at the closed doors, ignoring the comfortable-looking couch and armchairs. Hayley followed his lead.

Soon, one of the doors opened, and a tall, broad-shouldered man stepped out. "Detective."

"Mr. Forester," Finn said, approaching for a handshake. "This is Hayley Campbell."

"Good afternoon." Mr. Forester offered her a plaintive smile. His face was tan and his forehead lined with creases. A sprinkle of gray touched his otherwise sandy hair. He didn't invite them in. "What can I do for you?" he asked, swinging troubled brown eyes back to Finn.

"I'm looking into the murder of Katherine Everett," Finn said.

Mr. Forester nodded solemnly. "A true shame. She'll be greatly missed in this community."

"Couldn't agree more," Finn said. "I also couldn't help

noticing signs for your company all over the area where her body was discovered."

The soft sounds of typing ceased, and Hayley fought the urge to look at the woman who'd welcomed them. Instead, she kept her eyes on the man before her, as he seemed to pale at the mention of his company signs in conjunction with Kate's murder.

"We're planning to improve the area near the bay," Forester said. "The changes will bring in local businesses, reduce crime, create condos along the waterfront and single-family homes along the fringe. Parks. Playgrounds. The whole deal." His smile grew as he spoke, and his demeanor became congenial. As if he was reciting a canned pitch for the media or as a marketing speech, not explaining himself to a detective investigating a homicide.

Hayley struggled to keep her expression blank and guarded.

"Condos," Finn repeated, the disbelief in the single word making it fall flat. "In Old Downtown."

She understood the skepticism. The area in question was too raw and riddled with trouble. The criminal population alone would likely destroy or make off with any decent building materials before the things on Forester's list ever came to fruition.

Creating a community center and homeless shelter in an area was one thing. The people and the area were in desperate need of love and housing. Replacing everything with high-end housing and businesses was rubbing salt in a proverbial wound.

"Shopping too," Forester said. "Pubs, cafés, jobs. Whatever it takes to get families down that way."

Finn stared at him, silently scrutinizing. Hayley would've confessed to anything if she'd been on the other side of that look, but Forester kept up the unbothered grin. "How well did you know Katherine Everett?" Finn asked.

Forester rocked back on his heels. "Not well." He put his palms in front of him. "We weren't strangers, but we were friendly enough to say hello when we crossed paths."

"That happened a lot," Finn said. "I understand the two of you were friends. You did a number of things together. Boating. Golfing. Charity events and whatnot."

"Well." Forester chuckled. "That's what business owners do, isn't it? We lend a hand however we can. Golf outings, nautical events, dinners—they're all for a cause."

Finn sucked his teeth. "So you didn't have a personal relationship with Kate or her husband?"

Forester's smile slipped by a fraction. A ringing phone drew his attention through the open door behind him. "I'm sorry to do this, but I've been expecting that call. Would you mind?"

"Not at all," Finn said. "I'll be in touch if I need anything else."

Forester took his leave, pulling the door closed in his wake.

Hayley waved to the woman at the welcome desk on her way out, then they hurried back to Finn's truck. "Are you thinking what I'm thinking?" she asked.

"Depends." Finn opened the door and waited while she climbed inside. "Are you thinking he seemed extremely on edge beneath the forced smile?"

"Yeah, and I'm guessing Kate's plans would've put a big dent in the value of his condos."

FINN STRETCHED HIS aching limbs into cotton joggers and an old concert T-shirt later that evening, thankful for the rest of the night off. His team at Marshal's Bluff PD was working around the clock to find the missing boys and put the pieces of Kate's murder investigation together. Finn had no doubt they'd be in touch if anything significant came to light. Meanwhile, he needed to recuperate. He'd barely had the energy to visit with his mom and shower after the explosion. The trip to Lighthouse, Inc. had put him over the edge. But there was still one more thing he needed to do. Having a talk with Hayley about her confession the previous night, and their kiss earlier today, was already overdue.

He'd originally imagined her reason for confiding in him was simply to clear the air so they could move forward as friends. Especially since they'd become impromptu roommates. The kiss they'd shared, however, made him wonder if there was hope for more. It wasn't uncommon for people under extreme stress to find physical outlets, and all the things they'd been through certainly qualified as stressful, but he wanted to hear it from Hayley. Was her behavior a result of heightened emotions, or was there a chance they could find their way back to one another? He'd never forgive himself if the case ended, and she walked away because he hadn't taken the opportunity to set things straight while he had a chance.

Finn inhaled deeply, then released the breath slowly. He'd dreamed of being in Hayley's life again, and now she was living under his roof, sharing his meals and at his side in every moment of the day. He didn't want to screw that up or scare her away again. Whatever happened between them, he'd never stop protecting her in any way he could.

His eyes found her as he moved down the hall toward the living room. She looked like his personal heaven curled on the couch in a messy bun, oversize shirt and sleep shorts. She was so much more than a beautiful woman, human and friend. She was the place he wanted to get lost in, but he didn't have that luxury. Not while two boys were missing and a killer was at large. Hell, he wasn't sure he had that option at all. But it was time he and Hayley figured that out.

"Hey." She smiled as he entered the room. "How are you feeling?"

"Like I was in an explosion." He stopped in the kitchen and pulled two bottles from the fridge, then lifted them in question.

"Yes, please." Her eyes traveled the length of his arms and neck, pausing briefly on every cut, scrape and bandage, then on his swollen eye. "You look terrible."

"I feel terrible. How about you? You doing okay?"

Hayley pulled her bottom lip between her teeth. "I'm still hoping you want to talk." The blush creeping over her lightly freckled cheeks said she'd been thinking about her confession and their recent kiss as well.

Finn carried the bottles of water to the coffee table and took a seat on the couch beside her. She moved closer, leaning in and fitting perfectly against his side. He released a contented sigh and let his arm curve around her. This could've been their life.

If he'd gone after her that night.

If she'd found her voice sooner.

If he'd seen the signs of her pain and asked about them.

If he'd had a clue.

"Finn?"

He shook away the what-ifs and angled his head toward her, resting his chin atop her crown. "Yeah?"

"I hate that all of this is happening, but I'm glad you're here. We're alive today because of you."

He stroked her soft hair and inhaled her sweet scent, unsure of what to say. His every action today, and every day since she'd shown up unexpectedly in his office, were born of instinct and a bone-deep need to protect her at any cost. "You will always be safe with me," he promised.

"I know." She pulled away to look into his eyes. "I'm sorry I lost it last night when I was explaining myself. I wanted you to know all those things, but I didn't expect to be flooded with emotion while I shared. I definitely didn't think I'd be so embarrassed by the outburst I'd cry myself to sleep."

"You never have to be embarrassed with me," he said softly, meaning it to his core. "You can always tell me anything."

She gave a sad laugh. "I left you without an explanation last year. Then I dumped the whole story on you last night and left again. This is not who I'm trying to be."

Her words drew a small smile over his face.

"I know who you are, Hayley Campbell," he stated simply, stroking the backs of his fingers across her cheek. "I wish I'd known about your pain sooner, but I'm glad you told me. A lot of things make more sense now. And because I know, I can be more aware and sensitive to you."

"Do you have any questions?" she asked, gaze darting away then back. "I can try to fill in any blanks I left."

Finn opened his mouth to say he'd listen to anything she wanted to tell him, but he wouldn't pry. Instead, a different set of words rolled off his tongue. "Why'd you kiss me today?"

Hayley froze in his arms and pulled in a deep breath. "I thought you'd been hit by that car. The possibility I'd lost you again, forever and for real this time, was gutting. I never want to live in that reality. Even if you never speak to me again after this case ends, I need to know you're okay and happy somewhere. Nothing else makes any sense. You know?"

He pulled her against his chest and held her a little more tightly, because he knew exactly what she meant.

Chapter Sixteen

Hayley forced herself to push away from Finn's protective hold. She had more to say and needed to get it out before the phone rang or someone else tried to kill them. She tucked her feet beneath her and angled to face him on the cushions. "I want you to know I'm committed to healing. I don't want to hurt anymore, and I don't want to hurt anyone else like I hurt you. It's been a long road just getting this far, but I won't quit. I still meet with my therapist weekly to sort through the thoughts and feelings that make me feel unlovable. I have no intention of going back to where I was last year."

His kind eyes crinkled at the corners and he tipped his head slightly. Interest and something that looked a lot like pride flashed in his expression. "I believe you. Do you want to talk about it?"

She shifted, debating, but knew she needed to be brave and honest. "A little."

Finn nodded, holding her gaze. Then he waited patiently while she gathered the right words to continue.

"So far my key takeaways have been that my mother is an alcoholic. She has been for the majority of my life, and she will always be. She doesn't accept this as truth, and she is nowhere near the point of seeking help. Her behavior isn't my fault, and there's nothing I could've done better that would've changed her choices or healed her illness. She has to do that herself. I tried talking to her about it over dinner last fall, but she accused me of making slanderous accusations to hurt her."

Hayley took another steadying breath and swallowed, determined not to cry again. "I've accepted that my childhood was a series of minor and major abuses, and that I've both survived and thrived as a human despite her. Those unfortunate experiences have shaped and burdened every relationship I've had, including what I had with you. I'm distrustful and needy. Desperate to help others while neglecting myself. And a whole slew of other opposing concepts that keep me unsettled. But I'm working on those too." She pressed her lips together. "I will not pretend everything is fine like my mother."

Finn set a hand over hers as he'd done so many times before, an offer of shared strength. "How often do you get to see or speak to your mother now?" Finn asked, cutting to the quick of Hayley's pain. Seeing the thing she hadn't been able to say.

"I don't. Not since that dinner last year." Because until Hayley fully healed, interacting with her mother would only destroy the progress she'd fought so hard to make. She waited for Finn to say more, then tensed with each passing breath in silence. "What are you thinking?"

"I'm thinking that you used self-sabotage to avoid happiness," he said.

"I did."

"That's not uncommon when you spent so long being miserable."

Hayley nodded, thankful for the millionth time that Finn understood but never judged. "I should've trusted you with all of this sooner." She'd known in her heart that he wasn't like the others who'd hurt her, but her instinct had still been to run.

Finn opened his arms and raised his chin, coaxing her closer. She fell against him, immediately cocooned in his embrace.

"I'm broken in so many ways," she whispered.

"You are healing in far more." He pulled her onto his lap and pressed a kiss to the top of her head. "I'm glad you're on this path," he said softly. "You deserve happiness, Hayley. You deserve the world."

She tipped her head away for a view of his sincere brown eyes. "What if the only thing I've wanted in a very long time is you, and I ruined it?"

Finn's gaze darkened, and he lifted a palm to cradle her jaw. One strong thumb stroked her cheek. "I'm right here, just like I always have been. Like I always will be."

Her gaze dropped to his lips, and he angled his mouth to hers in response. The delicious scent of him encompassed her. The heat of his skin and tantalizing pressure of his embrace was instant ecstasy. When the kiss deepened and their tongues met in that perfect, familiar, sensual slide, she knew she'd finally come home.

HAYLEY WOKE ON the couch in Finn's arms the next morning. A call from his team roused them both from a deep slumber. It was the first truly good night of rest Hayley had had since the mess with Gage first began. Finn appeared astonished at the sight of the clock. She assumed he was feeling the same way.

An hour later, like the days before, they were up and out the door. Hastily dressed in denim capris, black flats and a white silk tank, she sat beside him in his pickup as they approached Katherine Everett's home. They rolled along the winding paved driveway that stretched between a posh gated entrance and the massive brick estate. The experience was a little like traveling to another world. "I had no idea homes like this existed in Marshal's Bluff," Hayley said, leaning forward to drink in the views. Majestic oaks lined the path, their gnarled, moss-soaked limbs stretching overhead, the road before them dappled in golden light.

"There are a few," he said. "And there are usually lawyers waiting for me when I visit."

She wrinkled her nose. "Frustrating."

Finn piloted the truck around a stone fountain outside the sprawling estate and parked near a sleek Mercedes convertible. He inhaled deeply, perhaps preparing himself for those lawyers. Then he opened his door.

Hayley followed suit and met him at the fountain, where they exchanged small smiles.

"You should get one," she teased. "Your yard chickens would love it."

Finn snorted before schooling his features into detective mode and leading the way to the home's front doors. He rang the bell and scanned the structure while he waited.

Hayley tried not to gawk as she admired the detail work along the eaves, around the windows and in the stylized shrubbery. Katherine Everett had always appeared so casual and down-to-earth online and during her television interviews. No different than those she helped. Clearly, that had been a mask.

Finn pressed the bell a second time and shifted for a peek through the beveled glass.

"Are you sure he's home?" Hayley asked. They'd come without calling after all.

"I believe that's his car of choice," Finn said, nodding toward the convertible. "One of a dozen registered in his name. Plus, it's still fairly early, and given his recent loss,

I'd expect a husband to be taking time off from whatever he does to grieve."

"What does he do?" Hayley asked, realizing she had no idea. Was being the spouse of Kate enough to keep a person busy?

Finn's eyebrows tented. "Not much as far as I can tell."

The door opened, sweeping her attention to a woman in black slacks and a crimson blouse. "May I help you?"

Finn flashed his badge and her lips turned down in distaste.

"The police have already been here to speak with Mr. Everett," she said, coolly. "I'm sure they have everything they need, and Mr. Everett's attorney's contact information for future inquiries."

Finn stepped toward her, causing her to step back. "I won't keep him long. I understand this is a sensitive time for Mr. Everett, but I'm sure he's as interested in finding his wife's killer as I am. Would you mind letting him know I'm here?"

The woman pulled her chin back and balked.

"My name is Detective Beaumont."

She turned with a huff. "I'll see if Mr. Everett is available." She left the front door open and stormed into the home.

Finn waited for Hayley to step into the foyer, then he followed the woman across acres of Italian marble and through sliding glass doors to a rear patio.

Hayley hurried along in their wake, devouring the delicious interior views. Each space she passed looked more like an image from a design magazine than the last. As if Pinterest had exploded and all the pieces landed in one magnificent array for the Everetts to enjoy.

She stole one last peek at the mind-bending gourmet kitchen before stepping back into the scorching summer heat.

It took a moment for her eyes to adjust as sunlight glinted off the water of an impressive in-ground pool. Gorgeous tropical-looking plants and landscaping ran the length of the space between home and cabana. An outdoor kitchen, bar, fireplace and rocky waterfall feature filled the area nearest a hot tub. Finn and the woman stopped short of the bubbling water, where a shirtless man was sitting chest-deep.

Mirrored sunglasses covered his eyes as he sipped from a tall glass. A few soft words were exchanged, and he rose, revealing orange board shorts and the physique of a significantly younger man. If not for the thinning gray hair, Mr. Everett might've been in his late thirties instead of his early fifties. Perhaps that answered the question of what he did all day as Kate's husband. Clearly, he worked out.

The woman presented him with a large striped beach towel, and he wrapped it around his waist.

"This way," she said, flipping her wrist as she passed Hayley near the patio doors. "You can wait in the study."

Finn slowed at her side and set a hand against the small of her back as they reentered the home. A few footsteps later, they arrived at a fancy office Hayley had noticed on her way through.

An executive desk the size of an elephant centered the room and mahogany bookshelves climbed from floor to ceiling along the back wall. Matching leather armchairs faced the perfectly clean desk. A single framed photo of Kate and the man from the hot tub adorned the glossy wooden surface. They appeared happy on a boat at sea.

"Wait here," the woman said, then pulled the tall double doors shut behind her.

Finn circled the room's periphery without speaking, and Hayley took a seat in an armchair. Something about the space made her think they might be on camera. The room was too pristine to be anyone's real office, too staged to be used as more than a prop.

This was most likely the enhanced, if not blatantly false,

image Mr. Everett wanted people to believe of him, Hayley realized. A middle-aged man's push-up bra and French tips. The idea only made her more curious about who he truly was.

The doors reopened, and the man from the hot tub entered. The sunglasses were gone, as were the board shorts. Now, he had on navy dress shorts with boat shoes and a salmon-pink polo shirt with a designer insignia on the collar. She couldn't help wondering if his shoes were the same ones Keith's friend had seen on the man chasing Gage through the rave.

"Mr. Everett," Finn said, offering his hand. "Thank you for seeing me."

Kate's husband nodded, frowning. "Of course. Call me Topper. Please make yourself at home."

Finn took the seat beside Hayley's, clearly unimpressed. "This is Hayley Campbell, a local social worker interested in your wife's project."

She smiled. Mr. Everett did not.

"What can I do for you today, Detective?" he asked, moving to the seat behind the large desk. "You have news on my wife's case?"

"A bit, yes." Finn angled forward, pinning the other man with an inscrutable cop stare. "I was hoping you could tell me about Lighthouse, Inc."

Mr. Everett leaned away, causing the spring in his chair to squeak. His eyes narrowed, as if he was deep in thought. "I believe they've worked with my wife on various projects of the past."

"What about her community center in Old Downtown?" Finn asked.

"I couldn't say." Mr. Everett's gaze roamed to the grandfather clock beside his window, to the ceiling and then to Hayley, before returning to Finn. "Kate had a number of things in motion all the time. No one could keep up." He forced a pitiful smile. "She was a force."

"Agreed," Finn said. "What can you tell me about Lighthouse, Inc. in general?"

"It's a local business."

"Investors?" Finn asked.

"Land developers, I believe."

"How well do you know the owners of the company?"

Hayley let her attention bounce from Finn to Mr. Everett and back, nerves tightening.

"We're acquainted," Mr. Everett hedged, swaying forward once more. He anchored his forearms on the desk and laced his fingers.

"I see. How did you meet, initially?"

"Conrad is a member of Ardent Lakes."

"Conrad Forester," Finn clarified.

"Yes."

Hayley recognized Ardent Lakes as the name of a local country club. She'd driven past the gates a hundred times, but had never been inside. "Mr. Everett," she said, pulling both men's attention to her. "Sorry to interrupt, but I'm wondering about the community center." She'd been introduced as a social worker. She might as well play her role. "A great many people will benefit from the completed project. I hope it will continue. In your wife's honor, perhaps?"

Everett cleared his throat. "As I mentioned, I don't typically get involved in Kate's work, so I can't say what will happen now. I suppose that will be at the discretion of the board of trustees." His attention flickered to the clock again, then back to Finn. "I hate to rush you, but I have somewhere I need to be." He rose and pulled a set of car keys from his pocket as if in evidence.

"Of course." Finn pressed onto his feet and offered his hand once more in a farewell shake. "Thank you for your time. I'll be in touch if I need anything else."

Mr. Everett hurried ahead of them to the office door, then

opened it and walked with them outside. He boarded the little blue car while she and Finn loaded into the truck.

She glanced in the rearview mirror as they motored down the lane, their pickup leading the way. Her eyes fixed on the strange man behind them. "That was weird, right?"

"Yup."

"Do you think he's hiding something?"

Everett's thinning brown hair lifted on the breeze, eyes hidden behind those darn sunglasses once more.

"Probably," Finn said.

"Do you think he killed her?"

"Statistically, the odds aren't in his favor," Finn said. "Realistically, I don't know. Could be he's just glad to inherit the kingdom. Everybody's hiding something, but most of the things we get squirrelly about as individuals are irrelevant outside our heads."

She relaxed against the sun-warmed seat back, certainly able to relate. "Should we visit the country club next?" she asked. "Or maybe drive past a few parks and look for the boys?"

Finn slowed at the end of the driveway, checking both directions and signaling his turn for the man behind them. "We can do all of that if you're up to it. The day's still young."

The sound of squealing tires on pavement turned Hayley's eyes away from Finn. Her heart lurched into a sprint as the black SUV from Old Downtown raced along the street in their direction.

"Get down," Finn yelled, one arm swinging out to force her head toward her knees.

Rapid gunfire ripped across the truck in the next heartbeat, shattering the windshield and raining a storm of pebbled glass over her back as she screamed.

Chapter Seventeen

A few phone calls later, Finn walked the crime scene with Dean, a pair of officers and a detective from his team. His pickup would be towed to a local shop for repair after the bullet casings were located. Dean and Austin had come to the rescue with a company-owned SUV. Dean would ride back with Austin. Hayley and Finn would keep the vehicle owned by the PI firm as long as they needed.

Meanwhile, Hayley sat in Austin's pickup, watching safely from a short distance. Austin, for his part, played the role of shocked citizen, gaping at the chaos, only there to comfort a shaken friend. He would see everything from his vantage point that Finn and those walking the crime scene would miss.

"What do you think?" Dean asked, folding his arms and turning his attention to Finn. "Everett followed you down the drive because he had some place to be. Was the shooting about you and Hayley or him?"

Finn rubbed his stubbled chin and scanned the broader area. His gaze slid over the squat navy blue convertible still parked behind his truck. The car's owner rocked from foot to foot several feet away, speaking with officers again. He'd made multiple phone calls, likely to his lawyers, and retreated into his home twice, but he kept boomeranging back. "Any idea where he was headed?"

"He had a reservation at the country club's restaurant," Dean said.

"Standing day and time?" Finn asked.

If Mr. Everett was a creature of habit, and someone wanted him dead, knowing when and where to expect him would make the work easy. It was the main reason Finn continuously warned women in self-defense classes not to create obvious routines in their daily lives. They never knew who was watching, or what motive they might have. For a determined killer, catching Everett leaving his driveway on a low-traffic residential road was far better than at the busy club.

Still, Everett had been in the hot tub when they'd arrived.

"Nope." Dean arched an eyebrow. "This reservation was set today."

"Who called it in?"

Dean shrugged. "My contact at the club didn't say. Only that the reservation wasn't on the books when she got there this morning."

Finn grunted. It was possible whoever wanted Everett dead had a contact at the club who'd tipped them off about his new reservation. Or maybe they'd simply been waiting outside the home for him to leave. Thankfully, Austin was keeping watch now. He would know if anyone on the street seemed suspicious and contact Finn as soon as he spotted them.

A rookie officer Finn recognized as Traci Landers moved in his direction, and the brothers parted slightly to make room for her in the small huddle.

"Learn anything good?" Finn asked, flicking his gaze in Mr. Everett's direction.

Officer Landers followed his attention, then turned back with a nod. "He thinks whoever killed his wife is targeting him now, and he's requested a patrol for his safety."

"I like that," Finn said. "Let's get him a babysitter. I want him safe if he's in danger, and if this is all some sort of ruse,

I want to know that too. Get someone good to watch him. Someone who'll pick up on anything that doesn't seem right."

"Will do," Landers said. "We've collected several casings from the shots fired. I'm taking those to the lab. If the same weapon has been used in any other crimes on record, we'll know soon."

More importantly, they'd know whether or not these bullets matched the one the coroner pulled from Kate.

Officer Landers's brow furrowed as she looked more closely at Finn. "You sure you don't want the medic to take a look at you?"

He forced his eyes to meet hers, determined not to look at the new cuts on his arms and cheek. Pebbles of broken windshield had nicked his skin, drawing fresh blood and staining his truck seat. "Nothing a little alcohol and peroxide won't heal." The windshield would be easy to replace. Bloodstained leather was another story. One he didn't want to think about. At least the cuts would take care of themselves.

Thankfully, Hayley had been physically unscathed. Emotionally, she'd been stunned silent, possibly in shock, though she'd also refused the medic.

Officer Landers tipped a finger to her hat and stepped away.

"How's Hayley holding up?" Dean asked, gaze drifting to Austin's truck. "I imagine social work isn't usually so brutal."

Finn gripped the back of his neck, hating that she'd been through any of the dangerous and heartbreaking things she'd experienced lately. "She's tougher than she looks." And he'd only recently learned the whole truth of that statement. Hayley had faced obstacles and had the odds stacked against her all her life. Yet here she was, a heart larger and warmer than the sun, proving that children weren't doomed to repeat the flawed lives of their parents and that sometimes those who'd had it the hardest learned to love the biggest.

Finn began to move in her direction before he'd made the conscious decision to do so. Hayley needed a safe place to recuperate, rest and heal. He wanted to be that for her. "I'm heading out," he told Dean. "Keep me posted."

"Where are you going?"

"I'm taking Hayley home."

No words had ever felt sweeter.

HAYLEY STOOD IN Finn's small bathroom, thankful for an incredible distraction from the sheer chaos of the last several days. Outside those walls, nothing seemed to be going her way. Inside, however, she couldn't complain.

Finn leaned against the counter, patiently allowing her to clean and rebandage a few of his deeper wounds. Some of the injuries he'd received during the explosion were out of his reach and in need of care following his shower. Hayley didn't need to be asked twice.

She swabbed each cut and puncture with an alcohol pad, then dabbed a fresh layer of ointment onto the angry, reddened skin before applying a new patch of gauze and medical tape. She tried not to steal unnecessary glances at his handsome face and bare chest in the still steamy bathroom mirror. And she refused the barrage of clear memories, reminding her of all the ways she'd touched and been touched by Finn Beaumont.

He winced slightly as she covered the worst of his cuts, and she paused before continuing her work. The kisses they'd recently shared, and the sweet words they'd exchanged, had meant a lot. But when the strongest man she knew humbled himself to ask for her help with something so personal, she knew she'd regained his trust. Trust was everything. And his willingness to be vulnerable spoke volumes.

Finn's strength and perseverance benefited everyone, but those same traits came at a price for him. Especially when accepting help with the little things. She'd seen him help his family build a pole barn in a week, but refused to get help tying his shoes after fracturing his wrist taking down a drunk-and-disorderly.

Her heart fluttered as their eyes met in the mirror's reflection. She set aside the tape. "Finished."

He swept his shirt off the countertop and threaded it over his head. "I appreciate it."

"Anytime. I appreciate all the things you do for me too."

Finn turned to face her, a smile playing on his lips. "I suppose I have to make you dinner?"

Hayley scoffed, eagerly playing along. "Of course, you do. Don't make me call your mama."

"Don't even joke about that." His strong arms snaked out, gripping her waist and moving her close on a laugh.

She arched as goose bumps scattered over her skin. The thrill of possibility burst in her chest. Finn's guard was down. He'd left the serious parts of himself somewhere else in favor of this precious, carefree moment with her.

She melted against him, hanging on with delight.

He buried his face against her neck, holding her as if she was his life preserver and not the other way around. "I am so sorry you were in that truck with me today," he whispered. "Or at that warehouse. All I ever want to do is protect you, and I'm failing miserably."

"You're not."

Heat from his nearness, his tone, the scent of him was all around her, igniting fire in her veins. She moaned as his lips drew a path along the rim of her ear. "Finn?" she asked, sliding her hands beneath the hem of his shirt.

He pulled back, blinking unfocused eyes, visibly struggling for control. "Too much?" he rasped.

"More."

Strong fingers burrowed into her hair, cradling her head. Then his mouth took hers in a deep, tantalizing kiss.

She traced the ridges of his abs and planes of his broad chest with greedy fingers, pushing the fabric of his shirt upward, exposing miles of tanned skin.

Finn broke the kiss, eyes wild and searching. His lips tipped into a wolfish grin at whatever he saw in her expression. Then he reached over his head and freed the shirt he'd just put on.

Emboldened, she did the same. Her shirt landed in a discarded puddle beside his, earning a low, toe-curling growl from Finn.

She tipped her chin in challenge and ran a fingertip down his torso to the waistband of his pants.

Another cuss crossed his lips, followed by a cautious plea. "Are you sure?"

She rose onto her toes, pressing her body against his warm skin. "Take me to bed, Detective."

Finn didn't need to be asked twice.

He gripped her hips in his hands and hauled her off the ground in one burst of movement.

A delighted squeal erupted from her chest as he swept her off her feet, and strode easily to his room.

She pulled him down with her, onto his sheets, and enjoyed the view.

He held himself above her, palms planted beside each of her shoulders, elbows locked. An expression of awe and admiration graced his handsome face. "I've missed you," he said softly. "So damn much."

"I've missed you too." She rose to meet him, kissing him slowly and drawing him down to her. She savored each mind-bending sweep of his tongue and expert stroke of his hand, feeling more beautiful and cherished than she had in far too long. Since the last time she'd been with him.

When there was nothing more between them, and their bodies rocked together to a perfect end, there was no denying her love for Finn Beaumont. As strong and resilient as the man himself.

She could only hope he might feel the same way again one day.

FINN SLIPPED AWAY from Hayley when her breaths grew long and even, her body taken by sleep. They'd talked for hours, clinging to one another and making up for a year of lost time. But when Hayley had drifted off, Finn's mind had begun to race.

Moonlight streamed through the window onto her beautifully peaceful face, and he kissed her cheek before he rose. His heart broke anew at the thought of losing her again. He probably should've taken things more slowly, not been so greedy. Shouldn't have risked scaring her away. But her sweet kisses and tender urging had reduced his logic to rubble. And he'd taken her at her word. She wanted him. He needed her. Shamelessly, he regretted nothing.

He only hoped she'd feel the same in the morning.

Finn tugged on his T-shirt and sweatpants, then padded into the living room, grabbing a bottle of water and his laptop from the kitchen on his way. He had files and transcripts to review. Lab reports and evidence photos to request. Maybe he'd even find a lead they could follow in the morning. Something that would bring them closer to locating Gage and Parker, or Kate's killer.

He took a seat on the couch and booted up his laptop, then waited for his usual browser windows to load. He logged in to his work email, forcing images of a climaxing Hayley from his mind.

He had a lot of work to do if he wanted to gain her love and trust again.

He'd have to be careful not to scare her away. He'd take his time and watch her for signs she was ready, because he couldn't lose her again.

The computer on his lap brought him back to the moment, to the awful reminder that he and Hayley had shared one too many near-death experiences this week. Until he found the culprit, it was only a matter of time before there was another drive-by shooting or explosion. And he needed to locate Gage and Parker before the killer found them instead.

Finn's inbox was full, as always, so he started at the top.

Several hours later, he'd worked through every message, reviewed every shared document, interview transcript and piece of evidence from crimes related to Kate's death. He'd replayed news footage and listened to audio files from interrogations until his heavy, scratchy eyes drifted shut.

He woke to the sound of his ringing phone and peeled his eyes open to blazing sunlight through the front window. His laptop rested on the floor beside the couch, where he'd accidentally fallen asleep.

Finn swiveled upright, planting his feet on the floor and searching the space around him for his phone. "Beaumont," he answered, catching the call before it went to voice mail.

"Are you sleeping?" Dean asked, his voice a tone of mock horror. "It's after seven."

Finn rubbed a hand over his tired eyes and mussed hair. "I had a late night."

"Oh, yeah?" His brother's tone implied the reason had been Hayley.

Finn supposed his brother was right on a number of counts.

A fresh bolt of panic lanced his gut. "Oh, no." He'd left her in bed so he could slip away and work. If she'd woken without him during the night, she was sure to think— "Hey, can I call you back," Finn asked abruptly, already moving toward the hallway. "Unless you've got news. Then let me have it, and I'll call you back after that."

"No," Dean said. "I was just calling to say Mama's on her way to your place with breakfast, and I'm hungry, so I'm coming too. I figured we can talk shop over cheesy grits and hash browns."

Finn spun back to face the front window. "How long ago did she leave?"

"I'm not sure. She was gone when I got there," Dean said. "Dad pointed me in your direction. Honestly, if I knew I'd have to drive all over town for my breakfast, I could've picked something up on my way to work."

"It's not too late for that," Finn said.

"I don't know," Dean said. "I'm committed to those grits."

"See you when you get here." Finn disconnected outside his partially closed bedroom door. "Hayley?" He rapped his knuckles gently on the frame. "Are you up?"

"Yeah."

Finn stepped cautiously into the room.

She sat on the edge of the bed, dressed in cut-off jean shorts and a faded blue T-shirt. She'd pulled her thick hair away from her face in a ponytail. Her expression was guarded and wary.

"Mom and Dean are on their ways over for breakfast." He smiled. "You sleep well?"

Hayley nodded and stood, her phone clutched in one hand.

"News?" he asked, looking pointedly at the little device, and hoping she planned to speak soon. He couldn't have ruined things for them already. Could he?

"Nothing yet," she said. "I was hoping, but—"

"Hey." Finn extended an arm as she approached, then wrapped it around her when she tried to pass him. "Can I make you some coffee while we wait for Mama?"

"That sounds nice. Thank you."

Finn sighed and let his head fall forward, tightening his grip a bit when she tried to get away. He raised his eyes to hers and waited for Hayley to meet his gaze. "I snuck away to work last night. I was trying to find a thread to pull on this case. I didn't mean to fall asleep out there. I was supposed to get back here after I finished reviewing files."

Her cheeks darkened, and she averted her gaze. "It's okay. I get it."

Finn raised his hands to cup her cheeks. "I mean it. I wanted to be right here with you."

She looked into his eyes, scanning, seeking.

The doorbell rang.

He held his ground for another long beat then pressed a tender kiss to her forehead before relenting. "Come on." He slid his hand over hers. "We'd better let Mama in before she jimmies the lock."

Hayley laughed softly, and a measure of weight rolled off his shoulders. "She wouldn't."

"Probably not," he admitted. "But she's fully capable, and I don't want to test her."

He led Hayley down the hall, and she broke away at the kitchen. He turned toward the front door. "Morning, Mama," he said, inviting her in a moment later with a hug.

"Morning, sweet boy." She patted his cheek and passed him a set of thermal casserole bags. "Breakfast is in there. Where's Hayley?"

"I'm here," Hayley called. "Making coffee. Would you like a cup?"

"Oh, yes, please!"

His brother's truck appeared at the end of Finn's driveway, so he left the door open and headed for the kitchen. "Dean just pulled up."

Finn unpacked his mom's casseroles while she pulled dishes from the cupboards and silverware from the drawer.

"Knock, knock," Dean said, stepping inside and closing the door behind him. "Something smells great." He greeted his mother and Hayley with hugs, then offered raised eyebrows to Finn. "You look beat."

"Sit," their mom ordered. "Let's talk over breakfast."

The meal became a business meeting, as expected, and Finn kept one hand on Hayley as often as possible.

She blushed and hid behind her mug when his mother looked in their direction a little too long, but she didn't make any effort to push him away. A good sign, he hoped.

"And now we're waiting for something else to come up," Dean said, concluding a lengthy list of places he and Austin had looked for Gage and Parker during the night.

"Do you have any other ideas?" his mother asked Hayley.

"No, ma'am. I wish I did."

Finn gathered her empty plate and cup, then pressed a kiss to her temple as he stood. "Can I get you anything else?"

His mother's eyes bulged and a smile wider than the Atlantic spread over her pink cheeks.

Dean shook his head.

"Well, I'm not worried," Finn said, setting their plates into the sink. The words were true enough, even if he wasn't sure what to do next. "Things always seem the worst right before a big break."

They still needed to visit the country club. See if anyone thought Mr. Everett and Mr. Forester were closer than they claimed. Or if there was anything else another member might want to share.

"True," Dean agreed, taking another swig from his mug. "It's some kind of phenomenon. Just when things start to look impossible in a case, they take off full-speed."

Hayley didn't look swayed. "What about all the cold cases out there?"

Dean frowned.

Finn tried not to smile. She had a point, but this case wasn't destined to go unfinished. Not if he could help it.

"Okay." She released an audible sigh. "Did anyone find out if Kate had a prenup? Her husband seemed squirrelly, and he had a lot to gain from her death."

"My team has confirmed the prenup," Finn said. "But not the specifics. According to a memo I read last night, they've put in a request with the Everett family lawyer and a local judge, hoping one of the two will comply. They've requested financial records as well."

Finn's phone vibrated, and he shifted to pull the device from his pocket. The name on the screen sent his attention to Hayley. "It's Eric."

She straightened. "The middle school's groundskeeper?"

"Yeah."

The room fell silent as he accepted the call using the speaker option. "Beaumont."

"Hey, kid, this might be a long shot," the older man said, bypassing a traditional greeting. "But Gage Myers has been on my mind since the moment you told me what's going on with him. And I recalled his father being an incredible artist."

That tracked, given the talent Gage had shown in his street art. "Go on," Finn said.

"Like I said, this might be nothing, but I remember the two of them spending a lot of time at a little art studio on the bay. His father used to lead classes there for students at the middle school. I'm not sure the place is used much anymore. He was the main volunteer, and the program was funded by an arts project that he organized."

Hayley covered her mouth, eyes springing wide.

And just like that, they had a new lead.

Chapter Eighteen

The art studio Eric had mentioned was a small rectangular building overlooking the bay. The clapboard structure was schoolhouse-red and perched upon tall wooden pillars that had been darkened and worn from weather and age. An abundance of windows faced the water, and a broad wooden deck stretched into the gravel parking lot out back.

A dense thicket of leafy trees cast heavy shade over the structure, effectively hiding it from the road. Hayley walked toward the deck stairs slowly, immediately thankful for a break from the sweltering sun. Multicolored handprints adorned the glass beside floating images of paint palettes, brushes and smocks. Wooden easels had been permanently anchored to the railing, securing them from storms and assuring they'd be there for any artist in need. Sunny yellow letters stenciled on a blue door encouraged guests to enter.

She climbed the steps and tried the knob, but it didn't turn. "Locked," she said, searching over her shoulder for Finn, who'd disappeared.

She moved to the window, scanning for signs of movement, then cupped her hands around her eyes to peer inside. A shadow outside a window on the opposite side of the quiet building peered back.

Finn's familiar face became clear, as clouds passed over the sun. He pointed to something in the space between them.

Hayley adjusted her hands and gaze to find a long table

covered in a blanket, the tip of a pillow poking out on the floor beneath. She straightened and hurried to the door, then knocked. "Gage? Parker? It's me, Hayley. Are you in there?"

Her heart jolted and hammered at the possibility she'd finally found the boys. They were safe, and they'd been well hidden in the old art studio. Protected from the sun and weather. They might've had access to running water and they'd had at least one blanket and pillow. It was more than she'd dared to hope. Images of the kids huddled together in a filthy, crumbling structure in Old Downtown had haunted her dreams. "Gage? Are you okay? I've been so worried. Please answer."

The wooden stairs behind her creaked, and she spun on a sharp intake of breath.

Finn stilled, palms up. "It's just me."

She pressed a hand to her chest and rushed back to the window for another look. "The boys made that blanket fort. Right?"

"I'm hoping," Finn said.

She tried opening the window, but it was secure. "How did they get in?"

"I don't know. The windows on the other side are all locked too." Finn gave the old blue door a thorough inspection, then dragged his fingers along the wooden trim overhead.

"Maybe Gage knew where to find a key," she suggested, recognizing Finn's attempt to do the same.

"Maybe, but I don't," Finn said, extracting a credit card from his wallet. "So it looks like I have to break in."

She returned to him with a smile. "I hoped you'd say that."

He slid the plastic rectangle between the door and frame, then wiggled the knob while he worked the card. A moment later, the door opened.

"You're actual magic," Hayley said, slipping inside while he put away the credit card.

"More like a reformed troublemaker, but I like your take a little better."

She flipped the light switch beside the door. Nothing happened. "I guess no one paid the bill lately."

"Judging by the layer of dust on the windows and countertops, I'd say it's been a while since the place was used as more than a hideout," Finn said.

The wide wooden floorboards were splattered with a rainbow of spilled paints. The walls were covered in murals of the sand and sea. Forgotten art projects hung from the hand drawn waves and surf. A countertop with a sink overlooked the rear deck. The rest of the building was an uninterrupted space, save for a room with an open door on their right.

Finn tapped his phone to life, and a moment later a beam of light illuminated the area. He headed toward the door.

Hayley wiped sweat from her forehead as she crouched to peek under the table covered by a blanket. Candy and snack wrappers littered the area inside the tiny fort. A second blanket covered the floor and empty water bottles had been flattened in the corner. A small notebook kept a tally of food and drinks, along with prices. On pages further back, a hangman game was in progress. Two words, four letters for the first, five for the second. The phrase *don't worry*, minus the two *o's*, had been revealed.

Her heart ached as she clutched the notebook to her chest and stood. "They were here," she said. "This is Gage's handwriting."

Finn returned to her, extinguishing the light. "There's a supply closet and restroom back there. The shelves are mostly bare. What's that?"

Hayley passed the book to him.

He examined the pages before returning the item to her. Then he squatted for a look at the space beneath the table. "Was he budgeting?"

"Looks like it. Should we wait for them to come back?" she asked, hoping the answer was yes.

Finn stretched to his full height. "I'll ask Dean to keep watch from afar. They might avoid returning if they see anyone nearby. You're probably right about Gage knowing where to find a spare key to this place since his dad spent so much time here. He's smart. I don't know who'd think to look for him at this place."

"Where do you think they got the snacks and water?" Hayley said.

Finn anchored his hands on his hips and shook his head. "I don't know."

"We should visit the closest convenience stores. See if anyone remembers them."

"That sounds like a plan," Finn said. He opened his arm in the direction of the door they'd used to enter. "After you."

Hayley bent to return the notebook, but as she placed it under the table, a new idea came to mind. "Can I leave a note for the boys?"

Finn smiled. "Absolutely. Make sure they have all our contact information. My folks' and brothers' numbers too."

She retrieved a pencil from atop the blanket, then began to write. She didn't stop until she was satisfied Gage understood the danger he was in and all the people who were on his side.

She sent up prayers for the boys' protection as she left the little studio, then climbed back into the borrowed SUV.

Finn navigated the scenic byway, the sound on one side, miles of marsh and natural sand dunes on the other. His attention bounced routinely from road to rearview mirror, likely watching for a tail.

Hayley kept her eyes glued to the coastline in search of a small shop or café. People were creatures of habit. If she and Finn found the place where the boys had gotten their snacks and water, they'd probably know where to expect them to shop again.

Less than a mile later, a small orange building appeared. The building's paint was faded and blistered by unhindered sunlight. An attached dock extending into the water was lined in stacks of brightly colored kayaks and paddleboards. The sign at the roadside declared the business to be Eco Exploration, Marshal's Bluff's premier nature-excursion-and-tour company.

"We have a tour company?" Hayley asked.

The SUV slowed.

"Three, believe it or not," Finn said, engaging the turn signal. "The others target fishermen and head out to sea. This place does dolphin-sighting boat tours and gets folks onto the water for exploring and appreciating the natural beauty here."

"Huh." She unbuckled when he parked, then joined him in the lot. "I forget to soak in the views sometimes. I need to make a point of it when this ends."

Finn slid mischievous eyes her way. "You still kayak?"

"Not as much as I should." She'd hidden behind her work since their breakup. But she was healing now, and all the near-death experiences were heavy reminders that she'd only live once. Her job helped a lot of people, but she needed to make time for herself. Take weekends and evenings to recuperate and soak up the beauty around her. "Any chance they sell snacks and water?" she asked.

"About one hundred percent." Finn stopped at the open shop door and motioned her inside ahead of him.

She crossed the threshold and plucked the fabric of her shirt away from her chest.

Box fans rattled in the open windows, and a pitiful cross breeze from one open door to the other stirred a dusting of sand on the floor.

"No tours today," a young woman at the counter called.

Her cheeks were ruddy from the heat, and she fanned her face with a clipboard. "Storm's coming."

Hayley envied the woman's string-bikini top and cutoff shorts, but doubted they were small enough to prevent her inevitable heatstroke if she stayed inside much longer. "We don't need a tour," she said as kindly as possible. "I'm a social worker looking for two missing children. We thought you might've seen them."

The woman's expression turned from bored to alarmed. "Do you have a picture?"

"Of the older boy," Hayley said. She flipped through the images on her phone in search of a recent shot of Gage.

"Have you seen a lot of children this week?" Finn asked, pulling the woman's attention to him.

Her lips parted, and she blinked.

Hayley fought a smile. The Beaumont men had that effect on women. The best part was that none of them seemed to know.

"Yes," she answered belatedly. "It's our busy season. Tourists," she added.

"The boys we're looking for are eight and fourteen," Hayley said. "They're in danger, and it's imperative that we find them before they're harmed." She found a selfie of Gage with a surfboard and turned the phone to face the woman. "They might've bought some drinks and snacks."

Hayley had taken Gage to the beach once, because he said that was where he felt most at peace, and it was his first summer without his parents to take him.

The woman's eyebrows rose and she levered herself off her stool. "I've seen them," she said excitedly. "They didn't buy anything, but they were in here yesterday hanging around when a tour was about to leave. I asked where their mom was, and the older one said she was already on the boat. So I told them to hurry up or they'd miss it, and they left."

A spike of hope and joy shot through Hayley. Gage and Parker had been in the same store where she was standing, only a day before. And they'd been okay. She turned to look for Finn.

He tipped his head in the direction of a wire display stand near the open door to the dock. The same snacks she'd seen in the blanket fort were represented. A small refrigeration unit hummed beside the rack. Bottles of water were visible beyond the glass door.

This was where the boys had gotten their foodstuffs.

She smiled as she realized the list of snacks and prices Gage had made wasn't a result of him managing a budget. He'd tracked the things he'd taken to survive. As if he might've planned to pay later.

"Thank you," Hayley said, turning back to the woman. "If you see them again, will you call me?" She extracted a business card from her bag and passed it to the woman. "Actually. Will you give them a note?"

The woman nodded, expression soft. "Of course."

Hayley wrote a similar letter to the one she'd left at the studio, then passed it to the clerk. "I appreciate this so much. And I'd like a bottle of water." She handed the woman enough money to cover the drink and the boys' snacks. "Keep the change."

She smiled brightly at Hayley. "I'm glad to help."

Outside, the breeze had picked up, and Hayley inhaled deeply, glad to be free of the stuffy building. Beads of sweat formed on her upper lip and brow as they moved toward their ride. The boys would need water soon. "We should wait here and see if they come back."

"I still want to visit the country club," Finn said, unlocking the SUV so they could climb inside. He started the engine and pumped up the air-conditioning, apparently not as impervious to the heat as he seemed.

Hayley wet her lips, anxiety rising in her chest at the thought of leaving this place. "We know the boys have been here and the art studio. I think we should split up and keep watch over both."

Finn frowned. "We're not splitting up. You've been in just as much danger as they have. More, as far as I know. So you're staying with me. Dean will stake out the studio."

"Finn—" Her protest was cut short by the ringing of his phone.

He raised a finger, letting her know he needed to take the call. Then he raised the device to his ear. "Beaumont."

Hayley scanned the nearby road, trees and parking lot while she waited, willing the boys to appear. She was so close to finding them. Practically walking in their footsteps. Separated only by a day.

"When?" Finn asked, pulling her eyes back to him. He shifted the SUV into gear and pressed the phone between his ear and shoulder as he drew the safety belt across his torso. "I'm on my way." He disconnected the call and dropped the phone into the cupholder. A heartbeat later, the SUV tore away from the shack with a spray of dust and gravel.

Hayley grabbed her seat belt, snapping it into place as the tires hit asphalt and they rocketed forward. "What happened?"

"Police Chief Harmen called a press conference. The team got a hit on the SUV from the drive-by. A doorbell camera belonging to one of Everett's neighbors recorded the shooting, and Tech Services pulled a partial license-plate number. It's the same SUV that was seen near the explosion and caught on the news near Kate's death site. The vehicle is registered to Lance Stevens. He's being picked up and hauled in for questioning."

Chapter Nineteen

Finn ignored the speed limit on the way back to town. The scenic byway they traveled was meant to be taken slowly and enjoyed, but there wasn't anything he'd enjoy more today than meeting Lance Stevens. The name of the man being brought in for questioning, possibly the one responsible for repeatedly putting Hayley in danger, circled in his mind. Had the man worked alone? Or was this crime spree his own? And if so, why?

Finn would've requested to perform the interview himself if he thought he was the better choice for the job. Unfortunately, he wasn't convinced he'd stop himself from flattening the suspect given an opportunity. And he couldn't afford to damage any chance they had at building a case that would put Mr. Stevens away for a very long time.

News of today's press conference was nearly as intriguing as news of a suspect. Finn could only assume one was directly related to the other. Police Chief Harmen wasn't one to waste time unnecessarily, or interact with the media when he could avoid it. Given the widespread interest in Katherine Everett's death, he expected everyone in town would be tuned in, and anyone with a camera and microphone would be outside the precinct, hoping for a front-row seat.

Unfortunately for Finn, he and Hayley had been as far from

the police station as possible without leaving Marshal's Bluff, and the return trip was infuriatingly long.

Traffic thickened as he reached the blocks nearest the station, slowing their progress further. News trucks clogged the streets and reporters hurried on foot toward the squat brick building in question. A row of cruisers stood guard inside the gate, looking authoritative and giving the impression of protection. The display of a formidable team. From the number of squad cars alone, he knew there were enough hands on deck to keep the conference orderly and peaceful.

"This is a lot of people," Hayley said, giving voice to his thought. "It's nice that so many folks care about what he wants to say, but I've never been a fan of crowds."

Finn completely understood. People were fine. People were smart. Crowds were often chaotic, thoughtless and emotional. A dangerous combination.

The station doors opened as Finn crept along behind a caravan of gawkers and rubberneckers. The chief of police strode onto the concrete steps and into view.

Hayley tuned the SUV's radio to the call numbers of a station represented by a nearby news van.

A female announcer's voice broke through the speakers. "...here for you live from the Marshal's Bluff police station, where Chief Harmen has called a press conference on the case of Katherine Everett."

Finn grimaced. He could only imagine what the details on his case would sound like through the filtered lens of local media. After everything he and Hayley had been through this week, he wanted the information firsthand. "Hang on," he said, turning his eyes back to the road. He pressed the gas pedal and turned the wheel, causing cars to honk and onlookers to complain.

"What are you doing?" Hayley asked, pressing a palm

against the dashboard to steady herself as he angled the vehicle onto the curb outside the station's open gate.

"Getting us a parking space." He unlocked the doors and climbed out, then waited for Hayley to join him. Dark clouds raced overhead as he took her hand and towed her past a set of uniformed officers.

Finn wasn't usually a superstitious man, but the sudden shadow cast upon this moment felt like a bad omen. He pulled Hayley closer in response. He flashed his detective's shield as he pushed his way to the front of the crowd, where an array of microphones on stands had been arranged.

Chief Harmen's eyes caught Finn's, and he gave a small shake of his head.

Finn straightened. Something had gone wrong.

"Hello," the chief said, effectively quieting the crowd. "I'm Police Chief Harmen, and this press conference has been called to update you on the investigation into Katherine Everett's murder. A male suspect has been identified in connection to that crime and several other crimes we believe to be related. We do not yet know if the suspect worked alone or in conjunction with others. Additionally, we are not releasing the name of the suspect at this time. However, you can be assured that despite his attorney's best attempts, we will not be swayed from finishing the work we've started. Katherine Everett, her family, friends and the community, will see justice served."

Frustration tightened Finn's muscles. He wouldn't be able to listen in on the interview of Lance Stevens today. Not because traffic had made him late, but because the criminal's attorney had likely already escorted him home. Either Stevens had money, or someone who did had interceded on his behalf. Kate's husband and Conrad Forester came instantly to mind.

"The investigation remains fluid and active at this time," Chief Harmen continued. "Anyone with information about the death of Katherine Everett, the warehouse explosion in Old Downtown or the recent shooting outside the Everett family estate should contact Marshal's Bluff PD. Thank you. Now, I'll take a few questions."

The crowd erupted in shouts, every member of the media vying to be heard and chosen.

Finn pressed the pads of his fingers to his closed eyelids.

"Hey." Hayley tugged his hands away from his face, meeting his tired eyes with her sincere gaze. "It's just a setback. Things always start moving fast when they seem to be at a standstill, right?"

His lips twitched, fighting a small smile as she returned the words of their earlier conversation to him. "I believe I've heard that somewhere."

Hayley held on to his hands as he let them drop. "I can't believe Stevens's attorney got here before we did," she said. "Summoning a public defender when I need one for a case can take forever."

He gave her fingers a gentle squeeze. "Money can't buy peace or happiness, but it can keep a lawyer on retainer."

Hayley frowned. "Who do you suppose paid for this one?"

"An excellent question." If the lawyer wasn't Stevens's, then whoever sent him over here likely had good reason. And that information would be priceless.

"Please!" Chief Harmen hollered into the mics, pumping his palms up and down in a failed attempt to regain control. "I'd appreciate your patience while I try to hear from a few more members of the media."

The rev of a motorcycle drew Finn's attention to the slow-moving traffic outside the gate. A driver in black leather with a matching helmet and mirrored visor slowed his ride to a crawl and set his feet on the ground to steady himself.

"Chief Harmen," a female voice called loudly, "can you comment on rumors that a fourteen-year-old boy is suspected in the shooting and bludgeoning death of Katherine Everett? Or that he is now considered a fugitive on the run?"

Hayley gasped, and Finn spun to face the crowd, attempting to identify the woman who'd spoken.

He needed to find that reporter and ask where she'd gotten that information. Someone had clearly fed her the lies to generate another narrative, or worse, to put the entire community on the lookout for Gage.

Sudden rapid gunfire blasted through the air, and Hayley dropped to the ground, pulling Finn down with her.

Screams and chaos erupted as he checked her for injuries.

"I'm okay," she said. "But they aren't."

He followed her trembling finger to several fallen crowd members. Honking horns and the sounds of multiple fender benders formed the backdrop to barking tires and the growl of a motorcycle engine.

The driver angled away, guiding his ride between stopped cars, seeking a path for escape.

"Stay here," Finn demanded, pushing Hayley toward the police station's steps. "Go inside. Tell them who you are and that I went after the shooter. He's on a black motorcycle stuck in traffic. Don't leave!" He freed his weapon and made a run for the waiting SUV.

The motorcycle jumped onto the sidewalk and rounded the corner, now out of sight.

Finn dove into his vehicle and gunned the engine to life. He squeezed the SUV between parked cars and a nearby shop, knocking off his passenger mirror in the process. On the next block, he had the motorcycle in his sights, and he lifted his cell phone to call for backup.

HAYLEY STARED AFTER FINN, stunned motionless as he climbed into the SUV and raced away.

Around her, people panicked, screaming and running

around mindlessly. Some toward the building. Some into the street. Others rushed to help the injured, who were lying in puddles of blood on the ground.

Several uniformed officers climbed into waiting cruisers, eager to give chase, just as Finn had. Except the cruisers were blocked by traffic and throngs of frightened citizens.

In the distance, ambulance sirens wailed to life.

Hayley shoved herself upright, struggling to process the horror. An armed gunman was on the loose, and Finn had gone after him. The realization of what might happen next gripped her chest and squeezed. Her breaths were short, and her head lightened uncomfortably. What if the next person to take a bullet was Finn? Who would help him?

A set of strong hands curled over her biceps and turned her in a new direction. "Let's get you out of here."

Hayley pulled back, intuition flaring. "No. I'm okay, thank y—" Words froze on her tongue as she took in the man at her side.

Conrad Forester, the CEO of Lighthouse, Inc., glared back, and his grip on her tightened. He appeared presentable and calm in a sharp gray suit and red tie, as if he'd only been present for the press conference like everyone else. "Let me rephrase. Come with me now, and do not cause any trouble, or those boys will die."

FINN KEPT THE motorcycle in view as he radioed for backup. Dispatch assigned two cars, but neither were close, and the cruisers from the precinct were several minutes behind. The motorcycle zigzagged through traffic, keeping a steady pace and changing directions frequently, trying and failing to shake Finn.

The vehicle darted into the shadows of an overpass, and Finn plunged in behind.

He blinked, adjusting his eyes to the darkness a moment before readjusting them to the sun on the other side. "He's getting on the highway near Mill Street," Finn called, projecting his voice toward the phone in the cupholder, Dispatch on the other end of the line.

A dozen similar motorcycles appeared in the space of his next heartbeat, all joining the first and forming a pack. Instinct raised the hairs on his arms, and suddenly he wasn't so sure he'd been a top-tier tail and not a detective engaged in a trap.

He pressed the gas pedal to the floor, determined to keep his eye on the motorcycle carrying the shooter, but the bikes began to weave in and out of lanes. An 85-mile-per-hour game of cups.

Then the central interchange appeared. A mass of twinning highways with multiple on-and off-ramps made it impossible to know which lane to stay in. Increasing traffic made it harder to maneuver quickly. But the pack of motorcycles split up, scattering in every direction, and Finn realized the whole truth. It didn't matter which lane he was in, because he couldn't follow them all.

He'd been tricked.

Chapter Twenty

Mr. Forester led Hayley through the chaos of a terrorized crowd to a waiting sedan. Her limbs felt numb, and all hope of rescue vanished as his threat settled into her heart and mind. He had Gage and Parker. And he'd hurt them if she drew attention to herself or tried to run away.

"Get in," he whispered. The words landed harshly against her hair. The heat and scent of his sour breath knotted her stomach, and she rolled her shoulders forward, wishing she could curl into a ball or hide.

She dropped onto the passenger seat as instructed, then flinched at the slamming of the door beside her. Outside the tinted glass, uniformed officers rushed to calm the crowd. They looked everywhere except in her direction, too distracted by the recent shots fired and a line of incoming ambulances.

Traffic moved, making room for the emergency vehicles to pass.

Forester shifted into Drive and took advantage of the cleared road, making a casual getaway.

She wiped silent tears from her cheeks as they left her only means of rescue behind. "Where are you taking me?" she asked.

Quaint shops and clueless pedestrians passed on historic sidewalks beyond her window.

"Somewhere you can't ruin my life." He stole a look in

her direction, head shaking in disgust. "All because some punk kid saw something he shouldn't have, and you couldn't let it go."

"Gage is a good kid," Hayley snapped. "He's alone and scared in this world, and he saw you kill a woman. Of course, he ran. What was he supposed to do?"

"He was supposed to mind his own damn business. And so were you!"

Hayley jumped at his sudden yell, the malice in his tone turning her blood to ice. Any chance she'd hoped to have at reasoning with her abductor was gone. He was clearly on a mission to silence her and nothing more.

He didn't even seem guilty or ashamed. Only outraged that he'd been caught committing murder.

"Why'd you do it?" she asked. *If I'm going to die*, she reasoned, *I might as well understand why.* "Why kill Kate? Was it because her plans for a homeless shelter and community center interfered with your plans to build parks and condos? Did you even consider trying to compromise before you bludgeoned and shot her?"

He pulled his attention from the road to stare at her for a long beat, eyes hard, expression feral. "She would've cost me tens of millions with that roach trap. People don't want to raise their kids beside a homeless shelter, or walk their little doodle dogs past park benches with junkies passed out on them. I tried to buy her out. I'm not the bad guy here. She refused to take my offer, and it was well over what she'd paid for her properties. She had something against other people getting rich. As if she was the only one in this town who deserved nice things. She was a greedy, selfish—"

Suddenly the sirens that had been small in the distance grew insistent and loud, interrupting Forester's tirade and pulling his attention to the rearview mirror. "Besides, this isn't all on me. Topper owes me. I couldn't reason with her, so he was supposed to."

Hayley twisted in her seat, craning for a look at the police cruisers racing into view behind them. Cars and trucks slowed and moved out of their way.

She dared a breath of hope.

Forester hit his turn signal and took the next right toward Old Downtown. The cruisers raced past, continuing toward the highway.

Forrester chuckled. "Those aren't for us. No need to worry."

She swallowed a lump of bile, worried again for Finn.

"I'm guessing your detective had a little trouble catching my friend," Forester said. "There's no shame in that. My friend is very good," he clarified. "Not your detective. If he was any good, you wouldn't be here with me, and those adorable boys you're obsessed with wouldn't be living their last day."

Hayley's stomach lurched at his words. She considered punching his face, wondering if the results would be anything other than him knocking her out in retaliation. "Your friend?" she snapped instead. "You mean the gunman who shot into a crowd? Probably the same one who performed that drive-by at the Everetts' house and blew up the warehouse."

Forrester shrugged. "Ever heard the expression 'you've got to do what you've got to do'?"

She curled her hands into fists on her lap. "People were shot today. Maybe killed. All so you could build some bougie condos? Get away with another murder? What is wrong with you?"

"Nothing I can't fix," he said.

She dragged her gaze over the familiar buildings of the waterfront. Broken and dilapidated. Uninhabited and unsafe. Tagged and spray-painted by lost souls and street artists. Like Gage.

Memories of the explosion that had nearly killed her and Finn crashed through her mind. The hissing stick of explosives from a nearby demolition site that sent them into the water. Her body shuddered in response. Their survival had been miraculous, but now she was back on the same block. Alone with a madman.

Signs with the Lighthouse, Inc. logo flapped and fluttered in the growing wind. The relentless sun was blocked by gray clouds of a brewing storm.

"All of this trash and rubble will soon be gone," he said, slowing outside a building surrounded by a chain-link fence. "I'm making sure of it. One building at a time." He parked and climbed out, then pointed his handgun through the open window at Hayley. "Come on. I've got somewhere to be."

She eased onto her feet, scanning the vacant streets, and holding on to his last few words. If he didn't plan to kill her immediately, she'd soon be left alone. And she could be incredibly resourceful. She wouldn't have survived her childhood otherwise.

The building behind the fence was tall and newer than most in the area. "Are the boys in there?" she asked.

"One way to find out," Forrester said, rounding the hood. He grabbed her by the arm and jerked, causing her to stumble.

Then he towed her onto the sidewalk and through an unlocked gate. No Trespassing signs warned that unauthorized visitors would be prosecuted. Other signage announced the property's scheduled demolition. Goose bumps tightened her skin as she read the date.

Tomorrow morning.

"The good news is you'll only be spending one night here," Forester said, tugging her along more quickly as they approached the entryway. "The whole place will be dust tomorrow, along with everything in it."

Her eyes strained for focus as she stepped inside. The loss of sunlight left her temporarily without sight. The space was silent. No indication they weren't alone. Were the boys really there? Or had she been duped? Believed the lie, and gone willfully to her death?

Forester led her down a hallway as her vision cleared. Then he paused outside a sturdy-looking interior door. He pulled a key from his pocket and freed a padlock from a heavy chain. He swung the barrier open to reveal a dark set of steps to the basement. "In you go."

Before she could protest or make a plan to run, the sound of his cocking gun clicked beside her ear.

"You don't want the kid to see another woman murdered, do you?"

She took a step into the darkness, and Forester gave her a heavy shove. Hayley screamed as she fell forward, clutching the handrail and pressing her body to the wall for stability. Her feet fumbled down several steps to a landing, before she crashed onto her hands and knees with a thud.

The door slammed shut behind her, and the rattle of chains being secured forced a sob from her throat. Suffocating heat covered her like a blanket. Sweat broke instantly above her lip and across her brow. There were a few more steps to navigate before she reached the sublevel and whatever awaited her down there.

Soft shuffling sounds sent her onto her feet, back pressed to the wall. "Who's there?"

A pinhole of light appeared, and the space became faintly visible. The room was lined with empty shelving. Maybe previously used for storage. A small window near an exposed-beam ceiling had been painted black and lined with bars.

"Hayley?" Gage's voice reached to her. The sound was thin and weak.

"Gage!" She rushed in the direction of the sound, down the final steps and around an overturned table near the light. Two filthy figures were huddled on the ground. "Parker." She gathered the boys into her arms and held them tight.

Gage winced and hissed.

She released them with a jolt of fear. "What's wrong?"

"He's hurt," Parker said. "He tried to get us out of here, but he fell."

"Fell?"

Parker pointed to the window high above.

"I think my arm's broken," Gage said. "This is all my fault. I shouldn't have been down here that night. I should've told you what I saw the next day."

Hayley squinted at his arm, cradled to his torso, scraped and bruised. "It's okay," she assured him. "Everyone understands why you ran and why you hid. No one blames you. No one's mad. I'm just so glad you're okay. We're going to get out of here, take you to a hospital and go home with the coolest cast you've ever seen. Okay?"

Gage nodded, but neither he nor Parker looked as if they believed her.

She refreshed her smile. "The good news is that the police are looking for you. They'll be looking for me now too."

"What about me?" Parker asked, his small voice ripping a fresh hole in Hayley's heart.

"They know the two of you are together," she said, stroking a hand over his hair. "We've all been very worried."

"I shouldn't have taken him," Gage said. "I knew he was scared, and I thought I could help. The Michaelsons were bad people. The next family might've been worse."

"No." She set a palm against his cheek. "The Michaelsons are the exception, not the rule. I'm so sorry no one realized sooner. Most foster families are wonderful and kind. Thanks to you guys, no children will ever be placed in that family's care again. I think that makes you heroes."

Parker beamed.

Gage snorted. "What kind of hero gets a woman and a little boy killed? Did you see the signs outside?"

Hayley nodded at Gage. "We can't wait around to be rescued. We're going to have to find a way out by ourselves." She scanned the boys in the little shaft of light.

Had they eaten since being brought here? Had they been given any water? Gage grimaced with each little movement, clearly in terrible pain.

"What were you doing when you fell?" she asked him. "What was your plan for escape?"

"I thought I could break the glass behind those bars and call for help, but I slipped and fell."

"What were you going to break the glass with?"

He lifted his uninjured arm to reveal bruised and bloody knuckles. "It's glass block under the paint. It's not breaking."

Parker burrowed closer to Gage, fitting himself against the older boy's side and winding thin arms around his torso.

"It's okay," Gage whispered. "I'm right here, and I've got you."

Hayley rose and walked the room's perimeter, evaluating the situation and attempting to clear her head. Her eyes returned to the pinhole of light, the result of a small hole in the exterior wall.

"We were staying at the art studio where my dad taught classes," Gage said. "We were going to be okay. I don't know how they found us."

"I was thirsty," Parker said. "It was my fault. I asked to go to the store again."

"It's not your fault, buddy," Gage soothed.

"He's right," Hayley said. "The only person at fault for this is the man who brought us here." She approached the shelves at the far wall, reaching a hand overhead and searching for something she could use as a weapon if needed.

"He caught us before we made it back to the studio," Gage said. "We tried to run, but—" His heartbroken expression said Parker was too small to outrun a grown man, and too big for Gage to carry.

She nodded. "You haven't done anything wrong. Neither of you. Right now, we have to think about how to get out of here. We can sort the rest later."

"The window is the only way," Gage said. "The door's bolted and chained."

"But the wall is weak," she said, pointing to the pinhole of light. "That brick is already crumbling. Any idea where we can find something to make that hole bigger?" she asked. "Maybe big enough for us to climb out?"

Parker's eyes widened. "That would have to be a lot bigger."

Gage pushed onto his feet with a sharp intake of air. He offered his hand to Parker, pulling him up beside him. Then he limped across the space to her side, left arm cradled across his middle. Apparently, he'd hurt his leg or ankle too. "Let's help Hayley get us out of here."

A few minutes later, they'd found an old piece of rebar, a few large nails and the broken handle of a tool Hayley couldn't name. She'd hoped for a forgotten sledgehammer, but she was willing to make do with anything that would save the lives of these boys.

"All right," she said. "Let's see what we can do about that escape."

Together, they attacked the bricks near the light, working steadily for what felt like an eternity in the heat, until the light outside began to dim. Distant sounds of thunder rumbled in the sky.

The boys stopped to rest, both saying they felt dizzy and weak.

Gage curled into a ball and heaved.

Parker cried.

Hayley offered soothing words and sat with them until they fell asleep. Then she got back to work. Tomorrow, the building was coming down. Today was all they had left and it was nearing an end.

Brick by busted brick, she had to get them out of there.

Chapter Twenty-One

Finn paced his small office inside the Marshal's Bluff police station, a cell phone pressed to his ear. Beyond the open door, his team sifted through reports from witnesses at the press-conference shooting. Thankfully there hadn't been any fatalities and only a handful of minor injuries. Unfortunately, no one had noticed Hayley leaving, but she'd been gone when he returned.

He never should've left her alone.

A soft knock sounded and Dean appeared. He waved from the threshold. "Any luck?"

Finn rubbed a heavy palm against his forehead then anchored the hand against the back of his neck. It'd been hours since the most recent shooting, and none of the resulting leads had panned out. The gunman had yet to be identified, and Hayley had become vapor. "I'm on hold with Tech Services," he said. "Someone called the tip line after we aired that piece on the news about Hayley's disappearance. The caller claimed to have been eating at an outdoor café when a dark sedan stopped at the light on the corner in the shopping district. A woman fitting Hayley's description was in the passenger seat. The caller didn't get a look at the driver and couldn't say whether or not the woman appeared upset or injured, but it's the only somewhat solid lead we've got.

Tech Services used the time and location to pull a partial plate from the car. They're running the number now." He motioned Dean inside. "What about you? Anything new?"

"Maybe," Dean said, stepping into the office and leaning against the wall beside the door. "I visited the country club where the Everetts and Forester are members."

"Yeah?" Finn asked. He'd been meaning to get to the country club for days but hadn't managed. "What'd you learn?"

"According to the bartender I spoke with, the Everetts were friends with Forester until suddenly they weren't."

Finn stilled. "Keep going."

Dean shrugged. "She didn't know why, only that there's a weekly poker tournament held after hours at the club. It's an invitation-only situation and only the wealthiest are invited. Lots of money exchanges hands, and big business deals are made, but no one talks about it on the record."

Finn sighed. "But the bartender knew and shared the details with you."

"She knew because she gets paid in tips to work the events," Dean said. "She shared because rumor has it I'm charming."

Finn sighed. "Go on."

Dean grinned. "Guess who lost a lot of money to Conrad Forester last month?"

"Tell me it was Kate Everett's husband."

Dean nodded. "I don't have specifics or proof, but that was the story making the rounds at the end of the night."

"Okay." Finn's mind raced with fresh theories. "So Everett owed Forrester. Any idea how much?"

"No, but they allegedly agreed to call it even if Everett got his wife to change the location of her community-center project." Dean's eyebrows raised and he crossed his arms over his chest, looking rightfully proud.

"Detective Beaumont?" The voice of the tech-services representative rang in his ear.

He'd temporarily forgotten about the phone in his hand. "Yeah, I'm here."

"Plates on that sedan match a vehicle registered to Conrad Forester. Would you like the home address and phone number on file?"

"Text it," Finn said, already headed into the hall to collect his team.

FINN NAVIGATED THE streets of Old Downtown, his heart in his throat and a storm rolling in off the coast. Forester hadn't been at his home or office, but Mr. Everett had started talking the moment Finn and Dean showed up at his door. He confessed his debt to Forester and explained that Kate had refused to change her dream over a game of poker.

Finn was willing to bet Forester hadn't liked that answer.

Now Dean was riding shotgun in Finn's borrowed SUV, the team close behind.

Forester owned enough properties along the waterfront to keep them all busy past nightfall, but it was the perfect place to hide two kids and a woman, so they wouldn't stop until they'd searched every square foot.

"So Everett owes Forester a gambling debt he can't pay up," Dean said, verbally sorting the facts. "At first he can't pay, because his wife controls the business and the money. Then Forester kills the wife, or has her killed, to stop the project, but Everett still doesn't control the business."

"He told me a board of trustees was handling things now," Finn said. "I'm unclear about his access or control of the money."

Lightning flashed as he parked the SUV on the street where it had all began. Three other vehicles followed suit, and his teammates filed onto the sidewalk. One side of the street contained the warehouse remains. Across the broken asphalt, yellow crime-scene tape denoted the location of Kate's murder. All around, signs with the Lighthouse, Inc. logo were pelted with falling rain.

Finn's phone dinged, and he paused to check the screen.

"News?" Dean asked, unfastening his safety belt.

"The lab," Finn said, scanning the message. "Bullet casings found after the press-conference shooting match those pulled from my truck after the drive-by and the one in Kate's body."

The same weapon had been used in all three crime scenes.

"And the case just gets stronger," Dean said.

Finn released a labored sigh. "Against Lance Stevens. We probably have enough to arrest him for the shootings and murder, but we'll need to prove Forester's connection to him and those crimes."

"So first we'll find Hayley," Dean said, opening his door against the increasing wind. "I have a feeling she's all we'll need to arrest him for abduction. And as soon as you do your cop thing and offer Stevens a deal, I'm sure he'll roll on Forester for hiring him as the gunman."

Lightning flashed in the sky, and Finn stepped into the storm. He'd bring Hayley home safely, whatever the cost.

HAYLEY WHIMPERED AS thunder rolled and she worked her bloody fingers over broken bricks, painstakingly tearing them free. Her hands were filthy and swollen from the work. Her arms and chest were covered in dust and dirt from the aged mortar and crumbling masonry. Tears streamed over her red-hot cheeks, and icy fear coiled in her gut. Her voice was nearly gone from continuous and desperate cries for help.

The boys rested on the floor, dehydrated and exhausted. Gage's pain had increased by the minute as he'd beaten the rebar against the wall, each whack reverberating through his thin frame and jostling his broken arm.

She was making progress on her own, but it was too slow to expect an escape before dawn. Even if she worked all night. The hole was large enough to get her foot through, but nothing more.

She swallowed a scream of rage at the unfairness of it all and reached again for the rebar. Her sweaty, blood-slicked hands slipped as she swung, tearing the skin of her palms and raising fire in her veins. "Dammit!"

Outside the foot-size hole, rain soaked the ground, creating mini rivers and mudslides that slopped over the brick wall and onto the basement floor. The rain would prevent any passersby close enough to hear her screams. If not, the thunder would surely cover the feeble sound.

She swung her weapon harder, funneling all the hate and fear inside her into each new swing. Every jarring thud wrenched a fresh sob from her chest until she couldn't lift the metal or her arms.

"Ms. Hayley?" Parker asked, wobbling onto his feet, fear in his wide brown eyes.

She wiped her face and forced her mind into caregiver mode. Their situation was dire, but Parker was only eight, and he needed her protection.

Before she could find the words to speak, a great, rolling groan spread through the structure above them. The wall she'd been assaulting began to shift, and the bricks began to fall. Dirt dropped onto their heads from the exposed ceiling beams and joists.

Gage pressed onto his feet with a sharp wince of pain. "What's happening?"

Hayley's heart seized in horrific realization as she watched broken bits of brick and mortar spill from the wall. Her failed attempt to save them would be the death of them instead.

She'd intentionally damaged a load-bearing wall.

"The building is unstable," she said, as calmly as she could manage.

Gage nodded in grim understanding. "What do we do?"

Parker peered through the growing hole. "Boost me up! I can fit!"

Hayley dragged her gaze from Parker to the opening as thunder boomed and lightning struck.

Sending Parker alone into the most dangerous area of town, into the storm and darkness, wasn't an answer she'd ever choose. But her choices had been erased.

Gage stepped into the space at her side. "Help," he instructed. "I can't lift him on my own. Parker, keep running until you find someone to tell we're down here. Then ask to call 911. Watch out for the man who brought us here. Look for his car. Be careful."

Parker raised a thumb, his attention fixed on the small opening in the wall. "Got it," he said. "I'm a hero."

"That's right," Gage said. "You're a hero. And, hey, don't come back here without an adult, understand? No matter what happens. Even if this building makes a lot of noise. Stay focused. Okay?"

Hayley swallowed a rock of emotion as she processed Gage's words of protection. If the building fell, Parker couldn't come back alone. Couldn't try to save them. Couldn't be hurt or worse by the unstable ruins. Whatever else happened, Parker would survive.

She helped Gage hoist the little boy into the storm.

Chapter Twenty-Two

Hayley swung the rebar at the shelving on the walls, dismantling it with every bone-rattling blow. "Gage, take these," she said, kicking boards and sections of fallen framework across the floor in the teen's direction. "Wedge them in the opening. Use them to support the wall."

A few busted shelves wouldn't stop a building from collapsing, but she could at least try to buy them some time. Give the miracle they desperately needed a chance to happen.

Gage had already been abducted and injured on her watch. She couldn't sit idly by and wait for them both to be crushed to death.

His face contorted in pain as he tried to place the boards between broken bricks.

"Let me help," she said, abandoning the demolition to assist in the new project. "Go ahead and rest. I've got this."

Gage stepped away, breathing heavily and pressing his broken arm to his torso.

Hayley stayed on task, working the boards into place between rows of still-sturdy bricks. The gap had grown exponentially with each ugly groan of the building, and a new realization hit with the next boom of thunder. "I think you can fit through this."

"What?" Gage returned to her side with a frown.

"Look!"

He squinted at the hole she'd braced, and a low cuss rolled off his tongue. "Sorry."

"Darling, I'm going to agree," she said. "Here." Gusts of cool, wet air blew into the basement as she laced her fingers together and formed a stirrup for his foot. "I'll give you a boost."

"What about you?" he asked, unmoving. "There's no one to boost you out if I leave. You'll still be stuck down here."

"I'll figure it out," she said. "Don't worry about me. You need to go look for help."

"I won't leave you."

The battering wind picked up, and the building moaned. Dirt fell in tufts from the space above their heads. Time was running out.

She needed to get Gage as far away as possible. Fast.

"I can climb out," she said. "I still have two good arms and legs. You're limping." She crouched and wiggled her joined hands. "Come on. Hurry."

Gage scanned her face, distrusting.

"Let's go," she urged. "The quicker you get out there, the sooner I can too."

Reluctantly, he set a foot onto her hands, and a tear rolled over his cheek. "You'd better make it out. I'm trusting you," he whispered.

She nodded, then she shoved him into the night.

FINN AND DEAN crossed the first floor of the third empty building they'd painstakingly cleared. There were dozens more and not enough law enforcement in the county to search them all in a short amount of time. "Maybe we need to arrange search parties," Finn said.

"We're not even sure they're in Old Downtown," Dean countered. "Lighthouse, Inc. owns a lot of properties in this area."

"We'd know sooner if we had more boots on the ground."

"Help!" The word seemed to echo in the storm.

Finn stilled, senses on high alert. "Did you hear that?" He focused on the sound, praying it would come again.

Dean raised his flashlight beam toward the open door ahead. "What?"

"It came from outside," Finn said, rushing through the building and onto the sidewalk.

In the distance, a small figure ran along a parallel street. "Help!"

"Hey!" Finn barked, projecting his most authoritative tone and hoping he would be heard.

The boy stopped and turned, then launched in their direction, arms waving. "Help! Help! Help!"

"Parker?" Finn met him in the intersection, pulling him into his arms. "Where did you come from? Are Hayley and Gage with you?"

Parker nodded. "They're in the basement. Gage is hurt."

"Okay, buddy." Finn said. "This is my brother Dean and he's going to get you out of the rain." Finn turned to pass Parker into Dean's arms.

"No! We have to help them!" Parker cried. "The building is getting blown up tomorrow. They didn't think I saw the signs, but I did, and I can read. I'm a very good reader."

Finn's chest constricted and his gaze whipped from building to building. "Which one?"

Parker scanned the street, wiping water from his terror-filled eyes. "We made a hole in the wall, and it started to fall apart."

"Which building?" Finn repeated, more harshly than intended, earning a stern look from Dean.

Dean pried the child from his arms. "Get your team out here," he told Finn. "We've got to be close."

Finn dialed his team and relayed the information while Dean ducked under a nearby awning with Parker.

Finn followed.

"You're okay," Dean said gently. "We're going to keep you safe and help the others. Can you show us where you were?"

Parker wound narrow arms around Dean's neck and whimpered. "I don't know."

"Do you remember which way you ran?"

Parker shook his head.

"What can you remember?" Finn asked, careful not to upset the kid further. "You said there were signs?"

"And a fence," Parker said.

"That's good," Dean encouraged. "Anything else?"

Parker buried his face against Dean's neck.

Finn patted the boy's back. "You did great, buddy. We'll take it from here, and you can get dry." He waved a hand at his teammates as they filtered out of nearby buildings, converged, then rushed to his aid.

Dean passed Parker into another set of hands.

"We need ambulances and the search-and-rescue team down here," Finn instructed. "Have him checked out and kept under guard." He nodded at Parker. "Don't let him out of your sight. We also need a list of buildings set for demolition in the morning. We're looking for one with a fence."

The group split up, and Finn caught his brother's eye. "SUV."

They both broke into a sprint for the vehicle they'd left behind. Within seconds, they were onboard and in motion.

Finn pressed the gas pedal with purpose, hydroplaning over the flooding roads.

"There are a few buildings behind fences at the end of the next block," Dean said. "I saw them the day of the warehouse explosion. I was looking for construction locations that might have explosives on-site."

Finn adjusted his wipers and heat vents, attempting to clear his view. Sheets of rain washed over the windshield, and storm clouds had turned dusk to night.

He leaned forward, peering over his steering wheel and straining for visibility. A moment later, he slowed, confusion mixing with hope. "I think I see someone out there." He veered to the road's flooded edge, sending a mini tidal wave across the sidewalk.

A narrow figure weaved in their direction, cradling one arm, head bent low against the wind and rain.

The Beaumonts jumped out and ran in the figure's direction.

"Gage?" Finn called. Could his luck truly be so good? To find not one, but both missing boys, in the middle of this storm?

The teen raised his head, stopping several feet away. "Finn!" he cried. "Help!" He swung an arm to point in the opposite direction. "Hayley's still inside, and the building's coming down!"

"We know," Finn said, erasing the final steps between them and projecting his voice against the wind. "Parker's with my team. He told us about the demolition tomorrow."

"No!" Gage turned back, eyes wild. "We broke a load-bearing wall and—"

Finn's ears rang as he raised his eyes to the silhouettes of distant structures.

And in the next breath, a building began to fall.

HAYLEY DRAGGED THE remnants of a broken shelving unit to the collapsing wall and climbed on to test its strength. Overhead, the building's complaints grew more fervent with every powerful gust of wind. She stretched onto tiptoe, reaching through the hole in search of purchase. There wasn't anyone left to offer her a boost. No one to grab her hands and pull her up. She'd demanded that Gage leave her and find Parker, then bring help.

She pressed the toe of one shoe into a crevice between bricks and thrust her torso outside with a harsh shove. The busted shelving crashed onto the floor, leaving her half inside and half out. The ground was slippery and soft from the storm. Each wiggle and stretch toward freedom threatened to land her back where she'd started.

If she died, two young boys would carry a lifetime of guilt with them for leaving her behind, and she would not allow that to happen.

Slowly, she got to her knees then pushed onto her feet.

She pulled in a shaky breath, stunned and elated to know she'd won. She'd gotten the boys to safety, and she'd beaten Forester at his twisted game.

A horrendous cracking sound filled the night and set her in motion toward the chain-link fence. She ran faster than she'd thought possible as the building came down behind her.

Hunks of busted bricks bounced and rolled over the sopping ground, crashing against her feet and legs. She stumbled and fell. Her body screamed with pain, and her forehead collided with the walkway. Then the world went dark…

Hayley. Her name echoed in her ears, sounding foreign, fuzzy. Her eyes reopened, mind aware of what she'd been through.

Rain had soaked and added weight to her clothes. Lightning flashed in the sky above.

"Hayley!"

She rolled onto her back, head pounding and heart racing as the remains of the building she'd escaped from came into view. Half of the massive structure was gone, revealing the insides, like a giant, ghastly dollhouse.

Emergency sirens warbled in the distance, and the glow

of searchlights danced over the rubble around her. She'd survived, and she was being rescued.

"There she is!" a male voice called. "Beaumont! I see her!"

Hayley twisted on the ground, seeking the man behind the name. She pushed up, onto skinned knees, then to her feet. Searching.

"Hayley," Finn said, striding through the storm like her personal hero. He moved faster and with purpose as their eyes met, erasing the distance between them until she was in his arms.

SIX MONTHS LATER, the summer heat had gone, but Hayley's nights were just as hot, and her days were filled with warmth and light. Today was no different.

Conrad Forester was in jail for conspiracy to commit murder, multiple counts of attempted murder and abduction, extortion, plus a whole host of other crimes. Most of which he'd readily admitted to in the hopes of a plea bargain. But a loose-lipped gunman and a rock-solid case by Finn and the Marshal's Bluff PD had put him away for life instead.

Katherine Everett's community-center project was well underway, and her husband was fully involved in making it everything she'd hoped.

Hayley had been promoted to a position for the routine reevaluation of foster families. And the job came with less overtime. All in all, it had been a pretty terrific six months.

She smiled as Finn parked the truck outside his parents' home and glanced over his shoulder at the boys in the extended cab.

"You guys ready?" he asked.

"Yeah!" Parker called.

Gage rolled his eyes.

Hayley turned and smiled at the pair.

If anyone had told her last summer that she'd be married

with two children before the holidays, she'd have told them they had the wrong woman. If they'd told her the children would be eight and fourteen years old, she'd have assumed they were off their rockers. But adopting Gage and Parker was the best, smartest, most wonderful thing she'd ever done.

Marrying the love of her life a few months prior was a possible tie.

Finn climbed out, then opened the rear door and grinned. "I can't wait to see everyone's face when they hear the news."

A mass of Beaumonts spilled onto the porch before Hayley made it to the steps. Gage trailed a short distance behind, carrying a neatly wrapped box.

"Grandma!" Parker said, running to Mrs. Beaumont's arms.

She kissed his head and tousled his hair with a smile. "What's this about exciting news?"

Austin, Dean and Lincoln moved to stand beside their dad.

Nicole, Dean's fiancée, and Scarlet, Austin's new wife, closed in on Hayley.

Josi brought up the rear. "Please tell me there's going to be a baby."

Hayley turned a bright smile on Finn. "Not yet."

He pulled Gage against his side. "We'd like to get this one into college first."

"So what's the news?" Austin asked. "It's freezing, and Mom said you wanted us all outside."

Hayley traded knowing looks with her family. "We aren't having a baby, but our family is growing."

Gage raised the box in his hands, and Parker whipped off the lid.

"We got a puppy!" Parker yelled, buzzing with the same excitement he'd had since Finn and Hayley had taken the boys to select their new pet.

"He's a hound dog," Gage said proudly. "He howls. It's hilarious."

Hayley wound an arm around his back, forming a chain with Gage and Finn, while the others oohed and aahed over Parker and the puppy.

"His name is Sir Barks-a-lot," Parker announced.

"I'm not calling him that," Lincoln said, swinging Parker under one arm like a football.

Josi cuddled the pup to her chest. "I think it's cute."

"I think it's cold," Austin complained, dragging Scarlet in for a hug. "Bring that little furball inside. Parker can come too."

"Hey!" Parker laughed.

The group filed into Mrs. Beaumont's kitchen, but Hayley and Finn stayed behind.

Gage shook his head and laughed, but shut the door in his wake…leaving them to do the thing they spent an awful lot of time doing these days.

Kissing and savoring the moments.

* * * * *